I0549638

RISKING IT ALL

A Romance and Suspense Novel by

Sara K. James

www.ten16press.com - Waukesha, WI

RISKING IT ALL
Copyrighted © 2015, 2020 Sara K. James

RISKING IT ALL by Sara K. James
ISBN 978-1-943331-08-6

For information, please contact:

www.ten16press.com
Waukesha, WI

Cover design by Therese Joanis
Rustic log cabin © Beth Van Trees/Shutterstock.com
Cabin in Woods © llaszlo/Shutterstock.com

Acknowledgments and Author's Note

First and foremost, a shout-out to my go-to guy for always having my back. To my first-draft readers, Jan, Jackie and Mary Ann: your encouragement and insight helped convince me that Emma and Max's story was a good one to tell. Also, special thanks to my team at TEN16 Press: Jenny Post, editor; Therese Joanis, graphic designer; and Shannon Ishizaki, owner.

Footnote: I hope that my readers will excuse any liberties I have taken with fictional references and location descriptions in order to enhance the continuity of the storyline.

For my family, who has always inspired me to do better.

PROLOGUE

Kennewick, Washington
Present day

She froze the moment she spotted him slipping into the air-conditioned lounge, expertly avoiding a collision with the couple that was on their way out. He paused long enough to hold the door for them and then turned his attention to the crowded room. She stood at the far end of the bar, shadowed in the dim fluorescent lighting above the mirrors, and everything around her seemed to blur and shift into slow motion.

The music coming from the jazz quartet.

The lively conversation from the lawyers and bankers who had loosened their ties and rolled up their sleeves, eagerly swapping corporate combat stories over shots of tequila.

The two overworked bartenders, courteously serving watered-down vodka gimlets and strawberry margaritas to the midlevel executives and secretaries who sat at the bar playing the mating game.

The only thing moving in real time was the man who was casually scanning the room, unnoticed by the other patrons at the Seabrook Grill. He'd always had the ability to blend in wherever he went and, more importantly, move about as if he were invisible—a talent Emma Cassidy would sell her soul to have at this very moment. Because it would only be a matter of seconds now before he spotted her. She shifted her body to sink deeper into the shadows and fixed her eyes on a crack in one of the floor tiles, willing him to just disappear.

How had he found her, anyway? she wondered. She had left over a year ago, changing her name and burying the life that had included the man standing across the room. A decision she was still convinced had been her only option in order to keep them both alive. She'd also taken steps to disguise her appearance by switching her natural hair color from strawberry blonde to a mundane brown, then cropping it so it now settled just below her ear lobes. She wore no makeup, and her soft hazel eyes were hidden behind brown, nonprescription contact lenses and plain, black-framed glasses. *Dear God*, she pleaded silently, *please let the changes be enough to fool him.*

She chanced another glance toward the front entrance and found him standing in the same spot, his attention now focused on her. His face remained blank, but when he didn't look away she was certain that he'd recognized her. And then he was crossing the room, and she literally felt the color drain from her face. Damn it, why had he come here? Why hadn't he just left her alone?

"Emily? Are you okay?"

She jolted at the sound of Tony's voice and turned to him with a questioning look.

"The order's up," the bartender said, pointing to the tray that held a pitcher of beer, five mugs and a plate overflowing with hot wings.

"Sure, I got it," she said, rummaging in her apron pocket for the ticket that went along with the order. She pulled it out, dropped it on the tray, and as she turned, bumped straight into Max Dunmore. She had to grab hold of the bar rail to steady herself.

"What are you doing here?" she began in a whisper that was harsh and shaky.

"Looking for you," he said in the same quiet tone.

"How did you find me?"

"I've got great investigative skills, remember? But I think the more important question is what are *you* doing here," he said, glancing around the bar to emphasize his point. When his eyes came back to settle on her, she was stricken with so many familiar emotions, she felt lightheaded. She knew that if she allowed herself the luxury, she could get lost in those brilliant eyes and pretend that the meeting here had been planned. Pretend that the time they'd been separated could just dissolve away, and it would be as if they were together again, enjoying a night out on the town.

But when one of the other waitresses dropped a glass behind the bar, reality came crashing through as it so often did. "I don't have time to talk to you," she said as she reached over to pick up the tray of drinks. "And even if I did, I'd have nothing to say."

"That's just too bad," Max said tightly, "because I've got plenty to say. And I think you owe me the chance to say it. This isn't a good time? Just name a better time and place."

"I don't think so. If you want to speak with me, you'll have to contact my attorney." She was getting worked up now and she could see Tony watching her as he continued to mix drinks. She set the tray back down and leaned closer to Max so only he could hear her words. "You couldn't manufacture enough evidence to make any charges stick, remember? That means I don't have to talk to you. Unless, of course, you found another dead body that you can't pin on anyone else, so you thought you'd just take a shot at pinning it on me. After all, it's all about closing the case, isn't it, *Detective*?"

He felt her words strike him like needle pricks but refused to let it go. "Don't, Emma."

Emma. She'd almost forgotten that Emma was her given name. It was strange to hear someone call her that after so long.

"Don't what?" she responded. "Don't believe that you were so short sighted that you couldn't see the truth? You didn't believe me, Max. You always had that doubt that maybe I did actually kill my husband." She shook her head and with a sarcastic grin said, "I never saw it coming, you know. If I recall correctly, not only did you shine when it came to investigative skills, you also had some handy interrogation techniques back then. Are you still using the one where you get a woman into bed so she'll give up all her secrets?"

"It wasn't a technique, and you know it," Max said. "It was real, Emma. Us being together—it was real."

"Well, you'll have to excuse me if I'm finding trouble wrapping my mind around that one," she said, experiencing a flashback of their short time together. She was being foolish, standing so close to him that she could soak in the scent of his aftershave. Foolish for losing herself in those dark, penetrating eyes that were watching her so intently she could feel herself crumbling, piece by miserable piece. Feeling what she had felt when he'd held her after making love. Those long, remarkably gentle fingers stroking up and down her back. She could still hear that deep husky voice as he spoke softly to her, when the world was safely locked outside and the only thing that mattered was his strong, solid body lying beside her. She closed her eyes again and silently begged him to stop making her feel so weak.

"Emma, let's get out of here," he said, laying his hand on her arm.

She jerked away as if he'd burned her with his touch, and the bartender was over in a flash. "Is this guy bothering you, Emily?"

"No, Tony, it's fine," she said as she laid her hand over the one the bartender had pressed to the counter. "Max is an old acquaintance and he was just leaving, weren't you, Max?"

But Max didn't move, didn't say anything for several long seconds.

"I think the lady asked you to leave," Tony said, leaning into the bar and giving Max a look that might intimidate most drunks but fell short on the unshakable Max Dunmore.

Sparing the bartender a glance, Max brought his attention back to Emma. "I need to talk to you, *Emily*, and the sooner the better. I'll be in touch."

With that said, he turned and strolled out of the bar. Tony waited until the man was out the door before saying, "What was that all about? If that guy is trouble I can take care of him for you. Just say the word."

Emma felt the side of her mouth curl as she pictured the two men grappling. Tony was quick enough to hold his own with the unruly customers, but she knew he'd be no match for Max, who would squash the kid like a bug. She also knew Tony had a crush on her, and wanted to impress her so badly, he'd go hand to hand with any man for no other reason than to defend her honor.

"That won't be necessary," she assured Tony as she picked up the tray. "But thank you for the offer. Max doesn't worry me."

Even as the words came out of her mouth, she knew they weren't true. He'd found her, and now she'd have to run again. Find a new place to hide. And this time, she'd have to go even deeper.

CHAPTER ONE

Kingsport, Colorado
Eighteen months earlier

Emma was standing at the kitchen sink washing the dinner plates. There was no automatic dishwasher, but that was fine with her. She enjoyed this quiet time, doing something that didn't require too much thinking or planning. In fact, when she was totally alone in the house she would indulge herself with listening to soft country music and watching the children play in the park through the window directly over the sink. But tonight she wasn't alone, so she kept her head down and her thoughts on the task at hand.

When Eric came into the kitchen, she felt her muscles tense as he opened the refrigerator door and grabbed for another beer. She remembered his defiant swagger when he had entered the house earlier, along with the pointed insults carelessly flung at her. All signs that he'd already had too much to drink before coming home. And even though she'd had dinner ready for him by five thirty—a request he had made on his way out that morning—he hadn't stumbled through the front door until nearly eight. Her fear now was that he was itching for a fight and she was going to be his unwilling opponent.

"Where were you today?" he asked, raising the bottle to his lips. "I tried calling you twice before I finally got a hold of you."

"I did the grocery shopping before picking up those boots you ordered. Then I took your check to the bank. The receipt is on the counter there," she said, making a motion with her head. She knew where his question was leading but didn't know how to derail it. Feeling the tears burning behind her eyes, she concentrated on blocking the paralyzing fear that was balling up in the pit of her stomach. "When I got back I spent some time in the garden."

"I suppose that nosy hag from next door was with you. I told you to stay away from her."

Emma's neighbor, Joan Adams, *had* come over. Although Emma didn't consider Joan and herself to be good friends, Joan was pleasant enough to her, someone who had a kind word on the few occasions they'd run into each other.

On this particular afternoon, they'd talked a bit about nothing in particular. At first. But then Joan had asked her how she'd gotten the bruises—the ones similar to those she'd always tried so hard to hide.

Emma had made light of her question, insisting they were the result of some remodeling work she'd been doing inside the house. She'd quickly changed the subject then, bringing the focus of their conversation back to the garden. Joan had gone along, even though Emma knew she hadn't bought into the excuse. It hadn't been until they'd started to part ways that Joan circled back to the bruises.

"I know it's none of my business," her neighbor had said, "but I have a knack for reading people. Those bruises tell me that maybe your husband has a violent side. I've seen you two together," she'd continued with total candor, "and I haven't always liked what I've seen.

"Now, like I said, you can go ahead and tell me it's none of my business. Just know that my home is always open to you. If you ever need a safe place, you come to me."

Emma had been speechless. On one hand she was taken aback by Joan's no-nonsense manner. On the other hand she had experienced a brief moment of relief that maybe she'd found someone who could truly understand Emma's situation. As her mind tried to sort through the pros and cons of disclosure, the ringing phone had slammed the confessional door closed.

Emma remembered that at the time she'd been convinced the caller had been Eric. That he'd somehow known what his wife had been contemplating. So Emma had made her excuses to Joan and hurried for the back door of her house, only to have the phone stop ringing by the time she got to it.

Now, based on his earlier comment, she was certain it had been him.

"No, Eric," she said in what she thought was a calm voice. "I didn't see Joan today."

Taking another pull on the bottle of beer he said, "You're lying. I always know when you're lying." When Emma remained silent, Eric slammed the bottle so hard on the counter that it sprayed liquid out of the opening. "You were out whoring, weren't you?" he bellowed.

She looked over her shoulder, wanting to plead with him to leave her alone. To go back into the living room and finish watching the game. But she saw it in his eyes. There would be no reprieve tonight.

"I don't sleep around, Eric. I wish you'd believe me. I did the shopping, picked up your boots and went to the bank. Then I came home. I swear."

He moved so quickly that she didn't have time to react. He had one hand on her throat and the other was wrapped tightly on her upper arm as he dragged her away from the window and the prying eyes of neighbors. When he had her in the dining room he threw her to the floor.

"Whore," he hissed as he slowly paced back and forth in front of her. "Nothing but a whore."

She didn't want to beg; it only fueled his temper. But so did her crying, which she was just barely able to control as she tried to crawl out of his reach. "Please don't, Eric. Not tonight."

"Please don't, Eric," he mimicked. "Not tonight."

His words were beginning to slur and his temper increased as his taunting continued. "Why *not* tonight, Emma? What difference does it make? Once a whore, always a whore." He took his cigarette lighter out of his pocket and started to play with it, clicking it until she could see the solid flame, then snapping the cover back down to extinguish the threat. "But I bet you can't even get that right," he added.

As he started toward her, she found that her efforts to crawl away had only trapped her between the wall and the dining room table. When he was close enough to crouch directly in front of her, she began to whimper.

"What's a guy to do? When he can't even trust his own wife?" He grabbed her by the wrist and pulled her arm until it was straight out.

"No, Eric," she pleaded. "Please don't."

Without another word he flicked the lighter one more time and when the flame burst up he held it out in front of her. She struggled to get free, knowing that if he wanted to inflict pain he'd have no second thoughts. But to Emma's complete surprise, he let go of her arm and stood up laughing. "You're pathetic. It's not even fun anymore."

Scrambling into the corner, she fought the sobs that were ready to explode, relieved that for now he seemed to have lost interest.

"Get up and finish the dishes. And bring me another beer," he said as he walked out of the room.

Emma cautiously stood, keeping her attention fixed on Eric as she moved into the kitchen. After delivering his beer, she hurriedly went back to the unwashed plates and then scrubbed down the kitchen counters before heading up the back stairs to the bedroom. If she were lucky he'd fall asleep in the recliner and stay there until morning. She didn't want to think of what the night hours would hold if she weren't so lucky.

Kingsport, Colorado
Somewhere across town

Detective Max Dunmore stood silently watching as the medical crew loaded the body of an eighteen-year-old stabbing victim into the waiting ambulance. As the vehicle left the back alley and headed for Mercy Hospital, the lights on top of the vehicle remained dark. He turned as his partner spoke.

"Looks drug related, Maxwell. They never learn, do they?"

Detective Roger Donnelly was shaking his head in mock sympathy as he glanced at the spot on the pavement where the boy's body had been lying before they'd first arrived on scene. The detective's long, angular face had no telltale signs of what he was feeling, but Max knew how to read his partner's looks. He was actually feeling compassion toward the young man whose throat had been sliced in one clean, quick stroke. Roger was good at mouthing off about how most street thugs got exactly what they deserved. But Max knew there was more to the man than tough talk.

He watched as Roger scratched the stubble on his right cheek, his keen green eyes composed and his blond wavy hair—streaked by the summer sun—looking a bit too tousled. Taking a closer look, Max honed in on the now-wrinkled khaki slacks, white cotton shirt, and casual navy jacket that he remembered seeing his partner wearing during their previous shift. He smiled at the thought that the great Roger Donnelly had been rousted from a bed other than his own to work this crime scene.

"Looks can be deceiving sometimes," Max finally said. "It's best we start the leg work and find out what that kid was doing out here at three in the morning."

"Always the optimist," Roger replied as he withdrew a notebook and pen from the inside pocket of his jacket. "Some people are just born with the scum gene. Can't escape their fate. Can't change it either. Face it, Max. He was a habitual criminal, going back to when he stopped sucking his thumb and started sucking on more interesting things. He was a known drug dealer to kids from the local grade school and a gang member who finally fucked up and paid the price."

"Ah, I see you haven't been paying attention to Councilman Janski lately," Max replied with a light slap on his partner's back. "Kingsport doesn't have any gangs."

Donnelly snorted as he started toward the apartment complex that loomed over the alley where the body had been found, accepting that the next logical step was to begin knocking on doors to determine if there was a star witness hiding behind one of them. "It's going to be the usual crap," he said as they swung into the lobby. "I can hear it now: 'I didn't see anything, sir. He was such a good boy with such a promising future.' Like saints have nothing better to do than go into alleys in the middle of the night to sell drugs."

"If I didn't know any better," Max said, "I'd say you were feeling a bit disillusioned about the fine upstanding youth in our fine upstanding community."

"Using the words *upstanding* and *youth* in the same sentence is an oxymoron, Maxwell."

"Well, that's a little harsh, don't you think? Don't you have a niece who'd fall into that category?"

"As you well know, college boy, there are exceptions to every rule. I happen to come from remarkably inspired genes, as do my sister and her offspring. Of course, that husband of hers is a whole different story."

"Are you forgetting that Malinda has both their genes? How do you know his don't dominate?"

"Bite your tongue. It's not possible and you know it. Unlike her idiot father, Malinda can actually carry on a coherent conversation."

Max had to laugh. It was a similar conversation to those they'd had at other crime scenes that were either drug or gang related. Most of the time it was a violent ending involving young men who hadn't yet seen their twenty-first birthdays. The talk was a way to expunge the disturbing images they were forced to deal with and prepare for the sometimes-tedious investigation that would follow. But as soon as they got back to the station, Roger would put more than the expected time into solving the case.

After spending the next two hours questioning residents that were brave enough to open their doors, they sat in a comfortable silence as Roger drove through the slowly awakening streets of Kingsport. A few blocks from the station, he pulled over to the curb and parked in front of an expired meter on Canal Street. "I'm running in for some good coffee," he said pointing to the small café at the end of the block. "Want anything?"

"Yeah, I'll take mine black, and pick up a couple of blueberry scones."

"You got it," he said as he scurried out of the car after killing the engine, leaving Max to review his interview notes and organize their next steps in the investigation.

Twenty minutes later Roger returned with two coffee containers, a white bag with the Star Café logo on it and a wide smile on his face. "Here you go, buddy," he said, tossing the bag into Max's lap and setting the cups in the plastic holder that pulled out of the dashboard.

Max waited until they were moving again before asking, "So, was Maria working this morning?"

Roger's smile widened, and Max had his answer. Maria was the latest in a string of young, eager women that Roger kept happy simply by being Roger. And even though this one had lasted longer than the others, Max had serious doubts that she was the proverbial *one and only*. The big difference between Maria and the others was that she wasn't a clinger. She could actually think for herself and didn't come running every time Roger snapped his fingers, which had proven to be both a curiosity and a challenge to the detective.

"Maria has a sister. Did I mention that?" Roger said. "She wants you to meet her, says you'd get along great. What do you think?"

"I think that I can find my own women," Max said firmly. "Besides, the last one you set me up with wasn't exactly my type. Did you know she had a collection of whips? That was one scary lady," he added with a dramatic shudder.

Roger released a manly snort. "I'll have to say that I misjudged a bit on Kisha. You were actually lucky to get out of that one unharmed."

"You think? So, thanks, but no thanks. Fix Maria's sister up with Dugan in Narcotics."

"Yeah, that might work," Roger said with some enthusiasm.

They were pulling into the parking lot of the Fifth Street police station when Max spotted a spry, petite woman in her mid-seventies coming out the front door.

"Isn't that your grandmother?" Roger asked, maneuvering the car into one of the few available slots.

"Yeah," Max said with concern in his voice. "Why would my grandmother be here?"

He stepped out of the car and headed straight toward her. When he called out her name she turned and he saw that she was smiling. That had to be a good thing, right?

"Hey, Nanna," Roger said as he bounced up the steps in front of Max. Leaning down to plant a kiss on her cheek and placing a hand over his heart he said, "My day is now complete. Please tell me that you've come all the way down here just to see me."

"You're a dreamer, Roger. And unfortunately, not a very good one if I'm the highlight of your day. Move aside so I can give my grandson a hug."

"Oh, I am wounded beyond words and I fear I will never recover," Roger said as he stumbled backwards a few steps.

"You need new friends, Maxwell," Joan said as she gave him a hug and a kiss.

"I'm trying, Nanna, believe me. What *are* you doing here?"

"I just wanted to talk to you about something, if you have a few minutes. It's about one of my neighbors who I think could use some help."

CHAPTER TWO

Emma was pacing herself as she strolled down the aisles at the Kingsport Grocery Mart. Every Thursday morning she would drive here—alone—and get the week's worth of shopping done. She would browse the windows of the small novelty stores that lined the strip-mall on the other side of Main Street and sometimes even stop in the café and enjoy a latte. Of course, that was only if she was sure Eric, an independent truck driver, wasn't expected back from one of his extended trips. During the past four months, he had picked up additional hauls that required him to be away for days on end, leaving her to guess when he would be back. And she'd learned the hard way that if she weren't at home waiting for him, the consequences could be harsh.

She rolled her cart out to the parking lot and when she reached her car, began unloading the groceries. After returning the cart to the receptacle she climbed into the six-year-old Honda and turned the key in the ignition. She heard the grinding noise, but the car didn't start. She pumped the gas pedal, hoping that would help, but after trying again even the grinding noise stopped. Every time she turned the key all she got was an ineffective click.

Emma sat back against the seat and started to feel an all too familiar panic. She suspected that Eric would be coming home today and she had to get the groceries unpacked and dinner started. Then there were the other household chores she had to get done and she knew she couldn't afford this delay.

As she sat weighing her options, a knock on the window caught her by surprise. Turning, she saw a remarkably attractive man leaning down, watching her through the glass. She guessed that he was somewhere in his early to mid-thirties and his face held a strong and determined quality. His skin was smooth and clean-shaven, although she could see that the dreaded five o'clock shadow could be his nemesis if overlooked. He had dark wavy hair that was cut short, and his eyes—which were just a shade darker than mocha— were closely focused on her. She could see his mouth moving but was so distracted by the tranquil movement of his strong, alluring lips that the words were lost on her.

She jerked when his knuckles gently rapped on the window a second time and watched as he took a step back, holding his hands up as if in surrender. When he spoke again he raised his voice to make sure she could hear him through the glass.

"I was just wondering if you needed any help."

Emma rolled the window down just a crack. "It won't start," she said, still feeling unnerved by the sudden appearance of this Good Samaritan.

"I know. I was getting out of my Jeep over there when I heard the grinding. I'm pretty good with cars, but to be honest, it sounds like the battery."

"Oh," she said at a loss for anything else to say.

"I've got cables, and as soon as one of these other cars moves, I can pull in and give you a jump."

"Yes, I suppose that would be all right."

"My name's Max, by the way."

Emma could tell that he was studying her now and probably thinking she was a total moron. She finally opened the car door and cautiously stepped out. "I'm Emma," she said, trying to appear relaxed. "I was doing my grocery shopping and when I tried starting the car, it just . . . didn't. *Start* that is. I'm not sure how old the battery is but I don't remember the last time we had one put in, so I guess that could easily be the problem. I only use the car for errands so I don't really think much about maintenance." She stopped talking when she saw the amused look on his face. "I'm rambling, aren't I?"

"Not that I've noticed," Max said, as he continued to observe her behavior. Definitely shy, although he also sensed some fear mixed in there somewhere. She was checking out her surroundings the entire time she talked to him, no doubt looking for a way out if she needed it. Always good to have a game plan, he thought, especially for a woman alone in a parking lot. She was also playing with the rabbit's foot that dangled from her key ring—something she no doubt did whenever she felt uneasy.

Just then a man and woman unlocked the car directly across from Emma's and started to load their bags in the trunk. "I'm going to swing my car around and pull in here. I'll be right back."

She watched him jog down the same aisle where the couple was parked, jump behind the wheel of a gray-colored Jeep, and with impeccable timing, back the vehicle out of that space and into the one that the couple had just vacated. Reaching over the seat, he pulled out a set of jumper cables and came around front to lift the hood on his vehicle. "Pop your hood and I'll take over from there," he said, as he began hooking one end of the cables to his battery. She followed his instructions and within minutes her car purred back to life.

"Thank you so much, Mr. . . ."

"Max," he said. "And you're welcome. You should probably look into getting a new battery though. You wouldn't want to be stranded in a less populated area if it happens again. In fact, why don't I follow you home just to make sure you don't have anymore problems?" Instantly, Max saw the panic cross her face and quickly added, "No, wait. I'm not a stalker or anything." He reached into the inside breast pocket of his jacket and pulled out his badge. "I'm harmless, really."

She gave him a nervous laugh and once again glanced around the parking lot while edging toward her car. "I'm sure I'll be fine. You don't have to follow me."

"I apologize, Emma," Max said gently as he walked to the front of the vehicles and started disconnecting the cables. "I didn't mean to frighten you. It's just my nature to want to help."

"Sorry," she said on a heavy sigh. "I'm the one who should be apologizing. I'm not used to strangers being so kind. I'm not all that outgoing and I have a hard time with people sometimes. Most of the time, actually." She smiled then, and added, "This is the longest conversation I've had with anyone other than my husband in months. But I'll be fine on my own. Thanks again for your help."

He smiled, giving her a half salute before dropping the cables in the back seat of the Jeep and driving away.

Maneuvering her way out of the lot, Emma was so preoccupied with the random act of kindness she'd just gotten from a complete stranger that she didn't notice the black Mercedes with tinted windows that pulled out behind her. But from his parked position at the opposite end of the parking lot, Max did. Well, it looked as if he was going to follow her home after all.

Emma pulled into her driveway, deciding to unload the bags before she garaged the vehicle. Keys in hand, she climbed out and turned toward the rear of the car. She'd only taken a few steps when a dark Mercedes pulled in behind her and idled.

She stopped dead in her tracks as she recognized Eric in the passenger seat. She had hoped for several more hours of alone time, but that didn't seem to be a luxury she was going to be enjoying today. She forced herself to walk to the back of the car and open the trunk. As she was leaning over for the first bag she heard the driver cut the engine and both doors opened.

"Emma. Sweetheart. Where have you been?" Eric asked after exiting the car.

Before answering, she glanced hesitantly at the driver who was now leaning against the hood of the Mercedes. He was taller than Eric by several inches and more muscular through the shoulders and arms. The sunglasses he wore hid his eyes, but the half-smile he was showing her combined with the thick black hair and perfectly manicured goatee gave her the impression that he was both disingenuous and dangerous.

"It's Thursday. I was grocery shopping," she finally said.

"Ah, yes. Thursdays are for grocery shopping," Eric stated pleasantly as he moved closer to Emma's vehicle. "Why don't we help you with these?" Grabbing a bag out of the trunk he added, "Stan, this is my wife, Emma. Sweetheart, this is Stan Hudson, a business associate."

Emma was becoming suspicious of the generosity her husband was showing. He hardly ever helped her with anything and certainly never did in front of other people. When he put his arm around her waist and gently moved her toward the house she felt the restlessness spread. He wasn't being attentive. He was up to something.

She preceded Eric into the house and lowered the bag of groceries onto the kitchen table. Placing her purse alongside it she said, "I should put the car in the garage so I don't have to do it later."

"That's not necessary. It'll keep." She could see that Eric's eyes were glazed, and wondered, not for the first time, if it was more than alcohol that gave him that look. "Stan and I are going into the living room to watch some tube. Why don't you start dinner?"

After the visitor set the bags of groceries on the counter, he started to follow Eric into the other room. But as he passed behind Emma he hesitated, caging her between his body and the kitchen table. He wasn't touching her, but she knew that just the slightest movement would bring their bodies into contact. He leaned down and spoke in a hushed tone close to her ear. "You're a beautiful woman, Emma. Eric didn't even come close to describing just how beautiful you really are. I'm glad I've gotten the chance to see for myself."

His arm brushed against hers as he moved around the table and headed for the living room. She fought to control the alarm that suddenly had her heart racing. Her hands clutched the back of the chair as she closed her eyes and concentrated on slowing her breathing, silently counting as she inhaled and then exhaled.

Steady again, she opened her eyes and found herself staring at Eric. "I don't see you making supper," he said in a sneering voice.

"I'm just starting it. It shouldn't take long."

"Good." He stood there for another half-minute before he gave her an amused grin and walked away. But Emma wasn't fooled. There was nothing amusing about the mood he'd come home with and she was sure it was somehow going to backfire onto her.

Max sat across the street and watched the dark Mercedes pull up behind Emma's car. When two men got out, he immediately pegged the one who'd been in the passenger seat as the husband, and the driver as an acquaintance. Although neither appeared to be a threat to Emma, and no alarm bells went off in Max's head, when they all disappeared into the house he decided to sit for another twenty minutes to see what developed.

His reason was simple. Earlier, his grandmother had told him that she was bothered by the fact that her neighbor, who had once been open and friendly, had become distant, rarely taking the time to say more than a few words. She'd also told him that not too long ago she had noticed bruising on Emma's lower back when the younger woman had been tending to her flowers.

"I saw a look in her eyes when I tried to ask her about it," his grandmother had told him solemnly. "The same look your Aunt Rose used to get when she lived with that horrible, abusive ex-husband of hers."

Max understood what his grandmother meant by the look. He'd seen it countless times in the eyes of the women he had to leave behind when he was dragging their husbands or boyfriends off to jail. Domestic calls were a cop's worst nightmare and they didn't get any better the more seasoned the cop became. Some hit you harder than others, but they all forced you to harden to the decisions you had to make in order to face another day. But you never forgot the look.

So Max had promised his grandmother that he would check into her suspicions without being intrusive, and that's why he had started his day off sitting outside Emma's house, watching for any unusual activity. When she had pulled out of her driveway, he'd kept up his observation by following her to the Grocery Mart, which had inadvertently turned into an opportunity to talk to her. Consequently, from what he had seen then and what he could see now, everything appeared normal.

After taking a final glance at the house, he reached down, turned the key in the ignition, then slowly pulled away from the curb. He'd have to tell his grandmother that there wasn't much more he could do other than work in a few drive-bys when he could. Beyond that, Emma Cassidy had the controls on this one.

By eight that night, supper had been served and Emma was once again standing in front of the kitchen sink washing dishes. She could hear the television blaring in the living room, and occasionally Eric or Stan would make a comment about the program. They seemed to be oblivious to her movements in the kitchen, making her feel marginally more relaxed.

After finishing the necessary chores, her intent was to slip up the back stairs and climb into bed. She started to reach over to draw the curtains shut when she felt his body trapping her against the sink, and heard that same hushed voice whispering in her ear as his hands grabbed onto her hips. She turned so fast that he was forced to take a step back. "What do you think you're doing?" she stammered, sliding out of his reach.

"Just getting a feel for the merchandise," Stan said as his eyes suggestively traveled up and down her body.

"My husband is in the other room and he wouldn't be happy if he knew you were doing what you're doing."

"I don't think so," he said as he made another move in her direction. "He's the one who sent me in here. Told me I should see if you needed any help."

"I don't, and I would appreciate it if you would leave now."

"Is that any way to treat our company, *darlin'*?" Emma turned and saw Eric standing just inside the doorway leaning against the wall. "Didn't your mama teach you any manners?"

"Eric? What are you talking about?" She couldn't quite grasp what was going on, and the fear she felt was making her legs weak and her heart pound.

"I told Stan here that you'd be more than happy to show him a good time because that's what you do best. Figured you can give away the package just as easy in our own home as you can in some dive downtown." He brought the beer bottle he was holding to his lips, keeping his eyes fixed on hers.

Stan was moving toward her again and she was fighting to breathe. This couldn't be happening, it just couldn't. She turned to run, but Stan caught her with one hand and spun her back into the room. "Where do you think you're going, *darlin'*?" Stan said, mimicking Eric's drawl. "Your husband said you're staying home tonight and giving me a little of what you got going."

Emma turned just in time to see Stan's hand swing out and make contact with her face. The pain was blinding as she fell sideways against the counter, her right hip taking the brunt of the impact. She could hear him laughing as she fought to stay upright and beyond arms length.

But before he could charge again, Stan's cell phone began to ring, and he moved off to the side of the kitchen to answer it. Eric, who hadn't moved during the encounter, continued to watch his wife with interest.

"That was Carl," Stan said as he disconnected the call. "It's a go for tomorrow."

"What time do I need to be there?" Eric asked as he took another drink from the bottle.

"Make it six. We need to be on the road by eight." Stan gave Eric an apprehensive look while slipping into his jacket. "I've got to go and get things set up. It's going to be a long trip, Cassidy, so I'd put it to bed for the night," he added, pointing at the bottle in Eric's hand.

As he headed toward the back door, he slowed down as he passed Emma. Giving her a perverted smile he said, "I'll take a rain check on the lady."

Emma closed her eyes and took a deep breath as she heard the door slam behind him. She quickly realized that although she had escaped the clutches of one monster, a second lay in wait just across the room.

When Eric started toward her she made a move for the stairs, but he was still able to grab her and drag her up against his body. She was physically helpless as he lifted her off her feet and threw her on top of the kitchen table. "Time you learn a valuable lesson on who runs the show around here," he said with a sneer.

Emma began to kick, scream and claw wildly, trying to fight off Eric's attack as best she could. But his strength overpowered her efforts, and he clamped one hand over her mouth as he used the other one to tear at her clothes and take what he thought was rightfully his.

Emma wanted nothing more than for Eric to die, right then and there, so that the pain and humiliation would finally stop. But as the assault dragged on, the fight went out of her and she made her mind go blank, freezing out everything that was happening in her quiet little kitchen in her quiet little neighborhood.

A short time later she found herself alone on the table, exposed and weeping. She sat up and pulled her skirt down over her knees and gathered what was left of the ripped blouse around her breasts. As she slid her legs over the side of the table and dropped her feet to the floor, she heard the indifference in Eric's voice when he said, "I'm going to bed. Be sure you lock up before you come upstairs."

The minute he left, she stumbled to the downstairs bathroom to clean up. When had their marriage gone so far off track? she wondered dejectedly. When had Eric turned so cruel that he actually took pleasure in hurting her? Hadn't they loved each other once? Or had she always just been blind to his total loathing for her?

It took another twenty minutes before she felt steady enough to move into the living room. Lowering herself onto the couch she lay motionless for over an hour, staring at nothing and desperately trying to regain just a shred of hope that tomorrow would bring an end to Eric's abuse.

When she finally accepted that hoping wasn't the answer—that only she could make it stop—she began to formulate a plan.

CHAPTER THREE

The next morning Eric found his wife sleeping on the living room sofa. Just as well, he thought. He was running late and didn't have the time or energy to watch her slink around the house while he was preparing to leave. Besides, he had a lot on his plate these days and needed to stay sharp in order to be ready to move when the time came. He was going to make it rich very soon now, and didn't want anyone, especially Emma, spoiling things for him.

As he started the coffee maker he thought about the haul he'd be making today and the profit the load would bring him. Who would have guessed that the out-of-the-blue meeting a few months back would have led to his big chance to strike it rich?

He'd just returned to the bar from one of the upstairs rooms at a dive in the outskirts of Denver where he had been enjoying the services of Michelle, a truly imaginative entrepreneur who ran a lucrative business entertaining truckers who were passing through town. Signaling the bartender for another drink, he glanced over and saw the unfamiliar man sitting two stools over, watching him through the mirror behind the bar. The man was ignoring the truly scintillating attempts from one of the other hookers as she tried to entice him to follow her upstairs. When he'd finally had enough, the man simply turned to her, and with a look that could kill, sent her on her way. Eric was totally impressed.

"They just don't give up, do they?" Eric said with a short laugh. "Business is business, I guess."

The man simply grunted in reply.

"You sure have a way of handling them, though."

The man lifted his glass and drained half of its contents. After setting the glass down on the bar, he went back to staring at the mirror.

"You a trucker?" Eric asked, taking a sip from his own glass.

"No," the man replied with no real emotion.

"I'm just here on a layover," Eric continued. "I'll be picking up a return load to Colorado Springs in the morning. Then it's back home to Kingsport."

The man glanced at him, and although Eric was well on his way to being unconditionally drunk he was still somewhat unsettled by the man's intimidating expression.

"Hey, sorry, man. Just carrying on a conversation, that's all. You want to be left alone, I understand." Eric turned back to his glass and drank.

Several minutes later he heard the man speak and once again met his stare through the mirror. "You're the guy driving that rig out back, right?"

"Yeah, that's me," Eric answered casually.

"Is it yours or a company rig?"

"It's mine. Why are you asking?"

"I'm trying to find someone to pull a partial load. You interested?"

"Could be. Where's it need to be and when?"

The man relayed the specifics and waited for a reply.

"Sounds doable," Eric finally said. "What's in it for me?"

The man threw out a price for the delivery.

After doing the math Eric quickly came to the conclusion that he could take the run for a couple hundred less, but who was he to

*argue if this guy wanted to overpay? "We can work something out,"
Eric said with a nod.*

*"Good. Let me write down the information you'll need. My
name's Stan, by the way. Stan Hudson." He reached over, offering
Eric his hand.*

"Eric Cassidy."

*"Why don't you leave me your number, Eric, and if this works out
I may have some future hauls for you. I've got a couple of irons in
the fire right now and we could use a reliable driver."*

The meeting had definitely had its rewards, Eric thought now as he
drained his coffee, debating whether he had time for a second cup.

"Eric?"

The soft cautious voice of his wife had him turning toward the
doorway to the kitchen.

"I was wondering how long you're going to be gone. If it's more
than a day or two I'm going to need some money."

He noticed the bruise forming high on her right cheek and felt a
moment of regret. Not because of the events that had led to it, but
because people might start asking questions about how it had gotten
there. And the answers she gave could lead back to him.

"You should get something on that," he said, pointing to her face.
Before she could move he opened the freezer door and grabbed a
handful of cubes from the plastic bin, dropping them into a hand
towel before passing her the makeshift icepack.

Emma took the towel and pressed it against her cheek. Her only
defense against the pain was to clench her teeth and accept it for
what it was. She knew how bad her face looked. She'd made a point
to check the damage before coming into the kitchen to talk to Eric.
But a pair of sunglasses and strategically placed makeup would hide
most of the discoloring when she left the house later. "I have to

take my car in and get a new battery and I'm low on gas," she said, clarifying her previous request.

"You don't need a new battery," he said, dumping the dregs of the coffee into the sink and rinsing his cup.

"The battery died yesterday and I needed to get a jump. I'm concerned that it will happen again and I would feel safer if I just replaced it."

He knew all this, of course. He and Stan had watched as she had accepted the help of the yuppie do-gooder. "Who gave you the jump?" he asked just to see what she would say.

"A man who noticed I was having problems starting the car. I don't know who it was. I'd never seen him before."

"And how did you repay this man's kindness, I wonder?"

She took a deep breath and let it out slowly. He knew she didn't cheat on him. Knew that his accusations of illicit affairs were nonsense and also knew how much it upset her when he made those accusations. Knowing that a defensive response would only encourage him to continue tormenting her, she decided to side-step his implication.

"If I can take the car in," she said in a slow, deliberate tone, "I won't have to worry about it anymore. And you won't have to worry about strange men offering me assistance."

Eric pierced her with a rancorous look, and after several uncomfortable moments she shifted her attention away from him. Satisfied that he had broken her once again, he pushed away from the sink and reached into his back pocket for his wallet. After laying three large bills on the table he glanced back at Emma and pulled a twenty out of the billfold, tossing it alongside the other bills. "That's for last night, sugar."

She fixed her eyes on him, recognizing for the first time that his face no longer held the charming good looks it once had. Gone, too, was the sparkle in those deep, exotic eyes that had always been so inviting. Unemotionally, she finally accepted that the love she'd once held for this man was dead.

Emma watched as he picked up his overnight bag and strolled out of the house. After the door slammed, she straightened her back and purposefully walked over to the table, taking the $300 and leaving the twenty exactly where he had dropped it. Turning for the back staircase, she headed up to the bedroom, intent on taking the first step toward breaking the hold Eric had on her, determined to be gone before he returned.

CHAPTER FOUR

Crystal Ridge, Colorado
One month later

It had been just over an hour ago that Eric backed his rig up to the double doors of a large climate controlled garage that stood adjacent to the main house located on a remote piece of property owned by Victor Manderfield. He'd been trying hard to look inconspicuous as four men carefully unloaded his delivery, wishing they'd just shake ass so he could get the hell back on the road. He nudged another cigarette out of the near empty pack and, lighting it, idly watched as the final crate was dragged out of the trailer with a forklift.

This was the sixth delivery he'd made for Stan Hudson since they'd met over a beer in Denver, and the second to this particular property. This evening's delivery, however, was probably more valuable than the other five runs combined. Tonight, the load included three rare paintings that had all been passed down from one Manderfield generation to the next.

The three pieces had, up until tonight, been on permanent loan to the Gunther Museum and Art Gallery—an arrangement made by the patriarch of the family, Marshall Manderfield, a week prior to his death several years ago. Dissatisfied with the arrangement, Victor had been discreet, yet vicious, in his fight to regain possession of the artwork, and his tenacity had finally paid off. All three paintings were back where they belonged—in the hands of the elder's first born—increasing Victor's net worth considerably.

But Eric knew that Victor's brother, Marco, had other plans for the paintings. There was a treacherous rivalry between the siblings that had gotten more intense after their father's death, and the deep-seated hatred only fueled Marco's desire to appropriate the artwork and add the pieces to his own private collection.

The ruse required an inside man—a role that Eric had been playing for the past several weeks. If everything went according to Marco's plan, this would go down in history as the most sensational swindle in the history of the Manderfield family.

From his position just outside the garage entrance, Eric could see Stan Hudson directing traffic and keeping notes on a clipboard. As he watched, he was hit with a sense of doom that stemmed from his fear that Hudson—or someone working in Victor Manderfield's organization—would discover that Eric was also working for Marco. And if that happened, he'd be a dead man faster than you could lay a two-bit hooker.

So all he needed to do now was keep it together and wait for further instructions on the when, where and how of the heist. Then, after the deal was done and he was paid, he intended to become a permanent resident on a very secluded island where women would be fighting over each other to be with him.

He ground out the cigarette and pulled the zipper of his jacket all the way up to ward off the cool air, consoled with the thought that in another week or so he wouldn't have to worry about hauling loads in the middle of the night.

"Mr. Cassidy?"

Eric startled when one of the shipping clerks said his name.

"I need your signature on this form. We're almost done here, and then you can pull out."

With little thought and no more than a cursory glance at the form

Eric signed and dated it at the bottom. The man ripped off the top copy and handed it to Eric with a final comment spoken in a mere whisper. "You're going to want to do more than pocket that." When Eric looked up, the man had already turned and was heading back inside the garage.

Eric glanced down at the paper and realized it contained his instructions. Written at the bottom was a phone number and the words "Call for package pickup" with a date and time. He allowed himself a satisfied smile as he folded the paper and slipped it into his pocket.

"By this time next week, I won't have a care in the world," he whispered into the night before walking back to his rig, leaving Stan Hudson and his crew behind.

Three days later, Eric was once again out in the middle of the night—this time as an employee of Marco Manderfield—waiting anxiously on an isolated dirt road roughly ten minutes from Victor Manderfield's Crystal Ridge residence. He'd been there just shy of an hour listening for the directive to move in. But the only conversation coming over the earphones was in Spanish, and Eric's lack of understanding for the language cost him the knowledge of what was being said. So he waited.

Eric's part in tonight's double-cross wasn't exactly brain surgery. He was simply the driver, although he had taken the precaution of slipping his loaded handgun into the waistband of his jeans. As a long-haul driver he'd learned early on that you could easily lose your entire load if you weren't prepared to protect it. And even though his contact, Lucas Ramos, had assured him there wouldn't be any trouble, he wasn't leaving anything to chance. A lot could happen out here in Nowhere Land while Marco's men disabled the security system and made sure that Victor's house wasn't occupied.

Drumming his fingers against the steering wheel of the rented cargo van, he once again went over the plan in his head: After the call came for him to drive to the house, the paintings would be securely packed into the rear of the van and he would take them back to his semi-trailer, where he would transfer them into crates that were specifically designed to transport the valuable artwork. Each crate would be hidden on the trailer, surrounded by similar-looking cargo, giving them the appearance of being legitimate freight. He'd then drive to a yet-to-be-announced location and drop the entire load. Sounded simple enough—as long as everything went according to plan.

Eric let out a slow, deep breath as he thought about how unsettled his life had been the past five weeks. Playing both brothers was not for the faint of heart, and twice he'd found himself living on the edge, needing to appease both sides with fast talking and carefully orchestrated lies. But he could finally see the proverbial light at the end of the tunnel and was convinced that this would be his last run.

The radio squawked again and he heard Lucas's voice. "We need a pickup. Move in."

Eric started the engine and cautiously drove down the narrow road, keeping watch for any unwanted surprises, knowing the Manderfield brothers could be deadly. Each had connections to organized crime, supporting Eric's belief that there were a number of bodies that would be found only if the cops made an effort to dig deep enough.

He spotted Lucas as he came into the clearing and drove to the back entrance of the two-story house that was rumored to be one of Victor's most valuable properties. Following the man's directions, Eric backed the van to the door and climbed out, leaving the motor running. "We need you inside to help load the paintings," Lucas said, waving Eric through the door. "We ran into a bit of trouble."

Eric instantly saw what Lucas meant by *trouble*. Two of the men who had gone in to clear the way were slumped over near a clump of bushes, their blood-soaked bodies motionless. Three other men that Eric didn't recognize were lying on the outdoor patio, their bodies also lifeless. The last man standing was crouched in front of the door that led into the house, working the elaborate lock.

"I take it the place wasn't empty like we were told," Eric said to Lucas.

"Not all information you get is accurate," he replied with a shrug. "The paintings are inside, second floor, the room facing the front of the house. Go with Alonzo."

It took another three and a half minutes for Alonzo to break through the locks, and once inside Eric was staggered by the treasures that were skillfully arranged throughout the first-floor rooms. There were tables displaying everything from delicately painted vases to crystal figurines and imposing statues. Original artwork occupied every square inch of wall space, and richly stuffed chairs and sofas that looked as if they'd once taken up space in European castles were stylishly placed in every room. Even the fireplace in the main room was a monstrosity. Combined, it gave the residence a real museum feel, Eric thought. Stuffy, overpriced and snobbish.

As they climbed to the next level, Eric ran his hand along a railing that had been constructed from flawless mahogany wood and polished to an almost blinding finish. It curled up and around a wide marble staircase with an oriental carpet running up the center of each step. More antiques lined the second-floor hallway, a blend of vivid colors and dignified luxury.

With Alonzo in the lead, they headed toward the end of the hall where they stopped in front of a door that was secured with a keypad entrance system. Alonzo punched in a series of numbers before hitting the play button on a mini recorder he'd pulled out of his pocket. Eric heard Victor Manderfield's voice clearly stating his name, and the locks clicked opened. "Who needs fancy technology," Eric mumbled mockingly.

The room they entered was fairly large and interestingly bare, the only piece of furniture being a long, padded bench running down the center. There were several other paintings, as well as sketches depicting landscapes and biblical scenes, adorning the walls, but the canvases they had been sent in to fetch were leaning up against the back wall waiting to be framed and hung.

Alonzo was already unlocking the three aluminum cases they had dragged up to use for transporting the artwork. Eric went to the first painting, a portrait of a woman and child, and slipped it into a soft, velvet sack before carefully packing it into one of the cases. Alonzo was doing the same with the second piece, this one a portrait of a single woman wearing next to nothing and lounging on a short sofa. The third painting was a portrait of a bearded man standing by an open window and looking off into the distance. As Eric prepared this painting for transport he scoffed at what people called talent. But if the three pieces were truly worth what his Internet search had indicated, who was he to judge?

After each piece was securely tucked away in its protective case, the two men made their way back through the house and out to the van, storing the paintings in the back. Lucas turned to Eric and said, "Get moving and radio if you run into any problems." He then followed Alonzo toward a battered pickup truck and the two took off in the opposite direction.

Once on the road Eric settled back, aware that he had two solid hours of driving ahead of him. Pulling out a silver flask, he took a satisfying sip of whiskey before raising the flask to his image in the rearview mirror in mock salute. "You're one lucky bastard," he said with enthusiasm. "One lucky bastard."

Eric was twenty miles out from the rundown barn where his rig was currently parked. He knew the exit he needed to take was fast approaching and checked his rear view mirror before changing lanes. What he saw reflected nearly caused him to lose control of the van.

A familiar black Mercedes racing for the exit forced Eric to change his strategy and continue down the highway, his eyes flitting back and forth from the road to his mirrors. When he reached the next exit he followed it to an old frontage road that led to the far end of the deserted farm land. Pulling off the road he cut the lights and came to a complete stop near a cluster of trees. He'd go by foot from here and check things out before deciding on whether it was safe enough to swap the paintings from the van to the trailer.

Moving as quietly as he could, he plowed his way through thickened grass and mud toward the area where he'd left his truck and trailer. But as he closed in on the exact spot, the sight of four men pointing large automatic weapons at Lucas Ramos and Alonzo Dias brought him to his knees. He crawled behind a rundown tractor that sat at the border of the property line, trying hard to regulate his breathing. And sure enough, there was Stan Hudson leaning against the same Mercedes that had passed him on the highway just over a half hour ago.

Eric couldn't hear what was being said—he was just too far away—but he could read the body language and judged that it wasn't going to be a happy ending for his two compadres. Suddenly, one of Stan's men grabbed Lucas and pushed him to the ground and Eric watched in horror as Carl Skinner, the most feared man in Victor Manderfield's organization, kicked him several times while the man's screams filled the empty night air. Alonzo, no doubt knowing his turn would be next, decided to take his chances and broke away, running in Eric's direction. As the headlights from the Mercedes lit Alonzo's face, Eric saw his anguish as the first bullet hit his thigh, the second his left shoulder and the third explode through his skull.

As the dust settled, there was absolute quiet. Eric turned back to where Lucas lay in a fetal position, his arms clamped around his head, and watched as Stan pushed away from the Mercedes and walked toward him. Squatting, he leaned over and said something that made Lucas tighten his body even more.

It wasn't until Lucas started to nod fervently and Stan finally backed away, that Eric was certain the crew boss was prepared to give up all the information he had on the belief that Stan would let him live. Eric also knew that the information furnished would include his own involvement.

After carefully making his way back to the van, he followed the frontage road to the first entry ramp leading onto the highway. Driving south, he thought about the rented three-room apartment where he was storing the few items he'd planned on taking with him when he headed for the beaches in the Caribbean. Even though he had continued to live in the house that he and Emma had shared, his paranoia had persuaded him to find a secure place to hide out in case he ran into trouble. He'd felt rather foolish at the time, forking over three months' worth of rent, but he wasn't feeling foolish anymore. Stan knew exactly where his house was, but Eric was sure that no one knew about the apartment.

But his first order of business was to get those paintings stashed and he knew the perfect place. Once that was done he'd pick up a six-pack and work out a new plan—one that at the very least would keep him alive.

It was nearly dawn before Eric finally settled into the apartment, located at the southern edge of Kingsport. He unscrewed the cap off a bottle of beer and strolled into the living room, plopping down on the worn recliner that his landlord had offered him when he'd moved in. The only light in the room came from a battered lamp with a dust-covered shade that had been left by the former tenant. The walls, which hadn't seen a coat of paint in the last ten years, were cracked and peeling, and the carpet was stained from the spoils of the various adults, children and pets that had occupied the space before him.

The heavy, flower-patterned drapes were drawn and the locks on both doors and windows secured, including the deadbolts he had purchased on his drive back and now installed at both the front and alley entrances. He'd also picked up two sensor alarms that would signal any unwanted intruders.

His mind drifted to the three stolen paintings that were tucked away in a storage unit at the Highland Self-Storage facility located about an hour outside of Kingsport near the Pueblo Airport. They'd be protected for now, but he had to make a decision about what to do with them, while at the same time assuring his safe passage out of this repulsive city.

He reasoned that he had only two options for unloading the artwork. He could try selling them through the black market—but his limited knowledge made that the less desirable choice. Or he could negotiate their return by either delivering the three pieces to Marco as planned, or make a deal to sell them back to Victor.

Eric's instincts told him that his best bet was to find a way to deal with Marco. After witnessing the brutality shown to Lucas and Alonzo, Eric would prefer not having anything to do with Victor Manderfield, which included his goons, Stan Hudson and Carl Skinner.

However, his plan needed a provision that would take the heat off his involvement and would still give him enough money to leave the country. It would take time to set things up and seal the deal, but he would find a way to make it happen.

He shifted his thoughts to Emma, who was going to play a prominent, although unknowing, role in his plans to hit it rich. She thought she had found a safe place to live after she'd left him, but it had only taken him a week to find her. And although up to this point he'd done nothing more than keep a watchful eye on her, that was about to change. She was going to innocently become his safeguard against the Manderfields.

He glanced toward the front door where he'd placed both his laptop computer and a large suitcase filled with an assortment of clothing and basic essentials. Beside the suitcase was a cardboard box—the bait in his creatively inspired plan. It contained odds and ends that didn't hold any particular value to him, but items he had grabbed on impulse during his last trip to the house. Included in the box was a silver tray that had been given to them as a wedding present by Emma's grandmother, two handcrafted Irish tablecloths and matching napkins that had belonged to her mother, and several stuffed animals from her childhood that she had kept on a shelf in the corner of the bedroom. One of the animals—a lion she referred to as Clarence—had been a sentimental favorite of hers. It had been given to her by her father when, at the age of three, she had spent a week in the hospital battling a severe case of pneumonia. Now, Eric was counting on that stupid stuffed toy to still hold an emotional allure for his dear wife. Because if it did, Clarence was about to become Eric's lifeline to a very prosperous future.

He took another swig, and closed his eyes while he mentally outlined his next steps. Within minutes his head lulled to one side and the beer bottle fell to the dirty carpet. For the next two hours he dreamed of sandy beaches, drinks with umbrellas and naked women.

CHAPTER FIVE

Max Dunmore and Roger Donnelly stepped out of the elevator at the Kingsport County Hospital and ran into one of the emergency room nurses. She stopped abruptly when Roger spoke her name in a soft and charming voice. "Mary Lou Speckman. Aren't you a sight for sore eyes?"

"Roger Donnelly. Haven't seen you around since you broke my sister's heart."

"Oh, come on now, Mary Lou. Give me a break here. What would you say if I told you that in fact it was the other way around?"

"I'd say that you'd be delusional. But I know my sister, so I feel no sympathy for either one of you." Starting back down the hall she said, "Are you here about the woman who was beaten by her ex?"

"Yeah. Do you know for sure it was her ex?" Roger knew that he'd get the official report from one of the two officers who'd responded to the call, but he also knew the talk around the water cooler had its value.

"Can't give you anything but hearsay," she said as if reading his thoughts. "And the word is that the prick was still beating on her when the cops arrived. They're treating him for cuts on his knuckles and some nasty scratch marks on his face and neck. Nick Fraley said it appears as if she tried like hell to defend herself."

"Officer Nick Fraley? I've got to admit that I find myself wondering why he's talking to the nursing staff about police business."

"I overheard him and Doctor Mike talking. So don't get your underwear in a bundle."

"No worries on that front," Roger said with a wink. "If you get my drift."

"Way too much information, Donnelly," Mary Lou replied. "How do you put up with this man, Maxwell?"

"It's definitely a cross to bear, Nurse Speckman."

She slipped her arm through Max's and said in a low but audible voice, "I always liked you best anyway." When they turned left and headed down another corridor, she released her hold and Max knew this was where the patients were treated. Everything, from the way hospital personnel acted to the sounds and smells, altered. The change in Mary Lou's manner was also noticeable as she straightened and took on the posture of a warrior.

"If you both wait near the desk for a minute, I'll find Dr. Waterman. He's the one who has been taking care of Ms. Cassidy."

It didn't take long before an impressive looking man in a knee-length white coat approached them. "Detectives. I'm Dr. Waterman," he said extending his hand. "If you'll follow me I'll take you to the patient's room. I can give you the extent of her injuries but you'll have to talk to the officers who escorted her in about what happened."

"We understand that the ex-husband was also brought in," Max said. "Do you know where he's being treated?"

"I believe Mr. Cassidy is one floor up. As his injuries are not as severe, another physician is overseeing his case."

"Thank you, Doctor," Roger said as they stopped in front of one of the treatment rooms. "We'll need some time alone with Mrs. Cassidy. If we have any questions as they pertain to her physical injuries, we'll buzz."

"Of course," Waterman said, turning toward the nurses' station as the detectives entered the room.

What Max saw was more vicious than he had expected. Emma Cassidy—the neighbor that Max's grandmother had asked him to check on—was pale beneath the bruising around her face, neck and arms. Her right hand and wrist were firmly bandaged and her lip showed a deep cut, no doubt caused by her husband's fist. There was also some dried blood along the cut above her right eye, and Max imagined that she was in a great deal of pain.

It had been weeks since he'd sat on Emma's street and watched her enter the pretty little house with the white and green trim, her husband's arm wrapped around her waist. He had to admit that he'd only thought of her once or twice since then. There had been nothing in her manner that day that would have suggested she lived in an abusive home. Or maybe that's just what he'd wanted to see, choosing to believe that his grandmother's imagination had just gotten the best of her.

He hesitated before approaching the hospital bed, taking a moment to collect his thoughts as the image of a rabbit's foot, dangling from a key ring, popped into his head.

"Mrs. Cassidy, I'm Detective Donnelly and this is Detective Dunmore," Roger began. "We're here to ask you some questions about what happened."

"I know you," she said to Max, "but I can't remember how."

"We met a month or so ago at the Kingsport Grocery Mart. Your car wouldn't start—"

"And you gave it a jump. Yes, I remember now." Shifting slowly to a more comfortable position she added, "Go ahead and ask your questions, Detectives. Dr. Waterman gave me pain medication and said that I'd be crashing soon."

"We need you to confirm who did this to you," Roger said, drawing Emma's attention back to him.

"Eric Cassidy, my soon-to-be ex-husband."

"This happened in your apartment, is that correct?"

"Yes. We're separated but he obviously found out where I'm living and decided to drop in unannounced."

"Why did you let him in? Or did he have a key?"

"No, Detective, he did not have a key. I didn't want anything to do with him. His abuse is the reason I left him and I haven't seen him since I walked out over a month ago."

Pushing past the sudden guilt he was feeling for not doing a follow-up on her, Max asked, "Why did you let your husband in if you knew he was a danger to you?"

"When I looked through the peephole Eric was standing there with a box of my things. Family heirlooms that meant a lot to me but that I'd had to leave behind. He was always a convincing son of a bitch and he said that he was moving and wanted to drop the box off because he knew how much those items meant to me. He said he was going to set the box by the door and leave. And I thought he had.

"I knew better, Detective. I work at a women's center, for crying out loud. I knew better. But I was having a difficult day and my spirits were at an all-time low and I couldn't resist holding something familiar. And I wanted to believe that even Eric could experience a flicker of kindness."

Emma brushed a stray tear from her cheek and without thinking, Max reached for her hand. "It's going to be all right. We have your husband in custody."

"For how long? I know how this works. I've seen it play out with other women who have come to the shelter for protection. And I've heard the do-gooders tell them they're safe and that their abuser is in custody. I know what you're saying is meant to make me feel better, but it doesn't. Because Eric will be out of jail probably before I'm out of this hospital bed."

Roger decided that he'd had enough with the drama. "Mrs. Cassidy. We're doing everything we can to ensure that Mr. Cassidy will be held responsible for what he's done to you. I strongly suggest you file a restraining order and when you're released stay with someone you know and trust. Don't go back to the apartment for a while. Because, yes, Mr. Cassidy will no doubt be released on bail. But he'll serve time if convicted of causing you these injuries."

"Thank you, Detective . . . Donnelly?" Roger nodded in acknowledgement. "I'm tired now and I can't answer any more of your questions. There's a slip of paper on the bed stand with my attorney's name and phone number. We'll come in and file a complaint after I'm discharged."

"You don't seem to be too shook up or concerned about this," Roger said, watching her closely.

"You're wrong, Detective. I'm extremely concerned about this. That's why I need someone who can support me through it. His name is Brian Reed."

As Max and Roger walked toward the elevator Roger said, "Let's go talk to the husband, see what his side of the story is." Stepping into the elevator car, Roger pressed the button that would direct them to the second floor. "You know, what has me puzzled is why she thinks she needs an attorney. She's the victim here."

"Maybe he's also a friend."

"Which makes me think that Mr. Reed may be the reason why Eric Cassidy is the soon-to-be ex-husband."

"You think she was cheating on the guy?" Max asked with some surprise. "Even if that's true, it's no reason to pound on her."

"Don't be an ass," Roger grumbled. "There's never a reason to beat up a woman. I'm just saying it's something that would anger some men enough to want to strike out."

"You're reaching, Roger. I don't see any reason we should play the affair card, based on what little we know."

"Well, here's his floor," Roger said as the elevator doors opened. "Let's get Mr. Cassidy's side of the story."

Emma had been right. Eric Cassidy had posted bail the morning following the attack—a full day before she left the hospital. Unfortunately, three days after that, they found his body in an abandoned building, his truck still burning behind the structure. He'd been beaten and then shot in the head.

Emma was the first person the police questioned in connection with her husband's death, and at her request the interview was taking place in her office at the Kingsport Center for Healing, a women's shelter where she'd been employed since leaving Eric. Roger Donnelly was taking the lead in the questioning while Max moved around the office space, observing.

"We need to know where you were last night between seven and midnight, Mrs. Cassidy," Donnelly began.

"I was at home, in my apartment. I ordered delivery from the Chinese restaurant down the block at about seven thirty and it came shortly before eight thirty. At about nine I phoned our director and we spent a half hour discussing details for our fundraiser being held at the end of next month. After that I was on my computer until around midnight. I've missed a lot of work in the past several days as you know, and I'm trying to catch up."

"I'll need the name of the director," he said.

"Delores Fairbanks. She'll actually be in around ten today and I'm sure she'll answer any questions you have."

"We'll be sure to talk to her." After a brief pause he continued. "When was the last time you saw Mr. Cassidy?"

"The night he came to my apartment, beat me and I ended up in the hospital."

"You didn't see him after that? Or talk to him?"

"No."

"Is today your first day back to work?" Max asked. He'd taken a seat on a scuffed-up wooden chair that sat off in one corner, taking notes.

"I returned yesterday, actually. I'm trying to put in as many hours here as I can, although there's a lot I can do from home."

"We're going to need your computer to verify you were on it at the time your husband was murdered," Roger said, drawing Emma's attention back to him.

"I'll contact my attorney. He may insist on a warrant."

Donnelly leaned forward in his chair and said, "Do you have something to hide?"

"Not at all."

"Did anyone else see you last night?"

"I don't know if anyone in my apartment building saw me come home," she said, trying not to let her dislike for Roger Donnelly float to the surface, "but I didn't see any of them. Of course, Martin saw me when he delivered my food. You can check with him."

"Maxwell," Donnelly said, his eyes never leaving Emma. "Do you have any other questions?"

"That should do it for now, Mrs. Cassidy," Max replied as he rose. "We would appreciate it if you would contact your attorney while we're talking to Ms. Fairbanks."

"And tell him that we'll be getting that warrant for your apartment, and your vehicle." Roger stood and headed for the door. "Oh, and Mrs. Cassidy? We'll no doubt want to talk to you again. So it would be better if you stayed available."

"I didn't kill Eric, Detective. I want to be off your suspect list as quickly as possible so I'll call Brian and we can meet you at my apartment whenever it's convenient for you."

"I'll let you know. Now, if you could point us to your director's office?"

CHAPTER SIX

A week after the police interview, Emma had been dropped as a suspect in Eric Cassidy's murder. She understood why she had been the logical choice for their primary suspect, but it was frustrating that she had been put in that position. Fueling her frustration was the realization that Eric had not only wielded a malicious power over her while he'd been alive, but had also found a way to manipulate that power after his death. Would she ever be free of his control, she wondered?

"What are you thinking about?" her friend, Zoe Brine, asked as they drove down Glenview Drive toward the house Emma had once shared with Eric.

"I want to be free of Eric and I've been having doubts about that ever happening. But before you say anything," Emma said with a grin, "I also have days when I feel totally liberated and I barely think of him."

"You're the only one who can break the connection," Zoe said with empathy. "Actually, going through the house is a great first step. Grab what you want, give the rest to charity and then put the house on the market. You won't even have to see it again after today if you don't want to."

"I know, and thanks for doing this with me, Zoe."

"Been there, done that and all the other rhetoric. We all need a good support system and I'm yours today."

"You're mine most days, and don't deny it. There aren't many people I call friend. And when Eric and I were together there was no one."

"Well, that's great. So, I'm the best among what? Two, three other people you've let into your life? That's quite the endorsement," she said with a laugh. "Cut yourself some slack, Emma. People are a funny breed and they tumble into your life at the oddest times. You can't rush it."

Zoe's words were lost on Emma as the house came into view. Slowly, she pulled into the driveway, flashes of the last night spent there, fighting their way to the surface.

"A quick in and out," Zoe said softly. "Let's use the front door."

Emma looked over at the friend she'd had since starting work at the women's center, grateful that Zoe understood the complexity of coming back here. She had a dark, unblemished complexion framed by soft, coal-black hair, and onyx-colored eyes that always seemed to have an amused look in them. Zoe's greatest asset, however, was her gentle heart and the deep commitment she had to the women at the shelter. As a volunteer who worked with clients needing legal advice, Zoe knew the steps that women recovering from abuse went through. Yes, Zoe understood—in more ways than one. "Been there, done that," is what she'd always say. Because she had been there at one time, and had survived. Now she helped others do the same.

"Front door. Quick in and out," Emma said flinging open the car door. "Let's do this, girlfriend."

Walking into the foyer was strange enough without witnessing the chaos that lay before her throughout the first floor. As the two women slowly made their way through each room, Emma was struck with the disbelief that Eric had completely ignored the upkeep of the place.

There were dirty dishes and beer cans stacked on top of tables and chairs in every room. On the floor next to the couch sat half empty bottles of liquor and plates holding the leftovers of unidentifiable meals. The couch cushions appeared to have been removed at one point and then indifferently tossed back where they sat crooked and out of place. Emma was appalled by the fact that she could have written her name in the build-up of dust on the furniture. She had always made sure the house was clean and uncluttered, working hard to make it a home for both her and Eric. And now it looked like a bachelor's pad that had seen more than its share of wild parties.

"I've got to say Emma, your ex was a real slouch," Zoe said as they started toward the dining room. "This place is going to need some work before you can sell it."

"More than some," Emma replied. "I hadn't expected this big a mess. I guess I'll need to come back next weekend and do something about it."

"We'll bring a couple of ladies from the shelter with us," Zoe said. "There's no way you can do this all by yourself. You pop for the margaritas and chips and we'll have us a grand old party."

Emma just shook her head and laughed, but knew she'd take her friend up on the offer. "Was there someone who supported you? You know, when you finally left your ex?"

"Nope. And it took me twice as long to get to where you're at emotionally so that's why I help wherever I can at the shelter." Zoe unzipped her windbreaker and flung it over the back of a dining room chair. "Let me see that list you made up and we can start packing up your things. I've got the stickers for any furniture you want to keep and Larry said he'd come over on Friday with a couple of his friends to move the heavy items out."

"Great. Let's get to it, and when we're done I'm buying dinner."

"Of course you are," Zoe said as she headed up the back stairs, noting that the upper floor wasn't in any better condition than the first floor. It took nearly four hours to get through every room, but it had been time well spent, Zoe thought as Emma locked up. The smile on her friend's face gave her hope that closure was just around the corner.

The phone rang early. Emma fumbled with the receiver, straining to see the clock on the nightstand. If she was reading it correctly, it was just past one in the morning.

The news wasn't good. The house she'd just been through ten hours earlier, and everything she'd left in it, had burned to the ground. Nothing had been spared. She was respectfully asked to report to police headquarters for questioning at nine.

By the time she arrived with her attorney, the initial determination was listed as a natural gas leak and by the end of the week she was being told that the investigation would be closed. Any further questions would need to be directed to her insurance company.

Four days after the fire, Max was reading the final report when Roger came into the squad room. "Emma Cassidy just can't get a break, can she?" Max said without looking up.

"Don't be fooled by that sugar and spice act," Roger replied as he took his suit coat off and slipped it on the back of his chair. Pointing to the folder he'd tossed on the desk, he said, "Victor Manderfield is involved with this, Max. And Eric Cassidy was knee deep in the kind of trouble that begins and ends with Manderfield. I have no doubt that poor little Emma, who just can't get a break, knows something."

"Wait, what are you saying? That if Cassidy was somehow involved with Victor Manderfield, that makes Emma involved by association? That doesn't make sense, Roger. Besides, we looked at Cassidy and couldn't make a connection to Manderfield."

"Maybe not, but the method used to kill him, and the fact that his truck was set on fire, then his house? That all fits with how Manderfield settles scores. The wife keeps professing that she and her husband didn't talk about his business, but you and I know that's a bunch of crap. I'll find the proof, and when I do, she's going down."

Max leaned back in his chair and watched Roger shuffle through a stack of message slips on his desk. He suspected that his partner's attitude toward the elusive Victor Manderfield was temporarily blocking his ability to see that Emma was innocent. "I know how bad you want Manderfield," Max said, "but Emma's not the bridge that's going to get you to him. With that said, why don't I stop by the shelter and unofficially talk to her again."

Roger leaned his elbows on the desk and sighed. "Fine. I guess she was always a long shot anyway. And if there was any proof of Manderfield's criminal activities that her old man kept, it's gone up in flames now." He stood, grabbing his jacket off the chair, and said, "I'm going downstairs for a sandwich. You want anything?"

"No, I'm good."

When he was alone, Max finished reading the report on the fire. His partner may still have doubts about Emma's innocence, Max thought, but he was convinced she had simply been a victim. He closed the folder and tossed it in the basket holding paperwork that would eventually be filed away.

CHAPTER SEVEN

One week later

Emma was on the phone finalizing the catering menu for the fundraising dinner that would be taking place the following Sunday evening. She'd been working nonstop ordering supplies, booking the entertainment, accepting donations for the silent auction, lining up sponsors and coordinating volunteers. She loved her job as administrative assistant to the shelter's director and cared deeply for the women and children who came through the front door looking for support. She knew what they were going through and understood how hard it had been for them to take that step in asking for help.

Just as she disconnected the call Emma heard the gentle knock on her open office door. She smiled when she saw Max Dunmore standing there, carrying two boxes, one that appeared to be loaded with toys and board games.

"Well, look at what the cat dragged in." She laughed as the calico cat that was the shelter's mascot slithered between Max's legs. She remembered Delores Fairbanks telling her that a young boy had brought the animal with him several years ago when his mother had sought protection from an abusive boyfriend. The shelter's director had given the cat a permanent home when—in a moment of regret for taking off—the mother had returned to her abuser and taken her son with her, leaving the cat behind. Sadly, the cat had been the sole survivor.

"I was nominated to act on behalf of the station and bring our donations down for the fundraiser. I also bought some toys for you to give to the kids here," Max said as he set the boxes on a worktable in the corner. "Actually, there's some really nice stuff for the auction. Our lieutenant has even donated his culinary skills in the form of a four-course dinner for six. He'll go to the winner's house, cook the food, serve the meal and even clean up after himself." He turned back to Emma and said with a smirk, "Hell, I'm even thinking about bidding on that one."

"That does sound like it could be a high-ticket item. For myself, I'd be hard pressed to find five other people I could invite over." Realizing what she'd just said, Emma shook her head and added, "Wow. That sounded grossly like an invitation to a pity party, didn't it?"

"Not at all," Max said as he sat down in the chair in front of her desk. "It hasn't been that long since you've been on your own. Meeting new people and making friends isn't always that easy. Give it time."

"You're right. When I left Eric, I swore that I wouldn't regret my decision no matter how bad things got, convinced it was the only way out. I never wanted anyone's pity. Still don't, for that matter." She sat up straighter and added, "And I still believe that. I don't need anyone's pity."

A knock on the door had Emma glancing up. "The meeting starts in twenty, Emma. Delores asked me to remind you that she'll want a report on how the fundraiser is going."

"Thanks, Anna. I'm on it."

When they were alone again, Max said, "My grandmother told me that you called yesterday. Said you guys had a nice talk."

Emma remembered how surprised she'd been when Max had popped in to see her a few days earlier, then casually mentioned his connection to her former neighbor. He'd claimed his visit had been a follow-up to the fire, even though he'd spent most of the time discussing everything but police business. She'd even suspected that if he hadn't been called back to the station, he would have asked her out. An invitation she would have enjoyed accepting.

"It was good to talk to Joan," Emma said now. "She's the one thing I actually miss about the old neighborhood."

"She has that affect on people," Max said, shifting in the wooden chair, hoping to find a more comfortable position. "Now, about what you said before. You know, about not needing anyone's pity? I hope you don't think I feel that way. On the contrary, I see a strong, determined, intelligent woman who's found a way to survive, with very little support from the outside world."

"Few people outside of these walls know about my past. I've wanted it that way. Not because I'm ashamed, but because I don't need it as a marker. I'm living for the now, with the past behind me and the future something to dream about exploring. It's simple, but that's the way I see it."

Max looked at her for several quiet moments, then said, "I'd like to be part of that exploration, Emma. What do you say about having dinner with me? Of course, I'll understand if it's too soon, or if you just don't want to go out with me. Although I'm hoping you'll say yes."

Emma treated him to one of her full-out, soft, and sexy-as-hell smiles when she said, "I'd like that, Max. Any feelings I had for Eric died long before he did, and I'm certainly not in mourning for him. So no, it's not too soon for me to be seen with another man. And besides, I don't really peg you as being someone who cares what other people think anyway. But I do appreciate you thinking about how I might feel about it. Thank you."

"You're welcome." He held her gaze, and returned her smile. "Are you free Saturday?"

CHAPTER EIGHT

Emma was walking up the steps to Max's townhouse where she would soon be treated to a home-cooked meal. For the past month, they had spent a considerable amount of time together and Emma was enjoying the getting-to-know-you phase of their relationship.

In addition to the movies, cozy dinners and weekend picnics, they'd also spent time talking about the struggles in Emma's marriage, and Max had proven to be a sensitive, compassionate listener. He hadn't judged, admonished, or changed the subject when the telling became difficult to hear. Instead, he'd held her when she cried and sat quietly with her when she was all talked out. What more could you want in a man? she thought.

Although every now and then Emma still found herself up against Max, *the detective*, which left her confused and just a bit apprehensive. She understood that when she had first met Max, Eric's abusive behavior and questionable business deals had created some uncomfortable moments for them, but they each had felt a connection to the other and had chosen to test the relationship waters. But there were times like this morning when, during a pleasant enough phone call, she was left feeling as if she were being interrogated by the cop rather than being courted by the man.

"I never want to lie to you," he had said in his easygoing and comforting voice, "or hold back anything that could hurt our relationship, Emma. But Eric's name came up today during the review of an investigation on a man we've been building a case against for a number of years. I really don't want to bring this up now, knowing how badly you want all those memories behind you, but it's important. Do you ever remember Eric discussing Victor Manderfield or his brother, Marco?"

She'd taken a deep, steadying breath, refusing to let Max's question upset her. "The names don't sound familiar," she'd said, keeping her voice steady. "I've told you a dozen times, Max. Eric never discussed anything with me, let alone the people he associated with."

Even as she'd spoken the words, though, her thoughts had flashed back to the night Eric had brought one of his trucking associates over to the house. Although she had told Max about Eric's attack on her that night, she had never told anyone but Zoe about the man Eric had called Stan Hudson. Besides, she couldn't see any connection between that evening and the link Max was searching for, so she'd dismissed it. "I wish I could help you, but I can't."

She'd remained calm as he asked her several more questions that she answered openly and honestly, and he finally ended the call by telling her he was looking forward to their dinner. She remembered feeling disappointed that their conversation had lacked the usual intimate nuance and wondered now if maybe she was expecting too much from Max. Maybe his feelings for her weren't as deep as hers had become for him. The pull to be with him was becoming too strong to ignore, and wanting to see him was slowly turning into a need to see him. Although her mind was telling her not to rush into what could become a strong, emotionally charged relationship, her heart was saying that Max was the man she'd spent her entire life searching for. This was the man who could show her the tender side of romance and would offer her everything he had, every time. She wanted to experience his touch, listen to his endearing words as they made love, and find contentment as they slept in each other's arms.

She was slightly startled when the door sprung open. "Why are you just standing out here?" Max asked as he looked around. "Did you ring the bell? Because I didn't hear it."

"I was just daydreaming, I guess," she replied, embarrassed that she had gotten lost in her thoughts of him. "Here, I brought a bottle of the finest red wine you can get for ten dollars," she said with a laugh. "It has a cork, so you have to give me points for that at least."

He took the bottle in one hand and gently pulled her toward him with the other. "A fine label indeed and one I've heard great things about, so I graciously accept your gift." He bent down and kissed her, taking his time to enjoy it. When he pulled back he added, "Come on inside before the neighbors start to talk."

"Like you would care," she said smiling.

"You've got a point. Hang up your coat and then come join me in the kitchen. We're having lemon chicken and rice with a side of mixed vegetables. Sound good?"

"Sounds and smells delicious," Emma said as she stepped into the kitchen and sat on a bar stool by the counter separating the kitchen from the living room. "Why so fancy?"

"I don't know about fancy. It's one of my grandmother's recipes and happens to be one of my favorites, so I usually don't screw it up. And speaking about my grandmother, she wants to get together with us sometime soon. I thought we could all go out to dinner and she could ask her friend Henry to join us. It sounds like that relationship is getting serious."

"I'd like that. I haven't seen Joan since . . . well, since I lived at the house. She was always nice to me, so yes, I think that would be a great idea."

"Done. I'll call her next week. Now, tell me how your day was."

Max uncorked the bottle of wine and poured two glasses, handing one to Emma. When he didn't get a response he looked at her and said, "What? Did something happen?"

"No," she said and took a sip from the glass. "You always do that. Ask me how my day was. And more importantly, you actually care how my day was."

Max had gone back to the stir-fried vegetables but now stopped and met her eyes over the kitchen table. "I do care, Emma," he said gently, knowing the meaning behind her words. "And I'm sorry that Eric never did."

"Water under the bridge, and it doesn't matter now," she replied with a shrug. "Thank you for asking, and to answer your question, my day was great. How about you?"

He watched her for another moment and smiled. "I did my part to keep the streets of Kingsport safe." He opened the oven door to check the chicken and, satisfied, picked up both glasses of wine and motioned to the living room. "Let's go sit and enjoy this wonderful vintage while we wait. Dinner should be ready in about twenty minutes."

She stood and led the way to the couch, making herself comfortable in one corner. Max set the glasses on the coffee table then slid down next to her, wrapping his arm around her shoulders. It felt good to be nestled next to her, drawing in her scent as he slowly ran his fingers up and down her arm. The feel of her was often enough to soothe him, but tonight his guilt about their earlier phone conversation was keeping the comfort at bay.

His day had been riddled with ups and downs, including Roger's badgering him to rattle Emma's memory regarding a lead he had received on a cold case involving Victor Manderfield. Max knew that Roger still believed Eric had worked for Victor, and therefore, had been privy to vital information pertaining to the man's organization. But there were cases with higher priority that needed attention, and with no hard evidence Max was of the opinion that spending time investigating a dead man was not the best use of time for seasoned detectives.

Unfortunately, Roger's continuous refusal to give up on finding a connection had put a strain on their partnership, not to mention their friendship. So he had made the call to Emma and was now feeling like a first-class jerk. He pulled her more tightly into his arms and, leaning down, pressed his lips to her temple. "I want to apologize for this morning."

She tilted her head and held his eyes, knowing exactly what he was referring to. "If I knew anything, I would have already told both you and Roger—who I know was the driving force behind your phone call. But I just don't know anything that could help you."

He kissed her softly before saying, "No more questions. I promise." He picked up her glass and handed it to her but instead of drinking, she laid her head on his shoulder and closed her eyes. Eric Cassidy had no place with them tonight and she was determined to banish his ghost before the end of the evening.

They were silent for several minutes longer until he said, "I have a confession to make, Emma."

She pulled back slightly so she could see his face. "Let's have it so we can be done with this whole thing."

"The reason we're having lemon chicken is because it's the only meal I know how to make. I hate to cook."

As her laughter filled the room, he smiled. The road that lay ahead of them wasn't going to be an easy one, but he was filled with the hope that they were both strong enough to fight their way through.

After dinner, Max suggested they take a walk around the neighborhood and enjoy the cool fall evening. Emma agreed, feeling foolishly relaxed after a perfectly prepared dinner and a second glass of wine. Max had been attentive and good-humored all evening and she was thankful that not once did the conversation veer toward his caseload.

As they turned the corner and began walking toward the townhouse, Max shifted slightly and began to gently rub his hand up and down Emma's back. "Do you have to leave right away?" he asked quietly. "I'm off tomorrow and if they don't have you working Sundays yet, you can maybe stay."

She slipped her arm through his and moved in closer to his body. "I'm actually free until Monday at eight."

"Great. I was thinking we could go back inside, put on some music and if everything goes according to plan, maybe share the funny pages in the morning. How does that sound?"

She looked up and saw that smile of his accompanied by a devilish shine in his eye. "You may have to be more specific on that plan so I can make an informed decision," she said in a voice dripping with mock innocence.

"Specifics would be lost in translation I'm afraid. I'll need to show you." He stopped at the door and turned so he was facing her, his eyes now revealing his true intentions. "Will you let me show you, Emma?"

She lifted her hand, resting it on the side of his face. "I'd like nothing more."

Once inside, Max quickly walked around the house making sure all the locks were secure, then led Emma into the bedroom. It was clean and uncluttered, Emma observed, no carelessly tossed clothing on the floor or bath towels pitched on the floor. The room was pure male with dark colors on the wall, black walnut furniture and a simple brown comforter resting across the bottom of the bed. No frilly curtains covering the windows and not a single knick-knack in sight.

When her gaze moved back to watch Max, she saw him slipping the gun and holster he'd been wearing on their walk into the drawer in the nightstand by the bed. "Am I to assume that's your side of the bed?"

"Only if we fall asleep," he answered with a crooked smile. "But I don't see that as being a huge issue tonight."

As he came toward her he began to unbutton his shirt, pulling it free from his khaki pants. Leaving it hang open, he unfastened the clasp on his belt and tugged it free from the loops that secured it. He thought he saw a flash of panic move across Emma's face, but it quickly passed. He silently cursed her ex-husband as he tossed the belt into the closet.

Taking three cautious steps toward her he said, "I want to make love to you tonight, Emma. We'll do it fast or slow, once, twice—or as many times as you want. Just know that there's no satisfaction for me in hurting you. My pleasure will come from seeing your pleasure when I touch you."

He stood so close to her now he could see her chest rise and fall with each breath she took. He slowly raised his hands and began unfastening the buttons on her blouse, making sure the back of his fingers brushed her skin as they moved downward. When each button was completely undone, he pulled the front of the blouse open, sliding it over her shoulders and letting it flutter to the floor. He then lifted the thin-strapped camisole over her head and dropped it alongside the blouse. Next to go was the lacy, taupe-colored bra.

"I'll keep going if you want," he said, pressing his lips to her forehead. "You only need to tell me it's too much and I'll stop."

She stepped toward him and laid both hands on his bare chest. "Don't stop. I want you to touch me, to make love to me and take me to places I've never been before."

"Emma," he said through a smile that held promise. "Your wish is my command."

His fingers moved with purpose—from her neck to her breasts and along her smooth, tight stomach—enjoying every caress of the journey. He watched the emotions drift across her face as he slid those fingers even lower, his touch just a whisper. There was first surprise. Then desire. And finally, that pleasure he'd been waiting for. She moaned softly as she pushed against his hand and tightened her grip on his shoulders.

He ran his free hand through her deliciously thick hair, then gently easing her head back waited for her to open her eyes. "I want to hear you say my name," he said in a throaty voice as he lowered his lips to hers and lost himself in a long and blistering kiss. When he felt her body tighten and her groan begin to explode against his lips, he pulled back slightly, just enough so he could see her face. "Say my name, Emma."

All she could do was hold on as indeed his name erupted from her lips and her nails dug deep into his skin. Her body vibrated as the shock from the orgasm spread and her legs weakened. Even before the mind-blowing sensations faded, Max was carrying her to the bed where he gently lowered her across the crisp cotton sheets.

Emma discovered that sex could be a source of healing rather than the cause of cruel pain. Max's hands were big, which made his gentle touch that much more exciting. He was playful and tender, both generous and greedy. His fingers stroked and his mouth explored until her body ached for release. Unashamed of her driving need she opened herself to him, craving everything he had to offer her.

Max was just as hungry and as he rose above her, he held her eyes and saw in them a raw passion that took him helplessly over the edge. The heart that beat wildly inside him was hers now, and he knew he didn't want it any other way. He was falling in love with this woman, and could only hope that she felt the same way.

When his mind started to clear he made a clumsy yet successful effort to roll onto his back, taking his weight off her. "Didn't mean to crush you," he said in a deep, nearly breathless voice. "The mind is sometimes the second-to-last thing to rejuvenate."

She laughed, which made him smile. He would never tire of that dazzling laugh, he thought. Pulling her close he leaned in to kiss her before settling back and absently running his fingers up and down her rib cage, occasionally skimming the side of her breast.

"You keep that up," she said with a grin, "you'll set a record for rejuvenation and we won't have a choice but to prove we can do even better the second time around."

"Ah, a challenge," he said through a delighted grin. "I'm always up for a challenge."

He took his time to discover more secrets to pleasing her and allowed her the same exploration until his willpower faded to the point that he could no longer think straight. It was then that he grabbed for another condom and proved without a doubt that yes, they could do better.

CHAPTER NINE

On Monday morning Emma found herself in the back of a patrol car as it made its way to the police station. She'd been told that the detectives handling her former husband's murder case had some questions for her and it would be best if the interview was done at the station. To make things worse, there had been no alternative but to accept the offer to be driven there due to the unfortunate fact that her car had refused to start that morning. She'd taken a taxi to work, but couldn't afford such an extravagant ride twice in one day. With no other means of transportation other than to walk or hitchhike the six miles, she'd been stuck.

The request to appear, however, had been particularly disturbing to her, as it came on the heels of a midnight phone call that had been riddled with threats and innuendos. The unidentified caller had mentioned Eric several times and asked her for things she knew nothing about. What had frightened her the most, however, had been his final threat—that she would die violently if she spoke to anyone, including the police, about the call. And now she was about to walk into the enemy's camp, not knowing who, if anyone, she could trust, terrified she would do or say the wrong thing.

She had called her attorney before she left her office and now as they drove into the parking lot she saw Brian Reed standing on the steps talking to another man in a business suit. By the time she was out of the car he was already heading her way.

Taking her by the elbow he spoke to her in a quiet, confident voice. "You didn't say anything, right?"

"No. And they didn't ask anything."

"Good. I'm going to insist we have a few minutes to talk privately before Detective Donnelly interviews you."

"What could he possibly have to ask?" she said in an exasperated voice. "There can't be anything he doesn't know about me already. He wants to pin Eric's murder on me, Brian—"

"Stop talking," the attorney said in a no-nonsense tone of voice. "Wait until we're alone."

They entered the police station and she spotted Donnelly laughing with one of the uniforms who stood behind the front counter. When he turned he briefly glanced at Emma and then talked directly to her attorney.

"Thanks for coming down, Counselor," he said as he pushed away from the counter and shook the attorney's hand. Intentionally choosing not to extend the formality to Emma, he simply dropped his hands into the pockets of his dark, pleated trousers and added, "I'm sure this must be an inconvenience, Mrs. Cassidy, but it shouldn't take long. We've had some new information come to our attention and I'm hoping you can help us clear up some points."

She could see by the look he was giving her that what he meant by clearing things up was to once and for all put her behind bars.

"I'd like some time with my client, Detective, before you begin the interview. I'm sure you don't have any objections."

"None at all. You can go into Interview Room B. I'll join you shortly."

Once they were in the room Emma looked nervously around. "Detective Donnelly's up to something," she said, looking straight into Brian's eyes. "He's always wanted me for this murder and he'll do whatever it takes to get me charged and convicted. It's been nearly five months, for Christ's sake. I don't know what I ever did to earn his wrath, but he's convinced I had something to do with Eric's death."

"You didn't kill Eric, Emma. You're the victim here. They've got nothing to hang on you because there's nothing there. You have to trust me. Okay?"

"I do trust you, Brian," she said. "I just want this to be over."

"Picking you up like this is bordering on harassment and if it continues we have options. Now, before Donnelly comes back in, is there anything I should know?"

"I have no clue why I'm here. When the police showed up at the shelter, they asked me kindly to get my bag and come down to the police station because they believed I could provide information about the murder of one Eric Cassidy. I didn't have to ask who'd sent them. I knew it had to be Donnelly."

"We'll give him some room and see what he has to say. But I don't intend on letting him railroad us here either."

She turned at the knock at the door and watched Donnelly poke his head in. "Ready for us, Counselor?"

"Yes. Come in," Brian said as he stood and moved to sit next to Emma.

Detective Donnelly entered, followed by a second man that Emma had never seen before. He was introduced as Detective Newton. As Donnelly took the chair across from her, the second detective moved to the corner of the room, where he casually leaned against the wall with his arms crossed, appearing to be uninterested in the proceedings going on at the table. Emma glanced in his direction, wondering why Newton was here instead of Max. Wouldn't Max have insisted on being here?

"You are not under arrest at this time and this questioning is voluntary," Roger began. "You're free to leave at any time. Do you understand your rights, Mrs. Cassidy?"

"Yes," she replied.

"And you've chosen to have your attorney present for questioning?"

"Yes."

"Then let's begin. Your husband, Eric Cassidy, ran his own trucking business, is that correct?"

"He owned his own truck, yes."

"How many employees did he have working for him?"

"None."

"So he owned and drove the truck himself?"

"Yes. You know all this, Detective."

"Just confirming it for the record, Mrs. Cassidy. How long did Eric Cassidy own his business?"

"About five years."

"So he had it prior to your getting married."

"Yes."

The next ten minutes were spent on the various places Eric Cassidy would drive, what he was paid to haul and who paid him. Emma tried not to become frustrated as her answers repeatedly came back to the fact that she knew little about her husband's business. At one point when Donnelly was interrupted by a uniformed officer who came to the door, she found herself thinking that maybe she should have made a point to know more about what Eric did. Of course, Eric had been the one who'd made that decision, not her. More times than not, he had gone out of his way to exclude her in anything outside the home.

Emma was jarred from her thoughts when she heard Donnelly's voice. She looked up, and realized that he had taken his seat once again and was staring at her, waiting for an answer.

"What did you say?"

"Was your husband's business successful?"

"It paid the bills, yes."

"It paid the bills," he repeated with a smirk. "It actually provided more than just enough money for the bills, isn't that right?"

"I didn't keep the books, Detective Donnelly, so I really don't know."

"But after his death, you inherited quite a sum of money, didn't you?"

"I wouldn't say that, especially since most of the money went to pay off Eric's debts. There was a small savings account and a life insurance policy. That's it."

"You weren't left a pauper though, were you?"

"Where is this line of questioning going, Detective?" Brian Reed said with a hint of irritation. "Mrs. Cassidy has admitted, for the record today and in past interviews, that she didn't have access to any financial information kept by Eric Cassidy in relation to his business, or personal financial information for that matter. If you have a point here, kindly make it."

Changing tactics, Donnelly asked, "Do you have an interest in art, Mrs. Cassidy?"

"Art?"

"Yes, art. Like Picasso, Rembrandt, Monet?" He sat back, watching for her reaction.

"I've been to the art museum, but I don't own any, if that's what you're asking."

"What about your husband? Was he interested in art?"

"We never discussed the topic of art so I'm not aware of any particular interest Eric may have had in it. If he wasn't driving the truck he was either at the bar or at home watching sports."

"Sounds like that bothered you."

"No. It didn't," Emma replied, keeping her eyes focused on Donnelly.

"While your husband was on the road he must have had some down time between hauls. How did he spend that time?"

"I don't know what Eric did when he was out of town. He didn't discuss his road trips with me."

"But you were married, Mrs. Cassidy. For what was it," he paused, looking down at the file folder he'd brought into the room with him. "Yes, four years. A wife must have some idea of what her husband does, or is involved with. I find it hard to believe otherwise."

"As I recall, you're not married, Detective Donnelly. So you have the luxury of believing anything you want. The reality is that not all couples share openly."

"And what didn't you share with your husband, I wonder?"

"Detective—"

"Okay, Counselor," Donnelly said as he held up his hand. He flipped a page in the folder, adjusting his reading glasses as he skimmed the information.

"Are you aware of any property your husband owned other than the house you shared?"

"No."

"After his murder, you must have gone through his documents, correct?"

"Yes, but there was nothing I found that indicated he owned anything besides the house and his truck."

Roger again glanced at the file resting in front of him on the table. "You stated in your previous interview that on the night Mr. Cassidy was murdered, you were at home in your apartment on Jackson Street. Is that correct?"

"Yes."

"Alone?"

"Yes."

"And five days before the murder, he came to your apartment saying he wanted a truce and had brought over some of your personal belongings that you'd left at the house when you . . . ran out on him. But according to your statement that night, he ended up assaulting you in a rather violent attack, is that correct?"

"You know it is," Emma said tersely, trying to fight off the increasing throbbing at her left temple. "You saw me. You took my statement. Eric was arrested." Turning to Brian she said, "Do I have to answer these questions again? This is ridiculous. We've gone through this how many times already?"

"We'll go through it as many times as it takes, Mrs. Cassidy. A man's been murdered. And no matter how rotten you say he was, we have an obligation to find who murdered him."

"I remind you that we're here voluntarily, Detective," Brian said now in his time-perfected attorney's voice. "Start presenting this new information or we're out of here."

Roger gave the attorney a composed glance before turning back to Emma. "You stated in one of your earlier interviews that Mr. Cassidy made frequent runs to different parts of Colorado, as well as to places like Nevada, New Mexico and Texas, is that correct?"

"Yes."

"What was he transporting on these trips?"

"I don't know."

"You don't know what he would pick up and haul back?"

"No, I don't."

"What about drugs, Mrs. Cassidy? Did your husband use drugs?"

"Drugs? Of course not," she said out of reflex. But then, realizing that she knew very little about the man she'd married, added, "Not that I'm aware of. I never saw him using drugs. He preferred beer or whiskey when he was home."

Emma watched as the door to the interview room opened and Max came through it. His eyes met hers, but he couldn't read her thoughts in the brief—and for him agonizing—seconds she gave him. Before he had the door completely closed, she had already turned her attention back to his partner.

Donnelly kept going with no more than a glance in Max's direction.

"Have you ever heard of Crystal Ridge, Mrs. Cassidy?"

"No, I haven't."

"You've never been to Crystal Ridge?"

"No. I haven't," she repeated.

"Did your deceased husband ever talk about Crystal Ridge?"

"No."

Donnelly took three photos out of the file and laid one on the table between them, facing Emma. "Do you know this man?"

"No," she replied shaking her head.

"What about this man?" he asked, placing the second photo alongside the first.

"No, I've never seen either one of these men."

"What about this one?" Roger laid the third photo down and watched for her reaction. He was pleased when she jerked back and lifted her hand to her mouth.

"What is it, Emma?" Brian asked as he laid a hand on her shoulder.

She couldn't talk. Couldn't seem to focus on anything but the photo. She had worked hard to wipe that face out of her mind. But here he was, smiling up at her as if to say, *I'm back, darlin'*.

"Eric brought this man to the house one afternoon. His name is Stan Hudson."

"When did this happen?" Donnelly asked.

"Shortly before I left Eric."

"Do you have an exact date?"

"No," she lied.

"What was your husband's relationship with Mr. Hudson?"

"I assumed that Eric was making a haul for him."

The fear she'd brought into the room with her had intensified to the point that her stomach hurt and her head felt as if it were being squeezed with a vice. Stan Hudson had surfaced for a reason. She was now convinced it had everything to do with the threatening phone call she'd received just hours earlier. All she had to do to stay alive was to control her reactions from this point forward, and just answer the questions. And then she could go home.

"I'd like to take a moment to talk to my client, Detective."

"I'm sure you would, Mr. Reed."

Emma laid her hand reassuringly on her attorney's arm. "I'm fine, Brian. I have nothing to hide." Turning to Donnelly she said, "And I really don't know anything more about this man than what I've told you. He hired Eric for a job. I don't know what that job was or where Eric would have driven for it."

"Tell me what you remember about the afternoon you met Mr. Hudson."

What she remembered was that Eric was more than willing to sell her off to this man, and when that didn't work out, Eric had raped her. Violently and with no remorse. But she wasn't prepared to share that part with the detective.

"What I recall is that Eric brought Mr. Hudson to the house for dinner and after dinner they watched the ballgame for a while. Then Mr. Hudson got a phone call and told Eric he'd meet him the next morning. It sounded to me like Eric was making a run for this man," she finished as she cautiously touched the edge of the photo of Stan Hudson.

"What happened during dinner? What did they talk about?"

"Sports, mostly. At one point Eric talked about his truck needing some repair work and that it might put him out of commission for a couple of days. Other than that I don't know because I didn't spend much time with them."

"How long was he there?"

"I'd say about three hours, total."

"Did your husband say anything to you after Hudson left?" Roger asked as he tapped his finger on the photo. "Maybe some deal they had going?"

"No, nothing."

"Anything else happen that night? Something you're leaving out?"

Emma kept her eyes on Donnelly. It was true that she had told Max about Eric's brutality on the night before she'd left him, but she'd never mentioned that Stan Hudson had been at the house at some point. Was it possible that Max had made the connection and that was why Donnelly was asking about it now? But even if that were the case, would Max have told his partner about Eric's attack? She wanted to believe that he hadn't, that he'd understood she had been telling Max her friend, not Max the detective.

It didn't really matter either way, however. Her lie to Roger Donnelly would be convincing.

"No, Detective Donnelly, nothing else happened that night. I've told you everything."

"When was the next time you saw him?"

"Today. When you showed me his photo."

After a brief pause, Roger slid all three photos back into his file folder, and said, "Do you know anyone by the name of Victor Manderfield?"

"Is he in one of the photos you showed me?" she asked. When Donnelly didn't reply, she added, "I recently heard the name through your partner but I don't know who the man is."

"What about Marco Manderfield?"

"Same answer," she said.

"What do these two men have to do with my client, Detective?" Brian asked.

Ignoring the attorney, Roger continued to address Emma. "So you're stating that neither of these two men had any connection to your husband."

"I don't know," Emma said, her frustration increasing. "Again, Eric never talked about his work and I never asked."

"I never said it had to do specifically with his work, Mrs. Cassidy."

She just gave him a blank stare and then said, "You've been asking me questions about what he does—did—for a living and now you're throwing out names. What else should I think?" Leaning forward in her chair and placing her arms on the table she added, "Or is there something else I should know?"

Roger hesitated, just briefly, before replying. "I'm asking the questions, Mrs. Cassidy."

"Oh please, Detective. You're sounding like a sitcom cop now." She turned to her lawyer. "I'd like to go. I need to get back to work."

"Do you own a gun, Mrs. Cassidy?"

"Unless you have some reason to hold my client, Detective, we're leaving." Brian rose, and Emma followed his lead. "If you feel the urge to call us in again be sure you can produce evidence of a crime because our days of voluntarily cooperating are over."

"Interview with Mrs. Emma Cassidy ended," Donnelly said for the recording. "We're through at any rate. Again, I regret having to inconvenience you, Mrs. Cassidy. Have a nice day."

His smirk was the last straw. "You're wasting your time with me, Donnelly, and you and your partner know it. Don't you think taxpayers' money would be better spent if you tried to do real detective work and find the person responsible rather than badgering me?"

"Come on, Emma," Brian said as he lightly grabbed her arm and pulled her toward the door.

"Oh, I'm confident the taxpayers will be satisfied with our investigation, and the eventual outcome of this case, Mrs. Cassidy."

Brian had her out the door before she could respond.

"Bitch thinks she can march in here and lie about her husband's dealings with Manderfield," Donnelly hissed, frustrated that he hadn't been able to uncover how much Emma knew. "Well, it's not over. Not by a long shot."

"What do you think you're up to, Roger?" Max said as he stepped up to face his partner. "Why wasn't I notified that you were going to be interviewing Emma?"

"I did contact you pal, and left you a voicemail. Can't blame me if you had court this morning."

"But why did you call her in?"

"Read the file," Roger said, tossing a manila folder onto the tabletop. "Replay the recording. I've got more important things to do than handhold you through this case."

Max was far from being satisfied with Roger's response, but was stopped from asking additional questions when his partner's cell phone rang to Rimsky-Korsakov's "Flight of the Bumble Bee." Glancing at the caller ID, Roger simply pushed his way past Max and stormed out of the room.

Max grabbed the folder off the table and headed in the opposite direction. He hurried toward the parking lot and caught up to Emma on the steps leading out of the police station. "Emma, wait up. I need to talk to you."

"I'm sorry, Detective. The interview is over and I've advised my client not to talk to you. She won't be answering anymore questions."

Speaking directly to Emma, Max said, "I just need a few minutes to talk to you."

"I have nothing more to say, Detective," she said, her back straight and her cool hazel eyes boring into him. "Not to your partner and especially not to you. After all, anything I say may be used against me later on, isn't that correct?"

"Let's go," Brian said as he gently guided Emma down the remaining steps and into some fancy foreign car that screamed lawyer.

As Max watched them drive off, he struggled to comprehend what the hell had just gone down.

CHAPTER TEN

Kennewick, Washington
Present day

When Emma stepped out of the Seabrook, Max was sitting in the back of the parking lot, partially hidden behind a box truck sporting the logo of a panther holding a paint brush between its teeth, with the name of a commercial detailing shop sketched in bold cursive letters below it. He saw her cautiously scan the area before being joined by the young bartender who stepped up behind her and placed the palm of his hand at the small of her back. Although Emma didn't seem to realize it, Max could see that the move was more a show of possession than protection.

She had her keys out by the time they reached the dark tan Caprice with the child's seat and stuffed lion in the back. The car sitting next to hers was a much older make and model and was littered with candy wrappers and discarded soda cans. Max knew all this because he had walked through the lot shortly after closing, inspecting each vehicle. He'd then waited as one by one, the other cars drove off, leaving only the two. He wasn't at all surprised that Emma had walked right past the unkempt one to the Caprice, even though he had no ready explanation why she'd be driving a car clearly used to transport a child.

He watched her shake her head as she reached for the door

handle. Max could all but hear Tony's pleas as he tried to convince Emma to let him take her home. But she wasn't having anything to do with the ludicrous suggestion, politely rejecting his offer.

"That's right, Mr. Big Shot," Max muttered to himself. "Just back off. This doesn't concern you and she obviously wants to keep it that way."

Max could tell that the little bastard wasn't going to let it drop that easily and he slowly sat straighter in his seat, preparing to leap out if things escalated. Emma just laid her hand on the young man's arm and smiled, saying something that seemed to take the edge off his argument. She climbed into the car as the bartender crossed behind it and squeezed into his own.

Max pulled out behind Tony, who had pulled out behind Emma. He knew how to follow a car without being tagged and figured it wouldn't take a great deal of effort to go unnoticed with this joker. Max was sure that Emma's new guardian wasn't smart enough to recognize a tail if it bit him in the ass. But he never took unnecessary chances and followed at a discreet distance, allowing other vehicles to slip in and out between his car and Tony's.

After going a good five miles, Emma hooked a left and headed south down a moderately busy road while Tony continued straight ahead. Max pulled into the left lane and followed her for another three miles before she turned again, this time onto a lesser traveled back road.

They landed in a quiet suburb where all the houses were small and similar in design. *Starter homes* was a term that came to mind as she pulled into the driveway of a single story residence that appeared to be well tended. There wasn't much of a front yard but the grass was trim and the garden overflowed with a colorful assortment of flowers he couldn't identify. There was a wrap-around porch that appeared lazy and used, with two wicker rocking chairs that had seen better days.

He continued past the house before circling back and parking just down the block where he would have an unobstructed view of the house. There he sat, staring out the windshield, debating on what his next move should be. It had been just over a year since he had last seen her, and although he had tried to forget everything that had happened between them, he wasn't surprised to find himself here, staked outside her home at two in the morning.

It hadn't been his initiative that had led him to Kennewick. No, searching for her had been pushed down on his priority list after several months of promising leads that had all ended in great disappointment. It had been the cryptic voice message left on the machine at his office where he now ran a private investigation business that had pointed him to her current location. And although he'd found her, he suspected he was being led down a path that would no doubt turn out to be another heartbreak.

The front door opened and Max saw a younger woman walk out, laughing as Emma followed. She turned with one last comment before swinging her backpack over her shoulder and heading to the compact car parked in front of the house. Emma waved as the car disappeared down the road then took a final look around before she disappeared back into the house. Max waited another two minutes before climbing out of his car and strolling casually toward the house.

He knocked on the front door and swore softly under his breath when she opened it without checking. A common mistake, but one that could be costly. "What did you forget this time, Molly?" he heard her say as the door swung wide. She had reacted just as he had suspected she would, believing it was the girl returning for something.

"You should never assume, Emma. Always check first," he said as he pushed past her and entered the front hallway.

"What do you think you're doing? Get out of my house."

He could tell that she was upset with his sudden appearance, which was understandable, but there was something more in the way she spoke. Something that made her nervous about his presence. As he approached the living room he took in the sight of toys scattered about, noting the playpen in the corner and a basket of baby clothes waiting to be folded. It appeared that she hadn't wasted any time after leaving Colorado in the middle of the night, he thought bitterly. Leaving him, with not so much as a so-long sucker.

"Well, I see you got married again," he said with a little too much accusation in his voice. He turned to look at her, seeing the unease burning in her eyes. She had never been very good at hiding her feelings from him, and now that he really looked at her, the realization of her discomfort struck him, hard.

Taking another look around, he could see no signs there was a man of the house. He walked through the living room and made the same cursory look into the small dining room. No framed photos, no discarded clothing hanging on the back of any of the chairs. Nothing that would say this was even partially a man's domain.

"Boy or girl, Emma?" he asked.

She hugged herself more tightly and looked away.

"How old is the child?" he asked as his gut began a low boil. When she didn't say anything he lowered his voice and emphasized each word. "How old, Emma?"

She slowly turned her head and he could see tears fighting to break lose in those brilliant eyes that could melt him in an instant. Without another word he started down the hallway looking for the room where he would find the baby.

Emma knew she should stop him. But she was just too tired of guarding the secret any longer. Instead she went into the living room and slumped into a chair, having little doubt that once he entered the room and did the math, he would know that Jacob was his child.

Max had no trouble finding the bedroom. The door was ajar and he quietly pushed it the rest of the way and entered. Stepping over to the crib he felt strangely connected to the boy lying on his stomach, peacefully sucking his thumb. Max's heart flipped and his mind clouded as he watched the child sleep. After several minutes he reached over and lightly touched his son's head, then gently stroked his back.

He was the father of this child, and she hadn't told him. He closed his eyes, trying to keep the feeling of betrayal at bay. He needed to be in control when he confronted her, because this was huge. Anger and hurt feelings just wouldn't cut it.

When he returned to the living room several minutes later he just stood there, looking at her, trying to find the words. "Why didn't you tell me? I had a right to know."

She swiped trembling fingers across her cheeks, knowing she wasn't prepared for this. "How did you find me?" she finally demanded, hoping she could lead the conversation in a different direction.

"We can get to that later. Now, I want to know when, if ever, you were planning to tell me I had a son."

She sighed, knowing deep down that he had a right to ask the question. And just as much of a right to hear the answers. "I'm going to make some coffee," she began as she stood and headed toward the modest kitchen off the living area. "We can talk in there."

As she busied herself with the coffee, Max stood by the rear door, looking at the house across the small backyard. He listened to the water as it dripped into the glass carafe, waiting for her to begin. After pulling two mugs out of the cupboard, she did.

"You sliced me in two, Max, when you walked into that interview room and just let your partner basically accuse me of being involved with Eric's dirty dealings. Of being responsible for his death."

He was facing her now and opened his mouth to say something, but she stopped him. "No, don't. If you want to hear what I have to say, then you'll just keep quiet until I'm through." She slammed the cups on the table and turned her back to him. She hadn't wanted it to be this way, and maybe that was why she had let each day go by without picking up the phone and calling him with the news that he was a father. After all the time that had passed, she still hadn't let go of the anger and regret. But he was here now, and she knew he wasn't going anywhere until he had the answers he was looking for. With a sigh she turned and said, "If we're going to get through this, we have to put aside the hurt feelings and accusations."

Max went over to the coffee machine, lifted the carafe and poured both cups. After returning it to the hotplate, he sat at one end of the table and motioned for her to sit at the other.

"I was feeling so lost and scared because I didn't know what was going to happen to me," she started. "I didn't know what had happened to Eric, who had killed him, and after you and I slept together . . . after Detective Donnelly ordered me down to the station . . . I didn't know what to believe. But the more I thought about it, I was convinced you had set me up. Eric used sex as power and I figured that maybe you weren't much different. But in your case you used my feelings for you to gain the information that Donnelly wanted. That's what I thought."

Max just sat across from her in disbelief, hearing the words but not able to totally comprehend their meaning.

"And then, when you walked into the room," she continued, "and didn't say anything, just let him beat at me and didn't even try defending me, I was crushed. Thinking that you had told him what Eric had done to me was just too much to bear. And I couldn't stay and face that—face you—another day longer than I had to. When my attorney confirmed that I wasn't an official suspect, I ran. I didn't even know I was pregnant until after I'd left. And I was still so angry and so lost that I wasn't about to ask you for help."

Max now understood why Emma hadn't trusted him. The night

he had promised her there would be no more questions he had taken their relationship to the next level by making love to her. And the following Monday she'd been escorted to the station and interviewed, leaving her to believe he had orchestrated the whole thing.

"I know your partner is still convinced I did it, or at the very least believes that I hired someone to have Eric killed." She took another sip of coffee and looked at him. "And I still can't be sure what you believe." Rising, she walked over to the sink and with a shaky hand rinsed her cup under the faucet, no longer wanting the coffee.

Max rubbed his hand across his mouth as his eyes tracked her movements. How could she not know? Had their time together meant nothing to her? That one night spent making love until sunrise—had it not convinced her of how strong his feelings for her really were? Didn't she realize that his silence that day during the interview was more help to her than if he had spoken out? Well, the answer was obviously no to all of the above.

"I know you didn't kill your husband and had nothing to do with his murder. Let's get that straight right now," Max said. "And as long as we're putting our cards on the table, you never told me that Eric knew Stan Hudson, even after I asked. That he had brought Hudson into your home, for Christ's sake." He stopped and took a deep breath, trying to rein in his emotions. "I still find myself wondering why you kept that bit of information to yourself until that day in the station." He shook his head and added, "Obviously we didn't know each other as well as I thought we did."

Not willing to share her reasons for wanting to forget about ever meeting Hudson, she said, "Speaking of Donnelly, I'm surprised he isn't with you. I can't imagine him passing up an opportunity to get me back into the hot seat. Does he even know you're here?"

"No. I haven't seen or heard from him in months. I'm not with the police department anymore."

He saw the surprise cut across her face. He'd seen the same look in more than a few of his colleagues when he had announced that he was quitting the force.

"Why?" she asked quietly.

"Long story," he shrugged. "I'm a private investigator now and the reason I'm here is because I received a call three days ago telling me where I could find you. It was a shocker, to say the least, but it was too intriguing not to follow up on."

Emma reached over to switch off the coffee maker, suddenly struck with an all-too-familiar feeling of panic. Her mind raced as she struggled to come up with a plan to get rid of Max. Even if she wanted to trust him, she had learned the hard way that the only person she could really trust was herself.

"Can we finish this later, Max? Let's meet somewhere and I'll bring Jacob and we can decide what to do from here on out."

"Is there something you're not telling me?" he asked, noticing how her body had tensed when he'd mentioned the call. "Does it have anything to do with why you left?"

"It can all wait," she replied. "It was a long night at work and I'm really tired. There's a small café two blocks over that opens early. Why don't we meet, say around eight?" She held her breath, hoping that she had carried enough sincerity in her voice to put him off for tonight.

He hesitated for just a moment before pulling a card out of his jacket pocket, writing something on it, and then handing it to her. "Here's my cell number. Use it if you need it." He stood and turned toward the bedroom. "I'll just say goodnight to my son."

The words almost broke her heart. Could he really want this child in his life? Or was he playing her, like Eric had played her in the past? Giving her hope that everything would get better, and then taking great satisfaction in knocking her down?

When he came out of the bedroom she was already standing near the front door. "You need a better lock," he said when he reached her. "And you should really invest in an alarm system."

"Thanks for the advice. I'll get right on it."

The grin he gave her was short and conveyed more amusement than anything else. "I'll see you both at eight, then."

She stood in the doorway and waited as he got into his car and drove away. When he was finally out of sight she shut the door and quickly got to work packing what she and Jacob would need for the immediate future, determined to be gone by morning.

Once she was finished, she glanced at the clock and decided to get a couple hours' sleep before leaving. She set the alarm for five but before crawling into bed walked back into the living room where she pulled up the floorboard by the front window and dug out the documents hidden there. The passport and driver's license showed her photo but listed the owner as Ellen Strong. The birth certificate claimed her son to be Matthew Strong. There were also two legitimate-looking social security cards bearing the same names. She tucked everything in the side pocket of the duffel bag that sat next to the two suitcases that were now filled with clothes and other essentials.

Going back to the bedroom, she checked on Jacob and leaned over the railing on the crib to gently kiss his forehead. Tomorrow they would have to start all over again. She just hoped this would be the last time.

Crawling into the double bed across the room, she started to doze, dreaming of better days.

CHAPTER ELEVEN

Max was brought back to life by the ringing of his cell phone.

After leaving Emma, he had returned to his motel room where he'd stripped down to his boxers and then collapsed into bed, confused and just a bit depressed. He didn't know how to feel about having a son, but it wasn't as much of a shock as he figured it should be. And what about Emma? How did she fit into the whole picture? Reflecting on the concept of instant family, he had fallen into a restless sleep.

Now, he groped for his jacket hanging on the bedpost and pulled the phone out of the pocket. He got to the call just before it dropped into voice mail and in a husky voice barked, "What?" as he dropped his head back onto the pillow.

"He's gone. Someone's taken Jacob." Emma's voice came through the cell drenched in panic. "I don't know what to do, where to look. They've got him."

"Who, Emma? Who's taken Jacob?" he asked as he quickly swung out of the bed.

"I don't know what happened," she said, ignoring his question. "But they found us and I have to get him back. I'm afraid of what will happen if I don't."

He could hear her sobbing now as he spotted his jeans flung over the back of the worn desk chair near the door. Struggling to put them on without dropping the phone he said, "I'm on my way over. Don't go anywhere. Stay right there and wait for me. Do you hear me, Emma?"

"Yes. You have to hurry."

"I'm only ten minutes away," he said and snapped the phone shut as he bent over to pull on his boots. He dragged on the same T-shirt he'd been wearing earlier, grabbed his keys and jacket and headed for the motel door.

He had gotten a room that exited directly into the parking lot and was thankful now that he hadn't sprung for a better hotel where he would have had to descend several floors and race through a lobby to get to his car. Climbing behind the wheel he glanced at the clock on the dash and noted that it was just past four thirty. He accelerated out of the parking space, mentally calculating that, with the limited traffic at this early morning hour, it should only take him half the time he'd told Emma it would take to reach her.

As he made the last turn onto her street and sped toward the house, he spotted her pacing the front porch. When she heard his car she quickly stepped back into the shadows but scurried down the steps when she realized it was him, reaching the car just as he slammed it into park. He jumped out of the vehicle and without even thinking gathered her into his arms.

"I want you to stay out here until I search the house," he said while trying to hustle her into the back seat of his car.

"I checked the entire house before I called you. I went out back, checked the garage. I thought that . . . I don't know what I thought, but I had to look. He's not here, Max. No one is. But they left a note." She was handing him a single sheet of paper as she spoke. "We've got to do something."

He took the note and read the message that was printed in block letters with what appeared to be a thick marker.

GIVE US WHAT WE WANT AND YOU GET THE KID BACK. NO POLICE. WE'LL BE IN TOUCH.

"What does it mean? What do you have that someone would want?" he asked as he looked up and saw that she had circled around him and was heading back to the house.

"I don't know."

When he caught up with her he grabbed for her arm to stop her, but it only managed to slow her down. "You've got to have some idea what it means," he demanded.

"We have to find him."

They were at the front door now and Emma reached out to open it. "Will you please wait a minute?" Max said, feeling the frustration that came along with trying to play catch up while not knowing all the facts. At least she had stopped her forward momentum and was now just standing there staring at him. "Talk to me, Emma. You know something and I can't help if you don't tell me what it is."

She turned and crossed the threshold saying, "Come inside."

He followed her into the living room and watched as she folded herself into the corner of the couch, pulling a colorful patch-work quilt around her upper body. Max took a seat in the recliner across from her.

"I left Colorado because I was being threatened."

"What? Jeez, Emma, why didn't you tell me?"

"The caller told me that the police were involved and I was convinced that I couldn't trust anyone, including you. We'd only been seeing each other for a short time, and before that the only time we spent together was me answering your questions about Eric."

"When did you get the call?" Max asked.

"The night before Donnelly pulled me in and drilled me about Eric's business dealings, and then showed me those photos. The caller said that Eric had double-crossed Victor Manderfield and that I had to make it right. I had no idea who Manderfield was, I'd told you that. But when Donnelly showed me those photos and I realized who was in them, I put it all together and it scared the hell out of me."

"Did you recognize the caller's voice?" he asked.

"No."

Max wasn't sure he believed her but let it slide. "What are you supposed to have that belongs to them?"

"The person who called said that Eric had stolen some paintings along with drugs and money. He insisted I knew where Eric had everything hidden and that he wanted it back. He gave me a deadline along with a warning that if I continued to hold out on him, I'd only be making it difficult on myself."

He heard the quiver in her voice, but let her continue without interruption, ignoring the impulse to go to her and offer comfort.

"Then he told me a few of the methods he was going to use to get the information if I failed to cooperate. Told me that Eric's partner had already been punished and that they'd left him in the woods for the coyotes to finish off." She wrapped the afghan more tightly around her body, and he saw a tear slowly trail down her face before she quickly swiped it aside. "He finished by saying I shouldn't bother calling the cops because there was no way for me to know who I could trust.

"The next thing I know, I'm being dragged down to the police station. I was too scared to say anything about the call. I didn't know what to do, so I played dumb. After I left the station I asked my attorney if I was going to be arrested and he said probably not. *Probably not* wasn't exactly the answer I was hoping for.

"When I got back to the apartment," she continued, "it was a mess. Someone had literally ripped through it, wrecking everything. I didn't know anything about what they wanted," she said with some heat. "I didn't have anything that even remotely resembled what they said Eric had taken. All I could think to do was run. So I packed my bags and waited for my attorney to call. When he finally phoned, he said that the police didn't have any evidence against me and that they'd been told by the DA to start looking for the real killer. I thanked him and left with what I could carry.

"I had an acquaintance that helped me get new ID under the name Emily Carter and after I left Kingsport I made connections along the way with others who gave me the means and opportunities to keep running."

She looked over at him and said, "But they've found me. It has to be Victor Manderfield. Someone he's sent here because of what Eric stole. I can't be sure the police here aren't part of it, too."

"That's why you called me and not the police," he said with a little tug at his heart, realizing that she had called him not as the father of her son but because he was the lesser of two evils. But what she had just told him had Max agreeing with her decision. "We'll keep them out of it for now. I want to call my partner, Cole Haywood. He's one of the most resourceful people I know. We're going to need help if we don't call in the police or FBI."

She didn't agree or disagree, choosing to sit quietly with her elbow resting on the edge of the couch, her head cushioned in her hand. Max pulled out his cell phone and went to the kitchen to make the call. Ten minutes later he came back, noticing that Emma hadn't moved.

"The bags in the hallway? You were going to take off again, weren't you?"

She lifted her head to look at him. "Yes," she said with little emotion.

Her admission angered him, but rather than lashing out he went to the front window and stood, peering out. "I'm not the enemy, Emma. We never had any proof that Eric was tied to Manderfield and certainly didn't know about any double-cross he was involved in. The fact that he was doesn't surprise me, but you have to know that I didn't lie to you back in Kingsport and I'm not lying to you now. I'm not the enemy," he repeated. "It's your choice whether to believe me, but if you want my help you can't hold back. Agreed?"

"Yes," she said softly.

"Jacob is my son, too. We'll find him, but we need to be honest with each other."

"I said I would." Throwing off the afghan she stood up and went to the bathroom, closing the door with a forceful slam. Max just stood there shaking his head. Did she honestly think she had a right to be mad at him? She was the one who'd been hiding the fact that he was a father. She was the one who, without even asking him, had decided he was part of some far-fetched conspiracy. On the other hand, he was the one who had decided to be stubborn and not go after her that day at the station. He should have tried harder to find out what had made her so upset instead of getting all pissed off. By the time he had cooled down it had been too late. She'd disappeared.

Twenty minutes later she reentered the living room and, although her eyes were red-rimmed, she held her head high when she asked, "What now?"

"Do you have a computer with Internet access?" Max asked from where he sat across the room.

Emma nodded as she walked over to where she'd set her luggage and picked up a small satchel, which she took with her into the dining room.

"We'll need to identify those paintings so we have some idea what we're up against," Max continued, as he followed her into the room and watched her set up the laptop on a student-sized desk sitting in the corner. "Why don't you start by getting anything you can find on the Manderfield brothers? I don't have access to the information I gathered on them when I was on the force so we'll have to start over. I know that Victor operates out of Denver, although I'm not sure where Marco resides. While you're checking public records, Cole will be digging up the not-so-public ones."

"Is he going to be coming here?"

"He's closing out a case right now but yes, he's going to try to make it here by noon," he said checking his watch. "That gives us about seven hours to get a head start. You mentioned someone that was Eric's partner. Did the caller give you a name?"

She thought for a moment before replying. "Lucas was the first name," she said and paused again. "I think the last name was Ramos. But I've never heard the name before and Eric didn't have a partner."

"I'm sure the caller was using the term loosely. Anything else?"

"I don't think so."

"Okay. Let's go back to the day Roger interviewed you. What do you remember?"

"Other than Stan Hudson, Roger only asked about Manderfield and his brother. But he also mentioned a place called Crystal Ridge. He wanted to know if I'd ever heard Eric talking about it, but I hadn't."

"I remember that. It's Victor's Colorado estate just west of South Fork. I don't know how that would fit in, but I'll have Cole check it out."

"Roger talked about Eric's assets and asked if we owned any artwork or property besides the house, but I still think he was just trying to establish Eric's net worth and whether it was enough for me to have wanted him dead. It was almost as if he was grasping at anything that would have given him cause to arrest me."

Trying to establish a plausible connection between Roger's interview and the threatening phone call, Max asked, "Did you ever tell anyone about the phone call? Your lawyer, maybe?"

"No. Nobody. But I don't understand why—"

As Max's cell phone buzzed, he cut her off with a raised finger. Checking the caller ID, he opened the phone and said, "Yeah, Cole. What've you got?"

An hour later, Max stepped into the dining room and stood quietly in the archway watching Emma work. It didn't take her long to sense his presence, and when she looked up from the computer, he could clearly read the worry in her eyes. Regrettably, he wouldn't be able to ease that worry any time soon.

"Cole checked on the name Lucas Ramos and through process of elimination, the one mentioned by your caller has indeed gone missing and is presumably dead. He worked as Marco Manderfield's head of security for the past four years and was one of his bodyguards for three years before that. Ramos has a criminal history dating back to when he was a teenager but his record's been clean since his hook-up with Marco. Which begs me to ask the question: how does little brother Marco fit into this whole thing?"

"He's certainly the flashier of the two brothers," Emma said. "Playboy extraordinaire who pays for his lifestyle from money he inherited when his father died. A father who inherited from his father, et cetera, et cetera. Marco has operating interests in two casinos in Reno and property in New York and California. Also keeps a swanky estate and winery operating in the south of France. He's been tied romantically to a number of big-name female celebrities as well as selective wives of notable politicians. He's a big spender, the life of any party and apparently has an ego to go along with the flamboyant reputation.

"On the other hand, I got very few hits on Victor," she continued. "He's been referred to as a recluse. Doesn't do interviews, doesn't serve on any boards, no favorite charities I could find. He's never been married and has no children. Both brothers, interestingly enough, share a passion for owning original and outrageously expensive art. Marco is very verbal about his collection. Victor? Not so much."

Max took a minute to think about that and then said, "If I remember correctly, Marco's married."

"Was married," she said. "Twice, in fact. The first one he divorced and his second wife died in a skiing accident about eight months ago. No kids from either marriage. But there is a sister," she added. "Not a lot of references to her, but the ones I've found have linked her more to Victor than Marco. Sounds like a family divided, if you ask me."

"Okay, so what does this tell us about the paintings you're supposed to have?" Max said out loud, more to himself than to Emma. "Eric owned his own truck. Did he ever work for anyone else, you know, driving for a company?"

"Not when I was with him. He drove mostly long distance but would also take short hauls," she said giving him a puzzled look. "You think he used the truck to smuggle for one of the Manderfields? Or maybe he was part of a theft ring?" She let out a short laugh. "I can't believe that he could have done anything like that for long without being caught. He liked to brag too much about his conquests," she added, looking away from Max. "He wouldn't have been able to pass up the opportunity to tell his buddies how smart he was, how tough he was, walking on the shady side of the law. Eventually someone would have called him on it."

Glancing up again she said, "I try not to think about that time in my life but I'll try to remember if there was anything that he said or did that could help us out." She turned back to the computer and started clicking away on the keyboard. "You're convinced that there's a connection between the Manderfield brothers and Eric, aren't you?" she asked quietly.

"Both Victor and Marco have an addiction to owning valuable artwork. Someone thinks you have paintings that Eric took. We know that at least Victor is involved in drug dealing, extortion and murder, and I bet Cole turns up a criminal history on Marco that will show the same thing. Someone thinks you have drugs and money that Eric took. Eric's dead. Lucas Ramos is dead." Max pushed away from the wall. "Yes, there's a connection."

"One of the brothers has Jacob, don't they?"

"It makes the most sense, which means we want all the information we can get our hands on. You've found a lot already in a very short amount of time and Cole will have more, but I think it's best if you keep at it." He cleared his throat. "I have to go back to the motel and get my things. I'll be moving in here until we're ready to move out. It won't take me long, but I really don't want to leave you alone."

She paused for only a moment and then said, "I'll be fine."

He remained where he was, not totally convinced she would be.

Emma stood and without saying a word walked past him, straight to her bedroom closet. She reached for a lockbox that was sitting in a corner of the lower shelf and took it over to the bed. From it she pulled a .22 automatic and a full magazine.

"Once I was on my own I decided I needed to make some changes in my life so I wouldn't end up a victim ever again. And when I found out I was pregnant, I knew I had to become stronger on both an emotional and physical level. I took a course in self-defense and personal protection. I know how to shoot and I have no problem with defending myself or my son, although I didn't do so well last night with that second part." Walking back to the computer she set the gun next to the monitor and said, "Go ahead and get your things. I promise I'll be here when you get back."

He held her gaze for a brief moment. "I didn't know that Roger had pulled you into interview that day. It was only by coincidence that I found out. And I never told Roger what Eric put you through the night before you left him. You need to know that."

He turned and started down the hallway. "I won't be long," he called back to her before closing the door behind him.

CHAPTER TWELVE

Cole was within an hour of reaching Emma's house in Kennewick. He was tired, ornery and hungry, although the last one was pretty much non-stop for him.

The case he was leaving behind in Montana had been particularly rough for him. The ones that involved kids always were. Thankfully this one produced a happy ending for Jim and Doreen Connor, who had hired Dunmore Investigations to find the birth mother of their adopted daughter, Amanda. The thirteen-year-old needed a bone marrow transplant and although the doctors had told the Connors that only thirty percent of donors directly related to a patient were matches, it was the collective opinion that Amanda's best chance for survival was a sibling or birth parent.

It had been a long and demanding search, but Cole had finally found the mother and convinced her to travel to Montana to meet with her birth daughter's family. He had even managed to keep her identity hidden, which hadn't been such an easy task. Alyson Somerville had a family of her own now—a family that she feared wouldn't understand her reasons for giving up her first child. But Amanda's adoptive parents had offered Alyson both financial and emotional support in order to save their young girl and in the end, Alyson was not only a match for the transplant, but also had decided to tell her family everything. By the time Cole had said his good-byes, the possibility was strong that Alyson would stay involved in Amanda's life—a blessing everyone could be happy about.

As Cole closed in on his final destination he drove slowly past the front of the white stucco house that boasted a comfortable porch, retractable green awnings and a meticulously well-groomed lawn. He didn't stop, choosing instead to continue down the road while checking out the surroundings and noting the handful of vehicles parked around the neighborhood. Satisfied with what he saw, he drove off to prepare for his grand entrance.

A half hour later, he pulled into Emma's driveway, climbed out of his car and headed up the walkway toward the house. The front door opened just before he reached the top step of the porch and although he couldn't see the hand Emma held behind her back, based on the report he'd received from Max, he assumed she was armed. His instincts, from first being a Navy SEAL and then a cop, warned him that this was a woman on the edge. So he moved cautiously to the doorway as he glanced down at the pizza delivery box he held in his left hand. He wanted to keep his right hand free just in case she decided to take exception to his being there.

"Pizza delivery for a Maxwell Jones," he said in his outside voice. In a quieter tone he said, "I'm Cole. Max called me."

He could see the emotions play out on Emma's face. The fear, the apprehension, the hope that maybe he really was one of the good guys.

"You must be Emma. He told me to tell you that he still kicks himself for losing out on his lieutenant's four-course dinner. Whatever that means. But he seemed to think that it would convince you I am who I say I am."

She seemed to relax a bit but still kept a defensive stance.

"The total comes to $25.65 not including tip," he continued in that loud, bored voice before lowering it again to say, "Tell me you didn't order a pizza."

She looked straight at him and shaking her head repeated the words. "I didn't order a pizza. You must have the wrong house."

"Ah, a quick study," he said quietly, pleased she had caught on to where he was going with this pizza scam.

"It says right here, lady. Eight-oh-eight Sycamore Street."

He turned the box so she could read what he'd written on the delivery slip—*Meet me at the back door in thirty minutes. We're being watched.*

"This isn't Sycamore Street. It's Sycamore Drive," she said shaking her head again. "Like I said, you've got the wrong place."

She shut the door and he heard the dead bolt click into place. Cole saluted with his middle finger before bouncing down the steps and back to his car. He made a show of throwing the box on the front seat and pulling a map out, spreading it over the hood of the car. After several seconds he muttered an obscenity, threw the map back in the car before sliding behind the wheel and peeling off down the street.

It actually took him forty minutes to return to the house. After driving around for ten of those to make sure he wasn't being followed, he'd hunted down a mega-warehouse store where he could leave his car parked unnoticed. On foot, he then hoofed back through three neighbors' backyards and over five sets of fences, all the while reminded that he wasn't as young as he used to be, or as agile.

When he reached her back porch, Cole immediately spotted Emma standing off to one side of the screen door, faintly lit by the mid-day sun. He stopped just long enough to announce himself.

"It's Cole, Emma. Just take it nice and slow. I know you're jumpy and I can't blame you. But I'm here to help."

As he slowly moved toward her he took a quick inventory of his immediate surroundings, realizing that if the woman in the doorway freaked and started shooting, his only survivable choice would be to leap into the flowerbed. Sending up a silent prayer that it wouldn't come to that, he settled his right hand on the butt of his Colt.

"You've figured out that I'm armed," Emma said, making Cole stop dead in his tracks. "I don't intend on putting it down until you show me some identification. Slowly take your right hand off your weapon and pull out your ID. Max also told *me* what to look for."

Cole knew what she was referring to and decided to trust that she wouldn't drop him before he could get to his wallet. He slipped the license out, transferred it to his left hand and held it up for her to see. "Coleman Fillmore Haywood." he said. "My mother practically lived at the Fillmore in San Francisco and actually went into labor at a Jimi Hendrix concert. Thus, I was blessed with my middle name."

As she examined the ID, her grip on the firearm relaxed, marginally. When Cole saw her flip the safety on, he allowed himself to feel a small amount of relief. She motioned for him to step inside, making sure to bolt the door behind him.

"If you're hungry there's some store-bought ham in the refrigerator," she said.

"You'll soon discover that I'm always hungry," he replied, moving deeper into the kitchen. "Sit down and I'll make us both a sandwich."

As he went in search for the packaged meat and mayo, Emma said, "I'm not really hungry so don't bother with me."

"It's no bother and you need to eat something." Finding plates in the cabinet he set two on the counter and began preparing the sandwiches. "Where's Max, by the way?"

"He went shopping for the stuff you requested. He told me you might be able to lift fingerprints so we can know who took Jacob."

"It's possible. We'll see."

He glanced over to where Emma now sat at the kitchen table and saw the sadness on her face. Although he didn't have any kids of his own, he thought he could understand exactly what she was feeling.

"After I got out of the service I worked in a private forensics lab for about two years," he said, trying to keep her mind engaged. "For me, it turned out to be a bit too tedious. I guess you could say not nearly enough action. So I joined the police force. Unfortunately, six years in, I was forced to take disability when I got shot on a drug bust. The injury slowed me up just enough that I couldn't give the job one hundred percent, so I got out."

"How long have you known Max?"

"About ten years," he said, placing one of the plates in front of Emma and the other one in front of the chair across from her. Returning to the refrigerator he found a carton of milk, poured two glasses, and handed one to Emma before joining her at the table. "Eat," he ordered gently. "Even if you don't finish it, you need to stay nourished."

Emma took a minute to study Max's partner as he devoured the sandwich and she nibbled on hers. He was an attractive man with a rugged face and dark hair that was just starting to show sparks of gray. The mustache he wore was full and still mostly black. His eyes, however, were what made Emma take a closer look. They were a cloudy gray that appeared to be almost transparent when he looked straight at her. Mesmerizing, really. Impenetrable, but compassionate. She suspected they were eyes that had seen more than their share of good and evil.

"Have you learned anything from your research about the Manderfields?" she finally asked, her voice sounding strained and uncertain. "Does one of the brothers have my son?"

"I've made some inquiries. I'll check my e-mail in just a bit. Then when Max gets back we can all sit down and compare notes."

"About Max," she began tentatively. "What has he told you about us?"

"He's told me everything I need to know, which includes why he's here. I know that he's the boy's father and that he'll do anything to get his kid back."

"What about you? Will you do anything to help me get Jacob back?"

"Yes," Cole said without hesitation. "I protect the people I care about—Max being one of them—and now, by extension, you and Jacob." When she didn't seem to be convinced, he set his sandwich down and tried to make his point clear.

"Look, you and Max have a lot of baggage you've been carrying around for a while. That's between the two of you. As for me, I consider Max my family and he's closer to me than any of my own brothers. I'll do whatever he needs me to do. That's the bottom line."

"Thank you for being so honest," Emma said, pushing her chair back. "I have some more research I want to do but I'd appreciate it if you'd let me know if you find anything in the other room."

Cole watched her closely as she walked out of the room. She'd hardly touched her sandwich but he figured that was only natural for a woman who was desperate to get her kidnapped son back. He, on the other hand, had completely wiped his plate clean. Carrying both the plates and glasses to the sink, he quickly rinsed them before placing them in the dishwasher. Then he grabbed the black duffel bag he'd placed just inside the back door, and headed off to the bedroom, ready to get to work.

CHAPTER THIRTEEN

Emma could hear Cole rummaging around in the bedroom. Before Max had left, he'd told her to stay away from the room's window and crib so if there were any prints Cole would be able to lift them. But if she hadn't even heard the kidnappers come in and take Jacob, she was sure they wouldn't have been careless enough to leave behind clues to their identities.

Frustrated, she moved into the living room, took a seat in the corner of the couch and began thinking back to the day she had been escorted into the Kingsport police station nearly four months after Eric's murder. She'd been torn between believing Max was an innocent spectator to Roger Donnelly's showboating, and believing that he had set her up to take the fall for murder. She had known even then that she was in love with him, but when Roger had spent over an hour questioning her about Eric's ties to Victor Manderfield—and Max hadn't stopped it—she'd been devastated. What else could she have thought but that Max had let her down?

Of course, Emma knew now that Donnelly had been fishing. He might have had a tip about some stolen art or some missing drugs but he didn't have any evidence that she'd been connected. He'd been trying to trip her up, make her say something that would have given him enough to arrest her. But the only thing she'd known back then was that her lack of knowledge was going to get her killed by an unknown player. So she had run.

Once she'd settled into her new location, Emma had considered calling Max and asking him to confirm or deny his involvement in the conspiracy that Donnelly had cooked up. To demand knowing if their relationship had been honest or just a way for him to keep track of her. Then she'd been given the news that she was pregnant, and every week that went by made it harder for her to pick up the phone. And after the birth of her son, her main concern had been keeping them both protected.

Sinking further back into the soft cushion, she closed her eyes, feeling the pain of failure sweep through her heart. How could she have let this happen? What had she done wrong? What had she overlooked?

"Wondering what you could have done differently won't help now," Cole said as he sat down at the opposite side of the couch.

She opened her eyes, damp now with the tears she had yet to shed and looked at him. "But I should have done *something* differently. If I had, Jacob would be here."

"I found this lying on the floor by the side of the bed," he said, lifting the syringe he held in his gloved hand so she could see it. "And unless you're a diabetic or drug user, whatever was in here was used to sedate you. Probably just long enough to get Jacob out."

"Oh, God," she moaned as she began to rock back and forth.

Cole heard a key turning in the door and quickly grabbed his firearm as he moved toward the front entrance. When he heard Max's voice sneak through the barely opened door he holstered his gun and grabbed the box his partner was carrying. "You're needed in the living room, buddy," he said before turning toward the dining room.

It took only seconds for Max to drop down next to Emma. "What is it, Em? What's wrong?"

When he didn't get a response and she didn't stop crying, he figured it had all finally caught up to her and the realization of what they were facing was a weight she was struggling to bear. He gently pulled her into his arms and held on.

"Oh, babe, I'm so sorry." He murmured the words without knowing whether she heard him or not, acutely aware of how sorry he truly was. Sorry that she had mistrusted him so much that she had been afraid to ask for his help when she'd first been threatened. Sorry that the wounds they both carried could in all likelihood be too deep—the love they once shared too broken—to ever be mended.

Minutes later she slowly pulled away, turning her head so he couldn't see her face. "I'm fine, really. I just lost it for a minute," she said, wiping the lingering tears from her cheeks. "I need to get something from the kitchen."

He let her go, knowing it was just an excuse. She didn't want the comfort he was willing to offer so there wasn't anything else he could do but let her go.

Cole had been watching the interaction between them and now stepped into the living room, shaking his head. "What did you expect, Max? That she would just accept you back into her life and forget about everything that's happened?"

If looks could kill, Cole figured he'd be a goner. He bravely crossed the room and sat on the edge of the tired-looking coffee table. "I'm on your side, partner. You know that. But she's believed for some time now that you misled her."

When Max started to speak, Cole held up his hand and continued over him. "Wait. Wait until I'm finished. She's wrong in thinking that. But there's a reason she does and it's going to take time to convince her otherwise. If you want a second chance with Emma, you're going to have to find a way to break through her defenses. And trust me, Max, when I say it ain't going to be easy."

"You're just full of optimism aren't you?"

"I call it like I see it," Cole replied as he stood and headed toward the bedroom. "Oh, you may also be interested in knowing they drugged her," he added.

Max bolted off the sofa and when he caught up to Cole, grabbed his arm. "What did you say? They drugged Emma?"

"Yep. I found the syringe on the floor by the nightstand. No way for me to know what was in it unless I get it tested, but it had to be something that would put her out quick, and probably not last for more than thirty minutes or so." After writing the identifying information on the side of a plastic bag, Cole placed the syringe inside and put it in his duffel. "No prints that I can find, and no other fibers or trace evidence. The crib, windowsill, even the window frame, have all been wiped clean. What I can't figure out is why they took the kid and left Emma behind, unharmed."

"They need Emma alive to insure that the paintings, money and drugs that Cassidy stole are returned. Kidnapping her son is a way to put pressure on her so she doesn't go to the cops, or just disappear like she did the first time."

"Makes sense," Cole replied. "But even if they get the stuff back it may not be enough, you know. They're going to be looking for payback."

"I know," Max said on a sigh and turned when he caught the movement in the doorway.

"That payback is me, isn't it?" Emma asked softly.

Max started toward her but stopped when she stepped into the room and moved to the side of the bed. She carefully laid the laundry basket she was holding on top of the checkered quilt. "It's me," she said more firmly, this time looking at Cole. "And it's time you both start talking *to* me rather than around me. The three of us are in this together and we need to work as a team. If you can't agree to that, then I'll find someone else who can."

"We're going to do our best not to let anything happen to you, Emma," Cole said. "And you're right. Keeping you in the dark isn't the way to do that." He looked at Max, who was looking at Emma. "We're both invested in the outcome here. Finding Jacob and keeping you safe isn't just a job to us."

"You mean finding Jacob and keeping me *alive*, don't you?"

"Semantics, Emma. And let's not play the word game. You want it straight, then okay. We mean to find Jacob and keep you both alive. You could find someone else to help, but they won't put the effort into it like Max and I will. And you don't have the skills to do it on your own. That's the reality."

As Emma and Cole locked eyes, Max shifted his stance and shoved his hands in the back pockets of his jeans, choosing not to state the obvious—that there was no way he was going to bail on Emma, or his son. After several seconds she said, "That was rather harsh, don't you think, Coleman?"

Giving her a crooked grin, Cole said, "I'm not really known for my savoir faire."

"I'll remember that. Now, get me caught up and tell me what I should expect to happen from this point forward."

CHAPTER FOURTEEN

Max, Emma and Cole moved into the kitchen, where Emma put on a fresh pot of coffee, and Cole began fiddling with the tracing equipment he had hooked up to the wall phone.

"Let's go over what you should expect when the kidnapper calls," Max said after everyone was seated at the chrome table, a throw-back to the 1950s. "They're going to demand you give them what Eric stole."

"We've been over all this, Max, and nothing's changed. I don't know anything," Emma said tightly. "How are we going to fool anyone into believing I do?"

Before Max could answer her question, the phone rang. Startled, Emma stood so quickly that her chair fell backwards and hit the floor with a crash. As she reached for the receiver Cole said, "Keep them on the line as long as possible, Em. You've got this. Go."

When she picked up the receiver she held it slightly away from her ear so that Max—who had moved alongside her, his head just inches away from hers—could listen to both sides of the conversation.

"Hello?" Emma said in a voice that was both steady and firm.

"Ah, you're awake. That wasn't quite the case earlier. I hope you slept well." The voice on the other end of the phone was deep and male and Emma could clearly hear the arrogance as he spoke.

"Where's my son, you bastard?" she said in reply, tightening her grip on the receiver.

Max shook his head and mouthed the words, "Don't upset him."

At the same time the caller was saying, "Now, now Emma. You want to be nice to me. I've never really had a great fondness for children, but this one? Fortunately for both of us he holds some value to me. Do you understand?"

"Yes. I understand. Please don't hurt my son."

"Do you have what I want?"

There was a white board hanging on the wall by the phone, and when Emma failed to respond, Max picked up an erasable marker and wrote, "Not here, need time."

"I don't have it here with me, but I can get it," Emma finally said. "I just need some time."

"I'll give you forty-eight hours, no more. You may have been able to slip away from me once, but you won't get very far if you try it again. And if you fail, the kid's as dead as your old man, and you'll be next. Forty-eight hours, *darlin'*. Clock's ticking."

Emma heard him laughing as the phone line went dead and she stood there, frozen in place. "We need to find Jacob, Max. Now."

As Max reached for the receiver she still clutched in her hand, he could see more than just fear in her eyes. "You know who that was, don't you?"

"Yes," she said quietly, turning so she was facing him. "Eric brought him to the house once."

"*Stan Hudson*?" Max asked with a look of confusion.

But before he could say anything more she turned to Cole and said, "Did you get it?"

Cole slowly raised his eyes to meet hers and smiled. "Hell, yeah. Right down to the zip code."

She returned his smile before turning to leave the room. "I'm going to make sure I've got everything packed."

"I'll do a background search on Hudson once we're on our way," Cole said as he began packing up his equipment. When Max didn't reply, he looked up and said, "What?"

"Nothing," Max replied, wondering what Emma was holding back about Hudson. "You need to be out of here in fifteen," he added, as he started toward the front of the house. "Call me when you're in place."

Max slammed the trunk shut and slid into the driver's seat.

Once Cole had traced the call, getting the address had been child's play for him. It matched the address of a Nevada property owned by Victor Manderfield located just south of Oregon's state line. Max had told Emma it was still too early to know for sure if Jacob was being held there, but reassured her that Cole would be making some calls to try and get confirmation. For now, the plan was to head south.

"Do you think Cole is set up yet?" Emma asked anxiously.

"I know he is. I got his call while you were packing up the laptop." He glanced briefly at her and added, "We've done this before, Emma. Just sit back and try to relax. This will work."

A little over an hour ago, Cole had slipped out the back door. His plan was to retrieve his car then circle back and position himself where he could keep an eye on the two-door sedan that was parked outside Emma's house. After Max and Emma drove away, he would hang back to observe whether a second vehicle was hiding in the shadows. Max's job would include losing the first tail, and Cole would keep track of the second until Max and Emma were clear. Eventually, the three of them would meet up at a predetermined location.

Pulling out of the garage Max turned right and headed out of the subdivision toward the main road into town. Right on cue, the sedan made a U-turn and slowly fell into place about four car lengths behind him. Max was confident in his abilities to lose the tail—after all, he and Cole had played this cat and mouse game before, and they were damn good at it.

Today, it only took twenty minutes of driving in a sporadic

pattern around the city to ditch their pursuer, allowing Max to turn toward the highway. Cole's phone call thirty minutes later conveyed that the car was still circling around the downtown area looking for Emma's Caprice. A second vehicle had rendezvoused with the first shortly after they lost Max, but Cole assured him that it was safe to meet up as planned.

Flicking a quick glance at Emma he said, "You should really get some sleep. It's going to be a long trip and you'll have to do a stint at driving."

"I know. I'll go down soon. Still a little wound up, I guess."

They rode in silence for the next several miles. Emma was vaguely aware of the steady rhythm the car tires were making on the pavement as she occasionally glimpsed a car or semi heading in the opposite direction. As they passed a road sign indicating they were entering Oregon's Umatilla County she said, "I have something to say, Max. And maybe this isn't the right time to talk about it, and I know you don't have to believe anything I say, but I was planning on tracking you down. I just needed some time. I wanted to make sure . . . to wait until—"

How could she explain the emotions she'd gone through when she'd learned she was pregnant? How it had frightened her to know she would have to bear his child without him. She'd been so confused, torn between the love she carried so deep inside for this man and her belief that he had deceived her. What could she say now to make him understand?

"I tried writing you shortly before Jacob was born, but ended up burning the letter. Then last month I tried calling your cell number, but it went to voice mail and I didn't think leaving a message was the best way to tell you about being a father." She let out a frustrated breath. "I still believe that I was doing the right thing by leaving, that it was the only choice I had. After that, well I can't change anything I did after that, can I?"

She watched him for any sign that he understood, but his face remained unreadable. Turning to the side window she felt a lump in her throat as she realized with great regret that any reconciliation was lost. The actions she had taken, justifiably or not, had put a wedge between them that was too entrenched to be removed.

Max wanted to say something. But the hurt had resurfaced and he was afraid that if he spoke now he would say something he couldn't take back. He was frustrated, angry and sleep deprived, and he knew from experience that the combination wasn't good. So he drove, and tried to organize his thoughts so he could maintain some dignified control over this conversation.

When he looked back at Emma, she was resting her head against the back of the seat, her body twisted toward the door, arms crossed defensively across her chest. It didn't take a genius to read her body language—conversation over.

He drove another two hours before pulling into the gas station where they would be reunited with Cole. Sometime during the drive Emma had fallen asleep but slowly began to stir when he parked next to Cole's Ford. He climbed out of the car and quietly closed the door.

"I just need to stretch a minute and take a leak," Max said as he continued past Cole and headed toward the convenience store. "Stay with Emma, okay?"

"Sure," Cole said as he leaned against the rear door. "I'm all filled up, but I'm going to need some more caffeine and something to eat if I'm going to take the first shift driving."

"Yeah, okay," Max muttered and kept walking. After using the men's room he bought some packaged sandwiches and chips, a large coffee, several bottles of water and, remembering Emma's weakness for sweets, a double-chocolate muffin. Walking back to the car he spotted Cole transferring the backpacks and duffel bags from Emma's car to his.

"Emma went to the lady's room," Cole said as he checked the briefcase holding his equipment. "I called an old FBI friend of mine, Lou Garrison. He's working on finding us help to get inside Manderfield's ranch house. He said he'll e-mail current photos of Victor and his sister Daria, who is supposedly living at the ranch. I asked him to also include a photo of Stan Hudson and Marco Manderfield. Although there's nothing saying that Marco is involved, I figured it's best to be prepared."

Max remembered Garrison from a number of joint operations he had worked in Kingsport. But Cole's connection to Garrison dated further back—to the days they had served together in the navy—but it was their history after those naval days that would forever tie them together.

It had been five years earlier, Max recalled, when Cole had been part of a clandestine rescue team that had gone into Mexico to rescue Lou's fourteen-year-old daughter. The teenager had run away with her boyfriend, a member of one of Mexico's fiercest drug cartels. Although Max didn't know all the details, he did know that one of the team members had died on that particular mission. He also knew that when Cole and a retired marine operative crossed back into the States three weeks later, Lou's daughter was with them. It was a story that never made headlines; in fact, he suspected there was no record of the team ever having gone in. Their mission had been personal, a way to pay back—or in Cole's case, pay forward—a former teammate.

During the years that followed, both men had relied on each other professionally. But today's request for information on the Manderfields fell into the personal column, and even though Cole would never have mentioned Lou's debt during the call, it would have been that indebtedness that influenced Lou's willingness to help him now. They both lived by a moral code that was honorable; a code the Manderfield brothers would never understand.

To Max, it didn't really matter whether the information shared was personal or professional. He was just grateful that Garrison was willing to offer his assistance. If memory served right, the man was an intelligent, thorough and take-no-prisoners kind of guy, and any information they received from him would be current and reliable.

"Does he know if Jacob is there?" Max asked.

"He just happens to have an undercover agent inside who thought there may be a baby in the house. He hasn't seen a kid, but said he overheard the maid talking about how Victor's sister was doing so much better now that she had a little one to call her own. He also said that there's a new staffer on site and he's gotten the impression that she's a nanny. Lou didn't go into why his guy thinks that, but you know how it goes. I know it's nothing solid, Max."

"We have to go with the odds," Max said, shaking his head slightly. "And seeing as it's our only lead, we'll follow it." Moving toward the car door he added, "We've gone in on other jobs with less intel."

"That's true," Cole agreed. "But this time there's going to be a lot of risk with the plan, and it's going to have to be a quick in and out. Lou won't compromise his operation, and he's not about to risk having his man's cover blown. Once we're in, he won't be able to give us any protection."

As Max moved to the front of the car to place the large coffee cup in the holder near the driver's seat, Cole took a quick inventory of what he'd stored in the trunk. "Why don't you bring Emma up to date while I go make a pit stop?" he said when he was satisfied he'd packed everything they'd need. "Be back in five."

Max broke the cap on one of the bottled waters and drank earnestly as he leaned against the trunk of the vehicle, watching for Emma to emerge from the restroom. When he spotted her crossing the lot, he pushed away from the car and waited until she reached him before speaking.

"Do you need anything from inside other than food or water? Something else to drink, maybe?"

"No, I'm good. Did Cole hear from his FBI friend?" she asked.

Max told her what he knew and then added, "We're back on the road as soon as Cole comes out. He's going to drive for a while, so why don't you take the back seat and you can stretch out."

She looked up at him and asked, "What's going to happen to my car?"

"Cole has found someone to pick it up and store it. We're taking precautions by taking his because the kidnappers don't know about him yet, or this car."

"I know. I was just wondering. Did you transfer the car seat for Jacob?" she asked, leaning down to look through the rear window. "We're going to need the car seat."

"It's in the trunk," Max said. "Everything's in the trunk." When she straightened, he could see the weariness in her eyes. "It's all going to work out, Em," he added as gently as he could. "All of it."

She just nodded and, opening the door, climbed in. By the time they were on the road again she was horizontal in the back seat clutching her jacket around her shoulders, her eyes closed tight. Max tried to make himself comfortable in the front but found it was difficult with the limited leg room the vehicle had to offer. Resting his head against the window he closed his eyes and tried to relax his muscles and his mind, convinced that sometimes life really sucked.

CHAPTER FIFTEEN

"Where's the kid?"

"Clara took him back to the nursery. Daria went upstairs to her room."

Stan Hudson stood behind a modest black walnut desk in his office at Victor Manderfield's Nevada ranch. He motioned for the other man to take one of the chairs across from the desk at the same time he lowered himself into a soft, executive style leather chair and lit one of the expensive cigars he kept on hand. He took a minute to study the visitor sitting across from him through the smoke.

Carl Skinner was an ordinary-looking man with short brown hair, a trim goatee and dark, corruption-ridden eyes. He'd been employed for Victor Manderfield for just over four years and was the guy Stan would call in when it came to dealing with unnecessary disruptions in their day-to-day business operations. At first sight most people saw a quiet, respectful man who—if they were broken down on the side of the road—could be trusted for a ride to the nearest gas station. But Stan knew for a fact that if Carl had gotten that close, he wasn't playing the part of Good Samaritan. On the contrary, if Carl was involved the body would never be found.

"Have you heard from Keagan?"

"Not since he phoned and said they'd lost the Cassidy woman, but I'm on it. I've sent Troy and his team out to locate Cassidy and Dunmore and instructed Keagan and the others to come back in."

"Victor isn't going to like this one bit," Stan said as he took another puff on the cigar. "Nephew or not, Keagan's a real loser, all the way around. At first it was just the little stuff, you know? Botched jobs that could be overlooked for family. But when he mucked up that drug exchange with the Folsoms? Inexcusable, for sure."

"That was a major misstep on his part," Carl said, sensing that Stan wanted a response.

"Family," Stan continued with some disgust. "I don't get it, but Victor thinks he owes the kid something. It can't go on for much longer, though. If Keagan has any brains he'll leave town now."

"Losing the one person who can lead us to those paintings could definitely be detrimental to the boy's health," Carl agreed.

Stan gave a slight nod. "Let me know when you get anything new." He leaned forward to shuffle some papers that were neatly stacked on the desk. Understanding that this was his dismissal, Carl left without another word.

When he heard the door close, Stan eased back and let out a sigh. He should have never let Victor talk him into putting his nephew in charge of following Emma. Even though Stan knew she was getting help from the ex-cop turned private investigator, he never thought the two of them would be clever enough to outmaneuver the men he'd sent with Keagan to Kennewick. The problem had been in underestimating Dunmore's skills. Or more to the point, overestimating Keagan's abilities.

He'd have to talk to Victor. Reason with him that Daria's son had messed up way too many times to be ignored any longer. And it wasn't like anyone would miss the screw-up, especially Daria. She'd gotten pregnant with him at the tender age of fifteen and because of her mental illness she didn't even recognize Keagan as her son anymore. Besides, she'd grabbed at the chance to take the Cassidy kid as her own, basically making Keagan an orphan.

But if Keagan wasn't dealt with soon, Victor would be losing more than money, drugs or his precious artwork. His nephew was damaging the Manderfield reputation, and by allowing him to skate, Victor was losing the respect of the men who really counted. Which would eventually lead to a loss in power. Stan had worked too hard all these years, getting to where he was in the organization, to allow that to happen.

He stood and walked over to the tinted window that overlooked the riding corral, reflecting on the night he'd received the report that Victor's paintings had been stolen. It seemed that Marco had staged a revolt of sorts and sent in a band of renegades to relieve Victor of some of his most prized artwork. But in pure Marco style, the men had been inferior and it hadn't taken long to track them down. When Stan had finally arrived on scene it had been easy enough to get the information he needed from Lucas Ramos, after pointing out exactly what would happen to him if he didn't spill everything. Of course, Stan had gladly followed through on his threat anyway, proving there was a sucker born every minute.

It had been somewhat of a revelation though when the information had led to Eric Cassidy, a man that Stan had never completely trusted but never thought would have the guts to steal from Victor Manderfield. He'd found Cassidy quite by accident about a week after the paintings were stolen, ironically enough, strolling out of a police station. Carl had been with Stan that day and together they'd followed Eric to a sleazy apartment in an even sleazier neighborhood where they grabbed him and took him to one of the several warehouses Victor's security team used to persuade people to share information. They'd convinced him to give up the pertinent facts surrounding the theft, which had led them directly to his estranged wife. He admitted giving her the key to a storage facility where the paintings were stashed, along with the drugs and money he'd been siphoning off for weeks. But before Carl could get the location of the unit, Cassidy had fought back and Carl had been forced to shoot him.

Lifting the cigar to his lips he contemplated the reason why Emma had chosen the ex-cop to help her. From what he'd heard through his police sources, she and Max Dunmore had parted ways and in a not-so-friendly way. So it was a bit disconcerting that he had reentered the picture, adding one more problem to the mix.

Stan knew they were close to pulling her in and, when they did, she'd give up the paintings in exchange for the promise of reuniting with her son. Unfortunately for her, once everything was recovered, he'd have to renege on that promise.

"A sucker born every minute," he mumbled as he moved back to his desk.

CHAPTER SIXTEEN

Max and Cole were stealthily making their way to a stone wall that stood behind the Manderfield ranch house. Max had instructed Emma to wait in the car, which was parked on a back road some distance away and hopefully out of harm's way.

It still made Max nervous, however, knowing she was alone on that deserted road and, in his mind, vulnerable. It was also little consolation that Cole had programmed both their cell phone numbers into the disposable one he'd bought for her before they'd hit the road. He knew that if she ran into any kind of trouble and managed to hit speed dial it would take too long for them to get back to the car, thereby limiting any help they could provide her. But he also knew that her call for help would mean aborting the rescue and giving up their one chance to get Jacob out. So, okay, the biggest part of his anxiety was that Emma wouldn't even use the phone—no matter what type of problem she encountered.

Reaching the small iron gate that stood at the end of the wall, Cole positioned himself on one side while Max crouched down opposite him. Both sat as still as hunters listening for any sign that Manderfield's men were patrolling the area. Lou Garrison had told Cole that his inside agent would disengage the alarm system precisely at midnight and leave it off for ten minutes. Anymore time than that would alert members of the security team. If Max and Cole got caught on the grounds after the system was put back on line, they would need to rely on their own ingenuity to find a way out.

At exactly one minute past midnight Cole slowly eased the gate open, and when no siren blasted through the stillness of the night, he joined Max in a race across the pristine lawn straight to the side door they'd been instructed to use. Garrison had said that this would be the only entrance left unsecured, and had given them the quickest way to find what had recently been confirmed to be the nursery on the second floor. What Garrison couldn't tell them was who would be roaming the halls at the precise time Max and Cole wandered through. Oddly enough, that didn't concern Max, and he accepted what needed to be done if they were exposed. His decisions from this point on would be made with no regrets.

With Max close on his heels, Cole slipped through the door first, turning left toward the back stairs. They reached the second floor unchallenged and stopped for just an instant to look down the hallway leading to the room they had targeted. Cole would go first, with Max hanging back to take out any threat that appeared from one of the other five doors on the floor. He scanned the hallway and saw that all but one door was shut tight. The nursery door stood slightly ajar and he could see the dim light just inside.

Cole moved quickly and when he reached the nursery, hesitated again, this time only long enough to see if the room was occupied. He glanced briefly back at Max with a smile on his face, and then slipped into the room. Trying not to be distracted, Max headed down the hall and quietly slid into the nursery, going directly to the crib.

"We've got to move, Max," Cole said from his position behind the door. "I don't like the fact that there's no activity on this floor."

Max understood what Cole was saying. He was feeling the same misgivings. Someone should be nearby, keeping an eye on the baby. But Max wasn't about to ask for any trouble by dawdling, so he gently lifted Jacob out of the crib, grabbed his blanket and turned to make his exit. And that's when he saw Daria, gun in hand and pointed directly at his head.

"Where are you taking my baby?" she asked from the doorway. "Victor said the baby was mine. You shouldn't be here."

Cole moved deeper into the shadows, waiting patiently for Daria to walk into the room. Although his mind was running through their options if she decided to turn and start running down the hall, he kept his own weapon trained in her direction, prepared to shoot if Max gave him the signal.

"You don't have a chance in hell of taking my baby out of here," she continued in a voice that was the total opposite of the sweet and mellow tone she'd just been using. "So return him to the crib before I put a hole right in the center of your fucking forehead." She slowly stepped into the room, and walked toward Max, never realizing that Cole was lying in wait.

"I'm afraid I can't do that," Max said as Cole stepped from behind the door. He placed a cloth, which was already coated with chloroform, over her mouth and nose, at the same time relieving her of her weapon. When she stopped struggling, he tucked her pistol in his belt, and lifting her limp body, carried it to the rocking chair in the corner of the room. "For anyone glancing in, they'll think she nodded off," he said, motioning Max out the door before closing it behind them. Taking the lead once again, Cole retraced their steps along the hallway, down the back stairs and toward the side door.

If they had been five seconds quicker it would have been a clean escape, but instead they ran straight into one of Manderfield's men coming around the corner of the house. He had a short-barreled rifle hanging off his shoulder and was concentrating on lighting a cigarette. The sudden movement of Cole and Max flying through the door startled him as he said, "Hey, man. What's your rush?"

Realizing too late that neither of them belonged there, the man grabbed for his firearm and Cole moved in quickly, easily disarming him. Then, with unquestionable precision, Cole used the butt of the rifle to take the guard down. As his body dropped motionless to the ground Max muttered, "Looks like smoking *can* be dangerous to your health."

Pushing Max forward, Cole said, "Move. This jackass won't be out long and we only have two minutes before the security system goes back on. We need to be through that gate before that happens."

They ran as hard as they could toward their only way to freedom, knowing that it was now a fifty-fifty chance they'd make it out before the alarm sounded and the gate went into lock-down mode. Cole was now three steps ahead of Max and as he yanked the gate open, Max never slowed his pace. He heard the gate rattle shut once his partner had joined him on the other side, thankful that the night remained silent. No sirens, no flashing lights, no gunfire.

The whole operation had been chancy from the beginning but now, with phase one complete, Max took a deep breath. One step at a time, he reminded himself as he ran through trees and underbrush toward the road where Emma was waiting, his son held close to his heart.

When they finally reached the car, Emma was waiting with the motor running. As she slipped into the front passenger's seat, Max handed Jacob to her, slammed the door shut, and jumped into the back seat. Cole, who was now behind the wheel, had the car moving as soon as Max pulled the rear door closed behind him.

Looking into her son's eyes, Emma's heart swelled. There had been moments leading up to this one, when she'd thought she'd lost him forever. Now, having Jacob back in her arms had her feeling absolutely euphoric. She smoothed back the blanket, touching her hand to her baby's heart, and let the tears trail down her cheeks.

Within minutes, they were speeding along the back roads, following the instructions of the pre-programmed GPS unit. They were all silent for several long moments until Max noticed the child's car seat sitting in the corner next to him. He also spotted the duffel bags they had packed in the trunk, tucked on the floor behind the driver's seat. Resting on top was a semi-automatic pistol. He held it up for examination and directing his question to Cole asked, "Where did this come from?"

"I've never seen it," Cole said as he glanced at the gun through the rear view mirror.

Emma gave it a cursory glance and said, "Oh, that. It belongs to the guard I've got locked in the trunk." She continued to coo at the baby and sweetly added, "You're such a brave boy, Jacob. Mommy loves you so much."

Max just stared at her as Cole moved his foot from the gas pedal to the brake pedal, bringing the car to a complete stop at the side of the road. "Emma? Explain the guy in the trunk."

"I didn't know where else to put him. He must have seen the car and came over to check it out. His radio should be on the floor back there and a cell phone, keys and a really big knife."

Max was rendered speechless as he rummaged through the other items lying on the floor. By now everyone inside the mansion would know there had been an intrusion and they were quickly losing precious time. "Cole. Drive. You," he said pointing to Emma. "What happened, exactly?"

Emma spared him a glance before answering. "I was sitting by the rear of the car watching for you to come back, and I heard something which turned out to be someone coming down the road. He was making an awful lot of noise so I was pretty sure it wasn't you. So I crouched behind the rear wheel and waited. And then I saw this skinny, bald guy walk right up to the driver's side door with his handgun pointing at the window. He didn't see anyone, obviously, so he opened the door and leaned in and that's when I—well, I guess you could say I disarmed him."

Cole glanced at Max through the mirror and grinned. Max just shook his head, unable to see the humor in the situation. "How did you disarm him and how on earth did you get him into the trunk?"

"Well, first I deflated his manhood with a well-defined kick to his lower region. Then I clocked him, just like I learned from my self-defense class, and he went down like a felled tree. That's the analogy they would use in class and I really never thought it would work, but shoot, it worked like a charm."

"And how did you manage to get him into the trunk?"

"Persuasion. After I knocked him out I took off all his clothes and used the duct tape in your duffel to bind his wrists and ankles. I was dragging him toward the trunk when he started to come around so I told him nicely to get in, suggesting that he'd be a lot worse off if he didn't. When he got his footing, he hobbled to the back of the car and I pushed him in. I think he'll have some cuts and bruises, but that couldn't be helped."

Cole was laughing now as he said, "You rock, Emma. My God, you rock."

"Please," Max said in an exasperated voice. "Don't encourage her."

"I wasn't going to let that scumbag ruin things. I knew that you had to be close to getting Jacob out and I couldn't let you walk into a situation that could have put us all in jeopardy. You did your part, and I did mine. Get over it, Max."

They were all silent for several minutes until Max said quietly, "Okay. You do rock, Emma."

She smiled and looked down at her baby. "Your daddy thinks I rock, Jacob."

Cole again glanced at Max and saw several emotions cross his face in quiet response to the *daddy* reference. And how interesting, he thought, that panic wasn't one of them.

"Thank you both for bringing Jacob back to me," she said before anyone else could speak.

When Max finally found his voice he said, "Cole and I will do anything it takes to keep you both safe, Emma. You need to believe that."

"I do, Max. But I'm still grateful."

CHAPTER SEVENTEEN

After leaving Victor's estate, it took Cole just over twenty minutes to find a deserted junk yard where he unceremoniously transferred their uninvited passenger into the back seat of a partially gutted Cadillac. Although the man was still naked, Cole graciously left his shirt and trousers on the dashboard. Of course, the clothing would be a moot point if the pinhead didn't succeed in getting himself loose before being discovered.

"We need to find a new ride," Cole said now from the driver's seat, as he continued to put distance between them and Manderfield's ranch.

"I'm guessing that won't involve stopping at a used car lot," Emma said from the back seat.

Cole turned his head and smiled at Emma, who was efficiently spoon-feeding Jacob from a jar of applesauce. "Affirmative on that," he said.

"So once Victor's man finds a phone, I'm also guessing the police won't be his first call."

"I'll wager the police won't be called at all," Max replied. "Not officially."

"And not when Victor already has plenty of cops on his own payroll," she muttered. "Max, could you reach around and grab my backpack, please?"

Max reached over the front seat and did as she had asked. "What do you need?"

"I packed some juice and bottles. Could you fill one of them for Jacob? You'll need to dilute it with some water, though."

Max gave her a questioning look as he did what she asked.

"It's habit. Whenever I leave the house I always pack some juice in case he gets cranky."

"This is why I don't have kids," Cole said. "I would have packed PB&J sandwiches."

Emma laughed. "You don't have kids because you don't want to settle down with one woman."

"Well, that may be part of it."

Max handed her the bottle and sat back to watch, his thoughts drifting to the fact that he had a son. Someone who would look to him for the impossible answers to the mysteries of life. A son he could help to shape into a strong and intelligent man. A son he could play ball with or take to a professional league soccer game or an NCAA basketball tournament. The reality, of course, was that he had to first get the boy and his mother somewhere secure so he could then go out and eliminate the threat against them.

They'd only gone about forty miles when Cole's subdued voice had Max on alert. "We've got company. Black SUV."

Max didn't have to ask Cole if he was sure. "How long?"

"For the last ten minutes. Hasn't varied the gap by more than a couple car lengths, speeding up when I do and doing the same when I slow it back down. Only the one car as far as I can tell. Best guess is that he's waiting for back-up. Check the GPS and see how far it is to the train station."

As Max complied, he could hear Emma humming softly as Jacob sucked enthusiastically on his bottle. "About twelve more miles," he reported to Cole. "You got a plan?"

"I figure I can distract them long enough for you and Emma to get out, but I suggest that we do it a couple of blocks away from the station. We'll look for a mid-size restaurant. There's got to be plenty of them within easy walking distance."

"If I recall correctly there's a bus depot close by. There will also be plenty of taxi stands in the vicinity, don't you think?"

"Enough to confuse them short term. So let's find the restaurant we need. You know the routine. In through the back door and out the front."

"And once they figure out we're not with you anymore they'll direct their reinforcements to cover all the escape routes. They won't know which transportation outlet we'll be heading for."

"Emma, are you getting all this?" Cole asked.

"Yes. Are we still going to take the train?"

"At this time of day there are business people getting on and off so you'll be safer with the train than you would be on a bus or in a taxi. And it's harder to stop a train en route than it is a bus. I already have people waiting on the other end, so yes. The train is still a go."

"Are you coming with me, Max?"

Cole looked at Max and said, "I think you should stick with Emma and Jacob. I'll meet up with you. I'll keep them off you for as long as I can. But there's the chance that we won't be fooling anyone, you know."

Max and Cole exchanged a knowing look before Max turned to Emma. "When Cole stops, you really need to move quickly. I'll bring your stuff," he continued as he slipped his firearm and two loaded magazines into his own backpack. He placed a second handgun in his belt so it was resting against his lower back. Emma knew that once he got out of the car it would be discreetly hidden under his shirt and leather jacket. "Once we're out," he was saying, "you have to follow my instructions. I know what to do and I won't have time to explain every little thing. Okay?"

Emma felt the car increase speed and, taking the bottle out of

Jacob's mouth, threw it on the back seat. She slid over as close to the door as she could and tucked Jacob inside her car coat before zipping it up, leaving only his head exposed. All she could do now was to wait for the command to jump out.

Cole was driving like a madman. He flew around corners, cut off city busses, scrambled down back alleys and just barely escaped mowing down a group of pedestrians crossing the boulevard against the light. As he pulled deep into the parking lot of a twenty-four-hour pancake place, he was calmly instructing his two companions to go, before he even came to a complete stop.

Max was out first and held the door for Emma, grabbing her arm before he quickly slammed the door shut. Without a backwards glance, Cole sped away, leaving Max and Emma dashing for the restaurant's back entrance which opened up to the kitchen. They were moving so fast that Emma didn't even have time to count the number of surprised faces that watched them fly through. But thankfully no one tried to stop them.

When they reached the swinging doors that led to the dining area he slowed down and put his arm around her waist. They were no longer racing, but still kept moving at a rapid pace down the far right aisle. They passed one waitress delivering an order, then a second. Emma kept her eyes focused on the front door, careful not to make eye contact with anyone, afraid that if she did someone would challenge their actions. In a flash, Max was propelling her out the glass door and onto the sidewalk. Again, they slowed their pace to more closely match the speed at which the other pedestrians were moving.

"Do you want me to carry Jacob for a while?" he asked as they made a left turn onto Commerce Street. She looked down and noticed for the first time that she was clutching him so tightly she was amazed he hadn't started to cry. Instead, she could see the wonder in his eyes as he took in the sights and sounds around him.

"Let's not stop. I've got him and he seems content to not cause a fuss."

"Let me know if that changes," he said giving her a warm smile.

She just nodded and turned her attention back to their journey toward the train station. She could see the building about a block ahead of them, and the nearer they got, the more anxious she became. "This is going to work," she murmured as they climbed the stairs to the public entrance.

As they made their way through the front doors, Max pulled her off to the side of the entry hall. Placing his hands on her shoulders he waited for her to focus on him. "Will you trust me, Emma?"

He saw the panic rising in her eyes, but couldn't back down. "There's a train leaving in thirty minutes that will take you to Nebraska. Cole's men will be waiting for you at the Lincoln station. You need to go to the counter over there and purchase the tickets," he continued, pulling money out of his wallet. "Buy two adults, and I think that Jacob can ride free, but here's enough money for whatever you'll need." He looked away from her for just an instant and then pulled her behind the huge marble pillar they were standing beside.

"You can't be serious," she said, already figuring out what he intended to do. Moving closer to him she lowered her voice. "If they're following us, they'll see you leave and—"

"And that's the point," he said, not letting her finish. "I suspect there's already someone here looking for us and I want to lead him away from you. Give you time to get Jacob on that train. If I don't make it back in time, get on the train and I'll try to hook up with you at one of the other stops, or for sure at the safe house."

Emma was stunned. She'd gotten used to having either Max or Cole there, providing her comfort and support. But she knew he wouldn't leave her unguarded if there were any other way.

She took a deep breath and said, "I stopped being a victim a long time ago, choosing to be a survivor instead. I'll be careful, but I need to ask you to do the same."

Max pulled her into a brief embrace, kissed Jacob on the top of his head and said, "Stay here for another five minutes and after you buy the tickets do not go anywhere where you'll be alone. I can't risk leaving you with a firearm, so you'll be vulnerable."

He bent down to kiss her lips. "Be careful," he said. "See you when I see you." And he was gone.

Emma heard the call come over the speaker requesting passengers holding tickets to Lincoln to begin boarding. In the center of the station were men, women and children gathering their belongings as they prepared to embark. Replacing them were others who had just arrived, being greeted by more men, women and children who'd been patiently waiting to welcome their loved ones home.

She sat in the center of it all, watching. She knew she should be heading toward the platform with the rest of the travelers, but the need to hang back was overwhelming. She stole a look at the wall clock, realizing that her decision to stay or leave could no longer be delayed.

"Is everything all right, ma'am?" Emma jumped as she looked up to see a man in his mid-sixties eyeing her suspiciously. He was dressed similar to the man who had sold her the tickets, indicating he worked at the station. "Can I help direct you to your train?"

"I'm fine, thank you. I'm waiting for my husband."

"If you'll forgive me, I'm aware that you purchased your tickets for the train leaving in—" he made a show of checking his watch, "—four minutes. If you don't hurry, you'll miss it."

"I appreciate your thoughtfulness," Emma said as she stood and glanced toward the main entrance. "But I'm going to wait." Decision made, she thought. "I'm sure he'll be here any second."

"My apologies, ma'am," he continued, as he took a step away from her. "I don't mean to be intrusive. It's just that I saw a young woman who appeared to be worried, traveling alone with a baby, and my radar went up. I've seen a lot in my job over the years and I just wanted to be assured that you weren't in any trouble."

"Thank you for your concern," Emma said, trying to keep her voice calm. The man was only trying to help, after all, and she didn't want to draw attention to herself. "We can always take another train if he doesn't make it here in time. We're going on vacation so it'll be okay. But thank you, really, for watching out for us." She glanced at Jacob, who had moved his thumb to his mouth and was now sucking it contently.

"I'll take leave, then. If you need anything, please don't hesitate to ask." He tipped his hat and strolled away.

Emma watched him stop and talk to a few more passengers before disappearing around the corner that led to the tracks. She sat back down on the hard wooden bench and listened as the final boarding call was announced through the overhead speakers.

Max walked into the rail station and saw her in the center of the room, gently rocking Jacob in her arms. She stood as he approached, swiping at the tear trailing down her cheek. He gathered them both into his arms and held tight. "I have a car parked out back," he said, releasing his grip and leading her to the rear door of the station. "Let me take Jacob."

Without hesitation she surrendered the baby, then followed him to the lackluster tan vehicle parked near the door. As they were pulling out of the parking lot Max said, "I thought I told you to get on the train if I wasn't back in thirty minutes."

Glancing over she could see the corner of his mouth twitch. "If you thought I'd do what you told me to do why did you come back?" she said with a smirk. "And why do you have a package of diapers and baby food on the back seat?"

"Our communication definitely needs work," he replied as they both settled in for the long drive to Nebraska.

CHAPTER EIGHTEEN

It had been close to five hours since Stan had been alerted to the break-in by Max Dunmore and Cole Haywood. And now, here he was with his assistant chief of security, Mark Flynn, waiting to explain to their boss exactly what had happened.

"How did they get through the gates—not to mention into the house—without the alarms going off or being seen by someone stationed in the security room?" Victor Manderfield's voice was menacing as he stood rigid behind his desk, demanding answers.

He was a tall, imposing figure of a man, with short salt and pepper hair that swept to the back. His eyes were black and penetrating, matching the intensity of his command, and the thin scar that ran from his right ear all the way to his lower lip was the only flaw in an otherwise handsome face. He'd received the badge of honor as a teenage boy who'd fought to gain the respect of an older rival at the boarding school in England where he'd spent the majority of his school years. He'd succeeded that day, and many days since, eventually learning that his mind was more powerful than his fists. Using that knowledge, he'd managed to build an empire that was far superior to what his father had amassed.

Of course, there were days when he recognized that the mind had its limits. On those occasions he relied on a well-paid army of men to do his dirty work. Knowing that today could very well be one of those occasions, he had summoned his second in command to provide a detailed report of what had gone down.

Stan now gave his security expert a slight nod, indicating that he should field Victor's question.

"Nothing showed up on the monitors tonight, sir. And the recordings showed normal movement both inside and out for the fifteen or twenty minutes we suspect the intruders were on the premises." Flynn knew this because he had already examined all of the security tapes, playing and replaying every second of every recording until he thought he'd go blind. "What we saw was the nanny checking on the baby shortly before eleven and then Daria going in the room at twelve fifteen and leaving five minutes later. There wasn't any other activity in that sector until after we discovered the security breach."

"But what's on the tape doesn't jive with what actually happened," Stan interjected. "From what we've pieced together the nanny decided to check the baby around twelve-twenty and found Daria out cold and the crib empty. At the same time one of the security guys spotted Dunmore leaving through the back gate with who we now know is his partner, Cole Haywood. I watched the tapes myself and nowhere do they show the two coming onto the property."

"Someone tampered with the live feed," Mark said. "I have Brody running old tapes to see if we can match up footage for the time frame we've identified."

"What will that get us?" Victor asked, his voice cold and controlled.

"Brody believes, and I agree, that what the guards were seeing on the monitors tonight was an old recording looped into the system starting around midnight. We think someone hacked into the computer and replaced our live feed with a recording from a previous night. In fact, he said that one of the men saw a screen jump right before midnight, but that's not unusual out here. There are often electrical surges that affect the equipment."

"Pull the files on all your men," Victor demanded angrily. "Do another background check on everyone. Find out who was where tonight, and who had access to the equipment. Find out who has the skills to set this up."

"I'll get right on it, sir," Mark said as he scurried out of the room.

"Once we discovered the kid missing," Stan said when he was alone with Victor, "Carl organized a search team to go after Dunmore and we've already had sightings of him. Haywood and the Cassidy woman are with him. We'll get them, Victor."

"The bastard who did this is dead," Victor said turning his rage onto Stan. "How the fuck did this happen? How the fuck did the best security system in the state of Nevada fail?"

The lethal look in Victor's eyes told Stan that whoever was behind the security system failure had best get his affairs in order, because his life was over. "Mark will get us the answers. He'll keep digging until he finds whoever did this. Count on it."

Several minutes passed before Victor spoke again. "Where's my nephew? If he hadn't lost the Cassidy woman in the first place, none of this would have happened."

"He's waiting out back, near the stables. Do you want to talk to him here or go out there?"

"We'll go to him. Bring Carl."

And with that order, Stan concluded that the Manderfield ranch was about to be a man short.

CHAPTER NINETEEN

Emma was driving as they made their final leg of the trip. Once Max had been satisfied they weren't being followed and had crossed into Utah in one piece, he relinquished the wheel and crawled into the back seat. Emma knew he hadn't gotten much rest since leaving her house in Kennewick, so she had insisted on driving for at least a few hours. Their destination had been changed due to the unexpected trouble they'd encountered back in Nevada, so they were now heading to a safe house in Wyoming, where Max's grandmother would be waiting to take the baby to an anonymous location. Max, Emma and Cole would then be free to search for the paintings, in hopes that by finding them, this nightmare might end.

She continued to follow the main highway east, while she listened to the soft classical music coming out of the radio. It was Jacob's favorite and she remembered how it had soothed him to sleep when she had first brought him home from the hospital. She glanced into the back and smiled at the sight of Max curled up next to his son, who was out like a light in his car seat. The music seemed to have done the trick on both of them.

When her cell phone vibrated against her thigh she grabbed it before it could wake Jacob. The caller ID read *Fillmore* and she grinned as she pressed the answer button. "I know it was unnecessary but I was beginning to worry about you," she said quietly. "Are you all right?"

"Right as rain, big momma. How's everything on your end?"

"The boys are catching forty winks in the back seat and we just passed through Salt Lake City about an hour ago. Max wants to keep going straight to the safe house, so we'll share the driving and work in a break or two. I figure it will take us another six hours." She could hear voices in the background and asked, "Where are you?"

"At a diner owned by Harriet Picard on Route 95 just south of Carson City. A few years back I helped her resolve a difference of opinion she was having with an ex-boyfriend who had pinched some cash and family jewelry from her. Seeing as how I was in the neighborhood, I stopped in for a bite to eat."

"This difference of opinion ended in a peaceful resolution, I presume?"

"Harriet seems to be at peace with it all. The dude was moving too fast toward the county line for me to ask what his thoughts were. Didn't even take the time to say good-bye, can you imagine that?"

Emma just smiled and shook her head. "You are one scary puppy, Coleman. By the way, what are you still doing in Nevada?" she asked, realizing that he'd headed south through the state instead of east toward Cheyenne.

"Needed to lead the wolf away from the sheep. It's put me somewhat behind schedule, but I plan on hopping a private plane out of Vegas. I may even beat you there."

"I'm guessing you have connections in the airline industry, too?"

"Babe, I got connections in most every industry. When you've been at it as long as I have, cultivating new friends just comes natural."

This time she laughed, and it felt good. "Anything we need to know before we arrive at our destination?"

"Just tell big daddy the wolf went back to his den with his tail between his legs. We managed to lose everyone. I'm going to try and get some rest on the plane, and we'll re-group when we're all together again. Take care, my beloved." With that, the line went dead.

"What did the mighty Haywood have to say?" Max asked quietly from the back seat, trying and failing to keep the sneer out of his voice. He couldn't say why, but he didn't appreciate that the mother of his child had gotten so chummy with his partner. Well, he did know why, but Cole's reputation with the ladies wasn't something he necessarily wanted to be analyzing right now.

"He's going to meet up with us at the safe house," she said, seemingly oblivious to the childish tone in his voice. She relayed the information she'd gotten from Cole.

"Sounds good. We'll just keep pushing on and we should be there by nightfall. We'll call Cole when we're closer so he can direct us in."

Emma didn't reply. She knew that as soon as they reached their destination she would have to give up Jacob. Although knowing that Max's grandmother and her companion, Henry Roth, would be the ones taking care of him made her feel slightly better. Max had also assured her there would be a bodyguard with them 24/7, so there really wasn't any other option that made sense.

"You can still decide to stay with Jacob," Max said as if reading her mind. "Cole and I will deal with this."

"But you could miss something if I'm not with you. You didn't know Eric. I did. There's a better chance that I'm going to see something—a *clue*, for lack of a better word—that you or Cole wouldn't even recognize as being important. Something we run across could jar my memory or lead us in the right direction to bring this to an end. I could be holding the answer to everything but if I'm here and you're there we'd never know it. Hell, I may know something that could save your butt out there."

"I have so many comebacks to that, but I can't use any of them with a child present," he said through his grin. "And talking about children, this little guy is awake and needing a diaper change."

"I can pull over in a minute and we can switch spots," Emma said as Max started to unbuckle the straps that held Jacob in the car seat.

"No, I got it," he said lifting the baby out and onto the back seat. "Hey there, J-man, let's see what we're up against here."

Emma laughed, and in warning added, "Boys have a tendency to spray when you least expect it, so you'll want the clean diaper out before you take the dirty one off. Be prepared to cover first. Cover or duck, sweetheart. Cover or duck."

Max laughed heartily, foolishly touched by her term of endearment. In his book, "sweetheart" trumped "scary puppy" any day. He followed her instructions, silently admitting that even if the whole baby thing was somewhat of a mystery right now, he still wanted to learn it all.

"Is it time for a bottle or something?" he asked when diaper duty was completed and he was bouncing Jacob lightly on his knee.

"I filled some bottles while you were at the wheel. Why don't you see if he'll take one of those?"

Emma drove, listening now to the murmurs, chuckling and animated baby noises coming from the back seat. After another two hours she announced that they were stopping for gas and food. Pulling into the next station, they agreed to take thirty minutes of down time and go in the café across the road for a sit-down meal. Finding a quiet booth in the far corner and a menu that served breakfast all day long, Max ordered coffee and scrambled eggs with wheat toast and Emma ordered her eggs poached with a buttermilk biscuit and a small bowl of oatmeal for Jacob, who was currently content with his pacifier.

"Do you think Tony has called in the state troopers yet?" Max asked, referring to the bartender at the Seabrook. "You not showing up for work must have caused him great distress."

"Hey, Tony is a good kid and even if he is a bit overprotective, his heart is in the right place." She made a face at Jacob that made him smile and wiggle in her arms as she continued. "I called him before we left and said my mother was ill and I had to go to Florida to be with her. Figured that if anyone went by the bar looking for me it was a good misdirect. Even if they didn't believe it, hopefully it would keep Tony out of the mix."

"I really don't think any of Manderfield's men would bother too much with him, even if they did discover that you worked there. They'd have gone in and asked a few questions but then realize it was a dead end."

Max leaned back to let the waitress drop their plates on the table. "More coffee?" she asked, giving Max her brightest smile.

"We'd love some, thanks," Max replied smoothly.

When she walked behind the counter to retrieve the glass carafe, Emma glanced down at Jacob and whispered, "Your daddy has an admirer, Jacob. It appears as if he's a real lady's man."

"Very funny," Max said just as quietly.

After their cups were refilled and the waitress moved on to another table, Max looked over at Emma. "Do you want me to take Jacob while you eat?"

"Please," she said, making the word drip with sarcasm. "You may be able to outmaneuver a band of thugs, but I am the queen of multitasking with a baby on my hip. There's not a lot of me-time anymore."

"Well, when this is all over maybe we can change that. You're not alone anymore, Em."

She took a bite out of the biscuit before changing the subject. "You and Cole make a great team," she said, shifting her attention to the eggs. "You both have an impressive knack for reading people, you're both shamefully devious, and yet you possess a keen intelligence that you don't feel the need to flaunt. I bet neither of you ever give up and you'll just keep digging in until something or someone breaks."

"Yes on all counts."

"So you're good at what you do." She'd made it more a statement than a question.

"Yes, we are."

After a brief pause she said, "Good."

When she didn't say anything more it was his turn to change the subject. "Why did you take the job at the Seabrook?"

"It was either that or working as a pole dancer at the Double Decker around the corner. But they weren't exactly warm to the thought of a fat pregnant woman shaking her assets on stage. Something to do with the liability insurance, I think."

He was giving her such a shocked look that she laughed. "I'm kidding, Max. I've never even been in the Double-D."

After a moment's hesitation, Max groaned and said, "The Double-D. I get it."

"Little slow on the uptake there. Or maybe I overstated my assessment of your intellect."

"You didn't answer my question," Max reminded her. "Why the Seabrook?"

Emma had traded her fork for a spoon and was feeding Jacob from the bowl of cereal. "A desk job would have been more up my alley, I know. And that's why I didn't look for one. If I wanted to disappear, I had to be the master of reinvention."

"Makes sense. Why Kennewick?"

"It's an unpretentious city with some beautiful scenery. I live in an area with neighbors who are friendly but not overly interested in where I came from or what I do. And it borders cities that are large enough that they would have provided me with cover for the short term if I'd needed it." She offered Max a timid smile. "I always had to stay two steps ahead. To be prepared to move if I was the least bit suspicious that whoever wanted me dead was close. And after Jacob, it was imperative."

"I'm sorry you had to go through all that. That you're still going through it. I wish I could have realized sooner what was happening so everything would have turned out differently." He looked at Emma and held her eyes. "But I'm going to make it right."

Emma didn't respond immediately, not really sure how she felt about Max's sudden confession.

"You'll need to multitask for a minute while I use the lady's room," she finally said, passing Jacob to Max and heading for the back of the café.

Looking down at his son Max said, "Your mom's one tough cookie, J-man, but we won't let that stop us from winning her heart back, will we?" Jacob gave Max one of his infectious smiles and burped. "I'll take that as a yes, then."

CHAPTER TWENTY

They were just crossing into Wyoming's Laramie County, with Max behind the wheel. He was on the phone with Cole.

"Are Nanna and Henry at the safe house?"

"They got here about two hours ago. I have two security guys who'll travel with them when they leave with Jacob. They've been keeping watch on the neighborhood and since I got here I've checked the area twice, both by foot and car. Haven't spotted anything out of place. Phil Herrick and I even checked the rooftops on the apartment buildings across the street. You can never be a hundred percent sure, but I don't think we've been followed. What about you guys?"

"We're clean. I've been driving around for about forty minutes and haven't spotted anybody, so I'm coming in."

Ninety minutes later Max pulled into the driveway of a small four-unit apartment building. There were kids' toys strewn on the front lawn along with a swing set that looked to be heavily used. As they moved up the side walkway Emma saw a pair of fisherman waders lying in the corner of the porch alongside a fishing pole that was standing upright against the porch railing.

"I thought you said this was a safe house. If other tenants live here, how secure can it really be?"

"Good," he said. "The facade works. The entire building is the safe house. The two units upstairs connect as do the ones on the bottom floor. The stuff out here is just for show."

Max had his hand inside his jacket pocket where Emma knew he had his handgun. "Stay behind me, okay? Do you have the extra set of car keys?"

"In my hand, just like you instructed me to do three times now. Running isn't new to me, Max. And believe me, if anyone other than Cole comes through that front door, I already have my escape route planned. Don't worry about me, just go."

He smiled and stepped up onto the porch, protectively shielding her body with his. The front door opened just a crack and Cole's voice came through the gap. "Don't shoot, big daddy."

Max heard Emma giggle behind him and ignored her. "Stop calling me that, you moron. Move your ass so we can get inside."

The door opened wider and Max stepped aside to let Emma and Jacob enter first. As he stepped over the threshold, he turned back to the street and inconspicuously made a final visual sweep.

By the time he followed Emma inside and secured the locks, Cole had taken Jacob, allowing Emma to drop the backpack she'd been carrying and remove her coat. Max dropped his duffel next to hers and stepped into the living area, where he found his grandmother standing near the couch. His face lit as Joan Adams walked toward him.

"Maxwell. I've been so worried about you. Tell me you're okay."

"Even better now. I hope you understand why I couldn't call you. We just couldn't take the chance." Pulling away from her embrace he added, "It's so good to see you."

"Max," his grandmother's companion said, offering his hand in greeting, "we're so relieved you're out of harm's way."

"Thanks, Henry," Max said, shaking the older man's hand.

Looking back toward the foyer, he saw Emma standing off to the side, cradling Jacob and watching the exchange. "Emma? I think you know Joan, and this is her good friend, Henry Roth." He extended his arm in invitation for her to join them, which she did.

"Joan, I can't tell you how good it is to see you again," she said warmly. "You must be Henry," she added. "I'm Emma Cassidy."

"It's good to finally meet you," Henry said with a kindly smile.

Joan stepped up to Emma and gently rested her hand on Jacob's back, the other on his mother's arm. "And this must be Jacob. Cole has told us what a sweet child he is." She smiled down at the baby. "He has your eyes, Max, and Emma's nose and chin. But that smile? That breathtaking smile is all his own, isn't it?"

Emma looked down now and stared at Jacob's face. She had always thought she could see Max in their son's smile, but now as she watched him, she realized that Joan was right. His smile lit up the eyes which were the color and shape of Max's, but if you looked at just the smile, it was all his own.

"Would you like to hold him, Joan?"

"I'd like that very much."

While Joan and Henry fussed over the baby, Max slipped his arm around Emma's waist. "Let's go into the kitchen. Cole needs to update us and I could use a soda."

Stealing a final look at Max's grandmother, she turned and walked toward the back of the apartment. She was already feeling miserable knowing she would have to leave Jacob behind, but she knew it was something she had to accept.

"Joan must be feeling on cloud nine to be finally meeting her great-grandson," Emma said distractedly. "Keeping him a secret certainly had its cost, didn't it?"

"It did, but I'm sure Nanna understands why. None of us judge you for the decisions you had to make."

"But you would have every right to, you know."

"Let's not go there now. Be satisfied that you have family who love Jacob and will continue to protect him while we're gone."

"Yes, you're right. We can sort out the rest once this is done."

Max didn't know quite what she meant by that, but let it drop.

They joined Cole in the kitchen and found him enjoying a sliced turkey sandwich and what appeared to be homemade potato salad. "You'll need to make your own if you're hungry. All the fixins' are in the fridge."

"Where are Herrick and Dragotta?" Max asked, referring to the two bodyguards.

"Phil is catching some shut-eye. Gabe is on patrol."

"Okay, good," Max said before motioning Emma to take a seat. "I'll make us a sandwich."

"I'm not really hungry," she replied as she sat across from Cole.

"Then we'll share one. We need something besides greasy eggs and stale toast to sustain us."

She didn't say anything, concluding that it wasn't worth arguing about. "Who owns this place, anyway?" she asked.

"I could tell you," Cole said between bites, "but then I'd have to kill you." He snorted at the overused and so not-funny comeback.

Emma just stared at him until he cleared his throat and said, "Right. It's just that I know what you're going through and the realization of what's happening has finally hit you. I'm not making light of it, just trying to make it less severe." He set his sandwich down and leaned his elbows on the table. "I really can't go into ownership about the building. We're not here, never have been. And we need to be gone by noon tomorrow, which gives us plenty of time to get set up.

"Lou Garrison said that Victor is incensed over the security breach," he continued, "and Stan Hudson is getting closer to finding the source of the hacked system. The FBI agent inside—who himself has some amazing computer skills—is actually helping Hudson find the source, which makes Lou believe that no one suspects him of being involved."

"Are you sure that nothing will point back to the agent?" Emma asked.

"Lou's man didn't really have any hands-on involvement. He just pointed me in the right direction and I'm the one who remotely accessed the surveillance tapes and looped them into the system the night we went in. He may have left the system vulnerable for a while, but I'm sure by now he's plugged the hole in the firewall and no one's going to be the wiser."

"What about you? Will they be able to track anything back to you?"

"Once they finally find the cyber intruder it's going to link back to a computer in Salinas, California. The operator will be one of Victor's oldest rivals who, coincidentally, is serving a life sentence in a federal prison. Eventually, Hudson will have to admit that the mystery hacking is one gigantic dead end."

"Where does that leave us? We still don't know where Eric hid everything."

"Hudson is convinced that you have—or at least know—where the paintings, money and drugs are," Cole said as he went to the refrigerator for a second helping of potato salad. "So we need to figure out what it is that he's so sure he knows." Glancing at Emma he said, "Question for you: what happened to your apartment in Kingsport?"

"I told the landlord that I was going to be out of the country for a year and that I wanted to sublease the apartment. He agreed and I paid for a year's rent."

"Who did you sublet to?"

"I didn't. I was afraid to let anyone near the place because I was sure someone would be watching it and might think that anyone living there would know where I'd gone. So it's been empty all this time. Although I'm sure that whoever was looking for me eventually figured out I wasn't coming back and no doubt broke in. But from the indicators I left they would have come to the conclusion that I took off in a hurry and that I was headed overseas."

"It's been more than a year," Max pointed out. "Are you still paying for the apartment?"

"No. I left instructions that if I didn't return after the year the landlord should contact Delores Fairbanks at the women's shelter to pick up all my belongings, and I would consider my rental agreement null and void."

"Did this Delores woman really know where you had gone?" Cole asked.

"I told Delores that I was leaving the country and wasn't coming back. I'm sure she knew I was running, but never asked me directly."

"Did you take anything with you when you left? Anything that may give us an idea of what we're looking for?"

"I took a suitcase full of clothes and little things like my jewelry box, some books, and a few family heirlooms. Other than the practical stuff, I left with things that had meaning to me, opting for quality rather than quantity."

"There must have been other things that you couldn't take with you but still didn't want to give to the shelter," Max interjected. "What did you do with those things?"

Leave it to Max to recognize that there would have been things she just couldn't bear to give away. "Most of what I took had to fit into the car so there were a few things I boxed up and gave to a friend to keep. But they were all memorabilia. Things I've had since I was a child or other things that I collected as a teenager and adult. There weren't any paintings or drugs and certainly no cash."

"A list of what was in the box would help us, and then maybe a second list of what you took with you."

"I can do that."

The three remained silent for several minutes until Cole said to Max, "It looks like our best option is to go back to Kennewick, see if there are any clues there, first."

"As good a place as any at this point." Looking at Emma he

added, "There's a crib set up in the back bedroom so you and Jacob should be comfortable. You can make the list up tomorrow and we'll decide if we need to stop at this friend's place first to go through what you left with her. It's a toss-up either way."

"Plane, train or automobile?" Cole asked.

"Let's start out by car and we'll play it by ear. Now that Jacob is protected, we've got some breathing room on time. We can always hop a commercial flight later on in the trip."

"I'll map out the best route in the morning, then," Cole said walking to the kitchen door. "Let's plan to be on the road by ten."

After he left, Emma said, "I'm going to turn in as well. You should stop in and spend some time with Jacob before you call it a night. I mean, if you want to, that is."

Touched, Max said, "I will. Thanks. I'll just say good-night to Nanna and Henry and check in with the security guys."

He sat alone in the kitchen for a short time before finding Gabe and then saying good night to his grandmother. His last stop was Emma's room. During the twenty minutes he was there, both Emma and Jacob fell peacefully asleep. He placed his son in the crib before moving to the double bed where Emma slept. He leaned over and touched his lips gently to her cheek then quietly shuffled down the hall to the last empty bedroom, where hopefully he'd be able to find his own way to slumber land.

CHAPTER TWENTY-ONE

As morning broke, Emma was the last person to wake. The first thing she noticed was that Jacob wasn't in his crib, but before she went into meltdown mode, she saw the note that Max had written in large, sloppy lettering: *Jacob is safe and in the living room with us.*

Taking a cleansing breath she decided on a shower before joining the group. Adjusting the water temperature, she stepped under the spray and let her thoughts drift to the succession of highs and lows she'd experienced in the past two days.

The constant through all of it, of course, had been Max. Even as she'd waited for him back on that deserted road leading to Victor Manderfield's ranch house, she had felt his strength through her fear. And when she saw him crossing the field with Cole—saw Jacob secure in his father's arms—her fear had been replaced with the realization of what she truly felt for Max. The sight of this tough, courageous man protecting their child while knee-deep in battle had touched her deeply, and she'd never loved him more.

Letting the water spill over her hair and back she wondered what the future held for the two of them. The hurt that she'd hung on to for so many months was beginning to thaw, and she now believed that Max had been an innocent bystander from the beginning, caught up in someone else's sick game. But did he still have some residual love for her? Sadly, she just didn't know. The bottom line was that Jacob needed his father and no matter how things worked out between her and Max, she would not deny him his right to be a part of his son's life.

Quickly drying her hair and getting dressed, Emma walked into the living room to see Joan, Henry, and Cole watching cartoons with Jacob and Max. Her son's extended family, she thought emotionally. A strong family who loved him, wanting nothing more than to give him the best they had to give. Looking at Joan and Henry she also knew that while she and Max were gone, they would protect her child as if he were their own son.

Joan glanced up and smiled. Rising from the couch she came over to where Emma stood just inside the arched entry to the living room. "Let's go into the kitchen for some coffee," she said quietly. "Let the boys be boys for a while."

She hooked her arm through Emma's and led the way to the kitchen. "Would you like something to eat?"

"I can make it," Emma said. "Have you eaten?"

"Yes. Henry and I are early risers. But I won't pass up another cup of that splendid java."

"Please, sit. I'll get it."

Emma poured two cups and then popped an English muffin into the toaster for herself. "I'm sorry that I kept Jacob a secret from you and Max," she said quietly, needing to say the words she'd held inside for way too long. "I had my reasons and maybe someday I'll be able to share them with you. But I can see how much you already love him and . . ."

Emma stopped, unable to finish. Turning away from Joan she whispered, "I'm so, so sorry, Joan."

Joan went to her and guided Emma to a chair at the table. "You just sit for a minute while I get your breakfast," she said, walking back to the counter to pull the English muffin out of the toaster. She covered it with a thin layer of honey before setting it on a plate, picking up Emma's coffee cup, and returning to the table.

"You'll feel better with something in your tummy and your first cup of coffee," she said in a soothing, motherly tone.

Emma pulled out a tissue and dabbed at her eyes and nose. "I'm usually pretty resilient, you know? I've always considered crying a weakness, mostly because Eric enjoyed making me do it so much. I'd fight the tears, feeling as if I'd won if I didn't break, even if I ended up with bruises in the morning." She looked up and saw understanding rather than pity in Joan's eyes. "You tried to help me," Emma added quietly.

"Yes," Joan said. "And I was pleased that you had found a way out."

They were silent for a bit while Emma nibbled on her breakfast and they both drank coffee. Eventually Emma said, "I'm sorry I didn't reconnect with you once I'd left Eric. Or after Max and I started seeing each other and I realized you were his grandmother. I should have made a better effort to see you. But then the ground fell out from under me and I found myself in survival mode."

"I know," Joan said sympathetically. "That's all in the past, and you and Max and that precious boy of yours need to concentrate on your future now. I'm just hoping that when this nasty business is done, you'll still let me see Jacob once in a while."

Emma's smile reflected the great fondness she felt for Max's grandmother. "Jacob is your great-grandson. He deserves to have you in his life, Joan."

With a sigh of relief Joan said, "That's settled, then. And when you both get back, we'll have a real family get-together. What do you say to that?"

"I say that's a terrific idea. Why don't you and Henry start making the plans while we're gone?"

"We will," Joan said as she took Emma's hand in hers. With tears in her eyes, she added, "Be safe out there."

Emma only nodded, not sure she'd be able to speak through her own tearful emotions.

Cole was busy loading up the car they would use for their trip to Emma's home on the west coast. Not that there was much to pack, but it kept him busy while Emma and Max said their good-byes.

"You're going to leave first," Max was saying to Henry. "Phil will take you out back where Gabe is waiting with the car. You'll be driven to a private airport where a friend's plane will be ready to fly you to West Virginia and then you'll be taken to a safe place. There should be at least one bodyguard with you at all times. Don't either of you go anywhere without your protection, understood?"

"You don't have to worry about us," Henry said, placing a strong and steady hand on Max's shoulder. "I'll protect your grandmother and your son, with my life if I have to. I'm not completely clueless to the dangers here, and I may have some years on me but I can still pack a punch and hit a target dead center at a hundred yards. Not that I'm going to need to do either," he said with a short laugh. "But I've got the skills. And I've got the motivation," he added, nodding at Joan and Jacob.

Max knew he was right. Henry was ex-military, with an exemplary record and the medals to go with it. Although he didn't talk about it much, Max knew that he had spent time in countries that didn't value the lives of their own citizens very much, let alone the lives of American troops.

"You need to go out there and end this," he continued. "And you take care of yourself and this beautiful mother of your child." Henry reached over and pulled Emma into a tender embrace. She held on for several seconds before pulling away and turning to Joan.

"Jacob likes the car, so hopefully you won't have any problems on your ride to the airport," she said, swiping at the single tear that ran down her cheek. "He's never been on an airplane, so I don't know how he'll react, but he's a good boy." She bent down and pressed her lips to the top of his head. Speaking quietly, she said,

"Be happy, my sweet boy. I'll be back as soon as I can. I love you, Jacob, with all my heart."

Max stepped up behind her and placed his hand on her back. He bent down to give Jacob a kiss as well. "I love you too, J-man, with all my heart."

Turning to Emma he gently said, "They need to leave now. Let's go find Cole and make sure we've got everything packed." Max knew how difficult this was for Emma, and the sooner they separated from Jacob the better it would be. "We'll be in touch when we can," he added as he kissed his grandmother on the cheek.

They met up with Cole in the bedroom that Max had used the previous night. Cole was on the bed leaning against the headrest, his legs crossed at the ankles, his arms folded behind his head. "Hey, big momma. What's shakin', big daddy?"

Emma laughed, thankful that Cole seemed to always know exactly what to say. He could be really scary at times, secretive and cunning, but he had a keen sense of being able to read a situation in seconds and react accordingly.

"Stop calling me that," Max said between clenched teeth.

"I really don't understand why it bothers you so much," Emma said, winking at Cole.

"It's the way he says it," Max replied defensively. "All smug and pretentious like." He walked over to the dresser to make sure the drawers were cleaned out, adding, "And I don't need you fueling his arrogance."

Cole grinned and rolled off the mattress. "We're ready to go any time. You should go check your room, Emma. Make sure you've taken everything. We don't want to leave behind any confirmation that we were here."

She did as Cole said, and combed through every corner of the room, glad she had. Stuck between the crib and wall was the stuffed lion that was Jacob's favorite. She grabbed for it and ran to the window facing the back of the building. The vehicle that Max had referred to earlier was nowhere in sight.

Hurrying down the hall to Max's room, her momentum abruptly came to a halt when she ran straight into him at the bedroom door. He grabbed her around the waist to prevent her from falling, the move resulting in full body contact. His strong, solid, totally masculine frame had her feeling breathless. Meeting his eyes, she realized that this slightly intimate connection might be having the same energized affect on him and she carefully pushed away as he released his hold.

"Are you ready to go?" he asked, still looking straight into her eyes.

"Have Joan and Henry left with Jacob yet?"

"Yes. I watched them pull away. Why?"

She held up the stuffed toy. "This is Jacob's. It fell behind the crib and I just wanted to give it to him if they were still here." She felt embarrassed now over the fact that she had been so concerned with getting the toy to her son.

"I'll just pack it," she said. "I'm sure Joan will find a replacement for it to keep Jacob happy."

Max reached up and gently laid his hand on the side of her face and rubbed his thumb on her cheek. Smiling he said, "What's the lion's name?"

The question threw her for a second but then she said, "Clarence."

"We'll just have to make Clarence an honorary member of our team. Sound good?"

"Sounds good. The J-man will appreciate it."

Max dropped his hand and turned her toward the kitchen. "Cole is waiting for us outside. Shall we?"

CHAPTER TWENTY-TWO

Cole was driving. They had been on the road for nearly two hours when he made the implausible announcement. "We've got company."

"That's not possible," Emma gasped from the back seat. Leaning into the window she tried to see through the side-view mirror. "How could anyone know where we are?"

"I don't know. But to be safe we need to dump the phones. It's unlikely that's how they got us but let's not take any chances."

Max already had his out, and was reaching into the back seat to collect Emma's at the same time Cole was dropping his on the front seat. Unceremoniously, Max ripped each one apart, smashing the internal mechanisms to unrecognizable scraps.

"Emma, in the duffel behind my seat, you'll find three new phones that Gabe picked up for us. Check them to make sure they're working, but don't do any programming."

As she bent down to rifle through the duffel she heard Max checking his handgun. "Do you have your .22 on you?"

"Yes. I need to pop the magazine in, though."

"Do that before you check the phones. I want you ready."

"I think there are two cars, and I see no alternative but to try and lose them," Cole said, increasing the vehicle's speed. "Buckle up, everyone."

Stan Hudson was riding shotgun in the first vehicle with his security man, Mark Flynn, driving. The second vehicle was a few car lengths behind them, driving a parallel course in the adjoining lane.

"He's picking up speed," Flynn reported. "He's tagged one of us, if not both."

"If we can just keep up with them for another ten minutes we'll have the helicopter in the air," Stan said. "Don't lose them, Mark."

"I'm doing my best, but jeez, this guy is good."

Flynn followed Cole's car onto an off-ramp and trailed behind him through a dozen or so city streets. As he expertly weaved the vehicle in and out of traffic his blood sang with the excitement brought on by the chase. But as good as this Haywood guy was, Mark Flynn considered himself better.

Down a few more streets. Around a delivery truck double-parked. And finally into the parking structure of the municipal building.

When Flynn reached the exit onto Main Street the car he'd been following was out of sight. He radioed to the second car to circle back around and head down Jackson Avenue, while he threw his car into reverse and slowly wound through the rows of parked cars. "It would have been a smart move to fly into the lot and right into an empty space," he said aloud. "The lot is big enough that Haywood could have pulled it off, no problem."

As they circled the structure, Stan kept his eyes peeled for any sudden departures. He also watched for cars with running motors. But after twenty minutes of maneuvering through the lot, Flynn slammed his fist into the steering wheel, knowing the parking structure was a dead end.

"Have you found them?" he growled into the radio.

"Negative," the driver of the second car said, his tone sounding as frustrated as Flynn's had been. "But there's a funeral driving through downtown, slowing up traffic. Haywood may have pulled into the procession. Hell, that's what I would have done. I'll stay put and check each vehicle as it goes by."

"Shit," Stan huffed as he glared through the windshield. "They're gone."

Another two minutes passed before he finally heard the helicopter circling overhead. "We're not going to find them on the ground," Stan admitted heatedly. "Contact the pilot and tell him we're heading out, but he should keep looking. If he sees anything, I want to know about it."

Cole felt marginally repentant about having to hot-wire one of the cars that had been parked behind the funeral home. Dumping the first car in the parking structure about two blocks east, they had hustled their way down an alley to the one-story, solemn-looking building that appeared to be packed tight with mourners.

"It'll be our luck," Cole said as they drove out of town, "that the funeral was for some retired law enforcement mucky-muck, whose sudden death from a heart attack caused the entire town to come out and pay their respects."

"And if that's the case, we should probably dump this car as quickly as possible," Emma chimed in as she continued to program a top-up card into each of the throwaway phones. "Because with our luck, you stole the chief's car."

"I'm going to believe it wasn't a cop and just an upstanding citizen who had a lot of friends," Max spoke up, "but I agree that we should find another car as soon as humanly possible. I'm sure we don't have much time before this one is reported missing."

"I agree," Cole said. "There's a theater complex not too far from here. A movie runs a couple of hours so we can wait for someone going in, and that should give us a good start."

After pulling into the theater's parking lot, they only had to wait ten minutes for the car they wanted. As Cole went to work getting the vehicle running, Emma stood guard while Max wiped down the interior and door handles of the car they had heisted from the funeral home.

When the engine on the hot-wired Chevy finally roared to life, Max quickly finished swapping the car's license plates with the vehicle parked in a neighboring slot. Emma had already started to drag the backpacks, duffel bags and equipment case into the back seat, and now slid in next to the gear as Max climbed into the front passenger seat.

"Okay," Cole said nonchalantly. "Let's try this again."

CHAPTER TWENTY-THREE

Max was behind the wheel of the beat up Chevy as Cole was busily working on his portable computer from the front passenger seat. They had detoured south after deciding that their most recent adventure called for a change in itinerary. Emma was sitting behind Cole in the back seat listening halfheartedly as the two men analyzed what had just happened, trying to figure out how they'd been discovered so quickly.

Thankfully, Joan, Henry and Jacob had been able to board the plane without incident. Earlier Emma had insisted that Max stop long enough to use a payphone to contact one of the bodyguards, and Gabe had assured Max that the chartered jet had departed safely.

The encounter had unnerved Emma more than she was willing to admit, and she was trying hard to deal with the reality that Victor Manderfield was out for blood and would stop at nothing until he had her in the crosshairs. For the first time since she'd left Jacob with Joan and Henry, the fact that her son would grow up without his real parents was terrifying. They had to find a way to end this so they could all go back home.

"The cabin is about another hour from here," Max was saying. "It's off the beaten track and hidden enough that we can trust the location. For now, I think it's better to stay out of sight for a day or two."

"I agree. We need a revised plan so we don't get ourselves killed," Cole said, glancing at the road signs as Max made the next turn.

"I had planned on waiting until we hit Washington before picking up gear and ammunition, but now that the situation's changed it's probably a good idea if we got it sooner rather than later."

"Not a problem."

"What about the cabin's occupants?" Cole asked. "Will they mind a couple of unannounced guests who are being hunted by psycho killers?"

"It's a family sanctuary but there aren't many of us left who need to get away to the depths this place is buried. So I'm sure we don't have to worry."

Cole glanced at Max now and after a moment gave him a quick nod. "Let's move it along then."

"It's right around that bend," Max was saying as they rode over a dirt road that ran parallel to a river he knew was running fast and furious this time of year. "There's going to be a one-lane bridge that signals we're two miles from the cabin. I don't know what shape it's going to be in so we may need to ditch the car and walk from there."

"If we can't get across in the car how are we going to do it on foot?" Emma asked as she stared out the window at the total seclusion that surrounded them. "That's what you meant, right? That the bridge would be out of commission."

Max glanced back at Emma. "If it's not passable by car it still may be okay by foot. And if not, there's a walking path along the back side of the cabin we'll take. It's just not wide enough for a car. I spent most of my summers as a kid here and I know all the ins and outs. I'll get us there," he said reassuringly.

She smiled faintly. "I'm sure you will. I'm just hoping you'll keep the adventure to a manageable level."

Cole had been assessing the isolated area as Max slowed their approach to the bridge. "Is this the only way in and out by car?" he asked.

"No. There's another road leading in from the north but it wasn't used much because it's even more untamed than this one, and driving it takes twice as long to get to the cabin from the main road." Straightening in his seat and leaning forward he added, "There's the bridge."

Cole had already spotted it and watched as Max came to a complete stop about two car lengths from the opening. "No one's getting over that any time soon," he pointed out as the three of them looked at the decay in the center of the structure. "It doesn't look like anyone's used it in years, Max. When was the last time someone was out here?"

"Can't say that I know for sure. The last time I was here was a good seven years ago. But Nanna still talks about the cabin on occasion so I've got to assume it's in better shape."

"Let's hope so," Cole said. "The area looks like it's secluded enough for us to hide out for a few days especially if you say the other access road is less known to anyone outside of the family. So how do we get to this homestead of yours?"

"It's going to take another two hours to swing around and backtrack to the other side of the cabin. You'll need to go through the town of Shay to get there and that's where you can pick up whatever you need in the way of supplies."

"Me?"

"Yeah. I might be recognized by one of the old timers. I'll draw you a map and then take Emma by foot from here and we'll meet you at the cabin."

Cole drummed his fingers on the dash board as he shifted his attention from the bridge to the land that lay beyond. Finally, turning back to Max he said, "They'll have what we need in Shay? Won't they wonder why a complete stranger is buying up ammo?"

"Stop at Farley's Outback on Cantor Street. They cater to the outdoorsman although you may have to show some identification—

Mr. Jones," Max said, sliding a deliberate look at Cole. He knew his partner carried false ID and was suggesting it was best if he used it at Farley's. "There's a lot of hunting that's done in these parts so you shouldn't have a problem. And I'm sure you'll come up with a plausible story if anyone asks."

Cole nodded. "When I'm on my way back I'll give you a call. Assuming I can get cell service."

"Sounds good." Max shifted in his seat to face Emma. "Are you ready for a hike?"

"Why not?" Emma replied as she opened the back door and dragged out the two generously sized backpacks that had been filled with snack bars, water and clean clothes.

Ten minutes later, Cole was backing down the dirt road, map in hand. When he was out of sight, Max turned to Emma and watched her stuff Clarence into one of the backpacks.

"It's Jacob's favorite toy," she said defensively. "I wanted to make sure I didn't leave it in the car. The way Cole goes through vehicles I couldn't be sure it would make it back to me."

Max let out a short laugh as he started walking along the tree line leading away from the bridge.

"How far from here?" Emma asked when she caught up to him.

"A half hour at most. Stay close to me, though. The path ahead will get a bit narrow at certain points and it can be tricky to navigate if you're not familiar with it. So you're going to want to take it nice and easy," he added, giving her a casual smile.

Although she wasn't a novice when it came to hiking, the rutted hillside on their right—mud-slicked from a recent rain storm and descending straight down to the river—gave her pause. Not to mention the six-foot-high embankment on her left, notched with jagged rocks. Added to that, the narrow trail they were following was riddled with more mud, loose stone and fallen tree limbs. Calling it tricky had been an understatement.

"Maybe this wasn't such a good idea," she said guardedly, glancing again to her right at the uneven overhang.

"We'll be fine. Besides, splitting up and approaching the cabin on foot gives us the chance to scout the surroundings. If we see anything out of place we can do an about-face and have Cole come back to pick us up."

But Max was having doubts now too, questioning why he hadn't insisted that Emma stay with Cole while he did a solo run on foot. He could justify his decision in so many ways, but none of that would matter if they ran into any trouble. He glanced back and just seeing the vulnerability hidden beneath the strength and determination she was carrying front and center, gave him the only answer that mattered. He didn't want to trust her safety to anyone but himself. Not even to Cole—the one person he would trust his own life to, and had on more than one occasion. He loved this woman, wanted to protect her, and couldn't do that long distance. It was selfish, he knew. But it was the God's honest truth.

He continued to carefully pick his way through the earthy debris along the trail, realizing they were close now. It felt odd somehow, coming back to a place that held so many memories. His parents had divorced when he was ten, and his father had moved out of state. His mother, recognizing she couldn't play the role of both parents to her children, had relied on her own father to provide some male guidance. So from a very young age, and all through high school, he'd come out here every summer with his brother and spent hours fishing, swimming and working alongside their grandfather who was an accomplished carpenter. He'd learned how to measure, cut, mold and carve everything from rocking chairs to cabinets and desks.

After his mother had died while he was attending college, he'd continued to come out here on his own whenever he could. It wasn't until his grandfather passed away that Max had gradually lost interest in the cabin, mainly because the memories had become more painful than soothing.

Lost in his reminiscing, he didn't notice Emma stop when her boot strap came undone. She removed her backpack, dropping it on the ground beside her, and crouched down to re-tie the strap. But when she stood, her foot landed on loose pebbles and wet leaves, causing her to fall to one knee. Her grunt pulled Max's attention back to the present and when he turned he saw her push herself up, lose her balance and stumble backwards. With a stab of panic, he watched as her feet ran out of room and she tumbled off the path and over the edge of the hillside.

He raced toward her, heart pounding furiously. He was within feet of where she'd gone over when he dropped low to the ground and started crawling toward the edge. He could see her hanging desperately to a willowy vine of sorts but he could also see that she was losing her grip, slapping the other hand against the mud wall, grappling for a second stronghold. He stopped just above her and lying flat, reached down. But when his hand grabbed for her wrist, it came up empty.

Her muffled scream hit him like an inflating airbag, momentarily taking his breath away, and the sight of her hitting the water below was almost paralyzing. He watched her fight against the current, recognizing it was a battle she would quickly lose. As the rapids picked her up and began carrying her downstream he could all but see the fear in her eyes.

Instinct and training had Max on his feet in seconds, grabbing both backpacks and sprinting down the path. Although the footing was difficult, he was making good time while praying he would reach Emma before the river opened up and it would be nearly impossible to get to her without a raft.

He kept her in his sights, wanting to believe that he was gaining on her. The path was now heading downhill and in just another several yards he would be on even ground with her.

As he picked up speed, he slapped at low hanging branches from trees that lined the river's edge and sought purchase several times when his boots slid on the mud-covered ground. He tripped once, then twice, but kept going until the third stumble took him down. He left the backpacks where they'd fallen and scrambled back to his feet, only to realize that he had lost sight of her. He released a string of profanity, forced to slow his pace so he could search the water for her location.

It was then that he heard his name called out in a weak but earnest voice. "Over here, Max. Hurry. I can't hang on much longer."

He headed toward the sound of her voice and when he spotted her, stripped off his overcoat and removed the gun and shoulder holster he'd been wearing under it. She had managed to grab on to a tree limb that had partially broken away from its trunk but he could see that weather had weakened the connection and if he didn't reach her soon, the branch would break away completely.

Certain the water was negotiable this close to the riverbank, he lunged in and half-walked, half-swam to her. Her jacket had snagged on the end of the branch and he tugged at the material in order to release the hold so he could drag her back to solid ground.

"Put your arms around my neck, Emma, and I'll do all the work," Max said once he'd gotten her free. "I've got you now and we're going to get you back to dry land, okay?" He waited for a response, concerned to see that her eyes were wide with fright and her skin pale from exhaustion. "Emma, tell me you understand what I'm saying."

"You're going to get me to dry land. I understand. Just make it quick. I'm awfully cold."

"The cabin's not far. It's got a fire place that I'll get going as soon as we get there. You still with me?" he added as he finally pulled her completely out of the water and laid her down so he could assess her condition. "Where are you hurt?"

"Oh, that's easy," she said with a wince. "All over should cover it."

"I'm so sorry, Emma. I knew it was slippery and I should have been paying better attention. Or better yet, I should have sent you with Cole." Taking her face in his hands he lowered his voice to a whisper and said, "Jesus, you scared me. Please tell me you're okay."

She raised her hand to cover one of his and said, "I will be as soon as you get me up off this cold ground."

He gave her a quick grin and, leaning over, helped her sit up. "You've got dry clothes in your backpack but if you can make it to the cabin it'll be better to wait and change there. Are you sure you can move? Do you think anything is broken?"

"I'm sure nothing's broken, just bruised."

Max made a quick detour to retrieve the backpacks, along with his coat and firearm, before helping Emma to her feet. With his arm around her waist and hers around his shoulder, they made their way gingerly to the cabin.

CHAPTER TWENTY-FOUR

After reaching the cabin, Max's first order of business was to start a fire as Emma went into the bathroom adjoining the master bedroom to change out of her wet clothes. When he eventually made his way down the hallway the bedroom door was open and he could hear the shower running. She'd placed the muddy backpacks on the floor near the bed and he started toward them with the intent of finding a pair of dry clothes for both of them. When he heard her cry out, he quickly reversed direction.

He could see through the glass shower door that she was holding her side, trying to stop the blood that was streaming through her fingers from a long, deep gash. Grabbing a hand towel off the counter, he slid the door to one side and said, "Here, hold this over the bleeding." Guiding her out of the shower and toward the bathroom door he added, "I thought you said you were fine."

"I thought I was," she responded weakly. "Until I saw the blood. I didn't even feel any pain until I saw the blood. It hurts, Max. Really hurts."

He saw the tears and felt her begin to shake as he half-carried her toward the king-sized bed, helping her position her body so she was lying on her good side. He hurried back to the bathroom for more towels and checked the cabinet for first aid supplies. Finding little, he went back to her and placed another towel over the one Emma was struggling to hold over the cut. He'd been in enough altercations of his own over the years to know he shouldn't be overly alarmed that she had already bled through the first one, but it was tough. Lucky for Emma though, he knew how to manage a bleeder.

"There's a first aid kit in the back and I need to go get it," he told her gently as he placed her hand over both towels. "You've got to hold this tight until I get back, okay? Apply some pressure."

She just nodded, making the effort to tighten her hold. After pulling the bed sheet over her body Max headed toward the back of the cabin, hoping the first-aid kit his grandfather had always kept stocked was still stored in the laundry room. It was, and he rummaged through it making sure it held the medical supplies he needed.

Back in the bedroom, he knelt down beside her and pushed damp strands of hair out of her face. It was even paler than it had been when he'd reached her in the river. Her eyes were closed and she was struggling too hard to breathe.

"Emma. Honey. I have to take a look at your side. I need to see how bad it is and what I need to do to get you all patched up."

His primary concern was that she'd need more medical help than he could give. But any call for help would mean disclosing their location to someone he didn't know and that was a risk he wasn't sure they could afford. A similar risk existed with taking her to a hospital—too many nosy people.

He lowered the sheet and moved her hand so he could check the towels. The blood flow had slowed considerably, and from the position of the gash, the branch that had sliced open her coat had also sliced her side. Faced with the probability of infection, he'd have to clean out the wound before doing anything else.

He pressed a clean towel over the gash and applied pressure for another five minutes, occasionally stroking her hair and using softly spoken words to soothe. When he was satisfied that he had the bleeding under control, he took her through what he needed to do next.

"I'm not going to lie to you, this is going to hurt. But I have to get it cleaned the best I can to avoid infection and I don't have anything to numb you up. You can scream as loud as you want and use every swear word you've ever learned. Whatever it takes to get through this. I promise I'll work as fast as I can."

Trying for a smile, she took his hand and gave it a squeeze. "I learned some pretty colorful language living with Eric for four years. Are you sure I won't make you blush?"

"Give it your best shot, kid."

And she did.

When it was over, he used several large bandages to cover the wound and helped her slip into a pair of hip-hugging sweatpants and one of his loose-fitting T-shirts. Once she was settled in, he pulled the blankets across her thin, battered body before pulling the old wooden desk chair close to the bed, settling in to watch over her.

It was just past ten in the evening when Max heard the front door open. He and Emma had been tucked away in the cabin for close to five hours now, the latter part of that time appearing to be restful for Emma. Although Cole had phoned earlier saying he'd be tied up for another several hours, it sounded like he had changed his plans.

Rising from his position alongside the bed, he stretched his back before reaching for his gun, which was sitting on the nightstand next to the dimly lit table lamp. Tucking it under his belt he picked up the flashlight he'd found earlier and moved toward the door leading to the hallway.

The fireplace had been on a slow, steady burn throughout the night and now illuminated just a small area in the front part of the cabin, leaving the remaining rooms in darkness. He flipped on the hallway light and stood motionless in the doorway, listening for any indication that he and Emma weren't alone, but the cabin remained still. It was possible he had only imagined the sound, but he wasn't about to take any unnecessary chances. He drew his gun and, after taking a final glance at Emma, stepped out of the bedroom, closing the door behind him.

Crossing the hall, he first checked the bedroom directly across from the master. Nothing seemed disturbed and he quickly cleared the room and the closet. He then crossed over to the laundry room, which was a small alcove at the end of the hall near the rear door. Again, the area was clear and the door remained locked and bolted.

He retraced his steps down the hallway and veered right, toward the kitchen. In the center of the room was an oversized island and breakfast counter with pots and pans hanging overhead on a rack suspended from the ceiling. He stepped over to the butler's pantry first, and when he was satisfied it was empty, continued to clear the rest of the room.

On his way to the final room in the cabin he detoured toward the front door. Locked, just the way he had left it after tending to Emma.

The living area, an open and uncluttered room with a large bay window, was now dimly lit by just a whisper of light as the full moon paused overhead. But like all the other rooms, no intruder lurked in the shadows.

The last space to check was a large walk-in closet off the main entrance. Cautiously, he laid one hand on the round doorknob and raised the gun he held in the other hand. Then, swinging the door out, he dropped low into a crouch and leveled the gun with both hands, aiming it into the room. He was surprised to see that the space was completely bare. During the summers he'd spent here, the closet had always been overflowing with stuff like fishing rods, spare clothes, an assortment of boots and discarded books and board games that no one wanted to throw out.

Max smiled at the memory as he closed the door and walked back into the living room wondering when the cabin had last been used. He had already surmised that someone had been taking care of it after finding the clean towels, sheets and blankets. The working electricity and running water were also an indication that his grandmother hadn't wanted to let the place go to ruins. He'd discovered some flannel shirts neatly lined up on hangers in the bedroom closet and men's underwear and white cotton T-shirts in the dresser drawer, so maybe the caretaker had even spent some time out here recently. From the lack of food in the kitchen and the dust on the furniture, however, he suspected it had been a while. And if anyone did come around, he would just explain that he had brought his girlfriend here to spend some quiet time away from the city. He was family, after all.

He moved to the window and took a minute to scan the acreage beyond, confident that there was nothing moving outside. Maybe the stress of Emma being hurt was causing him to imagine things, but it was always good to be cautious. Shaking his head, he started back down the hallway toward the bedroom, holding his gun loosely by his side.

With his mind once again on Emma, he realized too late that the door to the closet was slightly ajar—although he had closed it tight after clearing the space. The force of the intruder's body striking him had his gun skidding down the hallway and had Max crashing into the wall. Before he could turn around, the other man grabbed him from behind, clamping an arm around his neck.

Max knew self-defense—the kind you learned on the streets as well as the moves they taught in the classroom—but the man who'd taken hold of him was no lightweight. Max could tell instantly that he'd met his match.

"Who are you and what are you doing here?" a deep rumbling voice queried. "And tell me why I shouldn't just kill you now." The hold around Max's neck tightened.

"You got it all wrong, man." Max spoke in a strained voice, but knew it was still an asinine thing to say. How many times had he heard criminals and dope dealers say the same thing? "What I mean is that I didn't break in. Well, I did but I didn't. See, this is my place."

The man let lose a short laugh. "That's a good one. But try harder, because I know for a fact this isn't your place."

As Max listened to the man speak he was trying to recognize something in the voice that was just out of his mind's reach. Probably because his windpipe was slowly being crushed. "Ease up, man and I can explain. If you keep squeezing, all you'll be left with is a body to bury."

"Your point being, what?" Although he kept a strong grip on Max, the man did loosen it. Which should have given Max his opportunity to reverse the situation.

But before he could do anything he heard a soft voice say, "Let him go or you're dead."

Max was just marginally surprised that he hadn't noticed Emma before this, but he could tell the man behind him was totally startled. The hold once again tightened and he shifted his body so that Max was now his shield. "I've got a gun buried in this asshole's back so unless you want him dead, you'll be a good girl and drop the gun to the floor."

Max cringed at the man's use of *good girl* and only hoped that Emma wouldn't be insulted enough to shoot through him to take out her real target. Then that elusive detail that Max had been groping for popped, but not before Emma fired off a warning shot.

The bullet went into the doorframe of the second bedroom, so close that Max would have sworn he felt the breeze as it flew by. Reacting to the now escalated situation, both Max and his captor dove for the floor, and Max was able to break free. He rolled to his left and soared to his feet, racing toward Emma. "Emma, don't. Don't shoot."

She had repositioned her grip and was aiming the gun at the man who was still sprawled on the floor. A second before the next bullet left the barrel, Max was able to push her arm up and the shot thankfully missed its target. Taking her in his arms and relieving her of the gun Max said, "Emma, it's okay. He's my brother."

Emma was confused. She heard Max's voice, knew he was talking to her, but couldn't get her mind to understand the words. Why was she here in the hallway with him, and who was the man that was sitting quietly against the wall?

A gunshot. Yes, she remembered now. She looked down at her hands, sure that she'd find the gun there, convinced that she had fired that shot. But they were empty. She looked at the other man and remembered that he had been trying to hurt Max. If that were right, why was Max holding her and not plummeting this intruder?

"Emma, do you hear me? Look at me."

She did, and it was as if her whole world were spinning out of control. Her head began to pound, she felt both hot and cold simultaneously, and her legs were slowly losing the strength to hold her upright.

"Max. It appears as if the lady is bleeding."

Max looked down at her side and saw that Emma's cut had indeed begun to bleed through the bandage he'd put in place just an hour ago. He could also feel the heat of her skin through the T-shirt that was starting to soak up the perspiration. She was obviously spiking a fever.

"Shit," was all Max said before lifting her in his arms and carrying her back to the bed. He went into the bathroom to grab a clean towel, and when he returned, he saw Chris removing the tape that was securing the bandage. His first reaction was to push him aside, but the gentleness of his brother's touch stopped him. Instead, he dumped the towels on the bed and walked across the room to get the remainder of the medical supplies.

"Yep, ripped it clean open," Chris said as he replaced the bandage with one of the towels. "She's also burning up, which could be a sign of infection. Looks like she was at the wrong end of a knife at some point. Still like the dangerous ones, I see." But before Max could respond his brother added, "A slice this wicked isn't going to heal with a few strategically placed bandages. She's going to need real medical attention and some antibiotics."

He finally looked over at Max and held his gaze for a brief moment. "I know someone who'll come here and not ask questions," Chris said as he drew his attention back to Emma. "That's what you need right now, isn't it? A place to hide?"

Max set the first aid kit on the end table and said, "Not that I can afford to be picky, but does this someone you know have a medical license?"

"Same old Max. Just can't take an offer of help on face value." Chris had been holding one of the towels against the wound and replaced it now with a clean one. "Kyle runs a clinic just outside of Shay and he'll come here if I ask him to. And he'll keep a lid on whatever you're involved with—if I ask him to. It's up to you. But you better decide fast, because you're causing your lady undue agony by not getting her medical attention."

Max was close to losing his temper. When he looked down at Emma, however, and saw the suffering written all over her face, he relented. He could hash things out with his big brother later. "Get your friend here. But I mean what I say that if either of you hurt Emma it'll be the last thing you do for a very long time."

"Strong words for a long-lost brother, aren't they?" Chris stood and walked out of the room.

Max lowered himself to the side of the bed and checked Emma's wound. She was restless, and from what he could tell, in serious pain. He went into the bathroom and grabbed several washcloths, soaking them in cold water. Returning to her side he applied the compresses to her forehead and neck, hoping to provide some comfort.

An hour later, Chris walked back into the room followed by a tall, thin man who was in his mid- to late-forties and carrying a medical bag. He looked at Max and offered a hand. "I'm Kyle Brayton. Chris tells me you're concerned about my credentials. I'm a licensed, board-certified general practitioner and I run the family clinic in Jersey. If you'll move away from your friend, I'll see what I can do for her."

Max reluctantly stepped away from the bed, but took up position close enough to watch every move the doctor made. It was frustrating not being the one in control, but there was nothing more that he could do for Emma but keep an eye on the person who could. Chris had moved to the other side of the bed and, as if he'd done it a thousand times before, began to unpack the medical bag Dr. Brayton had brought, laying everything out at the foot of the mattress.

Chris hadn't changed much, Max thought as he studied his older brother. His unruly, dishwater-blond hair was longer than when they'd last seen each other, and he'd put on some weight, but both looked good on him. Unfortunately, he still had the same haunted look in his eyes, and a suppressed anger that lay just below the surface—from what, Max had never really figured out. There was something more, though, Max observed. He seemed happy, somehow, and for lack of a better word, content.

For the next half hour, Max kept watch as the doctor first cleaned Emma's wound then placed closure strips over the cut. After applying a clean bandage he finished his treatment by giving her a shot containing the first dose of antibiotic. It was only then that he gave his attention to Max.

"As nasty as the cut looks, we caught it before an infection could set in. Keep an eye on it and change the bandage as needed. I'll be back in the morning to check it myself, but if you run into any problems, give me a call." He handed Max his card along with a prescription bottle. "Here's the antibiotic. Make sure she finishes them even when she starts to feel better."

Chris had already dropped the used instruments and gauze into a plastic zipper bag and stuffed it inside the medical bag. Handing it to Kyle, he smiled and said, "Thank you for doing this."

The doctor just reached out and laid his hand on Chris's shoulder. "He's your brother. I know what it would have cost you if I hadn't."

Choosing not to respond, Chris turned and left the room.

But before Kyle followed, he stopped in front of Max and gave him a faint smile. "I can tell that Emma means a great deal to you, so I don't have to tell you to take good care of my patient. What I will tell you is that Chris means a great deal to me, so take as good of care with him as you will with her." Leaning in closer, his smile gone now, he repeated the words that Max had used earlier with his brother. "I mean what I say, that if you or your friend hurt Chris, it'll be the last thing you do for a very long time."

CHAPTER TWENTY-FIVE

Max put on a fresh pot of coffee and sat at the kitchen table waiting for it to finish brewing. After Kyle Brayton had delivered his warning to Max he'd promised to be back in the morning to check on Emma, then left with Chris who hadn't even bothered to give Max a backward glance. But Max wasn't planning on losing any sleep over the snub. It had been six years since he'd last seen his brother and for two years before that their relationship had been strained, to say the least. Besides, Emma was the one who needed Max's attention right now and he was determined not to let her down. Again.

Cup in hand, Max made his way back to the master bedroom. He stopped just outside the door and leaning against the jamb ran his free hand over the stubble on his chin. God, how she'd frightened him. First seeing her plunge into the water and then discovering how badly she'd been injured because of the fall. For now, all he could do was watch her helplessly as her body worked through the healing process.

He walked over to the small window and stood watch, shifting his gaze between her and the wooded area behind the cabin. When she stirred, he set the mug on the end table and carefully slid into bed next to her, cushioning his arm under her shoulders. It felt good when she turned into his body and settled into a comfortable position.

After several minutes her breathing became ragged and her

restlessness returned. "It's okay, Emma," he said in a smooth, reassuring voice. "I'm here and everything's going to be fine."

"It won't be fine," she whispered, her voice strained and raspy. "I'm so sorry."

"There's nothing to apologize for, sweetheart. Just try to rest now."

"I know you wanted more. I'm sorry I can't give you more."

Something inside Max's chest tightened. Was she really talking about their relationship *now*? With everything that had happened since he'd found her, could she really be reminding him that it was too late for them? And please, dear God, don't let the next five words out of her mouth be those every man dreaded to hear—*we can still be friends*.

He glanced down, wanting to believe that the fever was leaving her confused and unaware of what she was saying. "Go back to sleep now," he murmured as he lifted a strand of hair out of her eyes. "We'll talk about this when you're feeling better."

Although, if he were being honest, talking about it was the last thing he wanted to do. What he really wanted was to pick up where they had left off that glorious weekend back in Kingsport, when everything had been soft music, sweet wine and amazing sex.

As he continued to stroke her hair, Emma started to mumble softly and it soon became apparent that she was trying to tell him something important. When she braced her trembling hands on his shoulders, struggling to push herself into an upright position, he tried desperately to keep her still.

"Where's Jacob?" she finally said, the panic rising quickly. "We have to help Jacob."

Max laid his hand on her shoulder and quietly said, "Jacob is safe, Emma. Remember? He's with Joan and Henry."

She finally stopped struggling as the meaning of Max's words slowly reached her brain. But after several minutes, Emma's words, spoken in a weakened voice, had Max feeling uneasy. "Don't be angry with me about the other babies, okay, Max? We still have Jacob."

What other babies? he thought, unsure if he had heard her correctly. What was she talking about? There were no other babies.

Then, sitting very still beside the woman he was willing to lay down his life for, he realized the meaning behind her words.

There were no other babies.

And there couldn't be in the future.

It took less than forty-eight hours after Kyle had tended to Emma's injury for her to turn restless and argumentative. Max could hear her and Cole wrangling in the living room as he moved around the kitchen preparing lunch for the three of them.

"I can make it, Cole," she was saying. "I'm feeling fine and as long as I don't go climbing any mountains, I can keep up. I swear it."

"Well, swear all you want. You won't be able to keep up—no, let me finish," he said with a slight edge in his voice. "I've been in your position and I know the limitations an injury like this brings with it. And once we leave here and start back to Kennewick we won't have any medical help readily available to us. Max and I agree on this. You need another day or two before we move out."

"I don't," she insisted, leaping off the couch and wincing slightly at the pain the sudden movement caused. "I'm sure you didn't pay any attention to the limitations when you were hurt. You worked around them, which is what I intend to do."

"We're staying put, Emma. Discussion closed."

"This is Max's idea, isn't it?" she said, refusing to give up, even though she knew she was being unfair. "He hasn't wanted me along from the beginning and this is his way of getting rid of me."

Cole took a calming breath before responding. "I'll give you a pass on the attitude because you're scared and hurting right now. But you and I both know that Max totally agreed with the reasons you gave for coming with us."

"Maybe," she relented, but just a bit. "But that was then. Now he's just trying to totally control my involvement."

"Really?" Cole said, raising his voice slightly. "Let's review for a minute here. Max is the one who offered us his family home when we needed a safe place to hide. He's the one who saved your life and then got the good doc to come here and fix you up. And Max is the one who's had virtually no rest in the last two days because he's been a little busy cleaning your wound, changing your bandage and making sure you stay nourished. I don't know what your definition of control is, Emma. But from where I sit, those are the things someone does when they've got your back."

Emma didn't have a logical response because she knew everything Cole had said was right. Defeated, she dropped back down onto the couch and only then noticed that Max was standing just inside the entryway to the room.

"Breakfast is ready. It's on the stove. I'm going to take a walk around the grounds."

Emma stood, and started to apologize, but Max was already gone. "I didn't mean any of that," she said, turning to Cole.

"He'll figure that out, just give him some space."

"I'm such a bitch," she said more to herself than to Cole. "I'm not hungry right now," she added as she headed down the hallway, "but you go ahead."

"I don't think so," Cole said as he put his arm around her shoulder. "Max hates to cook. He won't even heat something up in the microwave if he can help it. And judging from the smell in the kitchen, it seems as if the man went to some trouble to feed us." While he'd been talking, Cole had led her into the kitchen and now pointed to a chair at the table. "Sit. I'll get you a plate and a glass of milk."

Max left through the back door and walked the perimeter of the property, starting with the wooded area behind the cabin. When he made his way to the front, he spotted Chris sitting on the porch but continued his search of the grounds, which took another half hour. Chris was still sitting in one of the rocking chairs when Max climbed the front steps.

"Haven't kicked the habit, I see," Max said pointing to the cigarette pack sitting next to a cup of coffee on a tree stump their grandfather had turned into a table.

Chris shook his head and let a smile escape. "Kyle keeps at me to quit, but it's been hard. I have cut down considerably and try to use it as a reward rather than a companion now. Doesn't always work out that way, though."

Max walked across the porch and sat in a matching chair on the other side of the table. "What do you mean by companion?"

Chris didn't answer right away and Max thought that maybe trying to engage his brother in conversation had been a mistake. But then Chris spoke. "I used to smoke because all the other cool guys did. I kept smoking for the added benefit of annoying mom. But then I started drinking, and everyone knows that when you pour a drink, you light a cigarette. Eventually it follows the chicken or the egg theory. Does the drink lead to the cigarette or the cigarette lead to the drink? But then it didn't seem to be all that bad a habit compared to the drugs. And besides, if I was smoking a cigarette then I wasn't snorting cocaine, and if I could put the cocaine aside I wasn't an addict."

He looked over at Max, who was sitting completely still with his elbows resting on the arms of the chair, his hands clasped tightly across his midsection and his face a roadmap to confusion. "Now that I'm sober it doesn't make much sense to me either," he added.

Max was taking a hard look at his brother. Chris was five

years older than he was and for as long as Max could remember, had always lived on the wild side. As a teenager he'd been best at making enemies, got hip-deep in a number of shady deals and had a police record that would have had their grandmother blushing if she'd known the whole of it. The last time Max had seen his brother he was being helped into a squad car in handcuffs. As much as he wanted to believe Chris was clean and sober, Max could only remember the years of tears and torment that he and his mother had suffered.

"How long have you been sober?" Max asked.

"Four years. I came out here after I decided to clean up. Nanna gave me the green light after I had my AA sponsor call her so she knew I wasn't lying about my sobriety. I can't blame her for wanting to be sure."

"She never told me," Max said, not all that surprised by the omission of information from his grandmother.

"Actually, I asked her not to tell anyone. It was easier that way."

"Where does Kyle fit in to all of this?" Max asked as he shifted his attention to the dense forest of trees at the end of the driveway.

"Kyle and I met in rehab," Chris began. "And don't freak. He's been clean for eighteen years. He led one of the support groups."

"But he wasn't always clean is what you're telling me? Did he become a doctor before or after the drugs?"

"Still go right to the core of it, don't you, Max? He was a resident when he started using so he could keep up with the others and to help combat the long hours. Later, after he joined a practice, his partners caught on to his drug use. They made him a deal that if he went into rehab they would keep his addiction as quiet as possible. Doctors tend to protect their own, but you'd know all about that, being a former cop and all," Chris said with little affection. "He lost his job, of course, and when he came out of rehab he moved here where he found a local doctor who was willing to take a chance on him. And when his mentor retired, Kyle took over the clinic. If anyone in town knows about his former drug problems, they've never said. All they see is a competent doctor they can rely on."

Again, neither spoke for several minutes.

"Kyle and I are together," Chris finally said. "Don't know how you or your friends feel about that, but I really don't care. We keep to ourselves because that's the way we want it, but I won't pretend I'm someone I'm not just because you might disapprove."

Max had already suspected that the relationship between Chris and Kyle went beyond simple friendship. He'd seen the looks they'd exchanged and Kyle's perfectly delivered warning the night they'd met confirmed that he and his brother had deep feelings for each other. Max could accept that.

"I'm happy for you," Max replied. "Kyle did okay by Emma and he seems to be someone who'll always be there for you."

What was left unspoken was that Max *hadn't* been there for Chris. During the hardest point of his addiction—his recovery—Max hadn't been there. Other than his grandmother and his sister Patty, who had disowned them after Chris's third arrest for drunk and disorderly, Max was the only family Chris had left. And since Max hadn't stuck by him, Chris had been left to sink or swim.

"I can see that you're blaming yourself for my indiscretions, little brother," Chris said, reading Max's thoughts. He knew that any reconciliation he and his brother were going to have would only come with time, but he wanted to make this point very clear to Max, now. "It wasn't your responsibility to save me, Max. Same with Nanna and Patty. I chose the black hat and you chose the white, just like we did as kids when playing cowboys. You were the good guy, and me? Well, I wasn't," he added with a short laugh. "But I like to think of myself as one of the good guys today. My life may not be as pure as the driven snow, but I know the difference between right and wrong and I try my best to choose right, every time."

Max didn't know how to respond. He felt a little uncomfortable with Chris's honesty. They'd never shared this type of openness growing up, and Max didn't want to say something that would hurt or discourage Chris. So he said nothing.

"Emma told me what she said before, and I'm pretty sure she didn't mean it," Chris spoke after several minutes of silence. "She's feeling helpless and that's making her cranky." Chris looked over at Max and waited until his brother turned to him. "You both love each other. I don't know why you're pretending you don't but I can give you some brotherly advice that you should consider. Don't let her go. Don't let her push you away. You need each other."

Max paused before he replied. "I have a son, Chris. With Emma. He's six months old and I just found out about him a week ago. Most of the hurt is gone, but when Emma pushes like she did today, it stings. And I wonder if we've just become two people who share a child and nothing more. I don't want it to be that. She's a great person and a fantastic mother. I just don't know what the future holds, I guess."

"Wow, I'm an uncle," Chris said displaying a huge grin. "I hope you'll let me meet him one day."

Max couldn't help but to grin back. "Yes. I'd like very much for you to meet your nephew. Of course, it'll have to wait just a bit."

"I'm guessing that your new-found family is part of why you're here. Are you going to tell me what's going on?"

Max leaned his head against the back of the chair and released an agonized sigh. "I don't know how much I can tell you without putting you in danger."

"Max. You're here. I'm here. If you're in danger, so am I. Don't you think it's better if I know what I may be up against so I can better protect myself? I may even be able to help."

"I don't want you anymore involved than you are, Chris. We aren't playing cowboys anymore. These are dangerous people and they're out for blood." Although, even Max couldn't deny there was some truth to what Chris was saying.

Deciding to go against his better judgment he said, "Let's take a walk and I'll tell you what I know."

CHAPTER TWENTY-SIX

After Max had finally crawled into one of the twin beds in the spare bedroom, he'd managed to get several hours of uninterrupted sleep. Now, feeling rested and fairly clear-headed, he pulled himself into an upright position, thoughts of stealing just another fifteen minutes of quiet time rambling through his head.

He groaned at the three short taps against the wooden doorframe, sensing that the luxury of a long, hot shower would have to be put on hold. Glancing up he saw Cole poke his head around the half-opened door then move into the room with an apologetic look on his face.

"You're awake," he said. "You got a solid five hours, my friend."

"Hurray," Max replied with little enthusiasm.

Cole lowered himself onto the edge of the second bed and said, "Hey, do you know anyone by the name of Zoe Brine?"

"Name doesn't sound familiar. Who is she?"

"Emma says she knows her through the women's shelter and she's a close friend. Says she was part of the network that helped Emma disappear. Seems she's a family attorney with some mid-sized law office and volunteers at the shelter a couple of times a month." Handing Max his cell phone Cole added, "She's left two messages on our office voicemail."

Max coded in to their business machine and replayed the messages. In the first, Zoe gave only her first name and asked that

Max return her call regarding an old friend. The second message had been recorded around seven that morning and sounded more urgent: *"Mr. Dunmore, I need to talk to you as soon as you receive this message. I'm concerned about a mutual friend. I've been trying to reach her and I'm afraid something's happened. I need to discuss this with you personally, so please call me."* The message ended with a phone number.

"Well, I recognize the voice. Our Zoe Brine is the person who led me to Emma's place in Kennewick."

"Then it sounds like the mutual friend she's talking about is Emma. Get dressed and we'll call her back from the living room. Emma's going to want to be kept in the loop."

"Yeah, give me a couple of minutes and I'll be out."

Cole rejoined Emma in the living room and less than five minutes later Max appeared. Emma looked up from the book she was reading as he sat next to her on the couch and dialed the number left in the phone message. After three rings a woman's voice answered.

"This is Max Dunmore. I'm returning your call?"

There was a slight pause before he received a reply. "Give me a phone number where I can reach you and I'll call you back shortly." Max did, and disconnected.

"She's calling back. Does anyone want anything from the kitchen?"

Getting a negative response from both Cole and Emma, he left the room and found a soda in the refrigerator. Grabbing a banana off the counter he headed back to the living room.

His cell phone rang. "Max Dunmore."

"Mr. Dunmore. We need to make this fast. Is your phone secure?"

"As secure as it can be. What is this about, Ms. Brine, or better yet, who is it about?"

"I'm breaking a confidence by talking to you, but I'm so afraid that something's happened to Emma. I've been trying to reach her for over a week and I can't get a hold of her. She gave me your name and number a few months ago in case anything happened to her, and maybe I'm being paranoid, but I don't think so."

"Why do you think something's happened to her?"

Zoe didn't answer immediately, and Max didn't push. He could outwait almost anyone. Finally she said, "I'm being followed. And someone broke into my apartment yesterday. I also think my home and office phones are being monitored. I'm making this call from a pay phone in the lobby of my office building."

"And you think these occurrences are happening because . . . why?"

"These occurrences, as you so smoothly put it, started shortly before I left the message telling you where you could find Emma. When I suspected that someone was following me I tried to reach her but when I couldn't I called you. And I'm hoping that the reason I'm still being followed is because you found her first and these guys have run out of ideas and are still willing to believe I know something."

"If that's the case, you could be in danger."

"And I'm hoping you'll be my knight in shining armor and get me out of here."

"Why don't you just call the police?"

"For the same reason Emma never did."

Max looked at Emma, who was only hearing his side of the conversation, but it was enough for her to look worried. He also knew she had suspected police involvement with the threats she had been issued before disappearing from Kingsport. He turned his attention to Cole, who simply gave him a nod. Even though he was only hearing one side of the conversation as well, he was already up to speed and knew what Max was thinking. They needed to get Emma's friend to safety.

"I need your help, Mr. Dunmore," Zoe was saying. Her voice

was nearly a whisper now and Max could hear the frustration. "The break-in wasn't random. It's connected to Emma."

"Why do you think that?"

"Because nothing was taken. But they did leave something behind for me. When I walked into my bedroom there was a calico cat lying dead on my pillow—the cat from the shelter—and its throat had been slit."

"Don't say anything more, Zoe," Max said as he abruptly rose from the couch. "I'm sending someone to get you but it's going to take several hours. Are you safe where you are?"

"Yes. There are at least fifty people on my floor, ten of those working in the same office as me. And the building has pretty tight security because our state senator's office is one floor down and he's in residence today. So as long as I stay here I'll be fine. People start leaving around five o'clock and the floor will thin out by eight."

"We can be there by six at the latest. Now let me describe the person who's coming for you and give you a password."

As Max continued to talk, Cole left the room for several minutes and returned with his black duffel. When Max disconnected, he relayed the full conversation and Emma remained quiet while the partners discussed their next step. She knew it would be tricky slipping into Kingsport and getting Zoe out. By now Manderfield's men knew that Cole was involved and they were obviously watching her friend's movements. But Emma was putting her faith in Max's partner to make it happen.

"What else do you need?" Max asked, while Cole double-checked to make sure his gun had a full magazine of ammunition.

"Nothing. I don't plan on spending much time there." Turning to Emma he said, "Zoe said that whoever broke into her place was looking for something that you'd taken. Assuming the break-in ties back to Manderfield, could she know anything about the paintings?"

"No. But Zoe is the friend I gave my things to before I left," Emma said thoughtfully. "But how could anyone know that? And why wait until now to start harassing her?"

"My best guess is that they don't know for sure she has anything," Cole replied. "They started harassing her to try and draw you out. For all we know she isn't the first person they've considered as a possible lead to you. Unfortunately, she's the one who really does know how to find you and her change in behavior is giving Manderfield hope she can point them in the right direction."

"If Zoe still has Emma's things, bring them back with you," Max said.

"Way ahead of you. I'll contact you as soon as we're on the road back."

After Cole left, Emma followed Max into the kitchen. "Max?"

He turned to her and waited.

"Is Jacob safe? And Joan and Henry?"

"Absolutely. There's no trail to them and Nanna told her neighbors that she and Henry were going on a cruise, so no one is going to be looking for them. Cole handpicked the men who are guarding them and they'll call if there's any sign of trouble."

"But something could still happen."

"Okay, yes, something could still happen. But, Emma. You can't go back until we finish this. I know it's difficult and I know you miss Jacob deeply." He crossed over to her and lifted his hands to cup her face. "Manderfield found us once. It's just too risky to go back right now. We need to finish this first."

"I know. I don't mean to be such a pain in the ass. I'm usually better than this at managing crisis."

"Well, there's a lot at stake here," he replied as he dropped his hands and shoved them into the front pockets of his jeans.

"I also didn't mean what I said earlier today." She stopped him before he could turn away. "And I should never have said it. You're not trying to control me and I'm so grateful you're here. Thank you for saving my life."

"You're welcome," he said, giving her one of his captivating smiles. "And because you're in such a grateful mood, you can fix lunch. I'm going to go walk the perimeter. Be back in thirty."

Max was sitting at the kitchen table across from Emma, enjoying a deli ham and cheese sandwich, a man-sized bowl of canned tomato soup and a tall glass of instant iced tea. He'd finished checking the property for any signs of intrusion and was satisfied that for now, the cabin remained a safe haven.

Watching Emma move around the kitchen he wrestled with the best way to bring up the night that Kyle Brayton had treated her injury, and the words she'd spoken as she had dropped into sleep: *"Don't be angry with me about the other babies. We still have Jacob."* But every time he tried to organize his approach his words got tangled up in his head.

Early on, he'd recognized that the fever had contributed to her ramblings that night. At first he'd thought she'd been telling him that she didn't see a future with him. That the family he'd been imagining wasn't going to happen. Now, not only did he believe that the strong connection they had once shared hadn't been completely broken, he was almost certain Emma was feeling the same way. So, had her words meant more? Were they actually a confession of loss?

Emma looked up to see him staring at her, and was puzzled by the tenderness she saw in his eyes. "You look like you want to say something to me, Max."

"I do. Well, it's more a question I guess." Taking a slow, deep breath he said, "The night that Kyle came here, you had really spiked a fever, and I spent the night in your room. You were in and out a lot and at one point you mumbled something about . . ."

Max paused, not quite sure how to ask the question that had been playing in his head over and over again. But he needed answers and decided the direct approach was the only way to go. "You said something about not being able to give me anymore children."

He saw first surprise, and then pain cross her face before she was able to conceal it. "Is it true, Emma? Are you not able to have children?"

Emma didn't remember very much about their first night in the cabin, although Cole had told her that Max had stayed with her throughout the ordeal. And now she realized that Max held information she had, up until now, managed to shove under the rug so she could ignore the reality of it. But he was looking at her with such compassion—and with what she could only read as love—that she couldn't bring herself to deny him the truth.

"Around my sixth month of pregnancy I became ill and was ordered on bed rest. That lasted until I went into premature labor five weeks before my due date. To make a long story short, my body couldn't handle the trauma of first the illness and then the difficult delivery. I was admitted to intensive care for a week and when I came out they told me that they'd had to perform a hysterectomy. But I didn't have time to deal with the emotion of that because I had Jacob to take care of. He remained in the hospital for another two weeks but his final prognosis was that he was healthy and growing at an acceptable rate for a premature baby, so I poured everything I had into making sure he stayed that way. It wasn't until he was about three months old that I finally broke down, and it was Zoe who stayed with me to help me deal with the sorrow of knowing I wouldn't be able to have more children."

During the telling, Max had reached over and taken Emma's hand in his. His heart was aching for her and he wanted to offer reassurance, but was at a loss as to how he could. As foolish as it was, he was also feeling responsible. "I should have been there for you," he said.

"Max, you didn't even know. And it wouldn't have changed anything."

"It would have made it easier for you. You would have had someone to hold on to."

"We can't look back. I've dealt with it, even if there are times when the realization I can't have more children hits me like a ton of bricks. But then I look at Jacob and see the light in his eyes and I feel blessed."

Max stood and pulled her into his arms. "I looked for you after you left. But I kept running into dead ends and I got frustrated and angry that you had just run off. So I finally told myself that when you came to your senses you'd find me."

"Thought about it, but I was too scared. I changed locations three times before Jacob was born and then once more after. Zoe was the only one who knew where I'd finally landed and even that was dangerous. I didn't know who had threatened me before I left, or if they were still looking for me. I worked hard to stay out of the public eye, Max."

"If I had known you were going through all that, I would have done anything to be there for you. You need to believe that."

"I do believe you," she said reaching up to briefly run her fingers through his hair. How could she have ever thought that he'd betrayed her trust? "I only hope you can forgive me. I want you to be a part of Jacob's life and I just hope you can one day feel comfortable enough to be a part of mine again, too."

He bent down and kissed her lightly on the lips. "You're right, we can't change the past, but I want you and Jacob in my future." He kissed her again, taking his time to enjoy the indulgence. When he finally stepped back he cleared his throat and said, "Why don't you go get some rest. I don't know when Cole will be back but we may have to move out, depending on what he learns."

"Okay." Before leaving the kitchen she said, "I'm guessing that

Zoe called you with where you could find me." When he nodded she continued. "Obviously I didn't know she'd done that, but in true Zoe Brine style it's proved to be in my best interest. I'm thankful you're here, because I don't want to do this alone anymore. I should never have done it alone from the beginning." Offering him a weak smile she added, "Wake me if you hear from Cole."

Max watched her leave the room, thinking how Zoe's visit to stay with Emma may have been the event that pulled Manderfield back into the picture. The timing was right, and even though Zoe had no doubt taken steps to cover up her visit, someone, somewhere, had recognized that her sudden departure from Kingsport had been out of the ordinary. So when she returned, Victor had put men in place to track her movements, proving that he'd never given up on looking for Emma.

Max calmly tapped a fisted hand on the counter as he considered what could have happened if he had been even a day later in finding Emma himself. "This is going to end, you bastard," he spoke softly to the empty room. "Count on it."

CHAPTER TWENTY-SEVEN

Several hours later, Max was talking to Cole on his cell when Chris and Kyle walked through the front door. "Brought groceries," Chris stated as he kept walking toward the kitchen. Kyle stopped at the entryway to the living room and gave Max a slight nod.

Here was a strong man, Kyle thought, as he listened to Chris's brother shoot off questions and then patiently digest the answers he received. Yes, Max Dunmore was a man who had spent his life going after exactly what he wanted and had no doubt succeeded more times than not. Unlike his brother, who had taken a wrong turn somewhere in his youth, and for years after, continued to make the wrong decisions. But every day Kyle thanked God that Chris had found the courage to climb out of the hole he'd dug for himself to fight for his place in life.

Chris walked out of the kitchen and joined Kyle. "Who's my brother talking to?"

"I'm not sure but it sounds like Cole."

"Have you checked on Emma yet?"

"No. I'll go in a minute." Kyle turned to Chris and smiled warmly. There were days that he still couldn't believe he and Chris had found their way to each other, and days he feared he'd wake up and realize it was all a dream.

When Kyle heard Max end the conversation he looked over and saw that he had been watching them. Kyle was ready to jump to

Chris's defense, but Max simply turned to his brother and said, "I heard something about groceries. I'd like to help pay for them. I know that Cole and I can't be too cheap to feed. Hell, the coffee alone could break you. What do you say?"

"I'd say that rather than giving me cash, you repay our generosity when Kyle and I come out to visit. Assuming things will eventually get back to normal. I have a nephew that needs spoiling, after all."

Max gave them both a warm smile and said, "You'll both be welcomed any time."

Kyle returned the smile, comforted by the acceptance. "You say that now, but when Chris says he's going to spoil Jacob, he has every intention of going overboard. Just so you're prepared."

"I only met my son a little over a week ago. Chris is going to have to step in line behind me. I plan on doing some spoiling of my own."

Kyle nodded and said, "Chris was telling me about the situation you're in and I may have some background information that could help. I'm going to go check Emma's laceration and then maybe we can sit down and talk."

"I think she's working on one of the jigsaw puzzles she found in the bedroom. Why don't you bring her back with you? I heard from Cole and she'll want an update, and this way we can share what we've got without having to repeat it later."

As Kyle headed toward the bedroom, Max said, "I just made fresh coffee. Do you want a cup?"

"I'll get us some," Chris replied and left the room.

Ten minutes later Kyle and Emma stepped into the living room to find Max and Chris laughing about some childhood calamity. "Granddad was so pissed at you," Chris was saying. "I thought for sure he was going to send us both back to Mom. But he just walked away, and I remember that when he came back he calmly sat you down and doled out your punishment for breaking the rules."

"Those were some great times, weren't they?" Max said with another chuckle.

Emma joined Max on the couch as Kyle took a seat in a solidly built rocking chair that Max's grandfather had made close to twenty years ago. "You'll need to catch us up on what's happening," he said. "It sounds as if there's been progress since last night."

After sharing everything from Zoe's suspicions that she was being followed to Cole's departure to pick her up, Max said, "When he called earlier, Cole said they were followed into her building's parking structure by a man who was in the lobby watching for her to leave. Three other guys were waiting near her car, but Cole and Zoe managed to get out unharmed." Turning to Emma he added, "Cole said your friend is quite the spitfire. Pepper-sprayed one guy and used some impressive kickboxing moves on the second."

"She's a survivor," Emma said. "When she finally left her husband, she decided it was time to learn how to take care of herself."

"It seems to have worked out for her. Anyway, once they left Kingsport they drove her car another sixty miles before dumping it in an auto graveyard and walking to a used car lot where Cole intended to appropriate yet another vehicle." Max sent Emma a playful wink. "This time a pickup truck."

"Knowing Zoe, I bet she refused to leave the lot until Cole broke into the office so she could leave some cash behind as a down payment."

"They're driving back, so it'll be well past midnight before they finally make it here," Max said. "Cole is going to want to make sure they're not being followed."

Turning his attention to Kyle, he said, "You mentioned you had some information to add. Care to share?"

"Chris mentioned three paintings that Emma supposedly has and that Victor Manderfield wants returned."

Max lifted his coffee mug to his lips watching Kyle over the ridge. "Go on," he said before taking a sip.

"What affects Chris, affects me too," Kyle said bluntly, "so don't think he's blabbed something he shouldn't have. Victor's threat to Emma extends to anyone associated with her, which now includes Chris and me. We've discussed it, and we're going to help you both in any way we can." After a brief pause he added, "With that said, I may know the paintings he's so eager to have back in his possession."

Max sat forward on the couch and slowly set his cup on the coffee table. "What do you mean? How do you know about the paintings?"

Chris rose from his chair, clearly miffed at his brother. "Kyle, Max is a cop first. Forever and always. So when he asks you what you know about the paintings—in that accusatory tone he's so famous for—you mustn't take offense. He can't possibly think you had anything to do with stealing them, let alone being involved with threatening Emma. He may think I could, but certainly not you. Isn't that correct, Max?"

Max slowly rose from his position on the couch and faced his brother across the room. After several tense moments he spoke, choosing his words carefully. "I apologize to both you and Kyle. I didn't mean to imply that either of you are involved in what's happening here. There may have been a time that I would have doubted you, Chris, but I see a different man standing in front of me today. A man who is strong and kindhearted and someone who, despite the trouble I've brought to his door, has opened his home to me and mine. And I see another man who has pledged his support to people he doesn't even know simply because his partner has asked him to." Walking to where Chris stood, Max said, "So, no. This shit of a brother does not think either of you are involved with Victor Manderfield, and again, I apologize if that's how it sounded."

He extended his hand to Chris and waited. Neither Emma nor Kyle had moved during the exchange, but when Emma saw the left side of Chris's lips curl up she slowly released the breath she hadn't realized she'd been holding.

Taking Max's hand Chris said, "Shit of a brother, huh? That's a good one." He tugged Max in for a brotherly hug.

When Max pulled back he extended his hand to Kyle. "If you can forgive my cynical cop attitude, we can start over."

Kyle took his hand and said, "Not a problem. Chris already warned me about the shit-of-a-brother side of you the first time your name came up in conversation. No harm, no foul."

Max returned to the sofa, Chris to his chair. "Go ahead, Kyle. Tell us what you know."

"I grew up in a privileged section of Manhattan and my family ran in the same social circle as the Manderfields. Although we didn't know them except in passing. Marshall could be a ruthless businessman but he wasn't mean-spirited like his sons, Marco and Victor. If Marshall took someone down it was because his company would profit, and in turn, his wealth would grow. He could play dirty and bend the law when it fit his needs, but he never buried a competitor's body. Watching them crawl away knowing he'd won was victory enough.

"But the brothers don't play by the rules. Ever. In contrast to their father's way of doing business they both want immediate gratification, trampling anyone who gets in their way. Marco still lives in New York, but Victor moved to Denver about fifteen years ago. In my opinion, he wanted to get out from under his father's thumb.

"When Marshall made an arrangement with the Gunther Museum and Art Gallery to indefinitely display a grouping of three paintings known as the Triad, Victor was reportedly livid. Art is a staple with the Manderfields and from time to time, pieces have been loaned to various museums and art galleries, but never with an open-ended agreement. And never the Triad.

"A week after the gallery received the paintings, Marshall died from respiratory failure and Victor began his fight for the return of the paintings. It was close to a year of lawyers going back and forth, but Victor eventually won. In fact, I don't believe the paintings were ever hung in the gallery. Victor made sure they stayed cased until a final resolution was reached."

"What exactly is the Triad?" Max asked.

"The Triad is comprised of three Nicolai Vesare paintings that were commissioned by Federico Rossi, a great, great, great ancestor of Marshall Manderfield. The first is a portrait of Federico painted around 1635. Then in 1638 he commissioned a second painting of his sixteen-year-old wife, Marta, and the third painting is Marta and their child, which was painted a year later. Three months after the final painting was completed, both Marta and the child died of diphtheria. Federico, not able to live without his wife and son, went crazy and burned down their chalet. The paintings were the only possessions that survived and have been passed down from generation to generation of Manderfields."

"I've never heard of an artist named Vesare," Emma said.

"Very few people have," Kyle replied. "But believe me, he was an extremely talented painter, right up there with Raphael and Rembrandt."

"Not to insult your intelligence, but how in the world do you know all this?" Max asked.

"Kyle is an accomplished painter in his own right," Chris said with genuine pride showing on his face. "His talent is off the charts."

"Spoken by a man who has no bias," Kyle laughed. "But getting back to the Manderfields, the three paintings have always been kept inside the family's domain."

"Until Marshall Manderfield decided to loan them to the art gallery," Max interjected, "breaking the family protocol of keeping them in a private collection."

"And Victor? Well, he's never been a man who likes to share," Kyle said. "He gets off knowing that his treasures are his alone. That's why he keeps Crystal Ridge. I understand it's loaded with antiquities that are for his eyes only. Oh, and did I mention? The paintings he thinks you have are rumored to be valued at around a million dollars."

"A million dollars?" Emma stammered, totally taken aback. "For three paintings?"

"For each painting," Kyle said, grinning.

"Each? That's just . . . unimaginable."

"Maybe, but it gives you some idea why Manderfield wants them back so badly."

"Okay, so if the paintings are what Victor believes I have," Emma said, "how did Eric get them?"

"I made some discreet inquiries and I had it confirmed that Victor had the Triad delivered to Crystal Ridge once the courts ordered the paintings be returned to him. But shortly after they arrived, someone orchestrated a break-in and the Triad went missing. And that someone had to know Victor's security system."

"But I can't believe that Eric had the resources to steal the paintings on his own," Emma said as she tried to digest the information Kyle had just shared.

"I don't think he did either," Kyle agreed. "But I've got a theory."

Turning to Max, he continued. "You mentioned that Eric occasionally worked for Victor's right-hand man, Stan Hudson. Is it possible that he was part of the group that delivered the Triad to Crystal Ridge? And somehow, Marco found out about Eric's involvement and made him an offer to steal the paintings away from his brother—an offer too tempting for Eric to refuse. I doubt that Marco cared about the history of the Triad and the family connection, but there's no doubt in my mind that he would have done anything to take possession of those paintings, simply because his brother had them. Added to that, he'd be able to sell them off and make a fortune. Unfortunately for Eric, something happened between taking the paintings from Victor and delivering them to Marco."

Max was up on his feet again, slowly pacing from one end of the room to the other. "Remember the name Lucas Ramos?" he said to Emma. "I'll bet you any money that Eric and Lucas were working together the night the paintings were stolen. Eric drove the paintings away from Crystal Ridge either alone or with someone else we don't know about, but Lucas didn't make such a clean get-away. Taking Kyle's theory a step further, Stan Hudson found Lucas, forced him to talk, and in the process he gave up Eric. They go looking for Eric, find him, and try to get the information they need, but he—"

When Max hesitated, Emma gave him a slight nod and said, "Go ahead. Finish it."

"The medical examiner found four slugs in Eric's body, one in his right knee, two in the back and one in the head. He'd been beaten pretty badly, so there's a high probability that he told Hudson that you knew something or had something that could lead them to the Triad. But that was only half the information they needed. He died before he gave up your connection to how they could retrieve the paintings."

To Kyle, Max said, "Can you get an approximate date for when the museum turned the paintings over to Victor and when they were stolen—keeping your inquiry under the radar?"

"I know someone I can ask. Give me a minute here." His cell phone was already in his hand when he headed out of the room.

"What's that going to tell us?" Chris asked.

"Eric paid me a visit shortly before he was killed," Emma said quietly as she watched Max. "If the dates Kyle is getting coincide with that attack, it's very likely that, unknowingly to me, Eric left something behind that night which will connect me to the Triad. Isn't that what you're thinking?"

"Yes," Max replied. "And if that bastard was still alive I'd go back and kill him myself, not only for putting you in that position but for giving you up so easily as the person who held all the answers. Even though you didn't have a clue."

Emma went to Max and folded herself into his arms. "We're close, Max. We're so close to having those answers, I can feel it."

"We just have to come up with the key to the mystery," Chris said from across the room.

After a brief moment of silence, Emma turned to Chris, who had already picked up on the importance of what he had just said.

"That's it," they said in unison.

Emma spun back to Max and said, "That's it, Max. The key. You said that Eric had to have stored the paintings somewhere. What if he slipped me the key to wherever it is he put them? It would make sense that when Eric found out Lucas was dead he would naturally assume that he was next on the list. By giving me the key he figured he was buying himself insurance until he could come up with another plan. Decide who to deal with. What an ass," she added with a disgusted tone. "And knowing Eric, I bet he actually thought he was going to be able to walk away unscathed."

"I've got some dates for you," Kyle said as he walked back into the room. He handed a slip of paper to Max.

Shaking his head, Max handed the paper to Emma. "The paintings were delivered to Victor a week before Eric showed up at your apartment. And stolen the day *before* he attacked you."

Emma fought off an involuntary shudder as she stared at the dates. "What I can't figure out is why Victor didn't come after me right away," she said in a shaky voice. "After he had Eric killed, why didn't they come for me?"

"I don't know but thank God they didn't."

For several moments no one spoke. Then Chris asked, "Is there anything else Kyle and I can do?"

"Nothing at this point. I'm going to contact Cole and get his take on what we've pieced together. Once he and Zoe are back with Emma's things we'll go through them and see what we've got."

"We'll go back to our place, then. You've got the number and we can be here within thirty minutes if you need us. Otherwise, I'll be back around nine tomorrow morning."

"Thank you both for everything you've done," Emma said as she hugged first Kyle and then Chris. "I don't know how I can ever repay you."

"We've already made a deal with Max," Chris said. Before releasing her he turned his head slightly to whisper in her ear. "Life's too short for regrets, Emma. Give my brother a chance." He pulled back and gave her his own version of the Dunmore smile. Grabbing his jacket and pointing a finger at Max he added, "Later, bro."

Emma sat on the edge of the bed in one of the oversized shirts that Chris kept in the bedroom closet. The book she'd pulled down from the shelf hadn't helped her to relax much, and the thought that what had happened to Eric could have just as easily happened to her, was beyond daunting. She knew that Eric hadn't loved her, but to deliberately put her in the line of fire? Why had he chosen her to be an unwitting player in his costly scheme to steal those paintings? She didn't have an answer and all she knew for sure was that he was dead and she was left to clean up his mess.

Rising, she began pacing the floor for the third time in less than an hour. When Max had stopped in earlier to tell her that Cole and Zoe were stopping at a motel for the night, she had been relieved that they were both safe and sound. Now, the fact that they wouldn't be arriving until morning left the cabin too quiet and gave her too much time to think.

Slipping on a pair of sweat pants she headed toward the living room where she found Max sitting on the couch, head back, eyes closed. His semi-automatic was tucked securely in a leather holster that lay on the cushion next to him and within easy reach. Even in sleep he looked alert, she thought.

"How are you doing?" he said quietly without opening his eyes.

"Jeez, you startled me. I didn't think you were awake."

"I was just taking a combat nap. I heard you coming down the hall."

Looking down at her bare feet she said, "Wow, not only can you go days on zero sleep, you have superhuman hearing."

"They're both perfected skills." Opening his eyes, he watched as she battled with the decision to stay or return to the bedroom. "You want to talk about it?"

"You need your rest, Max. I didn't mean to wake you."

As she turned to leave he sat forward and patted the cushion next to him. "I'm good. I'm used to grabbing rest when I can get it and wherever I can get it. Come sit and tell me what's on your mind."

She crossed the room and joined him on the couch, folding her legs under her and rotating her body so she was facing him. "I was just thinking about how much Eric must have hated me. To have dragged me into this the way he did? If anyone from Victor Manderfield's organization had found me, I wouldn't have had any clue what they wanted but they wouldn't have believed me. And I keep thinking about that first call back in Kingsport when the person described in detail what they were going to do if I didn't give them what they wanted."

Max pulled her close and said, "I'm here with you, Emma, and you need to stop worrying about what could have happened. With everything we've pieced together we're close to putting an end to this mess."

She smiled and rested her head on his shoulder. They were quiet for some time, content to just sit and offer each other a calming dose of solace.

When Emma finally pulled back she looked at Max and asked, "Would you mind if I stayed out here with you? I'm having trouble falling asleep in the other room."

"Of course I don't mind," he said as he pulled a blanket off the back of the sofa, spreading it over both their bodies. "Just close your eyes. I'll stay right here with you."

She nodded against his shoulder and tightened her grip around his waist. "I'm so tired," she said in a slurring voice. "I'll just go down for about an hour, okay?"

"Go down for as long as you need," he whispered as he kissed her forehead and ran his hand over her freshly shampooed hair.

Within minutes her breathing slowed and she relaxed into his arms. He tucked the blanket tighter around them and dropped his right hand so it rested just alongside his holster. He followed her into sleep, keeping a portion of his mind opened and poised for action, should danger dare to show its ugly face.

CHAPTER TWENTY-EIGHT

Zoe stepped out of the compact shower stall and ran her hand over the condensation on the mirror. The past two days had unleashed a whirlwind of emotions in her and she was still searching for the best way to keep her footing firm, determined not to let Emma's dead bastard husband be the cause of her friend's demise.

She scrubbed her short dark hair with a towel to soak up the excess water from the shower and considered her grooming complete. Looking at her reflection, she remembered how at one time the hair had cascaded down her back, most days fashioned into a French braid. But six months into her marriage it had become detrimental—a way for her ex-husband to literally grab her attention by grabbing her hair—and the day she'd left him she had cut it off with no regrets.

After brushing her teeth and flossing her gums, she pulled on the cotton tee and yoga shorts she had picked up at a discount store about three hours outside Kingsport. When they had stopped there, Cole told her it could be several days to a week before she'd be able to shop again, and advised her to make her selections wisely. In addition to her version of sleepwear, she'd chosen three casual tops, two pairs of jeans, a second cotton tee, some extra underwear and toiletries.

When she saw Cole approach the check-out with only a long-sleeve black tee, a single pair of jeans, boxers, socks, and toothpaste, she had simply shaken her head. "How in the world are you going to survive a week with only that?" she'd asked.

"I already have clothes back at the cabin. Besides, I tend to live an uncluttered life. In my line of work, jeans and a T-shirt are often enough, the socks keep my feet warm and the toothpaste makes it harder for a woman to resist my charm."

She gave him another laugh and just shook her head. "Think a lot of yourself, don't you?"

"I think a lot of my skill set which includes electrifying the ladies."

"My God, I believe you're serious."

"I don't lie. I only cheat when the opponent plays dirty. I can be secretive, which translates to being standoffish to some people, but I consider that their problem, not mine. And I've been known to lose my temper—on rare occasions—and only when I've been provoked to do so."

He paid the clerk and grabbed the plastic bags that held their purchases. Walking toward the exit he added, "But I've never hit a woman and never will unless it's to protect the people who are important to me. There have been one or two cases where a female opponent has been a threat, but I've always managed to find a way to disarm her without a physical assault."

Zoe thought about that for a moment and then said, "I take it the 'never hitting a woman' thing was for my benefit."

He didn't reply and instead simply planted those penetrating eyes on her as he opened the car door.

"It's a good rule to live by," she continued, "but I've learned to protect myself and if that means taking someone down in the process, I will."

"Fair enough," Cole said as she climbed into the passenger seat and he closed the door. Rounding the front of the pickup he threw the packages behind his seat before sliding in behind the steering wheel.

They'd driven then for well over an hour, taking the less traveled roads that were lit only by the glow of their pickup's headlights. Sticking to topics that were universal, Zoe had felt her attraction to this man growing. Not only because he had a great physical presence—which was by far the best she'd seen in a long time—but she truly believed he also had a kind and compassionate bearing.

He had proved her right when their conversation shifted to family. He'd spoken affectionately of his, which included three younger brothers scattered about the country, and parents who were currently residing in a retirement community in Florida. When the subject had turned to Max—whom she had yet to meet in person—the stories he'd shared about their friendship had her convinced that she would come to respect him as much as Cole did.

What had completely melted her heart though was the way he had talked about Emma and Jacob. Two strangers he was more than prepared to protect, even though they'd disrupted his life in a major way.

When Cole had finally turned back onto the main highway, he'd asked Zoe if she would be willing to find a motel and grab whatever sleep they could get before dawn arrived. She'd been on board with the idea, telling herself she needed the rest. Had she been totally honest with herself, she would have admitted that she'd wanted Cole in what her high school biology teacher used to call "a carnal way." There was no denying that she was finding it hard to resist Cole Haywood. A man who wasn't afraid to show his gentle side even though she suspected that he could make a grown man cry with one deadly look.

Now, as she stepped out of the bathroom, she found him on his cell phone. He watched her as she moved to the side of the double bed and removed first the blanket and then the top sheet. When she was convinced there were no uninvited guests crawling underneath, she shook out both and neatly replaced them. She then did the same with the pillows.

By the time she finished her ritual, Cole had concluded his call and was leaning against the wall, hands shoved into the pockets of his jeans, a silly grin planted on his face.

"What?" she said with a laugh. "This isn't exactly the Ritz."

"I didn't say anything," he replied raising his hands, palms out. "Whatever floats your boat," he teased. "In this place though, it's probably a good idea. Next time I'll have to find you a place with a higher star rating."

"I certainly hope you don't think of me as a prima donna," she retorted. "On the contrary, my taste tends to drift toward the simple and unadorned. I'm a straightforward city girl who has never gone in for flash, and is perfectly content to drink beer from a bottle rather than sip a hundred-dollar-a-glass imported wine."

"Talk like that tends to make my heart go thumpity-thump."

She laughed again, something she'd been doing quite a lot of since meeting up with this man. "Then I must ask if sharing the bed is going to be a problem for you and your out of control heartbeat."

"No problem," he said, pushing away from the wall. "No problem at all."

He continued to watch her as she dropped onto the bed and squeezed under the covers. "I'm going to take a quick shower," he announced as he walked to the bathroom door. Stopping just before he crossed the threshold, he gave her an amusing look before adding, "And then I'm going to brush my teeth."

She stared at the spot where he'd been standing until she heard the water start running. He hadn't completely shut the door, and she didn't know whether that was an invitation to join him or if he just wanted to be able to listen for any trouble. Wanting it to be the first, she nonetheless accepted that it was the second.

Besides, it was ludicrous to be thinking about having sex with Cole while they were in the middle of an intense hide and seek game with men who'd just tried to kill them. Hell, it wasn't a good idea, period. Sure, she was drawn to him, but who wouldn't be with those muscular arms, that rock-hard chest, and those charmingly irresistible eyes?

Swearing softly under her breath she turned onto her side with her back to the bathroom door and punched a fist into her pillow to fluff it. It was so unlike her to be this impulsive, she thought. Maybe she still had some residual adrenaline coursing through her body from the attack back at her office. That happened after a death-defying encounter, right?

When the mattress shifted from his weight, she realized that she hadn't even heard him come into the room. But she definitely felt his hand snaking around her waist and under her tee, finally settling on her bare stomach. And it would have taken a saint not to recognize his physical reaction to being so close to her.

"You need to tell me now if this isn't what you want, Zoe. Say no and I'll back off."

"And if I say yes?"

"You won't regret it."

She heard the smile in his response and turned to him, raising her lips to meet his. The kiss was soft, passionate, enduring, and his hands were soothing, inquisitive and imaginative as they did a slow waltz up and down her body. Time and space ceased to exist and when he finally entered her she could feel herself drowning in the pleasure of the moment.

He started slowly, keeping his rhythm steady and his movements controlled. There were no words of endearment, no assurances of forever. They both understood that, for tonight, they were simply two unrestricted souls who had come together to both give and receive, no strings attached.

When she heard his breathing become more rapid and the intensity of his movement increase to match his pace, Zoe lifted her hips as encouragement for him to go deeper. She wasn't a novice when it came to sex although she wouldn't have considered herself experienced either. With Cole, she found herself driven to do her best to rock his world. And in the end, she was damned satisfied with herself, not to mention her admiration for his creative talents.

Cole pushed up onto one elbow once he caught his breath, not ready to retreat but not wanting to overpower Zoe with his weight. He could see by the look in her eyes that she indeed had no regrets and in fact appeared to be sated. He knew exactly how she felt.

Zoe smiled and lifted her hand to his face. "Wow. I'm glad I said yes."

"Please, you're embarrassing me."

"I doubt you've ever been embarrassed."

"You could be right," he said leaning down to kiss her. "I just want you to know that I'm usually not this easy. At the very least I expect dinner first."

"I gave you a candy bar right around Castle Rock, if you recall. Doesn't that count?"

"When you get to know me better, you'll discover that a candy bar in no way qualifies as real food. When this is over I'll have to show you how to quench a real man's appetite."

"I thought I'd already done that," she said, smiling.

"That? That was just an appetizer. You have potential, though."

"As tempting as it is to prove to you just how true that is, time seems to be working against us, doesn't it?"

He saw the fear cloud her eyes as the realization that tonight was only temporary, and that soon they would have to go back out into the real world and right into the lion's den. He rolled onto his back and pulled her close. "I'm going to do everything in my power to give both you and Emma a happy ending to this. Trust that I will protect you with my life."

"That's a lot to promise someone you've just met, but I do trust you. And I'll take your protection and raise you a home-cooked meal when we've successfully banished the evil forces that have invaded our lives." He could tell that she was trying to stay upbeat but could still hear that doubt in her voice. "Did I mention that I'm an excellent cook?" she added. "After I left my ex-husband I took culinary classes and everything."

Cole took Zoe's hand and held it over his heart. "Feel that? You've just set off my thumpity-thump radar again."

Zoe laughed, settling in against his body. "That may be so, but I think we need some sack time."

"I think you're right," he said, tightening his grip around her waist.

With a final kiss they both surrendered to the night.

CHAPTER TWENTY-NINE

"Cole phoned and they'll be here soon," Max told Emma the next morning after breakfast. "Good news is, he hasn't spotted any trouble since hitting the road."

"Maybe once I go through the box of stuff they're bringing back, I'll have a clue about what I'm supposed to have," Emma said. "I just wish Zoe hadn't been dragged into this."

Max walked over to her and wrapped his arms around her waist. "Your friend will be safer here with us than on her own back in Kingsport."

Returning his embrace, Emma said, "I wonder how Jacob's doing. I miss him so much."

"I know how much I miss him, so I can just imagine what you're going through. And I'm sure he's fine with Nanna and Henry, not to mention the exceptional protection detail he's inherited." He smiled and bent down to kiss her. It was meant to be a kiss of reassurance, but almost immediately, Max was lingering, unwilling to break the connection.

He tilted his head and deepened the intimacy, the tip of his tongue grazing the inside edge of her lower lip. It was soft and inviting and he flashed back to a time when he would have simply lost himself in this kind of tenderness.

Without thinking, his hand drifted under her blouse and toward her round, firm breast. Her skin was smooth as silk and his fingers began to tease and excite, his thumb playing across her now extended nipple. Hearing a soft moan escape he pulled her closer, desperate to show her how much he wanted her.

He got busy unbuttoning her blouse as he continued his assault on her mouth and could have sworn that her unseen hands were busy with his belt buckle—although that could have been wishful thinking on his part. He gently backed her up to the wall that divided the living room from the hallway, and pressed his body tight against hers. Christ, it felt good.

Sliding her blouse off her shoulders he whispered her name as he trailed his lips down her throat toward that spectacular breast. When he took her into his mouth he heard her moan again and her hands slipped into his hair and held on.

He wanted her—writhing beneath him as he showed her how much he had truly missed her. How much he truly loved her. But it was more than want, he thought vaguely. It was need. He needed her.

"I think your pants are vibrating." Her voice broke through, all soft and sexy as hell.

"I don't doubt that in the least," he mumbled as he lifted his head back to her lips.

"Seriously," she chuckled as she slowly pushed him back. "Your phone. In your pocket." She was trying desperately to hide the fact that her breathing was uneven as her mind ran wild with vivid thoughts of ripping his clothes off so she could throw him down on the couch and . . . "You better get that."

"Damn," he said as her words began to make sense. Clearing his throat, he stepped away and with heroic effort snagged his phone out of his pocket. "It's Cole," he said to Emma as she bent down to retrieve her blouse from the floor. He backed away another two steps hoping it was enough to prevent him from reaching out to stop her. Turning his attention to the phone he answered with, "Everything still okay?"

"Actually, we're just pulling up outside. Just wanted to give you adequate warning that you had company."

"Sure. I'll, um, unlock the front door."

"Everything still okay there?" Cole asked, sensing something in Max's voice but unable to put a finger on it.

"Great. We're great."

"Okay. Great."

"Yeah, great. I'll get the door."

Cole gave Zoe a puzzled look after disconnecting from the call. "That was weird. He sounded . . . I don't know, distracted? Like he was surprised we were here even though I gave him our arrival time just twenty minutes ago."

"Maybe we're interrupting something," she said throwing him a knowing glance.

"Well, if that's the case all I can say now is, oops."

When the pickup came to a stop in front of the cabin, Zoe opened the door and climbed out, grabbing the two shopping bags. Cole walked to the rear of the vehicle and grabbed his duffel from the bed of the truck along with the box holding Emma's things. When he heard the front door of the cabin open, he glanced over.

Max stepped through the door first and surveyed the area before letting Emma pass. When he stepped aside she dashed down the porch steps and straight into Zoe's open arms.

"Oh, sweetie, I've been so worried about you," Zoe spoke first. "When I couldn't get a hold of you I freaked. Please don't ostracize me because I called Max. I just didn't know what else to do."

"You did the right thing, Zoe. I was in trouble and didn't even know it. If you hadn't sent Max, I don't know what would have happened. I'm so glad you're alright."

As the women joined arms and headed back in to the cabin— stopping briefly for introductions—Cole waited patiently by the pickup. When Max finally approached him he said, "How are things going?"

"Great. We're great."

"Is that why Emma's blouse appears to be buttoned wrong?"

Max whipped his head to see Cole's smile break into laughter. "That's what I thought. And before I start getting anymore bawdy thoughts in this pretty little head of mine, you should probably buckle up that belt, pal."

He laughed again as he strolled to the front door.

"Oh, crap," Max said as he quickly complied with Cole's suggestion and followed everyone inside.

"Before we do anything, I need food," Cole said walking directly to the kitchen. "I've been denied my daily requirement of carbs for way too long. I'm actually beginning to feel faint."

"He doesn't believe that a cinnamon bagel, candy bar and a bag of chips is real food," Zoe said following him to the kitchen. "Why don't you let me fix you something so I don't have to listen to your complaining anymore?"

Max glanced over at Emma and noticed that each button on her blouse was neatly in place. Had she fixed them once she was inside? Max wondered. Or had Cole just been messing with his head?

Emma looked up from where she was sitting on the floor and smiled. "Zoe mentioned the buttons if that's what you're wondering."

He let out a nervous grunt as he rubbed his hand over his face. "What can I say?"

"You? It was my lack of attention to detail that had me missing the obvious." She turned her attention back to the box that was positioned next to her. "Come help me go through these things. If nothing else, it will be a distraction."

He hesitated for just a moment then crossed the room and gingerly sat cross-legged on the floor opposite her. "I'm really not sorry about . . . you know. I wanted what happened to happen although better timing on my part would have been nice."

"I'll remember exactly where we left off, don't worry." She stopped rummaging through the box and reached over to lightly touch his hand. "You have nothing to apologize for, Max. I wanted it, too. And yeah, the timing sucks. Let's make sure to find a way around that, though. Soon."

He smiled on the outside while doing handsprings on the inside. "Okay," was all he could manage to say.

Cole and Zoe came back into the living area and plopped down next to Max and Emma. Taking the first bite of his salami sandwich he turned to Emma and said, "Did you know that Zoe is an accomplished culinary technician?"

"If you mean she can cook, yes."

"Skills like that are immeasurable to my way of thinking."

Zoe snorted and said, "It's just a sandwich. It doesn't even come close to giving you a true picture of my abilities."

They looked at each other, smiling like a couple of idiots, and Max caught Cole treating Zoe to one of his boyish winks. So, Max thought, he wasn't the only one who had had combustible thoughts in the past twenty-four hours. He glanced at Emma and caught her smiling, although she was trying to hide it by burying her head in the box of treasures.

"See anything that's promising?" Max asked. "Remember that even though our theory about the key may be a good one, we could still be wrong, so don't dismiss anything. If you have a feeling about it, speak up."

Emma started pulling items from the box one at a time, making brief comments about each one. "*This was given to me by my grandmother*," or "*My mother bought these candleholders during a visit to Ireland.*" She'd then pass them on to either Max or Cole for further examination.

It took another twenty minutes to empty the cardboard box, and the disappointment was clearly visible on Emma's face as she scanned the floor around her.

"This was always a long shot, Em," Max said compassionately. "But the fact that we haven't found anything here just pushes us toward our next move—we head back to Kennewick."

"I know. It's just so discouraging."

"But we won't let it discourage us for long," Zoe piped in. "We're survivors, Emma Cassidy, and we have pledged to overcome any and all obstacles that are thrown down in front of us."

"Hear us roar," Emma growled and pumped a fist in the air.

"Max? There must be something outside that needs our attention," Cole said rising from the floor. "Out back and away from these lunatics."

"Right behind you," Max said as he stood and grabbed his jacket. "Be back shortly, ladies."

When they were gone Emma started to pack everything back in the box. "Thanks for keeping these things for me, Zoe. I'm just sorry that it's put you right in the middle of this whole mess."

"Hey, who better than me to be your savior? Come on, grab that box and show me where Cole and I are going to be bunking tonight."

"There are only two bedrooms so I figured you'd be bunking with me."

"Not anymore. You and Max are going to have to work out your own deal."

"Why, Zoe Brine, I'm shocked. Cole's got a nice ass, though doesn't he?"

"Oh, you don't know how right you are."

Stepping into the bedroom, Emma laid the cardboard box on the floor beside the dresser and flopped onto the bed. "I keep trying to figure out what Eric would have done with that key. If that's what we're really looking for. But deep down, Zoe, I know it is. It's the only thing that makes sense. Where would he have hidden it, though? He would have needed to retrieve it at some point so it's someplace accessible but not obvious."

Zoe dropped down beside her and grabbed Jacob's stuffed lion off the pillow. "Cole said you think Eric told the bad guys that you knew where everything is being kept."

"Basically. It makes sense that's why they haven't given up on me. And I don't think even Eric would be so malicious as to point them in my direction just for the hell of it. But whatever he said before they killed him has put all our lives in jeopardy and that's why we have to figure this out, and soon."

After several minutes of silence, Zoe held the lion up and asked, "Why do you have this thing with you?"

"Oh, that's Jacob's favorite toy. I forgot to give it to him before he left with Max's grandmother."

"It looks familiar to me," she said eyeing the stuffed animal. "Oh, wait. When I came out to stay with you, Jacob wouldn't go to sleep unless this was in the crib with him."

Emma took the lion from Zoe and held it tight. "Nothing changed after you left. I'm not sure how he's getting on without it now." She smiled and added, "I remember when my father gave this to me. He told me it was a magical lion and I should—"

"What? What is it, Emma?"

Emma flipped the toy over and started to claw at the seam on the lion's underside. "This isn't new. I've had this since I was a child." She looked up at Zoe, adding, "It was in with the things Eric brought to my apartment the night he put me in the hospital. And one of the few possessions I took with me when I fled Kingsport."

Finding what she was looking for she showed Zoe the hidden zipper that was embedded in the material of the animal. "It's not all stuffing. There's space inside to hide things. My father told me I could keep all my mementos inside and no one would ever know."

As Emma lowered the zipper she continued. "But Eric knew, because I told him. I remember showing him once and he made a comment about how it was an ingenious hiding place."

She had her hand inside now, digging for any hidden treasures. When her fingers brushed against a serrated metallic object buried deep within the folds of the pouch, she froze. "Zoe," she whispered as she pulled the key out. Her excitement began to build as she handed it to Zoe. "Hold this," she said and dove back inside the lion.

"What else are you looking for?" Zoe asked, her voice revealing her own excitement.

"I'm hoping there's a map or something that will tell us where those damn paintings are. Got it!" she said triumphantly as she pulled out a single sheet of paper that showed the name of a storage facility, the address and the combination to the main gate.

"We've got it," she said as she grabbed the key back and sprung from the bed and out the bedroom door. "I've got to find Max," she yelled over her shoulder as she ran down the hallway toward the front of the cabin.

After leaving the cabin, Max and Cole went in separate directions making their routine search of the property. With that complete, they stood together at the end of the gravel driveway where Max was sharing his concern that it was only a matter of time before someone found the connection between him and the cabin.

"We've been here too long, Cole. We're just inviting trouble if we stay."

"What about your brother?"

"I've been thinking about that and I'm going to try to talk him and Kyle into leaving for a while. I think it's too dangerous to take them with us, but they can't stay here."

"Didn't you say that Kyle made some inquiries? He may think his source is secure but I think you're right. The two of them could be vulnerable if they stay. What are the odds that the doc is going to leave his practice, though?"

"Zero to none?"

"They may be okay if they just stay in town," Cole suggested. "It sounds as if Chris has kept a pretty low profile."

"Maybe," Max replied. "I'd feel better if they'd just take an extended vacation though."

When he saw the cabin door fly open, his gun was in his hand and he was running toward Emma before she even had a chance to reach the first step. Cole had dropped into a crouching position, gun in hand, sweeping the perimeter. He could see Emma waving her arm in the air, but wasn't able to make out her words as she continued to run toward Max. He could also see Zoe, still standing inside the doorway with a look that was more puzzled than panicked.

If Max understood what Emma was saying it didn't register, because when he reached her, he lifted her off her feet and, without missing a single step, carried her back into the house and slammed the door shut behind them.

"Max, what is it? What's happening?" But Emma's questions were drowned out by Max's own voice.

"What's wrong? What's going on?" He grabbed Zoe's wrist and pulled her down to the floor next to him. "Get down Zoe, away from the windows. Would one of you please tell me what's wrong?"

Zoe, the only level-headed one in the room answered. "You can let us go, Max. Emma was just a little over-excited when she found the key."

Max looked first at Zoe and then down at Emma and for the first time realized that he had her pinned into a corner, his body thrown against hers. Easing up, but just slightly, he asked, "What key?"

It only took three and a half seconds before it hit him. "You found the key? *The* key?"

Before Emma could answer, the front door flew open and Cole hurled his body through the entranceway. He kicked out his left foot and slammed the door shut. "Is everyone okay? Zoe, you okay?"

"Better than okay," she said with a smile. "Emma found the key. And the name and address of the storage facility the key supposedly goes to."

Max stood, reaching out a hand to Emma helping her to her feet. "Where did you find it?"

"I had it all along. Clarence," she said as if he would understand.

"Clarence? What about Clarence?"

"It was inside Clarence." She dragged him down the hallway and bent over to retrieve the stuffed toy she'd dropped outside the bedroom door. Showing Max and Cole the zippered compartment, she retold the story. "I could just kick myself for not thinking about this sooner, Max."

"There's no reason you should have. And it doesn't matter now, anyway. Finding that unit needs to be our priority, and the sooner we leave, the better."

"I can be packed in five minutes," Emma said as she turned toward the bedroom.

"Why don't you go with her," Cole said to Zoe as he ran the back of his fingers down her cheek. "Make sure she doesn't leave anything behind."

Zoe moved to Cole and ever so lightly touched her lips to his. Without another word she followed Emma down the hall.

Waiting until both women were out of earshot Max said, "I'm going to call Chris and tell him and Kyle to take off for a while." He pulled out his cell phone and after a brief conversation disconnected and turned to Cole. "They're just down the road. I forgot that Chris said he'd be back this morning."

Glancing out the front window Max watched for the SUV that Kyle drove. When it appeared at the end of the drive he headed for the front door. Standing on the porch stoop he surveyed the land for the second time in less than an hour. As a former cop he knew that the hair standing up on the back of his neck was a warning sign and had proved to be an ass-saver more times than he could count. He wasn't about to ignore it now.

Kyle and Chris climbed out of their vehicle and approached Max. "Let's go inside," he said while ushering them into the cabin.

"What's up?" Chris asked as he looked at Max's somber face. "Has something bad happened?"

"Just being cautious," he replied. "We've got some good news, though. Emma found the key."

"No kidding? Where is she?"

Max pointed to the bedroom and Chris rushed down the hallway. Kyle laid a hand on Max's shoulder and said, "You're a step closer to making a new life with your son, Max. I'm happy for you."

As Kyle left to join Chris and Emma, Max considered what he had just said, thinking that Kyle was indeed a wise man. There was a spot in Max's heart that had been empty ever since he'd left Jacob behind, and now he was closer to filling that void.

Thirty minutes later, everyone was prepared to leave. Max had pulled Chris and Kyle aside and stressed the importance of them staying away from the cabin, and thankfully they had agreed. For now, it was hugs and poignant goodbyes with promises to reunite as soon as possible.

The SUV was parked about fifteen yards from the front door. As Chris approached it, he opened the passenger door while Kyle started around the back of the vehicle, intending to get in on the driver's side. When the first gunshot rang out he reacted instantly, diving behind the car's wheel well for cover. Staying low, he crawled toward the spot where he'd last seen Chris, and saw instantly he'd been shot. Without hesitation he darted toward the front of the vehicle, hoping the still-opened passenger door would serve as a shield. "Tell me where you're hit, Chris."

Chris had his hand pressed to his stomach where the bullet had entered, not yet realizing that the worst of the bleeding was from the exit wound in his back. Kyle knew, and was struggling to get to his medical bag while staying out of the line of fire, knowing that he wouldn't be any good to Chris if he, too, were shot.

Inside Max and Cole were quickly assessing what had just happened. Cole yelled out to Zoe and Emma to hit the floor and stay where they were before joining Max at the front window.

"It looks like Chris has been hit," Max said with concern. "Judging by the strike to the side mirror, the shot had to have come from the wooded area off to the south."

"Max?" Both Max and Cole turned to see Emma crouched in the entryway to the living room. "The cabin's on fire."

"How bad?" he asked as he turned back to the window.

"Mostly smoke inside right now, but I can see the fire building right outside the laundry room window."

"We need to get out before they get in," Cole said as he stepped over to Emma. "I need you and Zoe to gather up what you can and wait near the bedroom window. I'll be there in a minute. Make sure you grab the shotgun Chris keeps in the closet and the knapsack with the ammunition for the guns. Even if you have to leave something else behind."

"Zoe has it already. We grabbed it when we heard the shots. She's also added a box of shotgun shells."

"Good. Then get on back there and gather up the rest of the stuff."

She acknowledged his instructions with a nod and took off toward the rear of the cabin.

Max had been listening to Cole's conversation with Emma while watching out the front window, and understood what needed to be done. "I'll get to the SUV and drive it around to the side of the house. Be ready for me because we won't have a lot of time. I'll drive as close to the window as I can."

"Copy that."

Cole turned and headed in the direction Emma had just taken, grateful that he and Max were of the same mind. Each had their job to do now, and he couldn't think about the danger Max was putting himself in. His job was to protect Zoe and Emma and get them in position to leave as soon as the SUV appeared. The plan had its pitfalls, but they both knew it was their only option to get to Kyle and Chris and escape the burning cabin.

When Kyle heard footsteps behind him he covered Chris's body with his own as he yelled, "Don't shoot, don't shoot."

"Kyle, it's Max. We need to get into the vehicle. Help me lift Chris in."

"I've got to stop the bleeding," Kyle said as he went back to helping Chris.

"After we get you both in the vehicle. Where are the keys?"

"I left them in the ignition."

Max was already in the vehicle pulling up under his brother's arms. Kyle grabbed his feet and together they got Chris horizontal on the back seat. While Kyle scrambled in behind them, Max dove into the driver's seat, turned the key and slammed the car into reverse. More bullets rang out, glancing off the fiberglass fender. But Max just kept going and managed to get the SUV to the protected side of the cabin. When he came to a complete stop he could see Cole, then Zoe, crawling through the bedroom window.

"How bad is my brother?" Max asked turning to Kyle.

"It's hard to tell the extent of the injury, but it's bad enough that I can't do much here. We need to get him to a hospital, fast."

The front passenger door opened and Cole helped Zoe into the vehicle. She threw his equipment case onto the floor and then reached over for the two duffels Cole had dragged out.

"Where's Emma?" Max asked when he realized she wasn't with them.

"Zoe will explain, but she's gone, Max. I'm going to track the bastards who took her. You need to get your brother out. Get everyone to safety. I'll contact you as soon as I can."

"Cole, wait." Max's voice was distraught and pleading.

"Go," he instructed as he slammed the door shut and took off with the shotgun and a backpack that Max assumed contained ammunition and other necessities.

Max sat frozen watching as Cole disappeared, but Kyle quickly brought him out of his trance. "Max, we need to go. Now. I'm losing him."

Turning toward Kyle's voice he took a hard look at his brother and the severity of his wound. His eyes were closed and Max couldn't see any signs that he was still breathing. He glanced over at Zoe, who was sitting at the edge of her seat, staring at Max. "Get down on the floor and hold on," he said as he put the vehicle in drive, and turning to Kyle asked, "Do you have my brother?"

"Yes. Just drive."

Chapter Thirty

"I told the doctor that it looked to me as if the injury was caused by a stray bullet from a hunter. That Chris and I were hiking along Captain's Peak when it happened and I was able to get him back to the highway. Then someone picked us up but refused to stay and took off when Chris was being wheeled into the emergency room."

Kyle was standing in the hospital parking lot talking to Max on his cell phone. "Chris is still in surgery but his chances don't look good. The police have questioned me and they're probably off checking my story because they're not here anymore. I overheard one of the detectives saying he was going to try and get a search warrant for both my clinic and house."

"They're going to need probable cause," Max said as he sat on one of the two beds in the frayed motel room where he had stopped with Zoe. "Just because you were with Chris when he was shot isn't enough. Do you own a rifle or a shotgun?"

"No. Chris kept a shotgun at the cabin for protection, but I don't have any firearms."

"Good. We found the shotgun and Cole has it now."

"The police are eventually going to tie the cabin to us, aren't they?"

"Yes, eventually. And that will just add to their suspicions that this wasn't an accident. When we left, the fire was spreading pretty fast and I think the cabin is probably a complete loss."

"It doesn't matter right now. Although Chris will be royally pissed."

Neither spoke right away, both trying to deal with the pain of someone they loved lying on an operating table, fighting for his life. Kyle broke the silence.

"I'm guessing we can't call your grandmother to let her know, but is there anyone else I should call?"

Max knew that Kyle was taking the necessary steps to put things in order in case Chris didn't make it. He rubbed his free hand across his face and worked hard to keep his voice steady. "I don't even know how to get a hold of my sister, and you're right, we can't contact my grandmother. Is there anyone you can call to be there with you, Kyle?"

"The only family left is my brother and he disowned me years ago. Besides, I'm better by myself. There are people here at the hospital that I know who have been stopping by as they get the news. Nurses, a few doctors, the chaplain." Kyle paused before asking, "Will they arrest me, Max? I can't leave Chris. I want to help you and Emma and I'll continue to stick to the story for as long as I can. But when the police don't find anything on that trail I'm afraid they're going to want me down at the station for the next round of questions. Is there anything you can do so I don't have to leave Chris?"

"I'll make a call and get an attorney friend of mine out there to deal with the police. Her name is Cassie Carlton and she'll be able to give you whatever support you need. When I've got it set up I'll call you back. I don't know what else to say, Kyle, except that I'm so sorry about involving you and my brother."

"You warned us off, if I recall correctly, but Chris wouldn't walk away. And I wouldn't walk away from Chris. Besides, the blame falls clearly on whichever Manderfield ordered that ambush at the cabin. What you need to do is put an end to this, and deal with the people who are responsible. They need to pay for what they've done. Do you understand?"

"I understand," Max said, his thoughts drifting to Emma. "After we get Emma back, I'll make sure there are no loose ends. You have my word."

"Thank you."

After another pause Max said, "I wish I could be there for Chris. Be there for both of you. But if I don't carry through with this I have no doubt that Manderfield will have Emma killed."

"I'll be sure to tell Chris that you wanted to be here, and he'll understand what you need to do. In just the short time you've been back, Max, your brother has found an inner peace that's been missing for as long as I've known him. He's received your forgiveness and that takes him another step closer to forgiving himself."

"He didn't need my forgiveness," Max said, startled by Kyle's words. "There was nothing to forgive."

"He would disagree. I do know that seeing you again has been good for him. I need to get back inside, Max. Please let me know when you have things arranged."

Max hit the disconnect button and began making calls to find a way to support Kyle. The cover story they had concocted during the race to the hospital had been weak, but Max couldn't risk having Emma placed in more danger because of police interference. Thankfully, Kyle had agreed. He'd lied to the authorities and the medical staff to help protect Emma, so now it was Max's turn to help protect him.

When he was satisfied that he'd done everything he could, he stretched out on the bed to think. After leaving Kyle to take care of Chris, he and Zoe had driven close to two hours, ending up at an out-of-the-way motel where they could wait for word from Kyle and Cole. With one call down, he had only to hear from Cole before moving forward. But first he had to find somewhere to tuck Zoe. No way was he going to put her in anymore danger, which would certainly be the case if she stayed with him.

"What did Kyle have to say?" Zoe asked quietly.

Max gave her the update. "Kyle will have an attorney to lean on in about an hour and she'll take care of anything else he or Chris needs." Glancing toward the other bed Max said, "Tell me again what happened back at the cabin."

Zoe didn't know Max very well, but she suspected that his anger was running wild just below the surface. He was blaming himself for not anticipating that someone could get so close, and because of that, his brother was lying in a hospital room fighting for his life. Added to that, he had no clue where to start looking for Emma.

So she would go through it all again and maybe this time something would click for him.

"When we started to smell smoke," she began, "Emma left the bedroom to tell you about the fire but she never came back. At one point, I heard some scuffling noises in the hallway and when I went to look, there was heavy smoke everywhere and I could see that the back door was open.

"Then I heard Cole yelling for me and when I started crawling back to the bedroom the heat from the flames was really intense and I could see that the fire was spreading. I told him what had happened and we started gathering up the cases and he told me that I was going to leave with you."

After a brief pause she said, "Max, they're not going to hurt Emma, are they? Someone's going to contact you, right?"

"They went to a lot of trouble to get to her so no, I don't think they'll do anything to hurt her." Not yet, anyway, he thought as he slowly rolled off the bed.

"I know you don't want to take me with you," she continued, "although I wouldn't mind watching you fry Manderfield's ass. But I understand what needs to be done. So call whoever you need to call to come pick me up, and then go. Get those paintings and then go get Emma."

Max nodded and left her alone in the room. She could see him standing near a row of cars in the parking lot as he used his cell. There wasn't anything more she could do except worry—a skill she had perfected over the past several years. It wasn't just Emma she was concerned about; there was also Cole. Sure, he could take care of himself but she still felt restless and on edge every time she thought about him, which was often. They hadn't heard from him in nearly three hours and she didn't know if that was good or bad. But Max didn't seem overly stressed about it, so she would take that as a good sign.

"I need a quick shower," Max said as he reentered the room and emptied his pockets, throwing everything in the side pocket of his duffel. Grabbing a clean shirt and underwear, he stepped into the bathroom. Zoe found herself grinning when he left the door ajar.

Deciding to make a quick change herself, she shuffled through her small bag for one of the clean T-shirts Cole had purchased for her. Just as she was pulling the new one in place, Max's cell phone started to vibrate. The shower was still running so she stepped over to the desk where he'd set it down and checked the ID, which showed an unknown caller. With the rising hope that Emma had escaped and found a phone, she pushed the connect button.

"Hello?"

"Tell me you're out of harm's way and I will be a happy man," Cole said in a soft and soulful voice.

"Tell me *you're* out of harm's way and I'll make you even happier next time I see you."

Giving her a manly chuckle, he said, "I'll hold you to that, missy. Is Max with you? I was sure I was calling his number."

"Yes, he's in the shower. Do you know where they've taken Emma?"

"Not exactly, but I know it's Victor's men who have her. And as much as I would love to just close my eyes and listen to your sexy voice right now, I really need to talk to Max. I don't know how much time we have before we get the call from the Manderfield camp. Can you put him on?"

"Of course, I wasn't thinking. Hold on." Zoe crossed the room and raised her hand to knock on the door just as Max was pulling it open.

"I've been thinking," he started. "We need to find someone—"

"Cole is waiting to talk to you," she interrupted, handing him the phone.

"Cole, thank God. Do you have Emma?"

Zoe stepped out of the doorway so Max could move into the main room. She listened to his side of the call, wishing she could also hear what Cole was saying on the other end. From the carefully chosen words Max was using and the unguarded facial expressions, she could tell whatever Cole was sharing wasn't good.

"I'll leave here shortly and meet up with you in about two hours," he said checking his watch. "I know you'll probably get there first, but wait outside for me. Although it will be less of a challenge for you, it'll still be easier to use the key." Disconnecting he slipped the phone in the back pocket of his jeans.

"Cole was able to track the men who took Emma to a private dock, about two miles east of the cabin. He got to the area just in time to see a speed boat pulling out and was able to get the registration number, which he traced to Victor Manderfield. We just have to hope they call us before—"

"How long do you think before Manderfield contacts you?" Zoe asked, not wanting to let Max finish that sentence.

"I don't know. I turned my personal cell phone back on after we left the hospital and Cole will start calling in to the office line every half hour or so to check for messages. We're doing everything we can to open up a line of communication with this guy."

"Where is Cole now?"

"On his way to the storage shed. I'll meet up with him there."

When the room phone sounded, Max picked it up on the first ring. Almost immediately he set the receiver back down.

"Shit," he said as he grabbed Zoe by the arm, directing her toward the bathroom as he picked up his cell phone, keys and both bags. He shut and locked the door behind them and went directly to the window above the toilet, which looked out over the back of the building.

"That was the desk clerk," he said as he climbed onto the toilet seat and unlocked the window. "Someone has just asked about us at the front desk."

Zoe looked up at him with unquestionable shock in her eyes. "It must be the men who are coming to pick me up, right? The ones you called."

"No. The men I phoned wouldn't ask questions in the front office and they're at least another thirty minutes out. Come on, we've got to move."

Max had already thrown the bags out the window and was reaching out a hand to Zoe. "It's a tight fit, but only for me. You'll have no problems sliding through. There you go, feet first." As he watched her drop to the ground, he was already wedging his body through the opening, and he too dropped to the pavement.

He was grateful now that during check-in he'd taken the precaution to ask for a room that opened up to the main parking area and had a window facing the back of the building. Handing the clerk a twenty, he had also asked for the qualifying room to be as far away from the front office as possible.

The clerk didn't seem to think the request was all that odd and told Max there was only one room like that and it looked out onto the motel dumpsters. "It get's kind of raunchy smelling if you decide to open the window," the kid had told him, "but otherwise, it's okay. Cable works too, so that's something."

Max had taken the room, then handed the clerk another twenty to call him if and when someone came around asking questions. It paid to be paranoid, he thought, as he and Zoe dashed around the dumpsters and sprinted across a back alleyway, heading for the SUV, which was parked three blocks down from the motel—another precaution he had taken.

As soon as they reached the car and he was driving toward the highway, he pulled out his cell and contacted Adler Security and Protection, the agency that he and Cole used when they needed additional manpower on a job. He informed them to abort their trip to the motel to pick up Zoe and that he would get back to them when he had worked out his plan B.

"So I guess I'm coming with you," Zoe said as she stared at Max.

"I guess you are, but just until I can figure something else out."

"I'll follow your lead, Max. Just tell me what to do."

He looked over at her and saw undemanding resolve on her face. Turning back to the road he said, "I could use a second pair of eyes on any cars that may be following us. You see anything that doesn't look right, you let me know about it."

"No problem," she replied as she crawled into the back seat, careful to avoid the blood stains that Max hadn't been able to completely wipe clean.

Max didn't really need her watching. He had just wanted to keep her occupied while he gave some serious thought about what to do next. And what he was going to tell Cole, who wasn't going to like this sudden turn of events one little bit.

CHAPTER THIRTY-ONE

Max drove past the Highland Self-Storage facility twice before he stopped along the back fence and waited in the idling vehicle. Two minutes later, Cole pulled alongside the SUV and through his open window said, "What is Zoe still doing here? I thought you were going to find somewhere for her to go. Why is she still with you?"

"A small glitch," he said before explaining what had happened at the motel. "I had to call off Adler because I didn't know when or where it would be safe to transfer her. I couldn't be absolutely sure that we weren't being followed or discount the possibility that someone at Adler tipped off Manderfield. Either way, I figured she was better off with me for the time being."

Cole glanced into the back where Zoe sat quietly before giving Max a curt nod. "Let's go. I'll follow you in."

Pulling the car forward, Max entered a series of numbers into the key pad that was positioned on a steel post directly in front of the storage entrance. When nothing happened, he entered the numbers a second time and the gate began to slide open.

Twenty cement block units were grouped into sections marked A through F, with an individual number clearly painted above each rollup metal door. He double checked the number Eric had written down and within minutes found the unit he was looking for—D23.

Killing the headlights, he and Zoe climbed out of the SUV and waited for Cole. Eric's unit had an expensive lock securing it in place but the key Max had gained them easy access. With both flashlight and firearm at the ready Max lifted the door and then moved off to one side while Cole covered the opposite side. Zoe stayed hidden behind the vehicle, per Cole's instructions.

The outdoor security light that hung from the opposite building provided them with a fairly good visual of what was inside and Max could see that the cubicle had a sizeable amount of unused space. Satisfied there was no threat present, he moved deeper into the unit and aimed his flashlight toward the corner, where three aluminum cases stood against the wall. Propped beside them were two suitcases and a large athletic bag. Max paused, glancing through the open door again listening for any signs that would indicate they weren't alone.

"I'll watch the lot," Zoe said as she bent down and pulled the handgun from an ankle holster. Tilting her head slightly when Cole started to say something she just spoke over him. "Max gave me his revolver. I know how to handle a gun, so let's not waste time debating. Do what you need to do so we can get out of here." Moving toward the open door she positioned herself in the shadows along the wall.

Cole just shook his head and turned back to Max, who was crouched down checking out the gym bag. "Cash," he said lifting a handful of bundled hundred dollar bills. "It's a real shame he didn't have time to spend it." Max had no idea how much cash could fit in a bag this size, but he wasn't particularly interested in knowing just yet.

Closing the zipper, he moved on to the first suitcase but noticed that it was secured with a built-in combination lock. He glanced at the other suitcase and found the same thing. Again, not particularly interested in what they held, he turned his attention to the remaining three cases.

He could see they also had locks but it was important to verify the contents. He reached into his jacket pocket and pulled out a small leather pouch that held specialty tools that would help him circumvent the lock. As he worked on the first case, he briefly glanced at Cole who was doing the same thing on the second case.

Once opened, Max lifted the lid and found a velvet sack holding one of the paintings he suspected made up a third of the Triad. He removed the unframed stretched canvas and found a flawless representation of what, in his opinion, a painting should really look like.

He wasn't a connoisseur of fine art, but if he had to describe this particular oil painting the only word that came to mind was powerful. It showed a young woman tenderly cradling a small child. The artist had captured the true essence of love in each stroke of his brush, and although it had a certain dramatic edge to it, the painting managed to reflect a quiet moment between mother and son. The mother's hand was gently resting on the child's head as he peacefully slept against her shoulder. Her head was tilted toward her son, her lips softly resting on his forehead. Her dark hair was pulled back, eyes slightly closed and her facial features were so immaculately captured that you could almost hear her humming a soft and soothing song.

Although it revealed a beauty that could never be reproduced, Max couldn't forget that what he held in his hands was the source of the pain that Victor Manderfield had inflicted on his family just to satisfy his obsession.

He returned the painting to its case and glanced at the canvas that Cole had removed. It was definitely another of the three they were looking for, and a quick examination of the third case completed the Triad.

"Let's get the whole lot into the truck," Max said, grabbing the two suitcases first and heading toward the overhead door. "We can take what we need from the SUV, then leave it parked in here."

After everything was transferred to the pickup, Cole snapped the cargo cover into place while Max secured the storage unit.

"What now?" Zoe asked as Max climbed behind the wheel and Cole motioned her through the passenger side door.

"We find someplace where we can wait," Max replied, trying to hide his anxiety. Turning to Cole he said, "Can you have a sky ride on stand-by? I'm not sure where we'll be heading but we'll need to be ready to move when the call comes in."

Cole nodded and pulled his cell phone out to start making calls, hoping that Emma was being kept at one of Victor's US properties. Even though he knew they could be holding her anywhere in the universe.

CHAPTER THIRTY-TWO

The large shopping mall, strategically located in a highly trafficked area in the city of Pueblo, was filled with more high-school-aged kids than it should have been. At least that's how Cole saw it. Most of the stores were just beginning to lift the gates that protected their merchandise during the nighttime hours, but the smell of greasy burgers, spicy tacos and three-topping pizzas, was already filling the food court.

"Why aren't these kids in school?" Cole asked, as he tracked five muscular teenagers in lettered jackets who were parading around the edge of the seating area. All boasting that testosterone-driven strut that most males learned at a very early age.

"It's a day off for them," Zoe said without looking up from the map she was reading. "I think they call it teacher convention."

"So the teachers go off, leaving their students behind to create chaos in the streets, or the mall, or wherever the damn place they want. Just doesn't seem right to me."

"Oh, my quasi-insightful friend. What you are a witness to this very minute is really quite innocent. A well-behaved and, okay, maybe a little too loud, but orderly gathering."

"And besides," Max added, "it's good cover for the time being."

"Good cover in that we blend?" Zoe asked with a chuckle.

"Very funny. It's a crowd, which gives us cover. Is that better?"

"Yeah, and we've got some great husky, well-defined, broad-shouldered macho boys who'll have our backs should the situation present itself."

"Hey," Cole mumbled around the huge bite of pizza he had somehow finagled from a vendor who hadn't even opened for business yet. "Quit checking out the competition."

"These young men threaten you, do they? What? You think that I'm going to all of a sudden get an urge to—"

The ringing of Max's cell phone stopped all conversation at the table. Although the noise continued around them, it was as if the three of them had suddenly been thrown into a dead zone and all that existed was that technical wonder vibrating in the center of the table.

Max reached for it, and breathed deeply before answering. "This is Dunmore," he said authoritatively.

Cole watched his friend's face as it first showed confusion, then concern and finally what appeared to be . . . grief.

"He's not with us, no. And I haven't heard from him." Max stopped to listen. Then, "I don't know him that well, Cassie. We just met a few days ago. How much trouble is he in with the locals?"

Cole and Zoe exchanged a knowing look and Zoe whispered, "Kyle?"

When Max finally disconnected the call, he set the phone down and said, "Christ, can this get any worse? Kyle took off." He looked up at Cole with heartache in his eyes and said, "Chris died early this morning."

Cole reached out and grasped Max's forearm. "Max, I'm so sorry."

Max just shook his head and pushed away from the table. "Give me a minute," he said as he marched out of the food court and into the general shopping area.

Zoe looked at Cole. "How does he usually handle grief? Should one of us go after him?"

"He's not going to shoot anyone if that's what you're asking. At least not yet."

Zoe reached out now and slipped her hand over the one Cole had resting on the table. They were quiet for another five minutes until the phone Max had left behind began to ring. Zoe looked around to see if she could spot Max, but he was nowhere in sight.

"You have to answer it," she said to Cole. "If it's Victor or Stan, maybe they don't know Max's voice."

Cole answered the phone. "Hello?"

He listened for a few seconds and then looked at Zoe and shook his head, but then surprised her by saying, "I'm sorry about Chris, but you're not helping yourself by taking off. And joining us maybe isn't the best idea either."

"I'm going to be a part of putting an end to this," Kyle said through the phone, "either with you or without, it doesn't matter to me. I know just enough to get myself in trouble if I go off on my own, and you know it."

"Where are you right now?" Cole asked.

"Nice try. How about you tell me where you are and I'll come there."

"Kyle, this isn't a game. These are ruthless men who will tear you apart if—"

"They've already torn me apart, you asshole," Kyle yelled into the phone. "And I will not rest until I know they've paid for killing Chris and hurting his family. Now are you going to tell me where you are or am I going to keep driving until I reach Victor's place?"

He did know enough, Cole thought. Enough to get himself killed. "Let me find Max and I'll call you back, let you know where we can meet." But his plan wasn't to invite Kyle into the fold. This was his chance to get both him and Zoe away from the danger of the situation.

Cole was closing the phone just as Max came down one of the mall corridors. When he saw Cole holding the phone he quickened his pace. Cole stood as he approached and said, "Not Emma, Max. It was Kyle. Sit down because we have some changes to make in our game plan. Kyle wants in and he won't take no for an answer. If we don't bring him on board he's going to go off on his own, and I believe him."

"This is unreal," Max spit out as he slammed his fist on the table. "This whole thing is spinning out of control."

The teenagers at the table next to them quickly gathered their belongings and moved to another seating area, one that was far away from the crazy people.

"I think we should bring him in," Zoe said emphatically. "He's smart, he's invested in what's happening and you won't have to waste time bringing him up to speed. And he's lived in the world of the rich and famous which could come in handy."

Max was shaking his head as she spoke but she just kept going. "We don't know what we're going to be facing once we get that call, Max. And yes, it's not the most ideal situation to have me and Kyle as your team, but it's better than having him go off on his own. I just don't think you should turn away from what we both can offer."

Cole hadn't said anything because he couldn't. He didn't know if having Kyle around was such a good idea but he knew for a fact that he wanted Zoe gone. Yet here she was digging in her heels and telling them both that she had no intention of going anywhere. It scared the crap out of him.

When Max agreed with her assessment Cole nearly blew a gasket. "What the hell are you talking about?" he said fiercely. "You can't be serious. How do you know what these two are even capable of dealing with? I don't mean to be insulting here, Zoe, but what Max said earlier is seriously dead on. These are dangerous, unpredictable people. Max and I have been in situations like this before and we know how to handle ourselves. I don't want to have to worry about you and Kyle when things heat up. I don't ever want to be put in Max's shoes worrying about where you are and how you're being treated."

He looked away from her, feeling unsteady and just a little too angry. "I'm sorry, Max, for being so blunt about Emma. But Zoe has to know there are consequences here that affect other people."

Max looked at Zoe and could tell she was trying to settle her emotions with a deep breathing exercise. He shifted his gaze to Cole and could see that he was doing the same thing. He hadn't realized how two of a kind they really were, until now. And neither of them was considering a compromise. More to the point, they were both trying to find the words that would sway the other one to their own way of thinking. So it was up to him to keep the sanity.

"Let's go. I'm going to call Kyle and set a meeting place. He needs to make his case before we proceed, and don't argue with me, Cole. I swear I'll knock you flat on your ass with few regrets if you so much as open your mouth right now. The same goes for you, Zoe.

"I need time to think without listening to the two of you. Not only did I lose a brother today but the woman I love is God knows where and yes, the fact that I don't know how she's being treated is terrifying me. We'll all take a time-out and I want you both to seriously think about what's best for Emma. If I have to use the devil himself to get to her, I'll do it. This needs to end."

With that he pushed away from the table for the second time and walked briskly toward the exit to the parking lot, his cell phone to his ear.

Cole and Zoe just sat for a moment looking at each other until Cole reached out for her hand. "Come on, let's go. We'll do what Max wants for now."

She rose and took his hand. She wanted to tell him not to worry about her. Tell him that she never wanted him to be put in the position where his fear for her could dim the glow in his eyes, like it had in Max. Instead, she smiled up at him and they walked out of the mall and into the bright morning sun.

CHAPTER THIRTY-THREE

Emma heard someone coming—footsteps scraping on the floor just outside the room where she was being held. She kept her eyes glued to the door, waiting. More than one person, she thought as she strained to hear the voices, muffled by the still unopened door. But when the groan of the hinges overpowered the voices she stumbled backwards, realizing that although her wait was over, the nightmare she'd been living had just gone up a notch.

Stan Hudson stood smiling in the lighted doorway, a military-style rifle hanging loosely at his side, although his finger was itching near the trigger. He had the same arrogant stance she'd seen when he'd come to the house with Eric, the same poisonous look in his eyes.

"Hello, *darlin'*," Stan said as he moved toward her. "Did you miss me?"

The words sent a chill through Emma and for the first time she could honestly say that feeling her skin crawl was more than just an overused saying.

"You don't look pleased to see me, sweetheart," he said in a voice dripping with false sincerity. "Carl, what do you think? Does Emma look pleased to see me?"

"What I see is a deer caught in the headlights, boss."

Emma remained silent with her arms pressed tight against her sides, her head held high. Although she felt her courage wavering she stubbornly kept her eyes glued to Stan's.

"Not going to talk to me, huh? Maybe it's because you don't particularly like me. Or maybe you're just afraid. Could that be it, Emma?" He took another step toward her but Emma knew she was trapped in place, already having backed against the wall when Stan had first appeared at the door.

"I can't say that it's good to see you again, Stan, because it really isn't. And being afraid of you? Not so much."

"Did you hear that, Carl? The lady speaks." Keeping his eyes fixed on Emma he said, "But tell me this, should she maybe fear me even just a little?"

"She should fear you a whole lot, if you're looking for my honest opinion."

Stan kept moving toward her. Slowly. Each step causing her heart rate to soar. But she would remain strong—for Jacob. For Max.

"Oh, honesty is always important, Carl. Do you believe that, Emma? Now, see, your husband didn't rate honesty too high on his morals list, which was a shame because ultimately it cost him his life. But I'd really hate to see that happen to you because even if you don't like me, I find myself liking you very much."

He lifted his hand and ran his fingers down the side of her face, her neck and let them travel between her breasts. He smiled a devious smile and said, "You have something I want, Emma. You also have something that Victor Manderfield wants. You know it, and I know it. So let's not waste any time playing games. Where are the paintings?"

"Eric never told me about any paintings. I don't have what you're looking for."

"You want to do this the hard way, then." Grabbing her by her upper arms he slammed her against the wall and she cried out as her head bounced hard against the cement surface. "Don't make me hurt you, Emma. All you need to do is tell me what I want to know and I'll let you go."

Looking him square in the eyes she said, "I thought we were being honest, Stan."

"Take this," he said as he handed his rifle to Carl. "I will hurt you, Emma, in more ways than you could ever imagine, unless you tell me right now what you know."

She could see the truth in that statement, written clearly across his venomous face. His hands tightened around her arms and the pain was making it hard to focus.

"I don't know where they are, but—wait," she said loudly as he raised a fisted hand.

"I want the truth," he spat as he waited for her answer. "Where are the paintings?"

Trying desperately to get each word out before he lowered the fist to her face, she stammered, "Max has them. Or at least knows where they are."

Emma was certain that Max had retrieved the paintings by now and that this was the only way to get Stan to contact him. But saying the words tugged heavily at her heart and it felt as if she were offering up the man she loved in order to save herself. She only hoped she was doing the right thing.

"He'll want to make a deal with you," she added, calculating the odds were in her favor that this was indeed what Max would be planning to do.

"Deal with me?" Stan said, the incredulity ringing in his voice. "Why would I want to do that? When I can just find him, kill him and take the paintings?"

"Because if anything happens to me, or he sees you coming after him, he'll bury those paintings so deep Victor will never find them."

Stan's reaction was immediate and Emma knew that she'd found his weak spot. Finding the missing paintings wasn't what was driving Stan so much as the fear that Victor Manderfield would be seeing red if they weren't returned in the condition they were in when they had been taken.

"All you need to do is call him, let me talk to him then trade me for the paintings. We'll both disappear and you'll never hear from us again."

Stan turned slightly to look at Carl, who gave him a brief nod.

Turning back to Emma he said, "Sounds so nice and tidy. What's the number?"

She gave it to him and saw Carl entering the sequence into his own phone. He walked over to Stan and handed him the cell while his eyes suggestively roamed up and down Emma's body. When he ran his tongue across his lips and smiled, she swallowed hard to prevent the bile from slithering up her throat. Although, she would have loved nothing more than to heave all over him.

CHAPTER
THIRTY-FOUR

"The three of you have to just deal with me being here, because I'm staying."

Kyle was sitting next to Zoe and across from Max and Cole at a picnic table in a rest area just off Interstate 25. They still hadn't received a phone call about Emma, and it was putting everyone on edge, especially Cole and Kyle, who had been going at each other for the last five minutes. Max had finally reached his limit at playing peacekeeper.

Before he could speak Cole said, "We could just hog-tie him and throw his body in that trash bin over there. It shouldn't take the state highway crew too long to find him. No more than a week at the most."

"You're a real sensitive guy, aren't you Cole? Have you even considered what I'm feeling right now?"

"That's exactly the point, Doc. You're making decisions based on what you're feeling. You lost your partner, your best friend. I get it. But you can't take on something this big with those feelings hanging around your neck."

"And if you lost Max? Someone who is as close to you as any biological brother? If you lost him to the same violence as I lost Chris, is that the advice you would take?"

He's got you there, Zoe thought as she continued to watch the traffic up and down the interstate. She had been wise enough to stay out of the way as the two men had battled back and forth, content to just sit back and observe. After that last volley, Kyle's score had him skyrocketing into the lead.

"Cole," Max said in a tired voice. "I understand where you're coming from, but I suspect that the real reason you don't want Kyle with us has nothing to do with his feelings or where his head is at right now. I think that maybe you want him to leave because then he can take Zoe with him."

"Hold on just one minute," Zoe said as she sat straight up.

"But you and I both know," Max continued, ignoring her outburst, "we don't have a clue what we're going to be up against. And let's say for the sake of argument that we can get them to leave. What's to stop Manderfield from sending someone after them anyway? Which means they may be safer right here with us. But if you've got a better idea, let's hear it."

Cole sighed and looked at Zoe. He almost laughed, imagining he could see the fumes escaping through the top of her head. "God, Zoe. You can't really blame me."

"Of course I can," she retorted sarcastically, although she was willing to cut him some slack on the issue. "Look, my life hasn't been rainbows and puppy dogs, by any means. Each struggle has taught me how better to survive, and I use what I've learned to teach other women how to protect themselves. You already know I have a license to carry and even though I didn't serve in the military, I fought my own domestic battle. And I did it alone."

Shifting her attention to Max she added, "If you and Cole decide that you don't want me along, okay, I'll leave. In my opinion, however, you would both be fools to let me go. And even bigger fools if you let Kyle go. The way I see it, you're running low on options here, especially when you're not sure who you can trust." She stood up and walked toward the ladies room inside the small shelter near the parking lot.

"Well, shit," Cole said as he too stepped away from the table, heading in the opposite direction.

Kyle stared at Max. "Relationships sure can be complicated, can't they?"

Max gave him a weak smile, but said nothing.

"I don't know if this is the best time to say this," Kyle spoke again, "but Chris regained consciousness shortly before he died. I was going to wait to tell you, but for some reason I feel it's important you hear it now. He wanted you to know that he loved you and asked me to tell you that you shouldn't be fooled by the color of the hat."

Max's smile widened as he shook his head, then lowered his eyes to the table top.

"Do you know what he meant?" Kyle asked.

"Yes, I do," Max said, as the image of his older brother in a worn out, black cowboy hat formed in his mind. "Thank you for telling me." Max looked up and watched Kyle as he stared off into the distance at nothing in particular. "He loved you, too."

Kyle nodded. "He did, yes. And I'll always be thankful for that. The attorney you sent is taking care of him until she hears from one of us."

"You can trust Cassie to do what's right for Chris. We met in college and have been friends a long time."

They sat in silence for several minutes more, each lost in his own thoughts. When Max's phone began to ring, Kyle jumped up and began waving his arms at Cole, who had already started walking back to the table. Max waited until he was in position, then pressed the phone's connect button.

"Max Dunmore."

"I can't tell you how thrilling it is to finally talk to you, Max Dunmore. Emma has been singing your praises here and telling me that you're going to be the man of the hour by handing over the paintings and saving her in the process. But let's take one step at a time, shall we? I want those paintings."

"Getting them to you won't be a problem, Stan. This is Stan Hudson, right? But I need to be sure you can also deliver. Let me talk to Emma."

"She said you might want to do that. And I'll give you the same warning I gave her. If you say or do anything I don't like, she's dead. And then I will hunt you down and you'll be dead. Do you believe what I've just said, Emma?" Max closed his eyes and strained to hear Emma's response, but there was nothing.

"I told her that maybe I would arrange for her to watch me kill you," Stan continued. "And if you don't play by my rules, I still may do that."

"You want the paintings and I want Emma. If you hurt her, I'm taking my knife to each one of them and I'll mail them to Victor piece by piece, making sure he knows it was your screw-up that allowed that to happen. Word on the street is that your boss is ready to fry someone over those missing paintings and you seem to be pretty high up on the list of menu choices. Now let me talk to her."

"You're really not in a position to be making demands, but I'll let that slip this time," Stan said, but with less conviction than the statement deserved. He put the cell phone up to Emma's ear but continued to cling tightly to her left arm.

"I'm here, Max."

"Has he hurt you?"

"I'm fine. Stan wants the paintings and then he'll let me go. He said—"

Max heard her wince and tightened his grip on the receiver, but stayed silent.

"Okay, that's enough," Stan interrupted as he pulled the phone away from her ear. "Hold her," he said to Carl as he walked toward the other side of the room.

"So you know she's alive. Now where are my paintings?"

"I'm not a fool, Stan. You'll get them as soon as I know that Emma is free."

Stan reminded himself that the primary goal was to get the Triad back even though he knew that Victor had no intention of letting Emma or Dunmore live. What *he* needed though was to keep them both alive long enough to get possession of those paintings.

"There's an old settlement church about fifteen miles north of Nevada's Battle Mountain," Stan finally said, giving Max precise directions to the meeting place.

Cole, who was sitting at the end of the table in front of his laptop computer—earphones in place as he listened in on the call—gave Max the thumbs-up, signaling that he had successfully traced the call.

"When you get there step out of your vehicle and start walking toward the church entrance. Leave the paintings in the car. I'll have someone with me who can authenticate them before we make the trade. And Dunmore, I know you won't come alone so I'd be wasting my breath telling you otherwise, but I hope I don't have to remind you what will happen to Emma here if you involve the cops. No locals, no FBI, no CIA . . . well, you get the picture. Just play it straight and you'll get Emma in exchange for the paintings and everyone can go home happy."

"I want to see Emma before anyone gets near those paintings."

"Just be at the church no later than midnight or you'll never see your bitch again."

The line went dead and Max closed his phone. "Where was he calling from?"

"The Nevada ranch," Cole said.

"Makes sense based on where he's set the meeting. Call the pilot and see how close he can get us to both locations. We can't be sure if Hudson was sincere when he said Emma would be with him so we'll have to split up and cover both the ranch and the church."

"What about back-up?" Cole said as he finished packing up the tracing equipment. "I've never had any cause to doubt Lou Garrison's loyalty before. Although I can't vouch for any of the other FBI suits he would choose to include. Our only other option would be Jim Adler's guys."

Max sent a hard, long look at Cole. "Hudson gave me the standard warning about bringing anyone in. And we still don't know who's been tracking us. Even if the leak isn't within the FBI and we ask for their help, they could charge in and put Emma's life in even more danger. Besides, they'll want to take too much time to organize a rescue." Looking first at Zoe and then Kyle he said, "Let's talk about it on the plane and everyone can have their say." Nodding at Cole he added, "Call the pilot and let's get out of here."

Zoe and Kyle appeared to be asleep in the back of the private five-passenger plane that had just been cleared for takeoff. Cole was up front with the pilot and Max sat by himself, knowing he needed to rest, but finding it difficult with Emma somewhere out there, alone.

Reaching into the back pocket of his jeans he pulled out a sheet of paper Zoe had handed him back at the motel. She'd told him that Emma had written it the day she'd found the key, with the instructions to give it to him if anything happened to her.

Carefully, he unfolded the note and read the words that would continue to haunt him until they finally found Emma safe.

Dear Max,

If you're reading this, I fear it means that things have taken an unexpected turn for the worst. Please do not blame yourself over any actions that are made by Victor Manderfield because whatever happens, I know that you have done everything in your power to get us all out safely. Just know that if I don't make it, you will need to rally around our son, loving him for both of us. He will need you to guide him as he grows up, support him with each new step he takes and make sure that he understands what it is to be an honorable man. Just like his father. Please talk about me often, and let him know how much I love him and that I am sorry I couldn't be there with him. Know too, Max, my darling, that I love you. I will not waste my time thinking about the mistakes I have made or the regrets I suffer. It will be you and Jacob occupying my thoughts—you and Jacob who I will be carrying deep in my heart. Always remember how much I love you.

Emma

Re-reading her words made his heart ache. He needed Emma in his life, needed her to be alongside him to raise their son. But he needed to find her first.

He took a slow, deep breath that was shaky at best, folded the note and returned it to his pocket. He glanced out the plane's window, seeing nothing but the blackness that surrounded them. Closing his eyes, his final thought before allowing himself a moment of sleep was that when they landed, it would be the beginning to the end of Victor Manderfield's reign.

CHAPTER THIRTY-FIVE

"Where are my paintings, Stan? I want my fucking paintings."

Victor was in a rage. A scene that Stan had seen played out many times before. But he couldn't remember ever having been the direct recipient. Yet here he was, facing Victor Manderfield in his office at the Nevada ranch, remembering the last time they'd been here. That meeting hadn't worked out too well for Victor's useless nephew.

"I'll have them tonight, Victor. I've sent my men to the church and they should be in place by now. If Dunmore's been foolish enough to plant an advance team of his own, they'll be taken out before Carl and I get there. Once he gives up the paintings, he's a dead man."

"And if he resists giving you the paintings?"

"Dunmore is a smart man. He understands that he only has one option."

"And the woman? This Emma Cassidy who seems to be holding all the power?"

"She's secure," Stan replied, ignoring Victor's not-so-subtle dig.

"That's good, Stan. Because there's one more piece of information you need to get from her. I need the location of the child."

Stan just glared at Victor, baffled by the unexpected mandate.

"Daria has gotten worse since Dunmore came here and took the boy away," he continued. "I don't like to see her so distraught and unhappy. She wants the child, so you will get the Cassidy woman to tell you where he is."

"Of course, Victor." Stan silently cursed his boss as his mind went into overdrive trying to figure out how he was going to pull this all off.

"Good. You'd best get started, then."

Victor lowered himself into his regal leather chair and started shuffling through an orderly stack of papers sitting in the middle of his desk. Stan recognized it as a dismissal—a move he'd made on his own men numerous times—and fought to control his irritation at being treated like an underling. Without speaking he turned and left the room, heading directly out the front door and toward one of a number of vehicles Victor kept available to move about the property.

Choosing one of the hybrids, he reluctantly considered the probability that he may not make it through this alive. Even if he did manage to get everything Victor had requested, he knew that he'd fallen out of the man's graces and was afraid to think about what that really meant for him. Dead or alive, the cushy life he'd been enjoying was in serious jeopardy.

What he needed was some major reinforcement if he wanted a decent shot at living another day. With that in mind he started the vehicle and, after pulling away from the house, made the necessary call on his way to Victor's helicopter.

Chapter Thirty-Six

Detective Jonathan Draper sat at his desk in the Fifth Street police station in Kingsport doing paperwork. Like every cop in the squad room, he detested paperwork, but as he lacked the seniority needed to weasel out of it, he was stuck.

His partner, Roger Donnelly, still had yet to return from lunch, and Jonathan glanced up at the clock for the third time in the last half hour. Since partnering with Roger, Jonathan's biggest fear was that when the bust of the century took place, he would be one of the greenhorns left behind—chained to a desk and scratching his ass—while Donnelly was out there securing his next promotion. Not that Jonathan was being paranoid or anything. He knew he was the youngest cop in the squad and the one with the least amount of experience, but didn't he make up for that with his dedication and tenacity? Obviously not, he thought now, because in this squad room experience was everything, and that's why he found himself working twice as hard, day after day, just to stay within reach of everyone else.

"Hey, Romeo," one of the older detectives said from across the room. "The coffee pot is empty."

Jonathan looked up and saw Gavin Turley emptying the remaining dregs into a chipped ceramic coffee mug that said *LIFE SUCKS IN SPADES* in bold black letters. Jonathan just shook his head and replied, "Get Melanie to make it. I hear women are good at that kind of stuff."

"I've made stronger men than you cry like little girls for making less insulting remarks, Draper," the only female member of the squad said.

"You're sitting right there, and besides, I don't even drink coffee."

"Which I can't understand," Turley said. "It just ain't natural. But that still doesn't get you out of your sworn duty to protect and serve. Protect your ass by serving up another pot, kiddo."

"Christ, when are we going to get someone new in this unit so I don't have to take all this crap from you guys?"

Turley gave Jonathan a broad smile and slapped him on the back as they passed in the aisle. Jonathan didn't really mind making the coffee or the jibes he exchanged with the other cops. It made him feel accepted even if his partner still didn't see his full potential.

After the task was done, he started back to his desk just as Roger came through the door, his walk a swagger and his voice loud and jovial as he greeted his colleagues. He removed his jacket, neatly placing it over the back of his chair, and started going through the messages on his desk. "How's it hanging there, Johnny Boy? Anything happening that I should know about?"

Jonathan scowled at his partner's twist on his name. No matter how many times he'd told Roger to call him Jonathan, the request was always ignored. Choosing not to make an issue of it again, he simply got down to business. "I put the Raggenstahl file on your desk," he began. "The DA says that we should—"

The sound of "Flight of the Bumble Bee" chirping from Roger's cell phone interrupted Jonathan's update. "Sorry, gotta take this," Roger said and headed for the hallway.

Jonathan wondered, and not for the first time, who was on the other end of that distinct ring tone. The call didn't come in often, but Roger always stepped away from prying ears to take it. He doubted it was someone associated with any of the criminal cases Roger was working, but on the other hand it didn't seem to be personal enough to be one of a number of girlfriends his partner juggled from week to week. Jonathan had even asked just the other day if it was one of his snitches reporting, and Roger had just brushed him off and changed the subject.

Shifting his attention back to the form displayed on his computer screen, Jonathan tried to concentrate. So many empty spaces, he thought with some annoyance. They should hire a secretary to do this kind of stuff. Wasn't the city better served if he were out on the streets? Glancing through the doorway he could see Roger leaning up against the wall, arguing with the person who'd called. He did not look like a happy camper, that was for sure. Watching for another full minute Jonathan was convinced that the call was definitely not work related and that Roger wasn't only angry, he was anxious.

When he returned to his desk, Roger grabbed his jacket and said abruptly, "I've got some things to check out."

"I'll go with you," Jonathan said as he stood and reached for his suit coat.

"No." Roger heard the sharpness in his voice and tried to smooth it out. "What I mean is that it's stuff I can do on my own. Besides, you got work here, Johnny Boy."

Jonathan lowered his voice and said, "Roger, I can help. What's going on?"

Roger glared at his partner for a full five seconds, his patience wearing thin. "If I need your help, I'll ask for it. For now, you do what I tell you to do." As he turned to leave he added, "I'll be gone the rest of the day."

Jonathan slowly lowered himself back into his chair. The other four detectives in the room as well as the two uniformed officers had gone quiet during the exchange and were now busily taking phone calls, updating records or reading files.

Turning back to the computer Jonathan started entering data into the report, not wanting to entertain the thought that everything he'd witnessed during the past several weeks could very well be an indication that Roger was a dirty cop. And that dirt was slowly burying his partner.

Roger could see the writing on the wall all too clearly. He knew the score, having worked both sides of the law now for nearly two years—receiving a regular paycheck from the Kingsport Police Department in addition to the extra, unreported income he collected for being Victor Manderfield's inside man. Now his days would be numbered if he couldn't figure out a way to stop Max Dunmore from doing any further damage.

Roger understood that he was a just small cog in the big wheel that kept the Manderfield operations going. But his position in the organization was, to his way of thinking, invaluable. Eliminate potential problems from inside the department by misdirecting investigations, supplying false information on certain cases that could harm Manderfield and his associates, and making sure evidence was misplaced or even destroyed. In return, Roger's offshore retirement account kept getting fatter. All he needed was another year, maybe two, and he could tell the chief to kiss his ass as he strolled out the door for good.

For now he needed to put in an appearance at the Nevada ranch if he didn't want to lose everything. All because Max Dunmore couldn't keep his nose out of other people's business.

As he headed out of town he took another hit of the exceptional cocaine that had been last week's bonus for supplying classified information on the whereabouts of a witness that Denver police had transferred to a safe house in Kingsport County. The information had led to the assassination of said witness, who could have put Victor behind bars for extortion and weapons charges. As far as Roger was concerned, the asshole was as dirty as Manderfield, so providing the man's whereabouts had been an easy decision.

Besides, it hadn't been him who had taken the guy out, so what did he care?

Leaning back in the car seat he smiled at the thought that if the truth be told, his involvement with Manderfield just gave him another outlet to help clean up the filth in his community. What was so wrong with that?

CHAPTER THIRTY-SEVEN

From his prone position at the highest point of a hilltop that bordered Victor Manderfield's ranch, Cole could see the security team that patrolled the property. Two members of that team stayed close to the house while the others fanned out and took up stations at various points. No one had come near his hiding place, foolishly assuming that there was no threat hidden out here in the overgrown brush, weeds and rocks.

The first time Cole had been out here with Max he hadn't had time to notice the enormity of the house. They'd had only one goal in mind and that had been to rescue Jacob. But now it was important to note every inch of space in order to safely extract Emma. Although there was no indication where in the home she was being held, it was easy enough to pick out the sectors that were exposed to a breach, as well as the weak links in the army of guards. That particular information gave him the exact route he would take to get to Emma.

He pulled out his phone and sent Max a text asking for his current location and providing him with the disappointing news that he hadn't yet spotted Emma. As he waited for the reply he downed an energy bar, imagining that a cold glass of water—or better yet, milk—would have complimented the snack quite nicely. When his phone vibrated he pulled it out and read the message: *30 miles out. all ok. will contact b4 I go in.*

Cole checked his watch. He figured that it would be another half hour before he heard back from Max so he made himself comfortable and continued to watch the house. Fifteen minutes later he saw a dark Mercedes drive up to the front porch. He pulled out his binoculars and when the door opened saw Victor Manderfield and two other men hurry off the porch and climb into the vehicle, which then quickly made its way down the road to the front gate. He sent a text to Zoe with the update and told her to stay alert even though the car was heading in the opposite direction. Her message back read: *Athena copies.*

He smiled, recalling how she had insisted on a code name, and he had obliged by giving her the name of the goddess of wisdom and heroic endeavor. He'd told her to use the name to let him know she was safe. He slid the phone into his pocket and tried to relax his cramping muscles.

He let his thoughts drift back to the discussion that had taken place on the plane when they had been finalizing their rescue plan. In the end Zoe had been sent with Cole to watch Victor's Nevada ranch and Kyle accompanied Max to the church. Zoe's job was to serve as the getaway driver if Cole located Emma. Kyle was riding shotgun to Max and would—if Emma was with Hudson—serve in a similar role as Zoe, keeping the engine running in order to facilitate a quick exit once the trade was made.

At one point Kyle had argued that it was time to call in the FBI to help with the exchange, but Max had strongly disagreed. He was convinced that Manderfield was keeping cops on his payroll, something that could easily extend to the FBI. They had all known that waiting to make the call was a gamble, but Max had taken responsibility for the final decision. Cole understood only too well the weight that decision carried for Max.

So in the end their plan hinged on getting Emma back on safe ground. Once that happened Cole would contact Garrison and the paintings would be turned over—the idea being that, at the very least, the bureau would arrest Manderfield for kidnapping and extortion.

Of course, any number of variables could easily derail their ingenious plan, such as the sudden departure of Victor Manderfield or the flurry of activity outside the ranch house that currently drew Cole's attention. Something was off, he thought, as he saw two of the security guards leave their stations and enter the house. That left only three guarding the outside perimeter.

He shot off a text to Max, cryptically telling him there was movement on the property and waited patiently for him to respond. After five minutes with no response, he tried again, but still no answer. He texted Zoe asking for the password and she responded immediately: *Athena*.

He tried Max one more time. *Where r u?*

Cole swore when he read the text that came back: *Arrived. Where r u?*

That wasn't Max asking because he already knew where Cole was, which meant that someone else had Max's phone. And if that were the case, someone had Max and Kyle, too.

Zoe sensed that something had gone wrong. Cole was texting her every couple of minutes asking her for the password and then reminding her to wipe their messaging. When she asked him what was happening, his only response was to stay alert. Now in his latest message he told her he was coming her way and would let her know when he was close.

She stepped out of the rented Explorer and circled around to the back where she crouched near the rear tire. She was dressed completely in black and held tight to the gun that Max had given her earlier. Her weaponry skills were probably substandard compared to Max and Cole, but she was confident that if need be she could hold her own.

When she heard rustling behind her, she turned, aiming the gun in the direction of the noise. She remained crouched, sure that she blended into the darkness of the night as much as she could. But then she silently cursed when her cell phone vibrated in her pocket. Painfully aware how freaked Cole would be when she didn't answer, she nonetheless ignored it, not wanting to chance the phone's backlight giving away her position.

She sat motionless, listening, trying to see beyond the brush and trees that lined the road. When she heard the whisper of words behind her she simply closed her eyes and slowly let out the breath she'd been holding.

"What are you doing outside the car, Zoe?"

At first she was relieved to hear Cole's soothing baritone voice but then quickly realized how hard her heart was pounding from the jolt of fear that had passed through her. She turned and smacked his shoulder hard with her fisted hand.

Saying nothing he wrapped his fingers around her elbow and guided her back to the driver's side of the vehicle pointing for her to get in. He hurried around the front and slid into the passenger's seat. When they were both securely inside he instructed her to start the car.

"Don't turn the lights on yet. Just drive slowly and I'll let you know if you get off course, but you should be able to feel when the tires go off the road."

Zoe continued to fume at his clandestine appearance but did what he said. Once they got to the first crossroad, he told her to take a left and then an immediate right. After about a half mile, the road opened up and she could see farmland on either side. Cole reached over and flipped on the headlights.

"You can pick up some speed now and just keep going south until I tell you to turn."

"What's going on, Cole? And why did you scare me back there?"

"Just drive so I can figure out where to go next. Please?"

He was angry, she thought. At her? What did he have to be angry about? But she kept quiet knowing he wouldn't talk to her until he was good and ready. After all, her job was to drive, but damn it, she wanted to know what in Moses's name was going on.

She drove another five miles before Cole instructed her to turn, again onto a back road that seemed to lead right back to where they'd just been. As she drove, the vastness of open land had her theorizing that owning property in this area wasn't for paupers and would require a magnitude of hired hands.

"Is this Victor's entire ranch?"

"Mostly, yes. We're coming in behind the house now, but we won't be able to get too close." Pointing to a grouping of trees, he said, "We need to hide the car, so keep your eyes open on that side of the road for a relatively flat place where we can back in. It needs to be deep enough off the road so it's not easily spotted."

"There," she said almost immediately, "by the weeping willow. We should be able to squeeze between those two trees."

"Okay, pull to the side of the road and let me jump out to see how far back we can go. I'll guide you in."

Once the vehicle was parked, Cole climbed back in and turned to Zoe. "You should have stayed in the car."

"But—"

"Stop talking and listen to me. If I hadn't gotten there when I did, you'd be dead." He saw her eyes go wide and she opened her mouth to speak, but thought better of it. "He was so close to you that it would have taken him just seconds to move in behind you and slice your throat."

She was paying attention now, trying hard to digest every word. When the impact of what he had just said hit her, she blindly reached out to take his hand in hers. It was only then she had the horrifying reality that his hand was covered in blood. She reached out to turn on the overhead light but he stopped her.

"No lights and it's just a scratch. Well, maybe slightly more than a scratch, but it isn't bad enough to require any stitching." He was reaching into his back pocket now and pulled out a bandana that he started to tie around his wrist.

Zoe bent over the seat and took the bandana from him, saying, "I have a bottle of water on the floor and we should try and clean it as best we can before we wrap it."

She could just make out the cut in the moonlight that filtered through the windshield. It didn't appear to be too deep and he was right—with the pressure from the handkerchief it should stop bleeding, which was actually minimal now. "I'm sorry I was the cause of this."

She was tying off the ends of the makeshift bandage when he finally spoke. "He was starting to make his move when I saw him. And all I could think was that I may not get to you in time. I know you have skills, Zoe, but you don't have the experience you need for what we're doing here. And now's not the time to be learning.

"You're a strong woman and you're smart. But this is too dangerous for you to be taking chances like that. If I tell you to do something, there's a reason for it. Because I do have the experience, I know what I'm talking about. I know what it's going to take to keep us alive. So please, will you please just do as I ask from now on?"

She hadn't looked up from his wrist the whole time he'd been talking, but now she did. The concern she saw in his eyes was almost enough to make her crumble.

Almost.

"I can do that, yes. And again, I'm sorry."

She leaned into him and kissed him gently. "Now tell me what's going on."

"That's it? No arguing? No telling me I'm a macho pig who thinks that women can't take care of themselves?"

"No, because this time you're right. You're right about my lack of experience and I should be listening to what you say." She paused just long enough to take a deep breath. "But don't shut me out now just because I've learned something the hard way. I can still be useful, so catch me up and let's move forward."

It was his turn to pause and let her words sink in. She was also right, he thought, and he could use her.

After telling her everything he knew, he said in his no-nonsense voice, "Out of the car, we're going in."

Cole moved effortlessly, weaving through trees, hurtling fallen timber, and dodging low-hanging branches. Zoe, on the other hand, fought for every gulp of air she could get.

"Do you want to stop for a minute?" Cole asked as he slowed his pace and watched her intently.

Even though her side felt as if someone had sliced a knife through it—even though her chest heaved from every heavy-footed step she took—she had a rhythm going and she knew if they stopped she wouldn't be able to get that back.

"I'm okay. Really," she added as he raised his left eyebrow. "I've got rhythm," she panted.

He smiled down at her, seeming to understand her plight. Taking her hand, they continued on. At first she thought the hand-holding was sweet but soon realized it was a way to keep her close as Cole once again picked up the pace. Why on earth, she thought, did people need this much land? Sure it was beautiful and private and all that crap, but when you had to skirt it in the dark of night it could be damn annoying.

She was rudely torn from her thoughts when Cole stopped and, not having time to register the move, she plowed into his solid wall of back muscle.

"Ouch."

He pulled her down behind the massive trunk of an oak and lifted his finger to his lips. She raised her arm to her face and tried to breathe slowly into the sleeve of her jacket. She didn't know if it helped to muffle the sound of her wheezing, but it was all she could do.

Realizing that Cole was pointing to an open field just beyond the ranch house she slowly raised her head and zoned in on the helicopter that had just touched down. The blades overhead were still moving, but the noise—which she'd thought at first had been her own ears ringing from what was surely a heart blip—had subsided considerably.

As they watched, a black minivan came into sight from around the side of what appeared to be a multi-car garage and made its way toward the helicopter. As soon as the vehicle pulled to a stop about thirty yards from the aircraft, the back door opened and two men jumped out. They ran to the chopper, reaching it just as the man who'd been sitting next to the pilot stepped down. The rear door opened and a second man stepped out before turning back to guide a third man to the ground.

Zoe couldn't make out who the players were but Cole seemed able to follow the action with the small pair of binoculars he'd taken from his backpack. She leaned into him and whispered, "Do you recognize anyone?"

His response was a nod of the head.

She continued to watch, squinting her eyes in hopes it would help give her a better view of the action. When she saw a body being lifted out and thrown over the shoulders of one of the men who had been in the car she felt a tendril of panic rise up inside.

"Who is that?" she said, keeping her voice low. "Is he dead?"

He responded again, this time shaking his head right to left. She turned back to the field and saw everyone but the pilot pile into the car before it slowly made its way toward the main house.

Cole tapped her shoulder and motioned her to move deeper into the woods. He stopped after several yards and spoke quietly as he returned the binoculars to his pack. "The first man out was Stan Hudson. I didn't recognize the second man but the third was Kyle. He didn't appear to be hurt or struggling in any way." He paused just briefly and then said, "The man they carried out was Max. I couldn't tell how badly he was hurt or even if he was. They may have only drugged him, but it was definitely Max."

He looked away from her, staring once again in the direction of the ranch house, knowing that if they had drugged Max they would have drugged Kyle too, which didn't bode well for his partner. This isn't good, Cole thought as he scraped his hands down his face. This is not good at all.

"We need help, don't we?" Zoe's voice was soft but strong as she watched the house.

"The FBI should already be nearby. Lou told me they had the ranch under surveillance."

"Lou? Isn't that your friend from the FBI? When did you—"

Without warning, Zoe found herself flat on the ground with Cole's body protecting her. "Stay quiet," he said in a low growling voice as he searched through the trees that surrounded them.

Cole knew the sounds of the backwoods. He knew the sounds that should be there and the ones that indicated something was off. He also knew that sometimes it wasn't the sound you heard but the sound you didn't hear that signaled trouble.

His gun was out and as he carefully panned the area behind them he listened for signs that would tell him they weren't alone. He'd always prided himself on being able to sense danger and outmaneuver his opponent, but with Zoe by his side he couldn't just slither out of reach and play a round of possum. Yet he couldn't just sit here either.

Then he heard the undeniable sound a shotgun makes when the

first round is pumped into the chamber, and the clarity that he and Zoe weren't going anywhere on their own was driven home.

"Drop your weapon, Mr. Haywood. There are two guns sighted in on your girlfriend there and you know how messy a shotgun round can be. Your hero days are over, my man."

Cole locked eyes with Carl Skinner, who stood behind one of the gracious oaks pointing a handgun directly at his head. He could also see a second man off to his left who indeed had his weapon pointed at Zoe. Not a whole lot of wiggle room here, he thought.

His decision to fight or surrender was made for him when the second man fired a shotgun round into the air, which had Zoe burrowing into his side. Cole tossed his gun to the ground and turned to her. "It's going to be okay," he said in a reassuring voice.

Carl and his men quickly moved toward them. One of the men roughly pulled Zoe to her feet and began patting her down as the other man did the same with Cole.

"Who else is out here?" Carl asked as Cole's hands were tied behind him.

"No one that I know about," Cole replied.

Carl gave the man holding Zoe a nod. With no remorse he shoved her down to the ground and held the gun he'd taken from her ankle holster to the side of her head. Cole took a step toward her and was also forced to his knees.

"Who else is out here?" Carl asked again in the same even tone.

"No one," Cole said as he looked over at Zoe. "It's just us. Just us."

"That's all I wanted to know. Shoot him," he ordered the guard who was keeping watch over Cole.

Hearing the order, Cole struggled to his feet as Zoe screamed. He looked straight into the eyes of the man ordered to end his life as the bullet from his revolver drove Cole back, causing him to twist and hit the ground hard. He lay face down, motionless at the foot of the tree.

But to Zoe's horror, it wasn't over yet. She watched helplessly as the same man walked over to where Cole lay and, standing over his body, took another shot. Although his own body blocked her view, Zoe saw the dirt around Cole's face fly and his body jerk.

The silence that followed was broken when Carl turned to walk away. "Take her to the house and throw her in the cellar," he said to no one in particular. "And be quick about it. We've still got work to do."

CHAPTER THIRTY-EIGHT

What the hell?

Max felt like he'd been run over by a train. The pain started at his head and continued on down to the bottoms of his feet. He raised his hands, trying to squeeze his temples, hoping the pressure would force the pain out his ears and onto the dirt floor.

Dirt floor?

What the hell?

"I was beginning to worry about you, bro. I'm glad to see you're still among the living."

Max tried to open his eyes but stopped when the light began to seep in. "Where am I?"

"I do believe we've gained access to the ranch," Kyle said in a humorless voice.

Making a second attempt to open his eyes, Max looked around the pain and saw Kyle sitting against the far wall with his legs drawn to his chest and arms resting on top of his knees. Awkwardly, Max pushed himself up into a sitting position, using the wall for support. It was pure willpower that kept him from losing the box of raisins he'd had for lunch.

He worked to clear the haze from his mind so he could piece together the events that had led to him being here, on this dirt floor, in this concrete room sitting next to his brother's—

His brother, who was dead.

The memories flashed through his head as if in fast forward and he felt the emotions of each moment as if it were happening in real time. He pulled his legs up, mimicking Kyle's position, and laid his head on his bent knees.

"Need me to fill you in on anything?" Kyle asked as he watched Max. When they had first been brought here, he'd tended to the gashes Max had received on his neck and arms when the car they'd been in skidded off the road and into a telephone pole. Of course, they'd been going at warp speed at the time trying to outmaneuver the four-wheel-drive truck that had managed to keep pace with Max's excellent driving skills. And they would have probably made it out unscathed if it hadn't been for the second truck that had unexpectedly appeared in front of them. Faced with the choice of a head-on collision that would have surely been a death sentence, Max had chosen to evade. The only problem with that plan had been the fact that they'd run out of places to evade to—enter telephone pole, stage left.

Max remained quiet and Kyle could see that he was taking slow deep breaths. He moved across the room to sit next to him and said, "You have some cuts and bruises from the accident that I've cleaned up as best I could. You have an injured rib that I'm guessing hurts like hell but I'm sure it's not broken, just bruised."

He waited for some reaction before he continued but Max just sat there, slowly breathing in and then out. "You hit your head pretty hard and that's why you're having a difficult time organizing your thoughts. You need to tell me if you have any problems with your vision or you start to get dizzy or nauseous. First, it may be a sign of a concussion, and second, I need to know if I can rely on you when we make our break."

That got his attention, Kyle thought, as Max turned his head so they were now eye to eye.

"Is Emma here?"

The desperation dripped from his voice and Kyle felt disappointment when he couldn't give Max any good news. "I haven't seen her."

Max continued to stare at Kyle and finally said, "So what's your plan, Einstein?"

"I don't like what I'm hearing, Stan," Victor said over the phone line. "What do you mean you don't have the paintings? Someone knows where they are. So what's the problem?"

"No problem, Victor," Stan replied as he shifted his cell phone from one ear to the other. "No problem at all. Dunmore didn't have them with him and they weren't at the church, but I'm certain we can convince him to tell us where they are."

"And just how much more time do you need to *convince* Mr. Dunmore?"

"No more than a couple of hours, I'm sure." God, he hoped he was right on that one.

"And when will I be able to reunite Daria with the child?"

"We're working on that now. Once I'm done with his mother she'll be begging to give me the information. Don't worry about that."

"Oh, Stan. I'm not worried about any of it." Victor's sardonic tone made Stan flinch. "You have one hour," he continued. "If you don't get results, I'll have to send in someone else to convince our guests that it's in their best interest to return what's mine. Is that clear enough for you, Stan?"

"Yes, sir."

Stan disconnected and wiped the perspiration off his forehead with the sleeve from his denim shirt. He couldn't tell which was stronger, his fear or his anger, but he did know that he needed to get those paintings. And the damn kid. Christ, this whole thing had turned into one huge fiasco.

He stepped out onto the porch and spotted Roger Donnelly climbing out of a sleek German sports car. The man sure had balls, Stan thought sourly. Working for Victor Manderfield had taught Stan that the best way to survive was to blend, and driving around in a car like that certainly went against that rule of thumb. What did it matter, though, just as long as he could help with the situation in the cellar?

"What took you so long, Donnelly?"

"Hey, I got here as fast as I could. Kingsport isn't exactly around the corner. If you'd sent one of the boss's planes I wouldn't have had to arrange my own airfare."

Stan didn't reply. The last thing he wanted Donnelly to know was that he couldn't afford to send up any red flags to Victor. He knew where the loyalty of each Manderfield Corporation pilot rested, and it certainly wasn't with Stan.

"Do you have Dunmore here?" Roger asked.

"Yes. And we have exactly an hour to break him, so let's go."

He led the way down the back staircase to the cellar. "The attorney friend is in that room," he said pointing to a solid wooden door ten paces to their right. "Max is at the end of the hall and we have him locked in with some other guy—Kyle something. I don't know exactly where he fits in."

"Where's Haywood?"

"Dead."

"And Emma Cassidy?"

"Resting comfortably at the location you suggested. Well, maybe not too comfortably, but she's still alive."

"I want to see Max first. I want to explain to him in detail exactly what's going to happen if he doesn't cooperate."

Roger headed for the room where Max was being held and motioned for Stan to unlock the door. Two of Stan's men stationed themselves nearby just in case the occupants decided to make a run for it. While Stan unlocked the door, Roger instructed them to shoot to wound, not kill. He wanted the pleasure of that all to himself.

Max heard the key turning in the lock and moved to stand up. Kyle reached out and helped him to his feet just as the door swung open.

Max's first thought was that he had actually suffered that concussion, although he didn't remember Kyle mentioning hallucinations as being one of the symptoms. But sure enough, there stood Max's ex-partner—Roger Donnelly.

Max and Roger hadn't seen each other since Max had left the police force. Even during his last few weeks there, they had avoided crossing paths whenever possible. Yet here Max was, face to face with a man he'd once called friend, a man who had taken that friendship and shredded it to pieces through his lies and callous behavior. Even through the slowly dimming haze of pain, Max realized now that Roger's obsession with Victor Manderfield had actually been the jumping-off point to the end of their partnership, and apparently it had all come full circle.

"Hello, Max. I know it's an old cliché but long time no see. You look a bit beat up there."

"I shouldn't be surprised to see you here, Roger, and if I gave a damn I'd even have to admit to being disappointed. Amazing how it all makes sense now—why we could never pull Manderfield in," Max said with a shake of the head. "When you have one of the lead detectives in your corrupt pocket it's easy to camouflage your criminal activities."

Roger simply smiled. "Stan," he said, never taking his eyes off Max. "Give me five minutes here, would you? Wait for me by the other room where the ladies are." Stan gave Roger a puzzled look but no one in the room appeared to notice. "Go ahead, I've got these two."

After Stan left the room Roger said, "You're trying to figure out how you can save the day and get all your friends out of here unharmed, aren't you? Not that you really have any chance of doing that, but you can always hope." Shifting his attention to Kyle, he said, "We haven't been properly introduced. I'm Roger Donnelly. Max and I were law enforcement partners once upon a time until Max decided to turn in his badge and go private. He couldn't take the heat of being one of Kingsport's finest anymore. Probably because he wasn't, isn't that right, Maxwell?"

"I think you may be confusing your record with mine."

"Whatever," Roger said, aiming his disgust at Max. "But there's no challenging the fact that you went soft. It's a demanding world out there and the strong ones learn how to deal with it. And then there are those like you who run off with their tails between their legs. You thought of yourself as some kind of saint, always on the right side of good and evil. Christ, it made me sick," Roger continued with obvious contempt. "But where did it get you, tough guy? Tell me, who's the one holding all the cards now? It's game over, Maxwell, and you lose."

The disdain that coated Roger's words was almost toxic but Max was only mildly surprised. When you went to bed with the enemy your perspective on life no doubt had to be altered. At one time his former partner had also been on the right side of good and evil, but it was apparent that was no longer the case. Game over? Not likely, Max thought. Not if he had anything to do about it.

"What's in this for you?" Max asked in a low, controlled voice. "Or is the real question how much is Manderfield paying you? Is it really worth tarnishing your badge?"

"Who are you to judge me? You're running some second-rate detective agency and just barely making ends meet, am I right? At least I'm living the dream and I'll be able to retire quite comfortably with what I've earned."

"What I can't figure out is how you manage to sleep at night,"

Max continued. "You were better than this once. What happened to you?"

Roger just scoffed. "Gallantry is for losers, Max. But enough small talk. Let's get down to why I'm here. The Triad. Tell me where the paintings are stashed and I'll let you see your precious Emma again."

When Max didn't answer, Roger calmly said, "If you're expecting any help from the magnanimous Haywood, I wouldn't get your hopes up too much. The poor guy's dead as a door nail. Shot in the back is the way I hear it. So with sweet Emma locked up tight and Haywood out of the picture you no longer have any bargaining chips." Pointing his gun at Kyle he added, "Although I'm still not sure how he fits into this whole thing."

"Let everyone go," Max said before Kyle could speak, "and the paintings are yours. Stan could have had them by now if he'd kept up his end of the deal. But now you and I can deal. The paintings in exchange for letting my friends go."

Roger laughed as he backed toward the door. "That's mighty heroic of you but that's not how it works. I'm betting one of these friends you're so desperate to save knows where you've hidden the Triad. Maybe I'll just start shooting them one by one until you finally figure out how serious I am."

The panic was burning inside Max but he kept his voice calm as he continued to talk. "Let everyone go and I'll take you to the paintings."

"Really? Why don't I just go down the hall and see if that's really true."

"Wait. We can make a deal. Roger—"

But he was gone and by the time Max got across the room the door had slammed shut. Taking a swing at it with his fist he yelled, "No one knows where the paintings are but me. Come back here, you bastard."

When no one on the other side of the door responded, Max took several steps back into the room and swore. "If I give up the location to those paintings everyone will be killed. The only chance we have is for me to convince Roger that I'm the only one who knows where they are. I'm the one he wants."

"Max. Listen to me. We have to find a way out," Kyle said as he slowly looked around the room for the umpteenth time. "It seems to me that this guy, Roger, wants to hurt you by hurting Emma—whether you tell him where the paintings are or not. Don't let him do that."

The anger was pouring out of Max now and he started back toward the wooden door, but Kyle stepped in front of him. "Screaming through the door isn't helping any of us," Kyle said clearly showing his frustration. "Think, Max. How do we get out of here?"

Chapter Thirty-Nine

Stan was stationed outside the room where Zoe was being held and when he saw Roger coming toward him, he pulled out his ring of keys. "You realize I only have one in here, don't you? And I don't know how much information we're going to get out of her," he said apprehensively.

"I don't care if she knows anything." Roger said casually.

"Then why aren't you working on Dunmore? We're running out of time." Stan was beginning to unravel as the pressure to retrieve those damn paintings continued to grow and wondered if Roger truly understood the severity of the situation.

"We are working on Dunmore," Roger said as he signaled for Stan to unlock the door. "The guy has a soft spot for vulnerable females and I'm guessing it won't take long at all to get the location."

Roger walked in the room and grabbed Zoe's arm, dragging her out into the hallway and pitching her against the far wall. At the last second she was able to throw her hands in front of her to avoid slamming her face against the stonework.

"Max knows where the paintings are but he's not willing to deal," Roger snarled at her. "Said he's going to take his chances because he knows what they're worth. I always knew he was a selfish son of a bitch, and unfortunately this time he's put you at risk."

Zoe had recognized Roger Donnelly the instant he'd opened the cellar door. She had gone to the hospital the night Emma had been attacked by Eric and had seen him leaving with Max. What she didn't understand was why he was here, although the real question right now was whether to believe what he was saying. A resounding *hell no!* echoed inside Zoe's head.

"I figure that all he needs is a little persuasion," Roger continued, "and I'm sure he'll change his mind."

Grabbing her now by her left wrist, he pulled her around so she was facing him. "Shall we begin to persuade?"

She couldn't help but to cry out as he twisted her arm behind her back and yanked the wrist upward, the pain sudden and enormous. She dropped to her knees, trying hard to break free of his grip.

"You hear that, Max?" he yelled out. "Your girlfriend here doesn't want to give me the information I want either."

Girlfriend? What in the hell—but then Zoe realized that he was trying to make Max believe she was Emma. She turned her head enough to see Roger smiling down at her, manic in his need to hurt her.

"What do you think?" he said in a loud growling voice. "What will it take before Max gives me the information I want?"

He still had hold of her wrist, and the pain increased as she struggled to get free. But then, with no warning, the pressure of his grip was gone, and she jolted as the chilling sound of a gunshot blast bounced off the walls, echoing even though the bullet had already hit its mark. She defensively raised her hands to her ears and lowered her body into a fetal position as another gunshot rang out and then a third.

She couldn't move, couldn't think straight for several long moments. It wasn't until Roger pulled her to her feet and roughly placed her between him and the shooter, that she first realized what had just happened. With one arm wrapped securely around her neck and the other holding a gun against her temple, Roger started to back down the hall, away from the shooter. "I thought you were dead," he stammered.

Zoe's heart pounded as she kept her eyes focused straight ahead on Cole—who was very much alive—and tried to ignore the blood that was slowly pooling out onto the grubby floor from the single bullet hole in Stan's head. One of the guards lay crumpled on the floor next to Stan and also appeared to be hit and dying, if not dead already. The other guard was already on his way to meet the devil.

"Let Zoe go, Donnelly. She doesn't know anything so she's useless to you."

"Well, I wouldn't say useless. If I let her go I've got nothing and you'll probably shoot me."

"Perhaps you're right, but if you don't let her go I'll definitely shoot you."

Roger applied pressure to the gun he still held against Zoe's head. "Maybe that's so, but either way, she'll be dead. You want her to live? You back off and just let me leave quietly."

They were wasting time, Cole thought. Any minute the group of men from upstairs would be storming the staircase behind Roger, and Cole would be outnumbered. As it was, Donnelly was still moving slowly toward those stairs, but Cole didn't have a clear shot to take the bastard out.

"I'll make a deal with you, hot shot," Roger was saying. "You drop your gun and I'll make your death real quick."

Before he could answer, Cole heard the undeniable sound of footsteps and watched helplessly as Roger relayed orders to God knew how many men.

"Your time's up," Roger said as he swung the gun in Cole's direction, still using Zoe's body as a shield. He got two shots off before slipping out of sight.

As Cole dove for cover, he heard the outside cellar door behind him open and just like that he figured he was under assault from both sides with absolutely nowhere to go. But he refused to concede the fact that his luck had finally run out as he turned the barrel of his gun toward the threat closest to him.

What he saw made his throat go dry and his mind race. The man who had shot him earlier was taking two paces at a time, coming directly toward Cole at lightning speed.

"Status," the undercover FBI agent said as he crouched behind Cole.

"Donnelly's taking Zoe out the other way, but we have an unknown number of assailants to get through before we can go after her."

"Don't worry about her. Lou said that his team was about to move in. Where are the rest of your people?"

"Down here somewhere, I hope."

Cole stole a glance around the wall and saw two men racing toward him, their guns raised. When they saw him they started to shoot. Cole ducked back and said, "On one," and dove toward the opening and began firing back. His momentum easily carried him to the other side of the entranceway and together, he and FBI Agent Brody Mannis defended their positions.

It took less than a minute to take down the four men who'd remained in the cellar. As Brody and Cole moved into the hallway that gave access to the secured rooms, they heard more footsteps on the stairs, but this time, accompanied by the words, "FBI. Put down your weapons."

Brody called out, identifying himself and cautiously held his gun at his side until he saw a man he obviously recognized. "Campbell, this is Cole Haywood. He's with me. Check these other rooms for civilians and bring them upstairs. Lou is going to want to talk to them." Signaling to Cole he added, "Let's go."

They took the stairs that Roger and Zoe had used and ascended to the first floor. Identifying himself once again, Brody led Cole through the door and into an organized although somewhat chaotic scene. It was clear who the federal agents were and who belonged to

Manderfield, and not just because the latter were in handcuffs. But Cole didn't care about all that. All he wanted was to find Zoe.

"There's Lou," Brody said as he holstered his gun. "He probably knows where Zoe is. I've got to check in, but you go ahead."

Cole started across the kitchen as Max and Kyle were led through the basement door without, he noted, Emma. He watched an agent escort them toward the main staircase to the second floor as he continued to head in Lou Garrison's direction. When he reached the FBI special agent in charge, he extended his hand and said, "Thanks for the quick response, Lou. Seeing Brody charging down those steps was one glorious sight, man."

"We'll talk about how you wouldn't have had to get your ass in such a tight spot if you'd just called me sooner, but it can wait. There are a few more pressing details that need my attention right now."

As Lou turned to leave, Cole blocked his path. "Wait. Before you go, you're holding a man by the name of Roger Donnelly. He came up with a woman, Zoe Brine. Do you know where she's at? She's one of the good guys."

Lou gave him a quizzical look before motioning to a younger version of himself. "Roger Donnelly. Name ring a bell? He came from downstairs holding a woman hostage."

"Negative. The first ones to come up were Brody and this one," he jerked his thumb at Cole.

Cole felt the fear boiling in his guts. He moved quickly back to the stairway looking for a secondary escape route and after several passes found a panel halfway up the staircase that slid open to an underground tunnel.

"Hold on," Lou said from behind him. "Take this so you're not accidentally shot because one of my men thinks you're with Manderfield." As Cole slipped into the Kevlar vest with large FBI letters printed on both sides, Garrison motioned for three of his agents to move through the open door ahead of both him and Cole.

The group carefully advanced single file through the narrow corridor, kicking up dust from the dirt flooring while communicating to each other with hand signals.

Halfway through, the muffled sound of helicopter blades intruded the silence of the tunnel. Lou glanced back at Cole, who begrudgingly nodded his acknowledgment of what needed to be done. In direct opposition to his personal feelings, his training told him the team first needed to eliminate any threats that lay between them and Zoe, clearing the way for a clean and safe rescue. He knew from experience they wouldn't be able to contain the situation if they were ambushed before they reached her. So he focused on the fact that every step he took brought him closer to getting her back.

At the end of the passageway they found cracked cement steps leading up to an iron gate that stood slightly ajar. On the other side of the gate were four more steps and then nothing but overgrown brush so thick that it was impossible to see what lay beyond. The thumping noise from the helicopter blades was now more audible and it sounded to Cole as if the chopper was damn near ready to take to the sky. Every muscle in his body was taut from the certainty that they were rapidly running out of time.

Again, hand signals were used, this time by the lead agent who directed each member of the team as they exited the tunnel. Cole had no trouble understanding the communication and took up his position alongside the others. Carefully scurrying through the brush, each man broke into the open at varying points, sticking low to the ground and guarding the other's flank. What they found made Cole's heart drop. The helicopter was already veering east, totally out of range of any firepower the FBI had in hand.

Cole vaguely heard one of the agents curse before Lou began to bark out orders, dispersing the team members to search various parts of the property. As each man disappeared from sight, Cole began to holster his weapon when he heard the rustling of leaves off to his left. Dropping to the ground and rolling toward the base of the closest thick-leafed bush he swung his handgun in the direction of the noise and called out. "Show yourself. Now!"

He heard footsteps behind him along with Lou's reassuring voice. Training his eyes on the area surrounding the brush he said, "Drop your weapon now and maybe I'll let you live."

"After everything we've been through, shooting me now would really suck." The soft voice seemed to blanket the space around him and the tension he'd been burying was unleashed.

"Christ. Zoe, is that you?"

"If I say yes will you point the barrel of that thing somewhere other than at my head?"

"Lou, it's Zoe. Cover me."

With Zoe's next words Cole was convinced she wasn't being coerced into getting him in the open. "I'm alone," she stated quietly. "And Athena could really use a hug."

CHAPTER FORTY

The Nevada ranch house was a deluge of activity. Each floor had been searched thoroughly, and to everyone's disappointment, there had been no sign of Victor Manderfield. Max now stood in the man's office, staring out at the stables, trying hard to keep his temper in check. After being released from the cellar he had searched the house from top to bottom with several FBI agents but Emma was nowhere to be found. He listened warily now as FBI Agent Brody Mannis reported to his boss.

"I was off shift when they brought Emma to the ranch," Brody was saying to Garrison. "When I came in last night I heard talk that Manderfield's overnight guest was going to be moved but I never saw anyone leave with her."

"Do you have any idea where they would have taken her?" Lou asked.

"None. As you know, Victor has property all over the US and overseas. She could be anywhere."

Everyone looked up as Cole and Zoe stepped into the room. Pushing away from the wall, Max walked straight to Zoe and asked, "Did you see Emma at all after they brought you here?"

"No. I'm sorry, Max. She's not here?"

"Not anymore."

Max saw the expression on Zoe's face change slightly becoming more intense and, what? Fearful? "What is it, Zoe? What do you know?"

"I overheard something Stan said to one of the men when they were transferring me from the car to the cellar," she said in a strained voice. "He said that someone was being flown to the fishing hut and that he'd be heading there tonight because Victor needed the information by morning. He also said they were using the place because there wouldn't be anybody out there to bother him. They never mentioned a name but it could have been Emma, right?"

Max turned to Brody and asked, "Do you know where that is?"

"Like I said, he's got property all over." He turned to Lou and said, "I'll go to the control room and get on the computer. Maybe I can find something that will help."

"Does Emma know where you hid the paintings?" Lou Garrison asked as Brody left the room.

"No. She only knew about the storage facility where Eric put them," Max replied tightly, turning once again toward the window.

"That could be a problem." Lou mumbled.

Understanding the implication behind the agent's words, Zoe moved to stand next to Max and in a compassionate voice said, "You and Emma did the research on the Manderfields. Do you remember any properties that are in a remote and unpopulated area?"

"There was so much data to sift through and Emma did most of the computer work. I don't really remember anything that fits that description." He glanced up at Cole and said, "Is there anything you can remember or something she told you?"

"Her computer was at the cabin along with any hard copy she might have kept. It probably didn't survive the fire." Facing Lou, he said, "If I can use a computer I might be able to help find something."

"I'll have a laptop brought in." Reaching for his phone, Lou added, "While you're working on that, I'll make some calls. When I get back, you need to bring me up to date with everything you know, Max."

After Lou's exit, Max turned to an agent that was stationed near the front entryway and said, "Where is Brody set up? I think I can offer some assistance."

"In the security room at the back of the house. I can show you where it is."

"Thanks, but I'll find it." Stepping in front of Cole he said, "Lou is going to want some answers, so maybe you could take care of that." He paused long enough to give his partner a knowing look and with a slight nod Cole said, "I'll take care of it."

"What was that all about?" Zoe asked after Max left.

"He doesn't want Lou to know where the paintings are yet."

"Why not?" she asked with some surprise.

"We still may need them as a bargaining tool if the FBI's rescue plan starts going south."

"Lou isn't going to like that."

"Don't I know it?"

When Lou returned, Cole filled him in on everything that had taken place, starting with their arrival at Max's family cabin and ending with how everyone ended up at the ranch. "Victor wanted the Triad back," he concluded, "bad enough not only to have ordered the kidnapping of Emma's son—which in and of itself is a little twisted—but then to kidnap Emma. And let's not forget the murder of Max's brother. To go to the lengths he's gone through to get those damn paintings? It's crazy. My money is on the fact that, simply put, Victor Manderfield is psychotic."

"Max mentioned that you also have a case full of money and drugs."

"Yeah, but I don't even think Victor realizes that, or if he does, isn't overly concerned about it. As long as he gets those paintings, everything else is expendable."

"Where are the paintings now?"

"Everything will be turned over to the FBI once Emma's safe," Cole said.

"This isn't a negotiation. Everything you've just told me supports the fact that what you have in your possession is evidence in the criminal activity of Victor Manderfield and I need you to tell me—"

"And we will," Max snapped as he reentered the room with Kyle. "Once Emma's safe. Somehow Manderfield has been kept informed of our whereabouts. We know now that Victor has informants within the Kingsport police department and there's no doubt in my mind that cops in Nevada and wherever else he operates his businesses are on his payroll. So for now the fewer number of people who know where the paintings are, the better. Besides, we still may need them to secure her release and I don't want to find out they've gone missing if that's the case."

"Are you saying someone on my immediate team is dirty?" Lou snapped.

"I don't know anyone on your team," Max responded with matching heat.

"Oh, so you're saying I'm the dirty one? I can take you into custody right now and—"

"Yeah, but you won't," Max said, raising his voice over Lou's. "And believe me, Agent Garrison, you don't want to try."

"That's it, Dunmore," Lou said in a thunderous voice as he pulled out a set of handcuffs. "Turn around and don't even think about giving me any trouble."

"Lou," Cole stepped between the two men and faced the agent. "We're on the same side here. Everyone just needs to take a step back for a minute."

Neither Max nor Lou moved. They continued to drill holes in each other, neither willing to be the first to blink. Using a smooth and non-threatening tone, Cole added, "Please, Lou. Step back."

Another five seconds passed before Lou turned away. It was then he saw the two agents standing in the entranceway, guns drawn and zeroed in on Max. "Stand down," he said with a wave of the hand. "He may be a royal pain in the ass but he's no danger to me."

The men slowly lowered their guns but neither holstered them.

"Max has clocked hundreds of hours studying and researching Victor Manderfield," Cole said, feeling comfortable enough that the situation was defused, "not only while he was on the force, but also after his son was taken. You maybe don't know Max well enough to want to trust him but you know me. And I do trust him."

Before Lou could reply, Brody came hurrying into the room. "Your suggestion paid off, Max, except it's not Donnelly but his wife that owns the property. It's near Glenwood Springs in Colorado. It appears to be a small fishing shack that's spitting distance from the Colorado River. And get this—not another dwelling within miles of the place."

"Donnelly? Why are we looking at him?" Garrison asked, turning his attention to Max.

"It was a shot in the dark," Max stated with some enthusiasm. "Roger is an avid fisherman and I remembered him talking about some property he acquired about four years ago. Said the isolation made it the ideal place to kick back and relax." Turning to Brody he said, "But Roger isn't married. What's the name on the deed?"

"Says here Angela Brighton Donnelly."

"That's not right," Max said, more to himself than to the others in the room. "Lou, we've got to confirm if there's activity at that shack."

Lou paused, but only for a brief moment. "Brody. Contact Peterson. Tell him to dispatch the closest agent to confirm if anyone is on site and to report back to me." Grabbing for his briefcase and suit coat he started out of the room. As he passed Max he said, "I'm not waiting until we get word on if your friend is there or not. It's worth checking out and we can either sit here twiddling our thumbs or do something constructive. Besides, my gut is seriously telling me this isn't just a coincidence. So unless you and Cole want to walk back to Colorado, I suggest you both be ready in five."

They'd been on the plane for nearly ninety minutes. Kyle and Zoe had stayed behind at the Nevada ranch to give their statements while being kept out of harm's way by no less than a dozen FBI agents— an added benefit, courtesy of the US government.

Max glanced up now as Lou made his way down the cabin aisle and slid into the seat next to him. Since takeoff he'd been busy up front conversing with the three agents traveling with them and making calls on the plane's phone. Cole was sitting directly across the aisle from Max and now leaned forward to participate in the conversation.

"Tell me what you know about Donnelly and his connection to Angela Brighton."

"Angela was a girlfriend Roger dated for about six months. He told me he broke it off with her because she was getting too serious and kept dropping hints about marriage and there was no way he was going to entertain that little fantasy. He broke it off and shortly after that she died from stab wounds she received in a mugging. When they autopsied her they discovered she was three months pregnant."

"I remember that," Cole interjected. "She was in Vegas with her new boyfriend, right?"

"Yep. Supposedly they were there to get hitched."

"Information you received from Donnelly," Lou guessed.

"Right again."

"Any reason you didn't believe him?"

"At the time, none. I'm having a hard time knowing what to believe now, though. I'd only met Angela twice and didn't even know she'd found a new boyfriend until they were both killed. But of course I never checked out Roger's story. I didn't have any reason to."

"Okay. Tell me about your ex-partner."

"He joined the Kingsport Police Department right around the

time he started to date Angela. Transferred from a small town up north. I'd already been with the force for three years and from day one we hit it off.

"We were assigned the Manderfield files after the detective who'd been working them retired. Roger was like a vulture. He spent hours building one case after another against both brothers, but was obsessed with Victor, scrutinizing everything that came in on him. But every time we thought we had him, his cache of lawyers blocked us. Arresting a few ex-cons we thought were connected to Victor was as close as we ever got to the man himself. It didn't stop Roger though. Whenever Victor was in Kingsport, Roger would park in front of his office building or hold vigil outside the house that Victor kept there. In reality, Manderfield accounted for just a small percentage of our investigations and I had to remind Roger more than a few times that we had to concentrate our efforts on the cases we could actually close.

"I don't know when Roger turned," Max continued pensively. "I only know that at some point, we started disagreeing on how to work the cases we were assigned. Not just Manderfield, but all of them. He started to make decisions without my input, conducted interviews that I only learned about after the fact. And every chance he got he shut me out. It was a gradual thing so I didn't even seriously consider it until he drew Emma into the mix.

"Just days before she left Kingsport, he pulled her in for questioning—once again without my knowledge. Badgered her about her ex-husband's business ventures and his association with Manderfield. I'm convinced now that he was already in Victor's pocket at that point and was trying to figure out what Emma knew."

"Did you ever file a complaint?"

"What do you think? He never put me or any other department personnel in harm's way, so no. He may have bent the line from time to time but I never saw any indication that he broke it. I just figured he had something personal going on or that the partnership just wasn't working anymore. It happens. But if I had known back then that Emma had been threatened and why, I would have handled things differently."

"What about Stan Hudson?"

"All I know is that he was a real hard-ass. High up in Manderfield's camp of outlaws. Emma was afraid of him."

Running a hand over his military-cut hair, Lou said, "Well, with Hudson dead, Donnelly has been handed a huge opportunity to move up in the organization. He also knows the benefit of getting those paintings, and that it will only serve to increase his position. If they are holding Emma at his place and that's where Donnelly is headed, we can't be that far behind him."

"But a lot can happen in a short amount of time," Max said. "He also has the advantage of knowing exactly where it is and all the short cuts to get there."

"Can't think that way, Max," Cole interjected.

"You're right," Max said shaking his head.

There was silence until one of the agents motioned to Lou. "There's a call for you, sir. It's Peterson and he says it's important."

Lou stood and hurried to the front of the plane. After several minutes he was back, reclaiming his seat. "My men found the fishing shack. They had the place under observation for about fifteen minutes before certain activities gave them cause to move in." Lou kept his eyes glued to Max, his voice steady and his face conveying none of the apprehension he was actually feeling. "Emma was found inside. She was roughed up, Max. She also sustained a fairly severe stab wound which will require surgery. She's been transported to the nearest medical center, which is where she is now. I'm sorry, but that's all Peterson knows. If he learns anything more before we land he'll contact me. I've checked with the pilot and we should be touching down in about forty-five minutes. There will be a car waiting to take you to Emma."

Max didn't respond. He'd heard the words but couldn't quite comprehend their meaning. He also knew he should be asking questions but didn't know what they were. He just couldn't think straight.

"Max?"

Cole, Max thought, as he redirected his attention toward the familiar voice.

"I need to get back up front," Lou said as he stood. "When I have more information, I'll let you know."

Cole moved into the vacated seat next to Max. "She's going to be okay, Max. Believe that. When we land, our priority will be to get to Emma."

"I know," Max said in a strained voice. "God, this whole thing is so fucked up. I let her down, Cole. This is my fault. I should have been there to—"

"Your fault? When did it start being your fault, Max? When Eric started abusing Emma? When he passed her that key knowing she'd have no clue that she even had it if anyone came looking for it? Or was it at your family's cabin when Victor's men grabbed her? If that's when it became your fault, then it's mine as well. And Zoe and Kyle and Chris. We were all there.

"Bottom line, partner? This is not your fault. It's not mine. The culpability falls squarely on Victor Manderfield. He's the one giving the orders."

Max's eyes were hard and deadly as he fixed his gaze out the window. "Not just Manderfield. Anyone who has laid a hand on Emma is to blame and they're going to pay. It stops here. We're going to stop it."

"I'm with you, but first things first."

"First things first," Max agreed, knowing Cole was referring to Emma. "Could you contact Gabe and check on Nanna and Jacob?"

Cole nodded and crossed to the back of the plane.

Max sat staring at the clouded space that seemed to float above both time and distance. Cole was right, he thought. They needed to put Emma first. But then what?

Well, he knew the answer to that one, didn't he? It would be time for Victor Manderfield to get his.

When they arrived at Clearview Medical Center, Emma was still in surgery. Max sat in the corner of the quiet waiting room, his head resting against the wall, his arms crossed in front of him and his eyes shut tight, mostly as a ploy to keep anyone from approaching him with more questions. Cole was sitting across from him and Max knew he would serve as a secondary barrier to stopping any unwanted intrusions.

They'd learned that Emma had gone into surgery immediately upon her arrival. After assessing her medical condition during the thirty-five-minute ambulance ride everyone had agreed that it would be best to fast-track her onto the surgical floor. That had been over three hours ago.

He sensed more than heard the shuffle of feet as someone entered the room. Opening his eyes, he pegged the man coming toward him as a doctor and pushed his body out of the chair.

"I'm Doctor Wright. Are you Max Dunmore?"

"Yes. Is Emma going to be okay?"

"There's no way for us to know for sure at this point. It's just too early." After explaining each injury in detail and answering several of Max's questions he said, "I'm sorry I can't spend more time with you now but I have another surgery scheduled. I'll be checking on Emma before I leave the center so I'll answer any other questions you have then. Let me just say that her injuries were severe and she lost a lot of blood from the stab wound, but she's young and she's determined. She's in recovery and it'll be a while before she's taken to a room in ICU. Why don't you go get something to eat in the cafeteria? I'll let the duty nurse know where you'll be."

After the doctor left the room Max said, "I'm going to stay here and wait for word on Emma."

"I think not," Cole said with some conviction. "And don't argue because we both need to refuel. I bet you can't even remember the last time you ate so let's take the doc's advice."

Before Max could disagree, Wright stepped back into the room. "Mr. Dunmore. Sorry. There was one more thing I wanted to mention. Do you know anyone named Jacob?"

Max felt as if the entire universe had started to spin out of control. "Yes, he's our son."

"Well, that explains Emma's agitated state. One of the critical care nurses said she kept asking where Jacob was. Asked for you as well." Seeing the concerned look on Max's face he added, "I don't know all the circumstances surrounding what happened to her tonight, but I've been at this job long enough to know her injuries aren't consistent with a typical mugging. And when a patient of mine is escorted in by the FBI? I guess what I'm saying is that you might want to check with the agent who rode with her in the ambulance. You may get some answers I can't give you."

"Do you have any idea where he is now?"

"I know he wasn't planning on leaving, so you might want to check the cafeteria. I also know that he wants to question Emma. I told him I'd let him know when that might be possible but I highly doubt she'll be able to speak with him until tomorrow." He gave Max a crooked smile and added, "I've left word with the nursing staff that you, on the other hand, should be given access to her room."

"Thank you, Doctor," Max said with relief.

As Wright left the waiting area and hurried toward a double set of doors at one end of the hallway, Cole silently led Max in the opposite direction and toward the bank of elevators.

CHAPTER FORTY-ONE

Kyle stood by the paddock fence with one foot resting on the lower rail, watching as the shadows that often circled the night began to fade, replaced by the subtle whispers of the predawn awakening. The turmoil that had surrounded the ranch most of the evening had settled down and all of Victor's men, including ranch hands and household staff, had been taken away in restraints. Remaining were four FBI agents, a handful of local law enforcement and a group of suits Kyle assumed were from various branches of the justice department.

Turning, he leaned his back against the fence and glanced at the house. Kyle was no stranger to the type of affluence Victor Manderfield had built here. Yes, he understood exactly what money could buy. And not only the material things but the assurance of staking claim to one's rightful place in society. The society of the rich and famous, that is. In Kyle's case he had also seen how money could take a man to the brink of destruction.

He'd been introduced to drugs at the difficult age of thirteen and had instantly embraced them. He could have easily blamed his addiction on his father, a partner in a large New York law firm, for the lack of interest he'd taken in his youngest son's life. Or on his mother who chose simply to ignore his addiction in favor of keeping her highly respected social status intact. Or on his brother, a Federal Court judge who was the golden boy in the family, always praised for his saintly deeds and obligingly excused for his missteps. But

Kyle had done none of those things, understanding that he alone had been the one to blame for the path he'd taken.

By the time he'd turned fifteen he was doing hard drugs, ignoring his studies, missing classes and trolling the streets when he should have been making plans for his future. At sixteen he was thrust into rehab and told in no uncertain terms that if he wanted to continue to live a privileged life he'd turn his life around and kick the drugs. So great was his fear that he would be cut off without a cent to his name and no future claim to the Brayton fortune, he'd walked out the doors of the facility clean, sober and determined to be exactly who his father wanted him to be.

Somehow, he'd made it into college—again, the power of money at play—and hunkered down enough to get better than acceptable grades. He went into medicine, because that's what his father had told him to do. And what his brother had endorsed. And what his mother believed was an acceptable profession. Each year his grades improved and when he began his residency he thought he had it made. The hours were grueling and the work more demanding than he had ever expected, though. Alone, restless and feeling totally overwhelmed, he occasionally popped an over-the-counter stimulant to help him stay awake and alert during the long, challenging nights. That had led to the intermittent use of weed to help mellow him out after experiencing a particularly punishing shift. The combination seemed to work and he got through the next few years rock steady.

The hardcore stuff didn't begin again until after he'd joined a prestigious Manhattan private practice. The transition from residency to a group of highly skilled and respected physicians had been challenging, and Kyle found himself back to his old drug habits. After three years of erratic behavior, a decrease in productivity and an increase in patient complaints, the other doctors in the practice were both unable and unwilling to accept his less-than-focused approach to medicine. Their ultimatum had been clear and delivered in no uncertain terms: *"Get clean or face the risk of losing your license. And by the way, your days as a partner are over."*

So for the second time Kyle had gone into rehab and worked diligently to make it stick.

Eight months later he moved away from his family in New York and headed west, eventually ending up in Colorado. There, Kyle met a small-town physician who had offered him an opportunity to practice medicine again. Dr. Vincent Monroe had taken a chance on him, despite his former addiction. The only condition of employment had been for him to volunteer once a week at a drug rehabilitation facility two towns over. He had readily agreed, and through his association with the center, had met Chris Dunmore. For the first time in a long time, his life had made sense.

The memory had Kyle doubling over and dropping to his knees. He'd never before experienced such heartache and inexhaustible pain. Not when his father had suddenly died of a heart attack or when his mother had been taken in a car accident a year later. Not when his brother had blamed him for both their parents' deaths and fought their wishes to leave Kyle a portion of their estate. Kevin had waged a battle to keep Kyle from receiving anything their parents had left, and had eventually won, mainly because Kyle hadn't really fought back. By then, he had discovered there were more important things that life offered besides being rich.

Even though he'd lost patients, lost friends—even though he had cried at the funeral of the man who had given him a home and a new beginning in Colorado—he'd never felt the unrelenting anguish that he was feeling now.

He jerked at the touch of a hand on his back. He'd been so lost in his grief that he hadn't even heard Zoe approach. Still a bit unsteady, Kyle mumbled the obligatory, "I'm okay," as he rose to his feet and stumbled against the fence. Zoe reached out but he quickly stepped away. "Give me another minute here, okay?"

She stepped back, but stayed close enough to keep him in her sight. She'd been watching him from the living room window of the house, knowing he was finally feeling the effects of losing the person who had meant the world to him. Understanding that such a violent act could easily break one's spirit, she was determined to stay with him, providing whatever comfort he might need.

Another five minutes passed before Kyle approached her. "Let's head back to the house," he said, giving Zoe a weak smile. "Maybe you could make us some breakfast while I try to get an update on Emma."

Kyle found Brody in the security room, seated in front of one of the computer monitors. His fingers moved briskly across an extended keyboard and his cell phone was flattened between his left ear and shoulder. Kyle didn't think he looked very happy.

"What's taking so long with the warrant on Crystal Ridge?" Brody asked as he abruptly stood and grabbed the phone before it slid to the floor. Seeing Kyle in the doorway had him lowering his voice. "I've backed up all the data here and sent some encrypted files to the field office in Denver." He listened to whatever the person on the other end was saying and then replied, "You know more about politics than I do, but we both know the meaning of justice. Let me know what you know as soon as you know it, Frank. I'll be finished up here by noon and would like nothing better than to have a green light to strip down Manderfield's Colorado property."

As Brody disconnected the call, Kyle said, "Do you have any news about Emma? I was hoping I'd hear something from Max or Cole by now, but I haven't."

"Let's take a walk," Brody said as he stepped out of the room and took the corridor that led to the back door. Once outside he reached for a pack of cigarettes and, lighting one, inhaled deeply before speaking.

"Emma was found at Donnelly's fishing shack. No one's sure

who gave the order but the two guys who were with her worked her over pretty good. Our agents got her to a medical facility and she's in surgery. Max and Cole are with her."

Kyle took a brief moment to digest what he'd just been told before saying, "You helped save our lives, Brody, and I don't think I ever gave you a proper thank you for that." Reaching out to shake the agent's hand, he added, "I'll be making arrangements for Zoe and me to leave as soon as possible so we can be with Emma."

"I'll have to talk to Agent Garrison about that," Brody said. "With Manderfield still loose, we have orders to keep you here where we can protect you."

"Go ahead and do what you need to do, then," Kyle said as he turned to head back inside the house. He went straight to the kitchen, where he found Zoe loading two plates with scrambled eggs, sausage and hash brown potatoes. He looked around the room for prying eyes before he sat at the table, signaling her to sit beside him.

After bringing her up to date, he said, "I'm not waiting for Garrison's permission to leave."

"Agreed," Zoe said as she gently squeezed Kyle's hand. "I can be ready to take off in five."

Max sat next to Emma's bed, watching the white sheet that covered her body rise and fall in concert with her ragged breathing. Every so often he felt her fingers twitch under his hand and he would softly murmur words that he hoped were comforting. He didn't know how much pain she was in, but knew if it weren't for the medication that was being administered through an IV, it would be unbearable.

When he felt his cell phone vibrate, he pulled it out of his pocket and glanced at the caller ID, recognizing the number as belonging to one of the bodyguards assigned to protect his son. It had been a long four hours since he'd last received a cryptic text message from Gabe Dragotta indicating they were all on the move. He'd tried several times to reach someone for an update but had been tossed into voicemail every time. Max knew that with Victor still unaccounted for and Donnelly on the run the prudent thing had been to switch his family to a new safe house, but he'd been sick with worry. As he pressed the connect button he moved off to the far corner of the room near the windows so he wouldn't disturb Emma's sleep. "Dunmore."

"Max, it's Gabe. We've arrived at the new location and we'll stay long enough for everyone to get a few hours sleep. But then we're on the move again."

"Are you being followed?" Max asked with some concern.

"Not that I can see. Just want to play it safe."

"How is everyone holding up?"

"Everyone's been great. Even the little guy. You got quite the kid there, Max, and my plan is to make sure he sees his daddy again. I'll call when we're settled. I've pulled in some additional back-up, too. Figured you wouldn't object."

"You do what you have to do, Gabe."

"Okay. How's Emma?"

"She's coming along. We're hopeful for a full recovery," Max mechanically repeated the words the doctor had used with him.

"Good. Well, I better hang up now. Don't want to stay on the line too long. I'll call."

With that, he was gone. Max knew it would have been risky to spend time talking to his grandmother or listening while she tried to make Jacob laugh, but, God, it would have been nice.

"Max?"

Her voice was weak and gravelly, and as Max moved back to Emma's side, he could see that she was struggling to open her eyes even though the left one was too puffed-up and bruised to allow in even a sliver of light.

Leaning down so his face was close to hers, Max took one of her hands in his and gently brushed his other one over her hair. "I'm here, Emma. Try to relax, now. You're in the medical center and they're taking really good care of you." Man, that really sounded lame. "Emma, you need to stay calm, okay?"

"What happened?"

"We'll talk about it later. Right now you need to rest. Don't worry about anything."

It stayed quiet in the room for several minutes before her voice cut through once again. "Is Jacob safe?"

"Yes, he's still with Nanna and Henry. We'll see him soon, I promise."

"What happened?" she asked again, her words starting to slur.

He rested his lips on her forehead and said, "Later, sweetheart. We'll talk about it later."

"Did Eric do this to me?"

Max was confused at first but then realized that in her drugged state of mind, she was associating her current pain with a time when it was all too often inflicted by her ex-husband. "Oh, baby, no. Eric is gone. He's never going to hurt you again." His voice hitched as he added, "No one will ever hurt you like this again."

"Thank you, Max," she whispered, and squeezed his hand as best she could.

As she settled back into sleep, Max continued to stroke her hair. When he was sure she'd gone under he again pulled out his phone, this time dialing Cole. "We need to talk," he said when Cole picked up. "Can you meet me here?"

"I'll need an hour. I've been playing phone tag with Lou and hopefully I'll have some information when I get there."

"Yeah, that's fine. Are Kyle and Zoe on their way?"

"They should be there sometime tomorrow."

"Good. I'll be in Emma's room."

"I'll get there as soon as I can."

"The warrant finally went through for Crystal Ridge," Lou was telling Cole. "The DA wanted to tread lightly and make sure she had a judge that wasn't on Victor's payroll. We're setting up a team now to go in. How's Emma?"

"She's still out of it. Max is with her. Have you found Manderfield?"

"No, but we've got some leads there. We're hearing that he's still in the States and still issuing orders. What we don't have is Donnelly. You got any idea where he might have gone?"

"Don't know him that well, but I'll check with Max. I'm headed for Clearview now."

"I'll keep an agent on Emma as long as I can. But eventually we'll have to switch that over to the local police."

"No, thanks. When you have to pull your guy we'll arrange protection until you have Manderfield and Donnelly in custody. I appreciate the offer, but we'll take care of it."

"Whatever you want. Like I said, though, my man will be there until he can get in and interview her. One more thing," Lou said, changing subjects. "It seems that Kyle and Zoe have disappeared. I would have worried about that normally, but Brody got a call from Kyle about an hour ago assuring him they were out of harm's way and he shouldn't bother looking for them. Don't suppose you know anything about that?"

"Can't imagine what those two kids are up to, Lou. What were they thinking, carelessly turning their backs on protective custody?"

"Yeah, my thought exactly." They were both silent for several seconds. Lou broke first. "Give them my best when you see them." And with that he hung up.

CHAPTER FORTY-TWO

Cole reached the medical center well past midnight but knew his way around the system. He approached Emma's room and stopped briefly to speak to the agent on the door before going in.

He found Max slumped in one of the visitor's chairs that he had pulled close to the bed. He held Emma's hand in one of his, propping his head up with the other. Although his eyes were closed, Cole knew he wasn't even close to being in a state of slumber. In fact, had Cole been a threat Max would have already been across the room with his hands around his throat.

He shifted his eyes to Emma and felt a tug of empathy. Her face was sporting a number of colors as the bruising began to heal. Her left arm was in a sling, her shoulder heavily bandaged. Lucky for her, the knife-wielding lunatic had had lousy aim, and had managed to miss both her heart and any major arteries—although she would still need time and rehab to heal from the muscle damage. Max had also told him that she had two bruised ribs and had endured a number of shallow knife cuts on her upper arms and body.

"The doctor was here not too long ago and said the injuries aren't as bad as they originally thought, although you wouldn't know it by looking at her," Max spoke quietly. "They're monitoring her regularly and for now she gets whatever amount of pain medication she can tolerate."

"Has she woken up at all? Have you had a chance to talk to her?"

"She's been in and out but I haven't asked her anything about what happened. She just keeps asking me what time it is." Cole heard a hint of humor in Max's voice. "I'm not really sure if she even knows where we are."

"What about the fed at the door? Has he been in here harassing her?"

"Have you had a recent head injury?" Max said dryly. "He's not getting anywhere near Emma until I'm convinced she's up to it."

Cole just grinned. "What does the doctor say about that?"

"Actually, he's on my side. What's funny is that Emma has had quite the effect on our Dr. Wright. He seems to be smitten with her. How that happened, I couldn't tell you, because as far as I know she hasn't been conscious long enough to win anyone over." Max looked down at Emma and smiled. "But she's always been a charmer."

"I managed to work my magic on you."

Max came out of the chair and moved into Emma's range of view. "It's not polite to eavesdrop, you know."

"What time is it?" she asked, making Max laugh.

"You ask me that every time you wake up. I just can't figure out why it's so important to you."

"I don't know," she said through a bent smile. "I'm having a little bit of trouble sorting things out."

"The doctor said that's not unusual."

"Can I get a sip of water?"

"How about some ice chips instead?" Max said as he reached for the cup. "The nurse gave me strict instructions. Chips only."

Holding a spoon to her lips, Emma maneuvered a small amount of ice onto her tongue. "I need to talk about what happened, don't I?" she asked after the chips melted in her mouth.

"Only if you're ready," Max replied as he smoothed her hair.

"I guess I am. Maybe it'll help clear out my mind." She turned her head slightly and saw Cole standing near the foot of the bed. "Hi."

"Hi back. You look like you've seen better days."

She gave him a tired smile and said, "You should see the other guy."

"That's my girl. How are you really?" Cole asked, taking the visitor's chair while Max sat down on the edge of the bed.

"Shaken. Frustrated. But glad to be alive." Returning her focus to Max, she asked, "Have you heard from Joan?"

"Everyone's fine. I talked to Gabe not too long ago and he told me that they're locked down tight."

"What about Kyle and Zoe?"

"They're on their way and should be here soon."

"Good. Did you ever find the paintings?"

"Yes. The FBI has them now."

"Good," she repeated.

Taking as deep a breath as her injured shoulder would allow, Emma began sharing the details about her original abduction, before moving on to her stay at the Nevada ranch house and finally her road trip to the fishing shack.

"I was tossed inside and left alone there for some time before the men who took me came back. They started asking where the paintings were, and not too gently. I figured you'd had enough time to find the storage shed but just to be on the safe side I only gave them the general location. Said I couldn't remember the name. When they were satisfied that I'd given them everything I knew, the bigger guy made a phone call but he didn't get through. They both left again for . . . I don't know, maybe an hour or more, and when they came back the same guy said that the information I gave was appreciated but that it wasn't over." Her voice cracked and Max could tell that she was fighting back the lingering fear.

"Take your time, Emma. Do you want to stop?"

"No, I need to get it out. Telling the story can't be any worse than having actually gone through it, right? Anyway, he said that he needed me to tell him who I left the boy with, that his boss wanted him back. And every time I didn't tell him, he hit me. And when that didn't work, he pulled out a knife."

"Wait," Max said, not quite able to comprehend what Emma had just said. "They wanted Jacob? Why?"

"Victor. Victor wanted him back."

"Christ, Emma. They did this to try and make you tell them where Jacob was? I'm going to kill them," he growled as he stood and crossed angrily to the darkened windows. "Who are they? Give me their names, Emma. They don't deserve to live for what they've done to you."

"Sit down, Max. I don't have their names."

"Cole, find out who—"

"Sit down, Max," Cole said calmly. "Let Emma tell it all before you go off the deep end."

Max walked back to the bed and reluctantly sat. "Okay, Cole is right. Finish it."

"At some point, one of them grabbed me and said he was going to take me to the river and maybe the piranhas could make me talk. I started screaming and tried to run but my legs wouldn't work and I fell. So I started to crawl, but I couldn't move very fast. Then I heard someone yelling from outside the cottage and the other guy kept saying they had to get out. When I looked up, the guy with the knife came at me, but I just couldn't roll away."

Reaching out for Max's hand Emma struggled to keep the panic out of her voice. "I know you said that Jacob is safe, but I need you to call and make sure. Will you please make sure?"

"I'll make the call, Emma," Cole said as he stood and walked out of the room.

Max reached over to gently run his fingers across Emma's cheek. Before knowing he had a son, Max could only have imagined the type of courage it took to protect your child in the face of death. But after holding his son, hearing his laughter, and seeing the light in his eyes when Max spoke to him, he had come to understand the whole of it, and he loved and respected Emma even more for bearing that courage.

"I'm so tired, Max," Emma finally said, as she tried to relax into the pillows. "Is it all right if I finish this later?"

Bringing her hand to his lips he said, "Of course it is. Just close your eyes and go to sleep."

"I will if you lie with me," she said quietly. "I need to feel you near me."

Carefully shifting her body to make room, Max slid into the bed and pressed his body close to hers. "You need to tell me if I'm hurting you."

"You're not. And if that changes, I will."

Neither spoke for close to five minutes. Max was hoping she'd fallen back to sleep but then her whispered voice broke the silence. "I love you, Max. I was thinking that when this is over, we should think about getting married."

Cole was sitting in the waiting room just outside the double doors that led into the ICU. He'd checked earlier with Gabe and got word that Max's family was fine. They'd changed safe houses again just as an added precaution, and even though he hadn't shared the specific location, Cole knew from the veiled clues what state they were in and the general region. Although he doubted that anyone who may have tried listening in on the call could have figured it out.

After that, Cole had put in a call to Lou Garrison to ask for an update. He wasn't surprised with what their search at Crystal Ridge was turning up, nor with the fact that Victor Manderfield had yet to be tracked down. He was concerned, however, with the news that Roger Donnelly was still on the loose.

In turn, Cole told Lou that Emma was still in and out of consciousness and hadn't been able to give her statement to the agent that had been assigned to protection detail. Of course that was stretching the truth just a bit, but he didn't much care at this point. He'd ended the call by telling Lou that he'd let his man know as soon as Emma was coherent enough to give her statement.

He stood when Max walked past the waiting area and into the men's room. Drifting toward the hallway to wait, Cole motioned to Max when he saw him come out. "Did she finally go to sleep?" he asked.

"Yeah. She's starting to feel the pain now and they just gave her another dose of pain killers. The nurse said she'll be out for a couple of hours."

"Let's go downstairs for a cup of coffee, then. I want to discuss something with you."

They took the elevator to the first floor and followed behind a group of weary medical students heading toward the cafeteria for an early morning shot of caffeine.

After getting coffee and muffins they took a table in the far corner of the room, away from the other diners. Cole spoke first, bringing Max up to date on the FBI's investigation. "Lou thinks they'll find Manderfield soon. They have the airports on alert and they're double-checking any flights leaving the country, specifically private transportation. They're not so confident about Donnelly."

"So where do they think he's hiding?"

"Lou doesn't have a clue and when I asked what inquiries they've already made, he was not forthcoming."

Cole broke off a sizeable chunk of his muffin and savored the taste. After washing it down with some coffee he said, "So, Emma told us that one of the men holding her at Donnelly's cottage made a phone call and had to wait more than an hour for a return call. She assumed he was calling Stan, but if we chart out a timeline we can make the assumption that Stan was already dead by the time the call was returned. So who was the guy trying to reach?"

"It could have been Manderfield. Or maybe Carl Skinner?"

"I doubt the guy holding Emma had a direct line to Manderfield, but yeah, it could have been Skinner."

"But you're thinking it was Roger."

"Yeah, I'm thinking it was Roger. It was his place where they were holding Emma, and it's possible we were wrong about his position in Victor's organization. Maybe he's higher up than we thought."

"When he confronted me back at the ranch he did all the talking," Max said. "Even told Hudson to wait in the hallway. But it's hard to say. Either way we can't afford to underestimate him."

"Agreed. So for the sake of argument, let's say he was the one who was on the other end of that call."

"Okay, but how does that help us?"

"It tells us where he's heading next."

"Right. To find the storage facility."

"And to retrieve the Triad."

"That he thinks is still there."

"But isn't."

"But he doesn't know that, because his information pipeline has been shut down by the FBI," Max concluded.

They both picked up their cups and sipped the lukewarm coffee thoughtfully. "Emma didn't give up the name of the facility, just the general vicinity," Max said. "So before he can do anything, Roger has to figure out which storage company Eric used. He'll be able to, of course. I'm sure he's got the connections. But it'll take time."

"Okay," Cole began. "Let's assume Donnelly was the person who returned the call to Manderfield's man at the shack. And that he started his search after he gave the order to eliminate Emma. And let's also assume he called the shack after he took off from the Nevada ranch house. Combine that logic with our timeline and he's pretty damn close to locating the storage unit. He'll also have figured that if either of us is still alive, we told the FBI where the paintings are. So the million-dollar question is—will he still try to go after the Triad?"

Cole finished off his muffin as he waited for Max's response.

"I say yes," Max finally said. "Whether it's for money or power, he wants his hands on those paintings and he's just crazy enough to try for it."

Cole nodded in agreement. "Should I call Lou?"

"Yeah," Max responded with a heavy sigh. "But tell him he should be careful who he involves. I'm real tired of always being three steps behind in this."

"I'm going to take this outside where I can find an unpopulated place to make the call."

"Do you still have the throwaway cell phone?"

"Actually, I went out and bought a new one. I'm good."

"I'll see you back in Emma's room, then. Thanks, Cole."

CHAPTER FORTY-THREE

Jonathan Draper sat slumped in his living room recliner watching a baseball game on cable and thinking about what a crappy day it had been at the precinct. He had known as soon as he stepped into the squad room that something was off, but hadn't realized how bad it was until Captain Hornby called him into the office. That alone should have sent up a huge red flag, but it had been the introduction of the two FBI special agents that had started his hands sweating and his heart pounding.

Roger Donnelly had been the focus of the meeting, and Jonathan had spent four hours answering questions and offering his observations on Roger's behavior over the past several months. He knew they'd wanted him to believe that his partner was a dirty cop, and Jonathan had felt torn between his loyalty to his partner and his soul-deep commitment to the badge. So he'd kept his answers short and offered only the facts as he knew them.

Later, the rumblings in the locker room were that Roger was in some deep shit and a good share of the other detectives speculated that he had ties to the criminal activities of Victor Manderfield. Of course, Jonathan had already heard that directly from the FBI and, if what was being said proved to be true, Jonathan knew his partner would get no support from his fellow officers. A dirty cop dishonored every man and woman on the force. Unfortunately, there would be those in the department who would forever doubt the integrity of the entire squad, albeit for the sins of one.

Jonathan finished his beer and got up to grab another one out of the fridge. Walking through the archway that lead into the kitchen he glanced at the wall phone, debating whether he should make yet another call to Roger's cell. He'd already left three messages since talking to the FBI, all short and asking for a return call, so the odds of a fourth call doing the trick weren't very high. He'd just have to continue to wait.

"Hello, Jonathan."

The voice floated out from the shadows in the hall near the back door and Jonathan knew instantly who the intruder was. "Why don't you come on in, Roger," he said as he opened the refrigerator door and leaned in for the beer. "I thought my locks were sufficient enough for this neighborhood but I see now I need to upgrade."

"I do apologize for showing up uninvited but your messages sounded somewhat urgent. I hope I'm not interrupting a spontaneous sleepover with one of your adoring supermodel girlfriends."

Jonathan turned to face his partner. "What's going on, Roger? Why is the FBI so interested in you?"

"Same old Jonathan," Roger sighed. "Avoid all the small talk and cut right to the core of things." Pointing to the beer can in Jonathan's hand he added, "I could use one of those."

Jonathan slid the unopened can across the kitchen table and went back in the refrigerator, this time grabbing a bottle of water. He waited for Roger to pull the tab on the can and take a healthy swallow before speaking. "I'm guessing you're in big trouble and it has everything to do with Victor Manderfield. Suppose you tell me about it."

Roger raised an eyebrow, surprised that the junior detective actually had the balls to be so direct. He was either trawling for information or had bought into the rhetoric the FBI was spewing—maybe a little bit of both. "What makes you think I have anything to do with Manderfield?"

"Because his name came up numerous times as the FBI was questioning me today. They wanted to know everything I could tell them about you and your association with him. Insisted that I was obstructing justice by not telling them where you were hiding out since you've failed to report to work. And also suggested that I was involved with whatever is going on with you."

Jonathan was on the brink of losing his temper, which just pissed him off. He had always prided himself on his ability to maintain control in any situation, but right now Roger was seriously testing his limit. Needing a minute to settle down, he twisted the cap off the water bottle he was holding, and took a long, slow drink. Warily he said, "I think you've gotten yourself into some ugly shit and you're way over your head now. Let me help, Roger. Talk to me."

Roger gave the detective a considering look before taking the plunge. "I'm being double-crossed by those fuck-ups at the FBI. I'm taking a huge gamble here, telling you what I'm about to tell you. But something's gone wrong and I don't know the good guys from the bad guys anymore."

Making a move toward his partner he said, "I've been working undercover as part of a joint operation that was going to bring down Manderfield for good. But it now appears that the FBI has left me swinging in the wind."

"Right," Jonathan replied irritably. "If that's true, why didn't the captain say anything when I was being drilled this morning?"

"Hornby wasn't brought into the operation. It was strictly need-to-know, and the brass figured the captain didn't need to know. I understand how off the wall this must sound, but you've got to believe me. You know how elusive Manderfield has been. For years he's slipped through the system and even the feds couldn't get him on anything that would stick."

Roger could see that Jonathan was weighing what he'd just heard and that he wanted desperately to believe every word. Could it really be this easy? he wondered. But then again the kid was still green enough to accept anything he was told, especially by a partner he idealized.

"So why you?" Jonathan asked suspiciously.

"I've been studying and analyzing and tracking the man ever since I got to Kingsport. I know him better than his mother ever did. So imagine my surprise when nine months ago Manderfield approached me with an offer to join his organization. All I had to do was supply him with information about ongoing investigations and occasionally slow down the system. I figured this was the big break we needed but didn't know who to go to with it. We'd always suspected that there were cops who were in Victor's pocket and I didn't know who to trust. So I went to an old buddy who just happens to be an agent with the feds, someone who believed in truth and justice."

"And no one in our squad knew?"

"No. I was told that there were a number of cops working for Manderfield and even though I didn't want to believe it, I just couldn't take the chance that someone in our house was involved. And if I told the wrong guy, the whole operation would be dead in the water. Right along with me. So, I signed on to help, and not just because I'd put so much of my life into stopping Manderfield. It went deeper than that."

Roger had to work hard to keep the grin off his face as he moved in for the kill. He knew Jonathan wouldn't be able to ignore what he had to say next.

"Last year Manderfield was responsible for the death of a Detective Alonzo Dias, who gained access to his organization by working undercover as one of Victor's hired hands. His body was found in a desolate area just outside Rio Grande County, and it was made to look like Al had been caught up in the middle of a drug deal that went bad. The assholes in Internal Affairs even thought it was the result of too many years spent in the Narcotics division. But I don't believe any of that. Dias was a good cop.

"A second body was found around the same time Al was killed, this one in a warehouse just south of Kingsport. Eric Cassidy. Word was that Cassidy was working for Manderfield and had stolen some drugs and money along with some paintings that were family heirlooms worth a great deal of money. He died before giving up the location where he was hiding the stuff. I've always been convinced the two killings were connected and knew if we could find the drugs and money we'd finally have a solid connection to Manderfield and could put him out of business once and for all.

"Then about a week ago I found it—Cassidy's hiding place. But by then I was convinced that I was being set up and didn't know who I could trust with the information. I even began to think I was being followed." Quickly recognizing the concerned look on Jonathan's face he added, "Don't worry. I made sure I was alone before I came here."

"God, Roger. Do you know how this sounds?"

"Of course I do. I sometimes wake up and have trouble believing it myself. But you've got to accept what I'm telling you, Jonathan, because I don't know who else I can count on right now."

In the silence that followed, Roger watched his partner closely. This was the make-or-break point and he needed the kid's help to get those paintings back. Because the one truth in his whole story had been that he really did think someone had put a tail on him. He just didn't know if it was the department, the FBI, or Victor Manderfield.

Finally, Jonathan flipped the plastic water bottle into the recycling bin and looked at his partner. "Tell me what you want me to do."

CHAPTER FORTY-FOUR

As Cole stepped back into Emma's room around dinner time he paused just inside the door and took a minute to gaze at Emma's visitor. The last time he'd seen Zoe was at Manderfield's ranch, and the sight of her now took his breath away. She was sitting in the chair that Max had placed at the side of Emma's bed, quietly talking to her friend.

It appeared as if she'd had the opportunity to shower recently, and her hair still glistened with delicate droplets of water. He assumed she'd also stopped somewhere for a change of clothes. He wasn't sure how, but she made herself appear both innocent and alluring in those formfitting black jeans and the red-hot turtleneck sweater. To Cole, she was simply beautiful.

Hearing Max's voice, he turned and waited for his partner and Kyle to reach the doorway. As Kyle stopped alongside Cole, Max went straight to Emma's bedside.

"Max has been filling me in on everything you've done to bring justice for Emma and Chris," Kyle said, extending his hand to Cole, "and I want to thank you."

"Well, I could say that no thanks are necessary but I understand how you may feel differently. And I'll add my thanks to you for taking care of Zoe. It means a lot to me."

"She mentioned that you were shot," Kyle said, tossing a meaningful glance at Zoe across the room.

"Just a flesh wound," he responded. "It was Brody Mannis doing the shooting so it just grazed me. We recognized each other from a previous case we'd both worked. I knew the FBI had an inside man at the ranch and I was praying real hard that it was him and that he hadn't gone over to the dark side. After he took the shot I knew for sure. Of course the second round into the dirt had my eardrums ringing for hours."

"I just wish I had known what was going on," Zoe spoke up. "I thought they'd left you for dead."

Cole crossed the room and gathered her into her arms. "I couldn't let on and I feel bad that you had to go through that."

She kissed him hard on the lips before pulling back and saying, "I'm just glad you're okay."

"Manderfield has to be taken down for what he's done here," Kyle spoke quietly from the corner of the room, taking in everyone with a sweep of his eyes. "And I'll help in any way I can."

Cole nodded and said, "Actually, Lou's working on Manderfield and he thinks that most of the people at the top of his organization are either already in custody or will be very shortly. It's going to take some time to sort everything out and build a case, but I'm confident they'll succeed based on what they're finding." Then turning to Max he added, "Lou said that if everything goes as planned, they'll be taking Donnelly late tonight. He asked if we want in."

"Why don't you go on down?" Max said.

"Aren't you going with him?" Emma asked.

"No. I plan on staying right here with you."

Emma sat forward, gritting her teeth against the pain from her injured shoulder. "Well, your plans have just changed," she said, lifting her good hand to stop any objections he might have. "What are you going to do here? Watch me while I'm sleeping or listen to me bitch when I'm awake? You can't do anything for me medically, and Kyle and Zoe are here to keep me company." She smiled now as she laid her hand on his thigh. "Go, Max. Go and finish this so we can get back to a normal life."

"Sorry to break this to you, Emma," Cole said casually, "but Max doesn't know the meaning of normal. If that's what you're after, you better dip your toes back in the dating pool. Maybe Dr. Wright would be interested."

"You're a real funny guy, Cole," Max mumbled.

"Actually, I ran into a proctologist before," Cole continued, not missing a beat. "Not literally of course, thank God, but he looked like he might be able to offer you some normalcy."

"We get your point, jackass," Max said through gritted teeth.

"And I bet his paycheck is substantially higher than the take-home pay of a lowly private investigator."

"Kyle, you're a doctor," Max pleaded. "Administer something to shut him up. Please?"

Emma was trying not to laugh. Nodding in Max's direction she said, "Well, I'm kind of stuck on this one, so your doctor will have to find someone else. But thanks for thinking about me, Cole."

"Hey, Zoe," Max said, "Maybe you're on the hunt for a tall, dark and handsome doctor? What floor did you say that proctologist worked on, partner?"

"Thanks Max, but I'll pass, too. I've already got my tall, dark and handsome."

"My teeth are starting to hurt with all this sweet talk," Kyle interjected, unable to suppress his own laughter. It felt good. "And not to put a damper on this whole love fest, but shouldn't you two get going?" Looking first at Cole and then at Max, his smile slowly faded. "I do have one request. Finish this thing as quickly as you can—for Chris. Donnelly's probably not the one who fired the bullet that killed him, but his involvement has caused a great deal of the heartache and pain we've all had to endure. He needs to pay."

"I know what you're feeling," Max said, "and you have my word that we'll finish this for Chris."

"For Chris," Zoe repeated as she slipped her arm around Kyle's waist.

"For Chris," Emma added as earnestly as she could manage. But then, fixing her eyes on Max she said, "All I ask is that you keep yourself out of trouble down there. Come back to me in one piece, will you?"

Zoe locked eyes on Cole and said, "That goes ditto for you."

CHAPTER FORTY-FIVE

The rain was drumming hard against the steel roof of Unit E24 at the Highland storage facility. Inside, Cole sat with Lou Garrison, Brody Mannis and Jay Slinger, who had flown in from the Denver field office.

Positioned on a five-foot plastic folding table were three view screens displaying the areas being monitored by cameras specifically installed for tonight's operation. The first camera covered the property's front gate, the second one was an aerial shot that covered the passageways between the buildings and the last camera had been mounted inside Unit D23, originally rented to one Eric Cassidy. That screen showed three aluminum cases and two dark brown suitcases, all sitting in the center of the floor.

No one spoke. Brody and Jay kept an eye on the screens while Lou read through some paperwork stuffed in a manila folder. Cole sat in a cheap folding chair at the end of the table, playing Solitaire with a deck of cards he'd found in the glove compartment of the last vehicle he'd hijacked.

Another twenty minutes went by with no activity. Lou had discarded his file and was now slowly pacing back and forth behind the other two agents, occasionally taking a glance at the monitors. After being cooped up in the small, stuffy unit for the past four hours, his patience was beginning to wear thin. He'd never been good at waiting, especially when he was a police detective covering the streets of Washington, DC. Back then, when he found himself spending hours on one surveillance op or another, he'd use the feel of a cigarette between his fingers as a temporary diversion. Of course, back then you could light up anywhere without the fear of being fined. At any rate, he'd finally kicked the habit, primarily because he got tired of his wife's constant nagging. But whenever he found himself in a situation like this he could still conjure up the taste and smell of that tobacco as it battered against his senses. God, those were the days.

He was brought back from his reminiscing by the ringing of his phone. At the same time, Brody pointed to the first screen and said, "A silver hatchback is pulling up to the gate."

Cole pushed out of his chair and stepped over to the table. He could see a man reaching out the side window and punching a series of numbers into the entrance keypad. The gate slid open and the hatchback proceeded onto the property. The cameras monitored the driver as he slowly steered the vehicle between the buildings—whether looking for the correct unit or trying to ascertain if he had company was anyone's guess—and finally circled twice around the building that housed Eric's unit. He cut the lights as he parked in front of D23 but kept the engine running.

After exiting the vehicle he took a minute to sweep the area. Satisfied there was no one around, he walked up to the unit's door and everyone watched as he reached into the breast pocket of his jacket and pulled out a pick-style tool that he expertly used to disengage the padlock. It didn't take long, which told the group that it wasn't the first time the Kingsport detective had used the skill.

"Are we going to make contact before he leaves?" Cole asked. "Or are we going to let him deliver the paintings?"

"We'll let him go. We have enough eyes on Donnelly that he won't get away and we've got tracking equipment in the cases. And let's not forget the listening device. We'll have a stronger case if we can record the delivery."

Lou continued to watch as the unit's belongings were loaded into the vehicle, and the driver took off. Stuffing his files into a side pocket of the briefcase he said, "Brody, you stay with the cameras here just in case anyone comes back. Keep recording. I'll take Cole and Jay back with me."

Checking the monitor one final time to make sure the hatchback had exited the property, he motioned to the other two men and the three left the unit, walking to the front gate where they were met by a black minivan. After everyone was inside Lou told the driver to take them to Kingsport.

Jonathan entered his fashionable two-bedroom condominium and flipped on the kitchen light. He tossed his keys on the counter and went right to the refrigerator to pull out a high-octane soda. It was close to two in the morning but he didn't care if the caffeine kept him awake. At this point, what difference did it really make?

He moved into the living room and sat on the leather couch. Not as comfortable as the recliner, but Roger Donnelly had already staked claim to that piece of furniture.

"How did it go? Did you get everything?" Roger asked.

"I emptied the storage shed. I didn't take the time to look at anything, I just hightailed it out of there. Geez, Roger. I thought for sure that at any minute some goon was going to clip me and bury my body so deep no one would ever find me."

"Did you see anyone?"

"Not a soul, which just proves that you were right. The FBI is staffed with a bunch of dim-witted chumps. How on earth did they miss knowing where Cassidy stashed the evidence?"

"It doesn't matter. Let's go see what you got."

Jonathan led Roger to the parking garage where his car was backed into an assigned space in a secluded part of the structure. He pushed a button on the key chain and with a beep the vehicle's headlights flashed and the locks disengaged. Roger hurried to the rear of the automobile and raised the hatch just as Jonathan slowed his pace.

Pushing the suitcases aside, Roger grabbed for one of the larger cases. Without hesitation he punched in the combination to the lock and opened the case. His reaction was swift and lethal.

He pulled his Sig and spun in the direction where Jonathan should have been standing. But the garage was empty, and he realized too late—and with some irony—that he'd been set up. He quickly crouched between the car's fender and the concrete wall as he watched two squad cars come roaring down the ramp on his left. At the same time, three FBI agents poured out of a white van that was parked near the building's elevator, and two more agents took up sniper positions behind a barrier on the level just above.

All weapons were trained on the detective, but the only person Roger was really interested in was his former partner, who stood partially protected by the white van, his Glock pointed directly at Roger's chest.

Later, everyone would agree that Roger had made the conscious decision not to be taken alive long before ever entering that parking structure. A cop serving time in jail was not a good scenario and he understood the cost. Max had watched him struggle with the decision; saw in his eyes that he was weighing his options. Could he run? Could he strike a deal? Could he stay out of prison? And Max had also recognized the exact moment when his former partner realized that the answer to all three questions was no.

"Give it up, Roger," Max said as he adjusted his stance to get a better line of sight. "It's over."

"Yeah, I know. And we don't want to see anybody get hurt. So just put down your weapon and blah, blah, blah. Tell me one thing, Max—and don't lie, because I'll know. You want nothing more right now than to put that bullet through the center of my head, right?"

"Wrong. I want to put it straight through your worthless heart."

Roger laughed and said, "Ah, you always had a touch of the poet in you. So, I put my weapon down and then what? Are my fellow officers here going to take me in quietly or are they going to shoot me and claim that I resisted arrest?"

"You're forgetting that most Kingsport cops are clean and believe in upholding the law. Go ahead, Roger. Look at them. Look at what you used to be. Now it's your turn to tell me something. When did money, and the violence and corruption, overtake the goodness in you?"

"Oh, please. Any one of you would have done the same thing I did. The offer was just too good to pass up. But you always have someone who gets greedy and fucks it all up. Cassidy just got too greedy.

"And you, Max, you had a part in this too. If you had just been able to keep your hands off that whore, none of this would have happened. Emma would have given up the key, we would have had the paintings and everyone could have gone on with their lives."

"But that's where you're wrong," Max said. "Emma never knew about the key. Cassidy slipped it to her without telling her. So she would have ended up dead and you still wouldn't have known where the paintings were. And I don't think Manderfield is the kind of boss who accepts failure too well. How long do you think it would have been before he sent someone to take care of you? Permanently."

"Maybe. But it doesn't matter now. Hey, how did you get Johnny Boy to turn on me, anyway?"

"You misjudged his loyalty to the badge. When he called us on his way to the storage unit he said that up to that point he had wanted to give you the benefit of the doubt. But then you called him Jonathan. Said you never called him by his full name—not until tonight when you were trying to convince him to help you."

"Damn. That was a rookie mistake, wasn't it? I guess the kid's going places after all."

"Put the gun down, Roger. You're out of options here."

Roger knew better. He actually had two options left. He could either live with the consequences or die with the shame. He looked straight at Max, smiled and pulled the trigger.

CHAPTER FORTY-SIX

After giving his statement to the FBI, Max walked out of the parking structure, ignoring the curiosity seekers and reporters that had gathered just outside the main entrance. Walking down Santa Barbara Boulevard, his only focus was on getting inside his car and driving back to Clearview Medical Center to be with Emma. He'd been given the opportunity to fly back with the FBI, but the flight wasn't leaving until after the noon hour, and he figured he could make better time on his own. So he had decided to make the five-hour trip in the rental that Lou had arranged to be waiting for him.

Once he was out of rush-hour traffic and heading north, he used the hands-free speakerphone to call Kyle, leaving a message when he was dropped into voicemail. On one hand he was ashamedly relieved that Kyle didn't pick up, but on the other was grateful for the extra time to digest the conversation he'd had with Cassie Carlton about an hour ago.

"The investigation into Kyle's involvement in the death of your brother has been dropped," she'd told him in the quiet, sensitive voice she used when speaking to the clients she represented. "The locals have been in touch with the FBI, and Kyle doesn't have anything to worry about."

"That's great news, Cassie. I'll pass it along to him."

"Max, I know that both you and Kyle have been through a lot, but some decisions need to be made regarding Chris. I've gotten a number of recommendations for funeral homes with solid reputations. I can handle all the arrangements and make sure that Chris is taken care of until you can make permanent provisions. I just need some direction with what your wishes are."

He'd assured her that he would call her back by the end of the day, but her call had been another punch to the gut and one he hadn't been prepared for. She was right about decisions needing to be made and he wanted Kyle to be part of that process.

The speaker signaled an incoming call just as Max was changing lanes. After settling back into the flow of traffic he grabbed the call. "This is Dunmore."

"Max, it's Lou Garrison."

"Hey, Lou. Everything okay?"

"Sure. Cole told me you got the news that Emma's been up and walking around."

"He told me, yeah. He also told me that your guy is pulling out every trick in the book to talk to her."

"We need her statement, Max. You know that. Out of everyone, she's got the most information. But she said she wanted you there when we talk to her. We don't have to work it that way, but we will."

Max was aware that Emma wanted him with her and was thankful that Lou was willing to accommodate her request. "I appreciate that, Lou. I'm on my way back there now, in fact. Is that why you called?"

"Actually, no. We got a warrant for Donnelly's place. It seems he kept impeccable records of all his dealings with Victor Manderfield. Dates, description of the jobs he took, who in Manderfield's faction was involved. We got names of victims, names of shooters, and names of other law enforcement personnel who were involved."

"Wow, that's hard to believe. He hated paperwork when we were partners, and most of the time I was stuck with doing it."

Lou chuckled and said, "Detective Draper had the same thing to say. He just figured it was because he was the rookie on the squad."

"How's Jonathan doing, by the way? It must have been difficult discovering his partner had gone rogue."

"Yeah, it's been a kick in the pants, but Draper is holding up. He actually did better than I expected him to do when he was working Donnelly. Everything we got off the wire he was wearing is going to help."

"He's going to get flack from within the department," Max said.

"He'll handle it. He told our senior agent out in Kingsport that he was considering applying to the FBI."

"He's got a couple of pretty reliable references if he does."

"That's a fact," Lou said. "I'm going to clean things up here at Crystal Ridge and then I'm needed in California. Jay Slinger will be in charge of coordinating the remaining evidence collection. He may want to talk to you again."

"I'll help in any way I can. What about Victor?"

"Oh, didn't I say? Unfortunately, our boy was forced to change his vacation plans. We got him boarding a private jet that had already filed its flight plan to Chile."

"And Marco?"

"As far as we can tell he had nothing to do with this. He's being questioned, but I think he'll be found guiltless. He's been asking when he can get the paintings."

"No surprise there," Max scoffed. "A Manderfield to the end."

"We have Daria in custody, too. I'll tell you honestly, Max, she's a real piece of work. But she'll no doubt be sent somewhere that can actually help her rather than enable her craziness."

Max heard a beep through the speaker, signaling another incoming call. "Thanks for the update, Lou. Listen, I've got a call coming in that I have to take. Just let me know if you need anything more."

"Will do. Take care, Max."

Max disconnected from Lou and answered Kyle's call. "Kyle, thanks for calling back."

"Sure. I just got your message or I would have done it sooner."

Pulling off the highway so he could give his full attention to the call, Max told Kyle everything that he and Cassie had discussed. "Did you and Chris ever talk about what he'd want? Um, you know, any specific directives upon his death?"

"Yes, he executed a living will and it outlines his wishes. I don't remember everything, but I know he wants to be cremated."

"Okay. Cassie can arrange for that and maybe you and I can go back to Jackson County together. If you want a service or something, we can put that together."

"No. No service. Chris always said that in the end, it would be the end. And he definitely didn't want people standing around sharing cheesy stories about him at some sad memorial service. So if it's okay with you and your grandmother, I'd like to respect his wishes. If Cassie could arrange for the cremation, you and I can collect his ashes and spread them on your family's property. He loved spending time out at the cabin and said he could actually feel tranquility from the land."

"I think Nanna will be good with that," Max said. "I'll call her, and then take it from there."

"Thank you, Max."

"You don't have to thank me. We're family. I may have a lot of regrets when it comes to my relationship with Chris, but I believe deep inside that we made our peace. I don't want to ever have the same regrets with you." Max paused, trying to swallow past the lump in his throat. "I'm on my way back now so I'll see you in a couple of hours."

"We'll be here," Kyle said with quiet emotion. "I'll see you then."

CHAPTER FORTY-SEVEN

Emma was sitting up in bed waiting for Max to return. She was alone in her room on the fifth floor after having kicked everyone out. Although she loved them all, Zoe was being way too mothering, Cole too upbeat, and Kyle had become too withdrawn. But she refused to feel guilty about needing some peace and quiet.

She was facing the window now, watching the rain slap hard against the solid, wide pane. It had been drizzling most of the morning, slow and brooding drops that slid sluggishly down the glass, coming to rest in pools of water on the narrow sandstone ledge. Now it was coming down in sheets and Emma was hard pressed to even see the rooftops of the houses that lined the street across from her room.

"A penny for your thoughts."

Emma smiled as she turned toward the smooth, masculine voice. "They're worth far more than just a penny."

Max moved alongside the bed. "You're looking pretty exceptional today. Feeling better, I hope?"

"Feeling hopeful is a better description. Dr. Wright tells me it's going to be a slow healing process, but he thinks I'll be able to leave in a few days."

"That's good news, then," he said as he bent down and kissed her lightly on the forehead. "Hey, where did this come from?" he said as he picked up a stuffed lion that went by the name of Clarence.

"Zoe brought it back with her. It somehow made its way into one of the duffels she took out of the cabin."

Max handed it back to Emma and gave her an affectionate smile. "I'm glad he made it out with the rest of us."

Cradling the toy under her good arm she said, "Will we be able to join up with Nanna and Henry? I need to have Jacob back just as soon as possible."

"Actually, they'll be coming here." Reading the concerned look on her face he added, "Yes, it's safe. Everyone who had something to do with those paintings is either in custody or dead. Victor's reign has come to an end."

"I hear the words and trust the messenger but it's so hard to believe it's really over."

"I've checked everything out myself, made sure we're no longer in danger. We'll keep the bodyguards in place for the next few weeks, though. You've been through a lot and I think it will help you to readjust."

"I want to say that I don't need you treating me like an invalid, but instead I'm going to say thank you. A security team will make me feel better, at least until I'm steady on my feet again."

"Well, you can thank your ex-husband."

"What does Eric have to do with this?" she asked, totally perplexed.

"He's paying for the whole protection thing. Although it could be argued that it's Victor paying. They both owe us so it doesn't really matter, I suppose."

"Maxwell, what are you talking about?"

"When we went to the storage shed we found the paintings, a suitcase full of uncut cocaine and another suitcase filled with hundred-dollar bills."

"You can't be serious. I don't want anything to do with Victor's drug money."

"I'm with you there. That's why I only took the duffel bag before I turned everything else over to the FBI." He laughed when she gave him a look that would not only kill a weaker man but would pulverize him to ash. "There was a duffel bag in the shed that had some of Eric's things. Some clothes, new identity and cash. Along with the cash was a ledger—a personal ledger—of his finances. The cash in the duffel matches the bottom-line entry he made for income, although I don't think he was working exclusively for Victor. In fact, it makes more sense that he was still running his own truck and just doing select jobs for Manderfield. Either way, it just doesn't matter. The money belongs to you now."

Emma was speechless as she tried to sort out what Max was saying. Finally, she said, "He wouldn't allow me to work even though I wanted to. I wanted to contribute to our marriage but every time I brought it up, it turned into an argument that always came out badly for me."

"Even more reason to keep this money. He owes you, Em."

"Is it rude to ask how much money we're talking about?"

"I don't know for sure, but from what I saw, you can keep those bodyguards in place for months, replace Kyle's van that got shot up back at the cabin and still put something aside for Jacob's college education."

"Wow. I don't know what to say."

"Don't say anything right now. In fact, put it out of your mind. You're still pumped full of drugs so you can't be thinking straight yet. Once you are, you'll see I'm right."

"Did you tell Lou about the bag?"

"I figured it was none of his concern. He got the paintings, the drugs and his own case full of money."

"Okay."

Max leaned down and brushed a kiss to her lips. "Okay?"

"Yeah, okay. When I filed for divorce I told my attorney I didn't want anything from Eric. I just didn't have the strength to fight him and I knew he'd put up one hell of a battle. Then when he died we were still technically married so I ended up with the house and all its contents. But he also had a lot of debt, which I ended up with as well. I lost the value of the house when it burned to the ground—a direct result of Eric's association with Victor—and after the dust settled, I had nothing. Everything that's happened to me—everything that's happened to all of us—started with Eric. So yes, he owes us."

"Have I ever told you how sexy you look when you're all riled up?"

Emma laughed. She loved it when he made her laugh. "You didn't say why you're bringing everyone home now." But then she realized that his grandmother wanted to be here for Chris's burial. "Nanna wants to be here, right?"

"Chris is being cremated and his ashes will be spread on our family land."

"I'd like to be there if it's all right with you and Kyle."

"It would mean a lot to me if you were there. If you're up to it," he added.

She leaned forward and put her good arm around him. "Neither of us needs to be alone anymore. No more secrets and no more regrets. Our new life starts here and now. Agreed?"

"Agreed. By the way, I told Cole we're getting married. I hope that wasn't meant to be one of those secrets."

"No, in fact I told Zoe and Kyle. Oh, and Dr. Wright."

"You told your doctor you're getting married?"

"Just wanted to make sure he knew I was spoken for in case he got any ideas."

Max laughed and pulled her closer. "I love you, you crazy woman."

"Right back at you, big daddy."

EPILOGUE

Three years later

Max and Emma started their day with a strong cup of coffee and front row seats to the day's luxurious sunrise. Whenever they came up to the newly built family cabin, they made a point to spend the early morning sitting on the porch together to witness the beauty of the dawning day.

After breakfast, Max and Jacob walked down to the creek to do some father and son bonding over a rod and reel. Nanna and Henry, who had arrived late the previous night, were still lazing around the cabin while Emma headed into town for groceries with Morgan, a six-year-old—soon to be seven-year-old—spitfire of a child.

Morgan had at one time been a lonely girl who lived in a world of drugs and violence. Her biological father had died shortly after her birth, and her mother, Connie, had lived a scattered and unfulfilled life. After Connie had been arrested and jailed on drug and assault charges, Max and Emma had brought Morgan into their home as a foster child. It had been rough at the beginning, but as the weeks passed and the trust grew, the young girl began adjusting well to her new home and came to accept the love and attention that was given to her unconditionally.

Eight months after her incarceration, Connie was released with the chance at a new start with her daughter. But the temptation to go back to the old life had won out over caring for her only child, and two days before Morgan would have been returned to her, Connie relinquished her parental rights and took off for the east coast.

By then Max and Emma had fallen in love with Morgan and did everything in their power to change the girl's status in their home from temporary to permanent. In early spring the following year, everyone had cried when the adoption was finalized.

Now, as Emma drove back toward the cabin, the trunk loaded with bags of both junk food and healthy alternatives, the sight of Kyle strolling out the front door had Morgan wiggling in her seat.

"Look, Uncle Kyle is here. I told you he wouldn't miss my birthday party."

Emma smiled, happy that Kyle had decided to join them. He had dealt with the pain of Chris's death by throwing himself into his work, expanding the clinic and picking up more volunteer hours at the rehabilitation center in Fort Collins. It meant that she and Max didn't see him nearly often enough, but like most families, special milestone events always had a draw that even overworked members managed to attend.

When the car came to a stop Morgan unbuckled her seatbelt and exited the car on a run. "Uncle Kyle, you came."

Kyle had just enough time to brace himself as she took a flying leap into his outstretched arms. "Hey, munchkin. I wouldn't have missed this for the world."

"Mommy said I get to help her make my birthday cake and I can open my presents today and not wait until tomorrow." She tilted her head and gave him a sly look. "Did you bring me a present?"

"Morgan Marie Dunmore," Emma said, walking toward them carrying two of the bags. "You know better than to ask a question like that. Of course he brought you a present," she added as she gave Kyle a devilish look. Planting a welcoming kiss on his cheek she whispered, "So if you didn't you better go back into town and get her something."

Kyle laughed and, taking the bags, said, "I may not have any children of my own, but I totally understand the species." Looking down at Morgan he added, "My present, which undoubtedly will be the best present you get this year, is in the family room with the others. You've got quite the haul in there, kiddo."

"I know," she squealed as she took off up the porch stairs, singing the birthday song as she disappeared through the front door.

Emma had unloaded two more bags from the car and together she and Kyle followed Morgan through the house, turning left when they reached the kitchen. "I better not see any wrapping torn on those packages," Emma said, raising her voice. "Dinner first, presents after."

"Why do grown-ups insist on tormenting poor, defenseless children?" Kyle said as he started putting the groceries away.

"Because we've lost that innocence and know we're never going to get it back. Simply put, we're jealous."

"Poor baby. You're not going to be cranky all day, are you?"

Emma administered a gentle smack to his shoulder on her way to the pantry as she said, "Have you seen Nanna and Henry?"

"They were heading out for a walk as I came in. Said they'd be back shortly."

"Let's get to it then. It looks like you and I are going to be in charge of the festivities."

Over the next two hours, Kyle and Emma worked on making side dishes for the big celebration dinner. During that time, Joan and Henry returned and helped Morgan bake and decorate the birthday cake. When Cole and Zoe showed up, the men wandered down to the lake to join Max and Jacob, and Zoe was put on kitchen duty.

Sometime later, Emma began to set the outdoor table for dinner. "Morgan," she called out, interrupting her daughter's video game playing. "Go on down to the lake and fetch the boys, will you please?"

As Morgan trotted off, the women took a well-deserved break and, with wine glasses in hand, watched as their men walked up the gravel driveway, Max carrying his delighted son on his shoulders. Emma could only groan as she saw the two scrawny fish clutched in his tiny and no doubt smelly hand. She knew she would be making room on the grill for the catch of the day, even if it was just for show. No way was she allowing anyone to eat those things.

After dinner was consumed, it was time for Morgan to open her presents. Zoe and Cole had gotten her three new video games, which had earned them each an enormous hug. Joan and Henry had brought two boxes, the first containing a new blouse and skirt followed by a pair of pocket embroidered, vintage-washed skinny jeans (the kind that all the popular girls at school were wearing) in the second.

Then it was time to open her parents' gift. Inside the package was a deluxe art set that their little girl had been begging for since the beginning of the year. It was filled with colored pencils, tubes of paints, assorted chalk and a tray packed with different sized brushes. Running her hand across each item, Morgan declared, "I've wanted this my whole life."

Kyle's present rounded out the gift-giving portion of the day and when Morgan realized what was inside the box, her eyes grew twice their normal size. It was a magician's kit, filled with everything from magic cards, coins and interlocking rings to beautiful scarves, a black flowing cape and what every top-notch magician requires—a collapsible hat. She'd immediately flung the cape across her shoulders and ran around the room waving the magic wand at anything she thought she could make disappear.

When the excitement began to diminish, Henry went outside to build a small campfire in the area behind the cabin. Morgan took Kyle's hand as they followed the others through the kitchen, pulling on it until he bent down to her level. "I don't want to make anyone feel bad, so I have to whisper," she began. "Your present was the best."

Kyle smiled and kissed her on the forehead. "That's quite the compliment considering all the other great gifts you got."

"Oh, I love them all," she said diplomatically. "I just love yours a little bit more."

"I won't tell anyone, I promise," Kyle replied, leading her out the door toward the others.

When Kyle took the remaining empty seat—a rocking chair made by Max's grandfather—Morgan scooted in alongside him. "I've been thinking, Uncle Kyle," she said, no longer finding the need to whisper.

"That could be a dangerous thing, but let's hear what you've been thinking about."

"Why don't you come back to Kingsport and live with us?"

"I don't think that would be such a good idea, munchkin."

"Why not?"

"Well, I think your mom and dad have their hands full with you and Jacob."

In all seriousness she replied, "I'm not a handful. I'm going to be seven tomorrow. But you're right about Jacob. He can be . . . oh, yes—quite unruly," she finished in what sounded like a poorly imitated British accent.

"Where did you get that expression?" Max laughed.

"From my teacher. She says the boys are . . . quite unruly," Morgan repeated using the same accent.

"And what does she say about the girls?" Cole chimed in.

"I don't remember," Morgan replied shrewdly, trying to hide her smile.

"Hey, Max, are you sure your kid is only turning seven tomorrow? She sounds way more grown up than that."

Morgan giggled but turned back to Kyle, refusing to be side-tracked. "Come on, Uncle Kyle, it would be fun. I'm sure Mommy and Daddy won't mind. And you would get to see me and Jacob every day."

"As much as I appreciate the offer, I have responsibilities here, Morgan. I have people who count on me to help them. Sick people who need me to help make them better."

"We have sick people in Kingsport, too. You could help them."

"A child's logic," Cole muttered as he kicked his feet out in front of him and waited to see how Kyle was going to get out of this one.

"Where is this coming from, sweetie? Why do you want me to come live with you?"

"I just don't want you to be lonely," she said as she raised her head to look at his face.

"What do you mean?"

"Well, Mommy loves Daddy. And Nanna loves Grandpa Henry so much she married him. And I heard Zoe say she loves Cole more than anything in the world." Megan paused for a brief moment and then said, "Who loves you, Uncle Kyle?"

Kyle cleared his throat to give himself time to reply. Glancing over to Max he saw the slight nod as he reached over and joined hands with Emma. "You've heard us talk about Uncle Chris before, right?" he asked as he shifted his attention back to Morgan. "Do you remember that?"

"Yes. He was daddy's brother. He died."

"Yes, he did. But before he died, he was the one who loved me the most. And I loved your Uncle Chris."

"Oh," she said, giving some thought to what he'd just told her. "Okay. But maybe you should find someone new to love you now. I don't think Uncle Chris would mind."

"A child's logic," Kyle repeated Cole's earlier words. "So simplistic."

She looked up as Kyle smiled and shook his head. "I don't know what that means," she said.

"It's not important. Let's just say that you're very good at figuring things out. We adults manage to make things so complicated but you have the special gift of making things simple. Your way is better."

She smiled at him before resting her head on his shoulder and placing her hand on his heart. "Tell me about Uncle Chris, okay?"

Kyle placed his hand over hers and started the wicker chair rocking. "Chris was one of the funniest people I knew. And he had a heart of gold. I remember one time when we went out fishing on the lake—right over there, in fact, just beyond those trees . . ."

As the sun set slowly behind the cabin, the sounds of the night blanketed the Dunmore family homestead. The adults continued to share stories that included Chris, and they all laughed and cried at the memories.

Hours later the heavy-eyed children were carried to their beds. Cole and Zoe, who'd decided to stay over, also retired for the night, followed shortly by Joan and Henry.

"You can stay too if you'd like," Emma told Kyle as he prepared to leave. "You'll have to share a room with the kids, though, or take the couch."

"Thanks, but I'll go back home. I've still got some files to go through before tomorrow."

"It was nice remembering Chris tonight," she spoke gently. "But you know, Morgan was right. It is all right to start seeing someone again. Chris wouldn't mind."

"I know. I still miss him, but I'm not mourning him anymore. I'm not missing him every minute of every day. So stop worrying, Emma. I'll be okay." He smiled as he reached over for a hug, promising to return early the following morning for breakfast.

And in the morning, when Kyle returned, and Joan, Henry, Cole and Zoe awoke, they would all find Max and Emma sharing a cup of coffee on the front porch of the cabin, witnessing once again the miracle of a new day dawning.

ABOUT THE AUTHOR

Sara K. James is a Midwest born and raised author and *Risking It All* is her gripping debut novel. Her writing delivers unforgettable storylines of romance and suspense and her readers are sure to find page-turning excitement within each chapter. She is currently hard at work writing her next book.